FRAME 232

A JASON HAMMOND NOVEL

FRAME 232

WIL MARA

Tyndale House Publishers, Inc.
Carol Stream, Illinois

Visit Tyndale online at www.tyndale.com.

Visit Wil Mara's website at www.wilmara.com.

TYNDALE and Tyndale's quill logo are registered trademarks of Tyndale House Publishers, Inc.

Frame 232

Designed by Ron Kaufmann

Frame 232 is a work of fiction. Where real people, events, establishments, organizations, or locales appear, they are used fictitiously. All other elements of the novel are drawn from the author's imagination.

Library of Congress Cataloging-in-Publication Data

Mara, Wil.
  Frame 232 / Wil Mara.
      pages cm. — (Jason Hammond)
    1. Family secrets—Fiction. 2. Film archives—Fiction. 3. Kennedy, John F. (John Fitzgerald), 1917-1963—Fiction. 4. Conspiracy theories—Fiction. I. Title.
II. Title: Frame two hundred thirty-two.
  PS3613.A725F73 2013
  813'.6—dc23   2013006618
  ISBN 978-1-4143-8176-3 (hc)
  ISBN 978-1-4143-5951-9 (sc)

Printed in the United States of America

19   18   17   16   15   14   13
 7   6   5   4   3   2   1

O Lord, who shall sojourn in your tent? Who shall dwell on your holy hill? He who walks blamelessly and does what is right and speaks truth in his heart.

PSALM 15:1-2

What a pity that the human animal is not able to put his moral thinking into practice.

HARRY TRUMAN

For Tracey—who understood
And for Jan—who believed

Acknowledgments

YOU CAN'T WRITE a book like this without help. As we are famous for saying here in New Jersey, *fuggedaboutit*. So many good people gave freely of their time and talents, and I am deeply grateful to all of them.

First, there's Peter Snell, who read through an embryonic story treatment in the spring of 2003 and made it clear with his characteristic diplomacy that I was a fool if I didn't stick with it. Pete has since passed from this world to the next, and I miss him tremendously.

There's my magnificent wife, Tracey, who carried on Pete's faith with the occasional (but firm) "You know what story you should go back to? That Kennedy one." Similarly, my children—my girls, my treasure—never lodged a single complaint concerning the time I had to invest in the research and writing process.

In 2008, I made the wise decision to submit the first draft of the manuscript to Tyndale, and there I found Jan and Jeremy—as close to a pair of good angels as you're likely to encounter on this mortal plane. They are, in every way, the perfect editors—insightful, patient, and enthusiastic. Expanding further into the Tyndale universe, I have encountered an abundance of support, cheerfulness, and professionalism.

Sincere and heartfelt thanks also go to Patti and Jane for reading earlier drafts and providing valuable criticism, and to Allison for discussing matters of faith that are at once so mysterious and so ridiculously obvious.

And of course, my undying gratitude to the Lord, not only for giving me this gift, but also for furnishing the opportunity to use it to further his glory.

Author's Note

THIS IS A WORK OF FICTION, but the raw materials have been mined from the quarry of reality. Most of us know that President John Fitzgerald Kennedy was gunned down on November 22, 1963, in Dallas's Dealey Plaza and that former Marine and U.S. expatriate Lee Harvey Oswald would have been tried for the crime if not for his own shooting death at the hand of nightclub owner Jack Ruby two days later. We know that a group of seven civil servants, acting on behalf of succeeding president Lyndon Johnson and bearing the colloquial name of the Warren Commission, investigated the assassination and concluded that Oswald was the sole individual responsible for the president's death. And we know that literally hundreds of conspiracy theories have been put forth in the decades since, attempting to contradict the commission's findings.

But there are other truths that have escaped the notice of the general public, and the most pertinent to this book is that the Babushka Lady is a real person and not a figment of anyone's imagination. She is one of only a handful of spectators within close proximity to the president's limousine who has yet to be identified. If you take the time to search the Internet, you will see her there, as plain as day. And in some images she appears to be holding a camera. Many assassination researchers believe it was the type that took motion pictures rather than stills and that she might have captured something no one else did. This could explain why she has made the choice to remain in the shadows. If that is indeed the case, then we can only speculate on what she witnessed that tragic day and, in all probability, has witnessed again, in private, in the years since.

PROLOGUE

MARGARET BAKER FELT more than a little foolish in her makeshift disguise—an overcoat she'd found in a box of her late mother's things, the prescription glasses she never wore, and a pink headscarf she'd borrowed from a friend. The coat and scarf were far too heavy for such a warm day. They made it *look* like she was in disguise. Everyone else in Dealey Plaza was dressed appropriately—most of the men in shirtsleeves, the women in skirts of varying modesty. True, this was November. But this was also Dallas, where temperatures could easily reach into the seventies this time of year. The morning report said it would be in the high sixties at least, with a fair amount of humidity. Her heart sank when she heard this. But she had little choice in the matter. If someone recognized her . . .

It wasn't her husband she was worried about. She hadn't informed him of this little detour, but he wouldn't mind one way or the other. He wasn't particularly political, and he was about as even-tempered as a man could be. But Dr. Lomax was a different story. Being one of his receptionists had its perks, to be sure. The pay was decent, the hours comfortable, the office clean and neat, and the other girls were nice

1

enough. But Lomax could be a monster, demanding and unreasonable. And as a proud member of the John Birch Society, he loathed the Kennedys. Whenever the president came on the radio, Lomax would stop whatever he was doing and listen intently, his face reddening, then launch into a venomous rebuttal that often ended with him stomping off in a rage. When he heard JFK was coming to town, he muttered something about how nice it would be if Air Force One went down in a fiery blaze.

Margaret wasn't sure what Lomax would do if he found out she had come here just to see the president, but it certainly wouldn't be pleasant. She had lied to facilitate the opportunity, coming in for a few hours in the morning before claiming she didn't feel well. Lomax didn't like his employees taking time off regardless of the reason, and he was already in a foul mood, griping about the increased traffic and security in the area. She took this as a bad omen and shuddered. Nevertheless, she went into the ladies' room of a department store a few doors down to put on the scarf and glasses. Ten minutes later she found a suitable position in the plaza, about thirty feet from Elm Street, and whispered a prayer that no one had recognized her along the way. The crowd wasn't as thick as it had been along Main, but she was still within walking distance of the office. Too close for comfort, in her opinion.

These worries evaporated, at least temporarily, when the cheering on Main Street became noticeably louder. *He's coming!* she thought, and excitement swirled in her belly. She had liked Kennedy from the moment she first saw him, with his Ivy League good looks and boyish magnetism. The latter had been obvious even when she and her husband, Ron, watched the first-ever televised presidential debates on their grainy

Philco Admiral. Kennedy had the air of one who'd already been in the office for years, whereas challenger and former Eisenhower VP Richard Nixon bore the haggard mannerisms of a prisoner in an interrogation chamber. Beyond all that, however, Margaret believed Kennedy's dedication to America was sincere and absolute and that in spite of his youthfulness—which so many of his detractors considered a handicap—he possessed the innate wisdom to handle the job. The way he had stared down that corpulent thug Nikita Khrushchev during the Cuban Missile Crisis had proved her right on that score, and Lomax's begrudging silence on the matter provided a delightful bonus layer of confirmation.

As the crowd's roar continued to rise, Margaret reached into the pocket of her overcoat and took out an 8mm Paillard Bolex. She hadn't used it since she and Ron went to Galveston for his sister's wedding. She'd bought a virgin reel earlier in the week and loaded it just before she left the house this morning.

The cheering reached a near-deafening pitch, and she switched the unit on. Looking right, she saw the motorcycle-flanked procession ease off Main and onto Houston. The lead vehicle was an ordinary white Ford with four occupants. She recognized the driver as Dallas Police Chief Jesse Curry, a familiar figure in the area who'd been on the force since the midthirties. She did not know the other three men, and they were instantly forgotten when Kennedy's 1961 Lincoln Continental appeared a moment later, its two fender-mounted flags—Stars and Stripes on the left, the presidential seal on the right—flapping madly. There were three rows of seats, and she briefly registered Governor John Connally and his wife, Nellie, in the middle. As soon as the president came into view, however, her eyes locked onto him. It was surreal to see the flesh-and-blood man in such close proximity. He was smiling and waving in the afternoon sunshine. *The handsome young king among his subjects,* she thought. When he used his left hand to sweep his chestnut hair off his forehead in that familiar way, her heart jumped.

The limo turned left off Houston and started down Elm, rolling ever closer. She was aware of a near-hypnotic feeling of fulfillment, to the point where she was no longer conscious of the Bolex camera in her hand. She might not have remembered it until the president was long gone if not for a woman close to her shrieking, "Oh, oh, look at Jackie! Look how bea-*u*-tiful she is!"

Snapping out of the trance, Margaret brought the Bolex up and activated it. As she did, she noticed a man—who would eventually be identified to the world as Abraham Zapruder—standing on the pergola on the opposite side of Elm. He was holding a video camera, a Bell & Howell Zoomatic, and was aiming it at the approaching motorcade. Margaret kept the president and his wife in the center of the frame, remembering a tip she had learned from a photographer friend. She'd always had a steady hand and had been pleased with her film work in the past. *Between the sunlight and the unobstructed view,* she thought, *this should come out really well.*

The president faced her direction briefly, then turned to the crowd on the other side of the street. Margaret hoped more than anything he would turn back again. If he did, she decided, she would sacrifice a little camera stability and try to get his attention. He was known for making direct eye contact with people, often accompanied by a smile and a wave. If she got either from him . . . how incredible would that be? She'd be willing to blow her cover and tell Ron if that happened. He'd probably just laugh and shake his head, but it'd be worth it.

She continued to follow her subject through the lens, waiting for him to turn back, urging him to do so through sheer willpower. Then—

POP!

A sharp, firecracker-type sound echoed through the plaza. The thought that it might be a gunshot did enter Margaret Baker's mind, but the president didn't seem to respond to it. Then came the second one, and this time his reaction was unmistakable—through the tiny viewfinder she saw him raise his hands to his throat, his elbows sticking out like spearheads. At the same time, Governor Connally began sinking, jellylike, into his seat. Margaret froze, uncertain of what was happening, and the camera kept rolling. When the third shot arrived and the right side of the president's head blew out in a gruesome cascade of bone and tissue, she gasped audibly.

She finally looked up, the camera still held in place, and witnessed something that would replay in her nightmares for weeks to come—Jackie Kennedy, resplendent in her pink Chanel suit and matching pillbox hat, crawling on all fours across the trunk. Noticing the bloodstains on the First Lady's midsection and the fact that the president was now a motionless figure slumped down in his seat, Margaret intuited through her horror what the rest of the world would soon come to know as truth—that Jackie, in her shocked hysteria, was trying to retrieve parts of her husband's brain and skull.

No . . . dear Lord, please. . . .

Margaret watched in wordless astonishment as one of the Secret Service agents forced Jackie back into the seat with her dead husband. Then the limo's engine roared as it picked up speed and zoomed off. In the remaining chaos, sirens blared and terrified people took off in every direction. Some dropped to the ground in case the gunman decided to expand the assassination into a random turkey shoot. Several adults were lying atop small children.

This can't be happening, a voice in Margaret's mind insisted. *It just can't be.* She wasn't even aware that she had stopped filming and was now holding the camera slack against her thigh.

More police officers and Secret Service agents materialized. Some people came up alongside them and pointed to a spot high on the facade of the Texas School Book Depository, where the son of one of Margaret's friends worked as a night custodian. She looked up and saw several open windows but nothing more.

"Come on! Don't just stand there!" a man barked as he sped past. The crowd around her was migrating to the other side of Elm. Margaret began moving forward, barely aware her legs were in motion. Everything had become dreamy and muted, like being underwater.

What snapped her back to reality was the scatter of red spots on the macadam. The sight of John Kennedy's blood, like paint flicked off a too-soaked brush, brought her to a halt. It glistened in the same afternoon sunshine that had projected an angelic light onto the president's face just moments earlier.

She moved to avoid stepping in it and kept going.

• • •

Margaret's home, a modest Victorian, was located in the quiet suburb of Addison. The house sat well back from the sidewalk and was partially obscured by a pair of massive oak trees.

She pattered up the front steps and worked the key into the door with hands that were still trembling. Once inside, she had no less trouble twisting the lock back into place—an action she had performed thousands of times without difficulty. She tossed the keys onto a nearby table and continued up the carpeted steps to the second floor. One hand still clutched the wad of tissues she'd found in the glove compartment. They had dampened into a warm, solid mass. Her eyes were delicately swollen and thoroughly bloodshot, her makeup a disaster.

She strode past the second bedroom, currently reserved for guests but which would one day be transformed into a nursery, and went into the master bedroom. She removed the headscarf and glasses and set them down on the dresser, then shed the overcoat and laid it on the bed. She crossed the room and turned on the tiny portable television that was set on a rolling hard-wire stand. They only received five channels in this area, and two of them were snowy on the best of days. They were all broadcasting coverage of the shooting, which wasn't surprising, and she twisted the knob to CBS because that's where Cronkite would be. Like so many other members of Middle America, the Bakers never questioned the gospel according to Walter.

There was still part of her that harbored hope for a miracle. She knew what she had seen, but there was always that chance. She had analyzed the shooting in her mind and figured that such a young man could likely survive the first strike, the one that pierced his throat. Maybe it would permanently affect his speech; maybe he'd need some kind of medical equipment to assist with his breathing. *But that second strike, the one where his head . . . where it . . .*

She erased these thoughts and trained her attention on

the little screen. Cronkite was there, sitting at his anchor's desk in a white shirt and black tie, addressing the nation.

". . . policemen called in on their day off because there were some fears and concerns in Dallas that, uh . . . that there might be demonstrations, at least, that could embarrass the president. Because it was only on October 24 that our ambassador of the United Nations, Adlai Stevenson, was assaulted in Dallas leaving a dinner meeting there—"

He was interrupted, presumably by a news editor who had just pulled an Associated Press bulletin from one of the wire machines. Cronkite put on the horn-rimmed glasses that gave him the academic bearing of a nuclear physicist. He read through the bulletin once while America waited, then turned back to the camera.

"From Dallas, Texas, the flash, apparently official. President Kennedy died—"

At this point he removed the glasses again, and Margaret Baker let out a warbling, uneven cry.

"—at 1 p.m. Central Standard Time, two o'clock Eastern Standard Time . . . some thirty-eight minutes ago."

The glasses went back on again, and a clearly affected Cronkite took a moment to compose himself. "Vice President Johnson has left the hospital in Dallas, but we do not know to where he has proceeded; presumably—"

Margaret switched it off. She then covered her face and wept. Kennedy had offered so much hope, so much promise. He had fresh and exciting ideas that represented the dawn of a new age. *And it's all gone now.*

When the tears dried up, she went to the mirror and wiped her face with the hardened tissue mass. Then she found some busywork, putting the glasses in their case and back into the forgotten reaches of her top drawer and setting the scarf by her jewelry box so she wouldn't forget to bring it back to the neighbor who'd loaned it to her.

She took hold of the overcoat, planning to put it back up in the attic, where it had been stored. Then she felt the weight of it, of something semi-heavy that was—

The camera.

She stopped. Every function in the universe, in fact, seemed to pause while she digested the magnitude of the discovery. She reached into the pocket, found the hard metal shape, and brought it out. Sitting on the edge of the bed, she stared at it as if it were a living, breathing thing. Then the unavoidable question came. *The film—what should I do with it?*

A litany of possibilities marched through her mind, none of them palatable. From a financial standpoint, it would likely be worth a small fortune. She had been about thirty feet from the car when the president was struck, and she was certain the quality was above average. But . . . *No,* she decided. *I will not profit from this. Absolutely not.*

Should the film be turned over as evidence? *Maybe.* . . . Surely there would be a massive investigation. But what about the people pointing to the high window in the book depository? *If that really was where the assassin fired from, I never turned the camera in that direction. And even if I had, what good would it do now? Would it bring the president back?*

Realistically, then, there was only one option—keep quiet about it. That was almost certainly the safest choice. *Or is it?* Had anyone recognized her while she was there? She had friends all over town. She went out for lunch at least twice a week, and she did a fair share of shopping in the area. Some of the people she saw on a regular basis had to be Kennedy supporters. It followed, then, that at least a few of them had also come out to see him. *Did they see me, too?*

Of one thing she was absolutely certain—she would never watch the film. There was no reason to relive the experience. Besides, the film had to be developed, which presented an assortment of new problems. Sometimes the people who worked in those labs looked at the things they were developing. They weren't supposed to, of course, but they did. If some technician saw those images, what were the odds he'd keep his mouth shut? A person in that position might even feel it was his responsibility to say something to the authorities. If that happened, Margaret might be criminally liable for withholding—

Or . . . what if the film didn't come out right? What if it got "accidentally" ruined before I even had the chance to develop it? The story came together easily in her mind—*I was running with the rest of the crowd immediately after the shooting. I fell down. . . . The camera tumbled out of my hand. . . . It popped open, and the film was exposed.* Then she would show the police (or FBI or CIA or whomever) the exposed and ruined roll as proof, and that would be that. They wouldn't suspect her of anything dubious. Why would they?

She ran her hand over the camera and found the little ring that opened the protective panel. She sat staring at it for a long time, taking slow, measured breaths. Then she slipped her forefinger into it.

There was a metallic *clunk* downstairs—the lock on the front door being opened—followed by the familiar rattle of Ronnie's keys. The door squealed, and he called out, "Honey? Honey! Where are you?"

She took a deep breath and slid her finger back out.

"Margaret? Are you—?"

"I'm up here, Ronnie."

"In the bedroom?"

"Yes. I'll be down in a minute."

"All right."

She gave the Bolex one last look, hoping a decision would come. It did not, and she didn't want to marinate in the uncertainty for another dreadful minute. Ron would want to talk about the events of the day. That would be followed by hours in front of the television and dozens of phone calls from friends and family. The film could be dealt with later. When, exactly, she didn't know. Just . . . *later*.

She opened her bedroom closet and knelt down to retrieve the Bolex box. She laid the camera carefully inside, set the lid on, then stored the box in a far corner next to a shoe-shine kit.

• • •

The two people responsible for what she did next were her husband and a local blowhard named Ellis Clayton.

The capture of Lee Harvey Oswald did not sway her one way or another. She never had any doubt the authorities would make an arrest. The fact that the shooter turned out to be some defiant little pip-squeak didn't shock her as much as it did some people. *It's always a nameless face from the crowd,* she thought as she watched him whine to journalists about police brutality and being someone's patsy. *Another nobody with delusions of grandeur.* She found his own murder two days later at the hands of nightclub owner Jack Ruby as shocking as the rest of the nation, but more due to the fact that it occurred on live television than anything else.

The following week, Ron said he wanted to take a break from the media madness in the area and drive out to Granbury, a town southwest of Fort Worth where he'd spent his childhood. Then he added, "Let's bring the camera, too.

I'd like to take some movies that I can watch when I'm feeling homesick."

Margaret decided at that moment that the film would be disposed of. *Stuffed in the trash—and out of my life forever. The president's gone; his killer is gone. . . . Why hold on to it?*

What changed her mind was a routine trip to the supermarket the following afternoon. Standing in one of the checkout lanes, yammering to one of the clerks and slowing everyone else down as usual, was Ellis Clayton. Clayton was a retired municipal utilities worker who padded about town in shorts and a tank top. He had a harsh, growling voice that he used as if certain every syllable that fell from his lips was sacred.

When Margaret first spotted him, she deviated to the only other lane that was open and tried to tune him out. As she unloaded the carriage, however, her attention was drawn by something he was saying about a possible conspiracy in the assassination—that Oswald might not have acted alone, might in fact have been part of a larger organization—and that new president Lyndon Johnson was ordering a group headed by Chief Justice Earl Warren to look into the matter. Margaret was trembling by the time she reached the car.

She knew she could still destroy the film if she wished . . . but that option no longer seemed realistic. *What if it's true? What if there really were more people behind the killing?* From there her imagination sailed. *The Russians? The Cubans? Fidel Castro? Or maybe President Johnson himself?* Anyone who paid attention to politics knew Johnson had loathed being vice president. *That would make sense,* she thought, unaware that she was among the first to dabble in the kind of wild speculation that would occupy much of society for a generation. *The fact that he launched the investigation would give him good cover. . . .*

Regardless of who was responsible, of this much she was certain—these kinds of things occurred on a level of society so far removed from her own that it might as well have been part of a different universe. And if the president's murder had, in fact, been a carefully coordinated effort among multiple parties, then those involved were likely well connected, well funded, and frighteningly powerful. In other words, very, very dangerous.

The following Monday—the office was closed on Mondays so Lomax could play golf at his country club—she drove all the way to Plano because she'd found a developing lab listed in the yellow pages and, more importantly, because she didn't know anyone out there. She used a false name and paid in cash, including an extra fee to have the processing done within two hours. She was so nervous when she walked back into the shop that the technician, still wearing his rubber apron, asked if she was feeling all right. She lied, saying she was in the early stages of her first pregnancy and still experiencing the effects of morning sickness. He congratulated her as he handed her the change, the receipt, and the finished film in a brown paper bag. There was nothing in his manner that gave her the slightest impression he had looked at it. Nevertheless, she couldn't help asking, "Did it come out all right?"

The tech appeared to be horrified at the suggestion of such unprofessionalism—precisely the reaction Margaret was hoping for. "I wouldn't look at a customer's film, ma'am," he explained, with patience colored ever so slightly by prideful irritation.

Back home, Margaret made a point of securing the front door not just with the dead bolt but also with the chain. She didn't expect Ronnie to arrive home from work for a few hours, but if he came early for any reason, she'd be alerted when he had to ring the bell. She would explain that a salesman had come earlier in the day, so she had decided to put the chain on before opening the door and had neglected to remove it.

She went into the basement pantry, unfolded the stepladder, and slid one of the ceiling tiles aside. She had chosen the pantry because it was dark and cool—ideal for film storage. She never removed the reel from its flat yellow box, nor the box from its brown paper bag. She simply set the whole package up there, then moved the tile back into place. At no point did she feel the need to put the film on the projector they kept in the hall closet upstairs. Seeing John Kennedy murdered once was more than enough.

After refolding the ladder and wiping the dust from her hands, she whispered a little prayer that she would not have to take the film out of its hiding place for any reason.

And the Lord would grant this request . . . for a time.

• • •

April 1976

Margaret opened the basement door and felt around for the light switch. This simple action was not as easy as it had once been, as her diminishing vision made depth perception difficult. Also, abrupt shifts from light to dark gave her instant headaches, often compounding the chronic migraines that already arrived, unannounced, several days a week. Bright sunlight, which she had loved as a child, was the worst. One look into a clear sky at high noon sent knife blades into her eyes.

She found the switch and flicked it, shielding her face like a frightened animal. Compromised vision and paralyzing

migraines weren't the only manifestations of the hypertension that had become a relentless presence in her life. In spite
of being only forty-one, she had acquired obvious streaks of
gray in the thick wave of brown hair that had once shimmered with such radiance it earned the envy of many of
her girlfriends. And her face, which had retained much of
its youthful clarity well into adulthood, now bore the first
lines, blemishes, and discolorations that commonly flow in
the wake of unyielding anxiety.

She took the steps cautiously. There was a faintly electric
uncertainty to all her movements these days, resulting in
a clumsiness previously unknown to her. She had already
slipped and gone down this staircase three times, once
resulting in a badly sprained ankle and a chipped bone in
her right elbow.

When she reached the bottom, she crossed through the
laundry area and went into the pantry. She did not turn on
the bulb in here; there was enough light slanting through the
ground-level window set high in the corner. Summoning all
her willpower, she took the stepladder from its hooks and
unfolded it, setting it beneath the ceiling tile in question.

She sat down on the ladder and took a pack of Parliaments
from the breast pocket of her blouse, which was fashionable
for the times but fairly wrinkled. Ron didn't care much for
the smoking habit she'd acquired a few years back. She told
him she had smoked in college—therefore it wasn't really a
new habit—and that she only indulged occasionally. She was
pretty sure he knew she was lying on all counts, even if he
didn't say as much.

She fumbled with the lighter, eventually got the cigarette
going, and reveled in the curling threads of bluish gray. Her
thoughts inevitably followed those threads upward, settling

on that accursed tile and the even more accursed package that waited behind it.

She was struck again by the fact that there was actually a point along the timeline when she could go days without the film even entering her mind, when it had become all but forgotten. She had even determined an exact date when this "era" began—September 27, 1964. That was when the Warren Commission released their report to the public stating that Lee Harvey Oswald had been the president's sole assassin and had not been part of a broader conspiracy. Those who believed otherwise scrutinized the evidence to the subatomic level and volubly protested the commission's findings. But the eight-man team that produced it—which included future president Gerald Ford—stood their ground, and the lone-gunman theory became a matter of official record.

Margaret had been so overwhelmed with relief that she broke down in tears and thanked God for his infinite mercy. *It's over—at last. The verdict has been handed down and written into the ledger of history. That's that.* And thus, there was no longer any need to worry about the accursed film. It would never be needed as evidence and could be recategorized as nothing more than a personal curio. A remarkable record of a remarkable moment in history, but nothing that would send shock waves through humanity.

She had thought again about simply throwing it away but decided instead to keep it as a family heirloom. At some point she'd tell Ron about it—she didn't know when because it just wasn't that important—then label the box and put it with all the other reels: the road trip to New Mexico, camping in Arizona, and that wild weekend in New Orleans, where they recaptured the spirited times of their premarital courtship. It was no longer radioactive, and that's what mattered most.

Drawing in another lungful of smoke, she moved to the next significant point on that timeline—1969. It was a turnabout year in so many ways, with the needle swinging in a wide arc across the emotional spectrum. On the joyful side, there was Sheila Marie, born on January 15, shortly after midnight. She was pink and plump and perfect in every way, and Margaret could not have been more delighted. Thoughts of the assassination were so distant on that day that it seemed amazing to her, even a little ridiculous, that she had been worried in the first place. The conspiracy crazies still stuck their heads up from time to time, and Margaret would occasionally invest a moment or two to listen. But they never came up with anything convincing, so she dismissed them and went on with her happy life.

Her blissful contentment was shattered just two weeks after Sheila's birth when New Orleans District Attorney Jim Garrison hauled local businessman Clay Shaw into court in what would prove to be the only prosecution relating to the president's murder. Garrison accused Shaw of working with both right-wing activists and the CIA to facilitate the killing, but he could not prove his case, and Shaw walked. While conspiracy theorists were disappointed, one aspect of the trial had such a powerful impact that it went all the way to Addison, Texas, and landed in the center of Margaret's life—for the first time in any public forum, the Zapruder film was shown in its entirety. This "new" evidence reignited the conspiracy frenzy, and Margaret found herself powerless to do anything except tend to the benign hope that the furor would once again die down.

Instead, Americans began to reconsider their stance on the assassination. To Margaret's astonishment, the people who had railed for years about the Warren Report being the product of a crooked government trying to cover up a brutally implemented coup now found an eager audience in the general public. New theories were being explored and new technologies utilized in private but well-funded investigations. Reenactments of the shooting were carried out, documentaries produced, and dozens of books and articles published. Some ideas were downright idiotic, but a few others seemed entirely plausible—and from there public interest grew even further.

It was around this time that Margaret began to think of the assassination not as a historical event but a cancer that had awoken in her life on November 22, 1963. It had gone into remission for a while but was now active again. She also began to realize it had been one of the central governing factors in almost every major decision she had made since that sun-soaked Friday.

With the cigarette now half-gone, she glanced up briefly at the ceiling and shook her head. In her memory, she reached the most recent segment of this interminable nightmare. It also had a specific launch date—March 6, 1975, just over a year ago—and coincided seamlessly with the decline of her health. That evening, millions watched as two conspiracy theorists, along with host Geraldo Rivera, played the Zapruder film on ABC's *Good Night America*. The public's reaction was immediate and decisive, with renewed demands on the government to finally resolve the question of who really killed John Kennedy. This horrified outrage eventually led to the formation of the United States House Select Committee on Assassinations as well as a small army of neo-conspiratorialists, all of whom dedicated an abundance of time, energy, and money to the examination of virtually every piece of evidence that could be found. No stone went unturned, no theory unstudied, and no witness unquestioned.

This was also when a small group of curious persons began to ponder the identity of the woman, previously overlooked, whom they provisionally named "the Babushka Lady."

She was there in a few photographs, grainy and unfocused. One was taken a good distance behind her but clearly established her proximity to the president's limousine. Another had the woman in midstride across Elm along with several others exiting the scene. And she was there, albeit briefly, in Abraham Zapruder's grisly record of the killing.

Most researchers believed the Babushka Lady—so dubbed because of her distinctive headscarf—was holding a motion camera of her own and had witnessed the assassination from a unique angle. If this was the case, then perhaps her film had caught something equally unique. In particular, they wondered if there was clear evidence to support the growing theory that a second shooter was positioned behind the stockade fence that stood atop a tiny hill just a few yards away from the Bryan pergola, a region of Dealey Plaza that would eventually become known as the "grassy knoll." If so—if the Babushka Lady did, in fact, have such evidence—why hadn't she come forward with it? Had she been tracked down by the conspirators and killed, as many believed others had been? Or was she still out there now, waiting for just the right time to come forward? Perhaps she had already sold the film to some powerful media presence, like *Time* or *Life*, for an astronomical sum, and they were the ones sitting on it. There was also the suggestion that the woman in question wasn't even aware of what she had and that the film had been innocently relegated to a forgotten box in her home somewhere.

Whatever the case, two points were now very clear to

Margaret Baker. One was that *she* was the person known as the Babushka Lady. The other was that many people associated with the assassination wanted to find her.

• • •

She took a final puff and dropped the cigarette onto the cement floor, crushing it out with her shoe. A part of her had always suspected this day would come. In the end, it wasn't the film's potential implications or the quest for justice or even the thought of shadowy figures searching for her that brought about this moment—it was the blood she saw in the toilet three days ago following her morning routine. The hypertension that was gradually obliterating her strength had begun with the usual symptoms—fatigue, occasional dizziness—then moved to the more severe—blinding headaches, irregular heartbeat, labored breathing. They made life difficult, no doubt, but she had tolerated them. There was something about the sight of that blood, however—something about the thought of her insides *coming apart*—that pushed her past her limits. The time had come, she decided, to rid herself of this burden, to take the steps necessary to put the matter to rest once and for all. And the first step, she knew—against every instinct and desire—was to watch that film.

She let out a final, defeated sigh and placed her foot onto the ladder. With each step she felt increasingly sensitive to the sickness that was consuming her. It was as if the film still possessed a kind of emotional radioactivity after all and moving closer to it magnified the symptoms. Sliding the tile aside had a ghastly familiarity to it, like she'd stored the package up there only a day or so before. The actual interval between then and now shrank to zero, and she was reminded of the dim awareness she'd felt on that day—and which had never fully left her waking thoughts since—that she would one day have to do this.

She felt around on the gritty surface, and at first there was nothing. What followed was an almost-relieved kind of confusion. *Is this the right tile? Did I forget where it was?* Then, slightly more alarming—*Did Ronnie find it and do something with it?* And finally, almost inevitably, the paranoia—*The men in the shadows . . . They found me and searched the house one day. . . . They know everything, and they know that I know.* This got her heart pounding like a parade drum.

It was only after she moved to the stepladder's top rung that her fingers found the wrinkled paper bag. It had been there all along, right where it was supposed to be. She supposed she had subconsciously lingered on the lower step as a kind of passive self-sabotage.

Like everything else up there, the bag had been dusted by time. She gave it a shake before bringing it down. She could feel the hardness of the box inside, and it filled her with revulsion.

Stepping to the floor, she unrolled the bag and took the box out. A part of her fantasized that it had been damaged somehow, perhaps from a pipe leak. The box would be corroded, the film warped and water-stained. . . .

No such luck. The box was firm and solid, its corners sharp. When she lifted the lid, the reel was so healthy it still bore malodorous traces of the chemical processing that had been performed twelve years earlier. The first few inches of dark celluloid hung out like the tail of some sleeping beast. *Waiting for me,* she realized angrily. *It has* always *been up there waiting for me.* Once again, she entertained thoughts of destroying it, more aggressively than ever before. *Douse it with gasoline and throw a match on it, then pour the ashes down the drain. If anyone asks, deny it all. There won't be any evidence, so what can they do?* But it was too late for that now, and she knew it.

In another eerie reenactment of 1963, she went upstairs to lock the front door and secure the sliding chain. Ron had moved into a management position in 1971 and was rarely home early . . . but still. Their daughter was down the street with a retired schoolteacher who supplemented her income as a neighborhood babysitter.

Margaret went back to the basement with the projector in hand and set it up on a folding snack tray, aiming it at one of the bare walls. Her shaking hands made it difficult to feed the film through the spools. When it was finally in place, she took a deep breath and summoned all the nerve she had left. Then she turned the switch.

For a moment there was nothing but the purr of the projector's gears and a run of scrambled letters on the wall. Then came the first images of the president's motorcade as it flowed onto Houston.

Margaret was overwhelmed by sensory recall—the warmth of the sun on her cheeks, the scent of grass in the plaza and a nice perfume that the afternoon breeze had carried from one of the other women nearby, and the uncomfortable sliminess of perspiration mounting under her too-heavy outfit. She also remembered, for the first time, what she had planned to do with the rest of her day once Kennedy had passed—put the camera and her disguise back in the car, then return to the office and say she felt a little better and wanted to carry on. Lomax would've liked that. And if Kennedy had waved to her, she would've confessed everything to Ron over dinner that evening and laughed when he shook his head.

The motorcade eased onto Elm, and the president came

into view. It occurred to Margaret then that the film's quality was, as many researchers had theorized, outstanding. The images were sharp, the colors vivid, and her hand had been remarkably steady. *A hundred times better than the Zapruder film,* she thought. *And closer . . . much closer. . . .*

As the president and First Lady drew nearer, she could see Abraham Zapruder clearly on the Bryan pergola with his receptionist, Marilyn Sitzman, behind him. As Margaret had suspected all along, there was no view of the sixth-floor window in the book depository building in her film. And the assassination was mere seconds away.

She could not bring herself to look at Kennedy as he was struck. She had been unable to pull her eyes away twelve years earlier, but she would not witness it now. *That's not why you're watching anyway, is it?* Of all the conspiracy theories that had been put forth over the years, one that had really gained traction concerned a supposed second shooter behind the fence atop the grassy knoll. When that area of the plaza came into view, Margaret fixed on it. When the president was hit—she was aware of it even though she wasn't looking there—she searched for any signs of that elusive second shooter. A rifle barrel being leveled between the pickets, perhaps, or the head of a man in sunglasses. Even a puff of smoke as a shot was fired. . . . But there was nothing, nothing at all. Just the trees and the shade and the few bystanders who had long since been identified. There was no one there.

She smiled with an unpolluted elation she had not felt in ages.

Nobody. All those nuts who've been poring over blurry photographs with their magnifying glasses have been—

Then she saw something else, something well away from the stockade fence and the grassy knoll and Abraham

Zapruder and the book depository building. Something unbelievable.

She rewound the film and played it again. Once again the motorcade turned onto Elm. . . . The president and First Lady waved cheerfully to the adoring crowd. . . . Zapruder lifted his Bell & Howell and began filming.

And again she saw it.

"No," she said in a tone soaked with dread. *"No . . ."*

She watched it again, just to be sure, then a fourth time.

When she went into the upstairs bathroom a short time later, there was more blood.

● ● ●

Margaret had never been to Texas First National before. She and Ron did all their banking at Dallas Fidelity, on the other side of town. That was exactly why she had come here.

She went to a teller window and asked to see the manager. The woman, with a turtleneck sweater and a beaded eyeglass chain, gave her a once-over. It was highly unusual for a female customer to make such a request. In fact, it was unusual for any married woman to come in without her husband. What was this lady up to?

"I'm not sure he's available right now."

"He's expecting me."

The teller's carefully drawn eyebrows rose. "Oh?"

"Yes."

The appraisal continued. Then, in a tone that suggested she wasn't ready to admit defeat just yet, the woman said, "I'll see if I can find him."

"Thank you."

Margaret retreated to a quiet corner so as to not attract further attention. The teller returned a moment later, followed by a tall, well-built man in a pin-striped suit. His black hair was combed like that of a child on school-picture day. The rest of his all-female team stopped what they were doing when he appeared, their faces drawn with concern. He was the rooster of this particular henhouse.

"Can I help you?" There was no attempt at friendliness. His precious time was being wasted.

The teller hung around until Margaret shot her a look, then stalked off.

"I believe you spoke to Mr. Moore earlier this morning?"

The manager, whose name tag read *Kelso*, said, "Moore?"

"Henry Moore. The attorney?"

Kelso stiffened; he clearly did not like being contacted by attorneys.

"He's a friend of my husband's," Margaret said, her stomach tightening, "and handles all of our legal matters. I think he told you I would be coming here to put some things in our new box."

"Box? You mean—"

"A safe-deposit box."

"Oh, uh-huh. And you are . . . ?"

"Margaret Baker."

"Margaret Baker, right."

"It was opened for us yesterday."

"I believe I remember that."

He paused to study her, the faintest trace of a smile on his otherwise-dour face. Margaret felt fear begin to crawl through her. The struggle to maintain a casual air was beginning to slip out of its leash. *He's seen women do this before. He's going to call Ronnie. . . .*

"Do you have the items with you?"

"Yes, right here."

She drew a small cloth bag from her pocketbook and held it open for Kelso to inspect. Inside was an impressive cache of gold coins, dull-shiny and in various denominations that Ronnie had collected over the years. He kept them in a small lockbox under their bed.

Kelso's face brightened, revealing the actual—and unabashedly greedy—soul underneath. "Well, look at those."

"They belonged to my grandparents, and I don't feel comfortable leaving them around the house."

He reached in, removed one, and admired it. "I wouldn't want these lying around either."

"So is it all right if I . . . ?"

"Hmm? Oh yes." He tossed the coin back in the bag resentfully. "Follow me."

He led her to the bank's spacious vault. The safe-deposit boxes were in a separate, smaller room on the right.

"I believe Mr. Moore reserved number 423 for us."

"Number 423."

"I have the key right here."

Moving to the far right corner, Kelso opened the little door and then pulled the box out by its loop handle. It was auto-primer gray and about the size of two shoe boxes set end to end. He carried it to the small table in the middle of the room. The lid opened like an alligator's mouth.

"Here it is."

"Thank you."

Kelso lingered until it became obvious that his guest was not going to do anything while he was there, then left.

• • •

Margaret put the cloth bag back into her pocketbook and took out the film. Just having the box in her hand again made her feel nauseous. She also took out a standard-size envelope with the words *For Ronnie or Sheila* written across the front. The flap had been sealed.

She wondered for the millionth time if this was the right thing to do. It could be that this was just one of those situations where there *was* no perfect solution and you simply had to go with your best guess. *If that's true, then please, God, please let this guess be the right one.*

She felt tears coming on again, so without further hesitation she placed both items into the receptacle. It slid back into its cavity easily, and she locked the swinging outer door. Then she returned to the lobby, where Kelso was making time with his harem.

"You're finished?"

"Yes, thank you."

"Will there be anything else today?"

"No, that's it."

When she stepped onto the sidewalk, she paused to scan her surroundings. This had become a habit now, born from the fear of being watched or followed. Every stranger had become a threat, every glance in her direction a cause for concern. Were they really out there, searching for her? Were there really men in dark shadows, monitoring her every move, listening to her every conversation? Were they waiting for an opportunity? Did they plan to eliminate her, as they had apparently done to so many others associated with the assassination?

It was a beautiful clear day, cheerful under ordinary circumstances. But then November 22, 1963, had started out the same way. Margaret couldn't remember the last time she'd felt anything even close to cheer. It seemed like a part of someone else's life, a long time ago. She didn't want to think about it anymore. She had done what had to be done; whatever happened now was out of her control.

She took one last look around, then hailed a cab and disappeared into the afternoon traffic.

1

IT WAS NOTHING but a waiting game now, a cruel and macabre waiting game.

Sheila Baker watched her mother's face, framed within the hospital pillow. The eyes, reduced to sunken orbs covered by parchment skin, had been closed for a while now. Her nose and mouth were trapped inside the oxygen mask, clear plastic with pale-green straps. Her breathing was erratic, as it had been for the last two days. A drip bag hung nearby, filled with fluid that streamed into her ravaged body, and a mile of gauze ran around her wrist to hold the needle in place. The room was kept immaculately clean by the hospital staff, the sheets changed daily. Yet the reek of death hung heavy in the air. The clinical-looking clock on the wall held no relevance; time was measured in here by the rhythmic hiss of the respirator. For Margaret Baker, who had turned seventy-eight nine weeks earlier, this room was her universe now, her gateway from this world into the next.

She had smoked for years, a habit she'd first picked up in the 1950s, when smoking was considered safe and fashionable and people puffed away in airplanes, offices, restaurants, and elevators. The idea that you could die from it was as distant as the notion of committing gradual suicide from the sustained consumption of fried foods, the use of dirty needles, or living down the street from certain types of power plants. By the time academics started publishing their studies proving otherwise, she was hooked. When she finally mustered the willpower to break free of its grip, the cancer had already set up shop. Doctors were summoned, friends rallied round, and a spirit of cautious hopefulness arose. But lung cancer was almost always a nonrefundable ticket to the grave, and the light of optimism first dimmed and then flickered out. Margaret had accepted the truth and, with characteristic courage, focused not on fighting a losing battle but rather on making the final stage of her journey as uncomplicated as possible.

She'd been a patient at Parkland twenty-six times over the last three years. The first few visits were overnight stays for observation and an endless litany of tests. Then they became longer—two days, four, six . . . Names and faces of the hospital staff became familiar. The need to stop at the information desk faded. One of the nurses in the oncology section, it turned out, had been a year behind Sheila in high school. People from the past came to visit in a depressing revival of *This Is Your Life*—the owner of the pharmacy in downtown Addison, several church friends, a former coworker, a few others. But no relatives. Sheila was Margaret's only child, and her husband had passed away in '98.

Sheila was pleased they finally moved her mother to a private room. She'd had roommates in the last three, all in worse shape. Each one was an elderly woman, and they were all deceased now. The first had been clearheaded for a few weeks, the other two in various states of delirium. Sheila was haunted by one in particular, who stared maniacally at the ceiling and produced an endless stream of glossolalia. It wasn't her deteriorated mental state that affected Sheila so deeply but rather the fact that no one came to see her. There were no balloons, no flowers, no cards. A forgotten soul in a world of billions. Someone from the local church had left a prayer card—but then her mom received one too. So did every other patient, most likely. Then one day Sheila came in and found the bed empty, made up with fresh sheets. One of the nurses said the woman had died the night before. *With no one there to hold her hand, no doubt,* Sheila thought with a touch of anger.

She stroked her mother's white hair, kissed her on the cheek, then sat in one of the ridiculously uncomfortable guest chairs and opened a cooking magazine she'd spotted in the lobby. No sooner had she found a recipe for sesame apricot chicken than her cell phone vibrated. Removing it from the holster, she found the following text message on the screen:

Sheila,

The guys are here with the new arc trainer and they're setting it up. Is there anything else I need to do?

Vi7cki

Sheila rose from the chair and walked into the hallway before dialing. The call was answered on the second ring.

"That was quick," Vicki said.

"I'm here at the hospital and it's pretty quiet right now."

"Oh, I didn't know. I'm sorry."

"No, that's fine. I asked you to let me know when they got there."

"Do I need to tell them anything?"

"Are they actually working? Sometimes Eric's guys need the whip cracked over their heads."

"No, they're doing it." Vicki laughed. "I think they're afraid of you."

"That can be useful sometimes."

"I don't know. . . . You're the best boss *I've* ever had; that's for sure."

"Vying for a raise again?"

"No, really. I—"

"I'm just kidding. How are things going otherwise?"

"Okay."

"Busy?"

"No more than usual, but no less, either."

"Any new recruits?"

"Yes!" she said. "I signed up four new people this morning. *Four.*"

"That's excellent, Vick. Terrific work."

"And I re-upped two others."

"Re-upping is just as good. As long as they come to *my* gyms, I don't care how or why."

"We're the best."

"Better believe it."

"Oh, and that guy stopped in again, too. . . ."

"What guy?"

"That Doug guy."

Sheila rolled her eyes. "Did you tell him I was out of town?"

"Yeah. I don't know if he believed me, but he said he'd be back."

"Lucky me."

"He's creepy."

Sheila agreed, but she was also at a point in her life where she wasn't interested in a relationship with any man.

"Okay, let me get back to Mama."

"How's she doing?"

"Not that great. It's just a matter of time."

"How are *you* holding up?"

Sheila wasn't sure how to reply to this. She'd been through every emotion on the spectrum since the cancer had quietly entered their lives three years ago. Truth be told, she felt like a towel wrung of all moisture. It was torture to watch her mother suffer like this and to know the end of her life was mere days or even hours away. But there was still that hope, like a little flame that never burns out, for a miracle. Of course it was ridiculous now, but that wouldn't stop her from tending it.

"I'm doing okay," she said, more to keep the silence from winding out than anything else. "As well as can be expected under the circumstances." A tear rolled down her cheek, and she wiped it away before anyone else in the hallway noticed.

"I wish there was something I could do."

"I know. I appreciate it."

"Is there anything you need? Anything I can send you?"

"No, I'm fine."

"Really? Honestly?"

"Honestly. Hey, she was the greatest mom I could've asked for. She and my dad were always there for me, gave me everything I needed, and let me find my own way when the time came. I couldn't have asked for much more. And they really loved each other, so she had a good life too."

"You were all very lucky."

"We certainly were. But let me go, okay? I want to stay by her side."

"Sure. And don't worry about anything here. I've got it all under control."

"Thanks, Vick."

Sheila ended the call and put the phone away. As she crept back into the room, she thought about how lucky she'd been to find Vicki, too. She had more than two dozen employees, and Victoria Miller was the best of them. No formal education beyond high school, yet she had more natural business sense than any of the arrogant MBA geniuses Sheila had interviewed. Vicki was hardworking, tough, and—best of all—trustworthy beyond all doubt. That was something they didn't stress much in postgrad courses, Sheila noticed.

She was just about to return to the magazine when her mother groaned and rolled her head back and forth. The oxygen mask didn't follow—the tube got caught under her arm. This caused the edge of the mask to press her nose down crookedly. Sheila hastened to fix it, and Margaret's eyes opened. They were red-rimmed and watery, like those of a child who'd been crying.

"Sweetheart," she said, her voice muted behind the clear plastic.

Sheila was stunned by the lucidity of her tone. They were medicating her heavily to chase off the pain. She slept most of the time, talked nonsense the rest. She usually confused the past with the present, referring to long-dead friends and family as if they were standing in the hallway. Every now and then she produced a coherent thought, but they were growing scarce.

Sheila leaned down and smiled. "Yes, Mama?"

Margaret lifted the arm with the gauzy wristband and, with surprising strength, took her hand. "I'm sorry," she said.

This came out shaky and labored, but the eyes were suddenly bright again. The abruptness of the change was unsettling.

"For what?" There was still a faint trace of the Texas accent in Sheila's voice, in spite of not having lived here for almost twenty years.

Margaret's eyes closed again, and she sank back onto the pillow. This simple exchange had drained her, it seemed. Sheila thought she might fall back to sleep.

Then her mother took a deep breath and swallowed to clear her throat. Her eyes reopened. "For the burden. The burden of it."

Puzzled, Sheila studied her for a long moment. "What are you talking about?"

"This burden that I'm leaving you. I'm sorry, Sheila. I'm so sorry."

"Mama? What burden? What do you mean?"

"Just get rid of it. Get rid of it."

"What? Mama, I don't underst—"

"I'm sorry. . . ."

The eyes closed slowly this time. Her breathing became deep and heavy.

Margaret Baker had just two more rational moments—one the next day in which she said that she loved her daughter more than anything in the world, and a second on her final day, when she asked Sheila what she thought God might have in store for her. When Sheila said she didn't know but was sure it would be wonderful, her mother managed a weak nod before slipping into unconsciousness. Her suffering came to an end less than two hours later.

2

"THEIR OBJECTIVE was to blow up four synagogues in upstate New York. All on the Shabbat, all at the same time."

As assistant deputy director of the CIA, J. Frederick Rydell wouldn't normally deliver this briefing. But the agency's number two, the only man superior to Rydell aside from Director Vallick himself, was still overseas. Rydell was thin and smallish, with silvering hair that still bore random streaks of its former shoe-polish black. He was dressed in a dark suit with a tightly knotted tie and was leaning slightly forward with a manila folder in his lap.

"These were large congregations," Rydell went on, "mostly wealthy and well-to-do. The planners wanted a high body count. Plenty of children would've been involved too."

"And it was only six men running the operation?" Director Vallick asked from his side of the desk. The CIA boss's personal feelings on most issues were usually a matter of speculation; it was impossible to tell exactly what was happening behind those gray eyes. But his focus was already the stuff of legend, and it was a mistake to think he wasn't paying attention. He missed nothing.

"Yes," Rydell replied. "Six men, five of Middle Eastern descent, and one illegal from Coahuila."

The individual seated next to Rydell, the national security adviser, shuddered. "Savages," he said. He was sickly thin and wore large glasses that augmented his already-academic bearing.

"Where, specifically, did the Middle Easterners come from?" asked the only other person in the room, a woman in her early forties. This was the president's chief of staff and former campaign manager. She was attractive in spite of her reserved, bookish stylings. "The president will want to know."

"Three were Saudis, one was from Syria, and the fifth was from Pakistan."

"And our friends in Germany helped us with the intel, I understand?" This was Vallick again.

"Yes, they did. Above and beyond the call of duty, in my opinion."

The plot would likely never have been uncovered if not for some patient monitoring of a suspected terrorist safe house by the Bundesamt für Verfassungsschutz, Germany's domestic intelligence group in Cologne. Two months earlier, they caught three of the conspirators on tape discussing the target locations. Prior to this, the CIA hadn't even been aware of the cell's presence in Europe or America.

"I will make sure that's mentioned in the next press briefing," the chief of staff announced, "but I will also let them know that your people made the arrests. The agency will get full credit."

"We appreciate that," Vallick said. "Is there anything else?"

Rydell said, "No, that's it."

Everyone rose. The director came around, waited for the others to leave, then put his hand out. "Thank you, Freddie. Excellent work."

"My pleasure."

"Seventy-four and still blowing steam out the stack. Incredible."

Rydell smiled. He had known the director since the mideighties, when Vallick was still a field agent building files on Unabomber types.

"Not as much steam as I used to," Rydell pointed out. "And none at all come this time next year."

"When's your last day?"

"In four months, give or take a week."

The director smiled warmly and crossed his arms. "And you're still heading for the Keys?"

"Yes."

"White shoes, leisure suits, shuffleboard, that kind of thing?"

"I'm thinking more along the lines of fishing, reading, and finally learning how to cook."

"That doesn't sound too bad. Are you feeling the work-load growing smaller? Less weight on your shoulders?"

Rydell laughed. "Not one bit. I keep promising myself to scale back. But that never seems to happen."

With a dismissive wave, his boss said, "You love it. You'll always love it."

"Probably."

"Within weeks you'll be wishing you'd never left."

"Oh, I don't know about that." They cackled like crows at this bit of comedy.

The director walked back to his chair but stopped before sitting down.

"You know, it could just as easily have been you behind this desk. About a half-dozen times over the years."

Rydell's smile didn't vanish, but it changed into one colored less by humor and more by soulful reflection. "Perhaps, Pete. I don't know. . . . I'm just not a spotlight type of guy. Putting up with the media nonsense. Look at all the noise you have to deal with."

"A royal pain to be sure."

"I wanted to serve the agency without distractions like that." Rydell brightened again. "Just serve, you know?"

"Sure, of course. And you've done that amazingly well."

"A lot of people have served this government honorably."

"But not too many for more than half a century."

"No, I guess not."

The director waited for his guest to say something else but didn't appear surprised when he didn't. Rydell, who was barely known to the rest of the world but was an icon within the intelligence community, had never been one to let his words runneth over.

"Okay, old friend," the boss said finally, "get back to your glorious retirement plans, and let me get back to my first heart attack."

"You mean you haven't had one yet?"

"Out."

• • •

Rydell arrived back at his office ten minutes later. His secretary, an efficient woman of fifty-four who'd been with him since the first President Bush, held up a pile of phone messages. She also gave him a beaming smile.

"Thank you so much for your thoughtfulness," she said, nodding toward a crystal vase with a pink ribbon tied around its midsection and an explosion of spring flowers out the top.

Taking the messages, Rydell said, "Oh, of course, Theresa. I'm just sorry Greg can't be here to share them with you."

Her husband, a career infantry officer, had been killed by a sniper in the Gulf War during a routine patrol. The grim irony was he had less than two weeks before he was due back in the States. Today would have been their thirty-third anniversary. She had never taken her wedding ring off, and she kept her husband's service photo in a large frame on her desk.

Turning to it now, she said, "He did like flowers. He certainly would've liked these. Thank you."

"You're welcome. If you need me, I'll be inside."

He closed his office door gently, tossed the briefing file on a table, and got behind his computer. His in-box was overflowing, as usual. He scrolled through the list rapidly, giving the subject lines a cursory scan. Most messages were ignorable, destined for the recycle bin unread. Half had the red "Important" flag. *Everyone thinks their problem is priority one,* he thought. Even those messages of genuine concern, he had come to realize, wouldn't prevent the world from rotating if disregarded. It made him think back to his early days in the agency, when he was fueled by the mortal conviction that every little thing mattered, that the world truly would stop spinning if every agency employee didn't run at full throttle all the time. *What devotion,* he remembered. *What fanatic, maniacal devotion.*

His focus drifted away from the e-mails and further into the past. These sentimental journeys had become more frequent in recent months. He was well aware of the habit but never made any attempt to coax his concentration back. The simple fact was he was gradually unplugging himself from the job. It was perfectly normal, he had decided, to become nostalgic about the beginning when one was so close to the end. And there had been nothing wrong with his gung ho approach during those formative years. The agency needed boys like that. He'd caught the attention of the intelligence gods, and he'd wanted them to know that his dedication was absolute. Opportunities had arisen with gratifying regularity, and he had gone to great pains to cultivate the right image and reputation. He'd made as few enemies as possible, steered clear of controversy, and become known as a man of quiet, competent reliability. His rise had continued unabated until, in 1988, he was named assistant deputy director. Then, he decided, he would go no further. He had been offered the top job on five separate occasions in the years that followed, and he had declined each time with appropriate grace and etiquette. His formal explanations always seemed sound, even noble—he did not crave the spotlight, did not want to deal with the media, did not cherish the thought of stepping onto the political battlefield that was home to all who were vested with such awesome power.

His true reasoning, however, was never revealed.

He did not want anyone watching him too closely.

As third in command, he knew he could still wield a fair share of power while remaining invisible. It was true that all of Washington's elite would have his number in their digital Rolodexes, but few beyond the Beltway would even know his name. One average citizen in a hundred might be able to identify the director; one in a thousand knew the guy right behind him. The number three man, though, was basically a nobody. That kind of anonymity meant no *Meet the Press* appearances, no tabloid pictures of him walking to his car, no editorials cooking him alive to satisfy the public's voyeuristic gluttony.

And it also meant he could get away with things. Rydell's list of transgressions—ranging from thinly legal to outright criminal—was extensive. Some were carried out in the good name of the agency and the American government. Others, however, had been personal. Those were the ones he found most gratifying. By the midpoint of his career, the holy line of moral demarcation had been blurred out of existence, and he found this liberating.

A tiny smile appeared on his lips, and his thoughts shifted from the past to the future. There was the new house in the Keys, a little Cape by the channel with the Boston Whaler 255 Conquest moored outside. Three bedrooms, two bathrooms, a garage, and a patio with an inground barbecue. Reasonable, modest, humble. The kind of retirement home that would draw no attention, raise no eyebrows. He had already invited some of the agency boys down, held a housewarming party and a handful of poker games. He got to know a few of the neighbors, too. Again, cultivating a certain image, striking just the right note. He even went to pains to mention the down payment on the boat and grumble about the local taxes.

But it was all a ruse. Because Frederick Rydell was sitting on millions that no one knew about.

• • •

Rydell opened a folder on his computer, went two more subfolders deep, and clicked on an Excel spreadsheet. The name of the file was similar to that of the other seventy-seven in there, and none were password protected. There were several columns, and in one the dollar amounts ranged from $52,117 to $632,080. The total at the bottom was $4,779,186. Again, very similar to those in the other files.

Thus, to anyone who might one day examine it, it would appear as just another boring march of financial details—which was exactly what Rydell intended. He inserted a new line and typed in $285,331. The total adjusted itself automatically—$5,064,517. He sat back and let out a long sigh of relief, and a broad smile spread across his face. Really, he wanted to laugh out loud, but that wouldn't be prudent in this setting. He admired the figure for a while and even took to shaking his head in self-satisfied amazement.

The money had been gathered over the years. *Accumulated* was the word he preferred, as it was more civilized than *stolen*—not that he would ever speak about it to anyone. He felt no guilt, no need to rationalize it. Some of the funds had been skimmed from criminal enterprises of various types, including drug cartels, terrorist organizations, crumbling foreign governments, and so on. Others had been part of operational expenses that went unused. The best situation in that category, he had discovered, was when large sums were passed to field agents who were killed before they could use them. Everyone simply assumed the money had been withdrawn *before* the agent in question died, so no investigations were ever launched. Rydell knew such investigations were rare even under normal circumstances—it was taxpayer money, and those in government who sounded the alarm when taxpayer money was wasted were a very rare breed.

As it came in over the years, he tucked it away in offshore accounts under names of real people who had no idea they were so wealthy. The ability to manipulate information was one of the advantages of his position. If the money ever was discovered, it would lead back to an actual person—but not him. The cash was spread over nearly a dozen accounts, so the chances of it all being found were slim to none. Since he began the scheme more than three decades ago, his luck had been remarkable—he hadn't lost a cent. It was easy to beat the system when you were one of the people running it.

The best part was that the money was only one component of a larger plan; the rest was what really got him out of bed in the morning. After his official retirement, he would move down to the Keys and burn a few months, just long enough to do the requisite debriefings, tie up a few other loose ends, and create the illusion that he was settling into the sunset of his life.

Then, when the time was right, an accident would occur. He was leaning toward the Boston Whaler exploding in a spectacular column of flame a mile or so offshore. The following inquiry would suggest he had been out fishing and become the unfortunate victim of a crude bomb, likely planted by someone seeking to even an old score. Considering the number of years and volume of raw energy he had poured into tripping up the bad guys, the list of potential suspects would be endless. No body would be found, of course, so a memorial service would be held. Hundreds would attend, tearfully recounting the exemplary career of this true-blue American. His legend would grow into myth; they might even name a building after him. And all the while, following a meticulously planned alteration of his appearance, he would be sitting on a much larger vessel in the heart of the Caribbean, catching marlin, drinking tequila by the gallon, and learning to forget his previous life until it seemed like some fairy tale he'd read as a child. No more liberal policies aimed at exposing the agency's doings to the public because the average American had "a right to know." No more regulations against torturing prisoners. And no more academics in the president's inner circle promoting heavily revised political history and whispering that drugs should be legalized, African Americans should be compensated for slavery with tax dollars, and Bobby Kennedy should replace Alexander Hamilton on the ten-dollar bill. Rydell had had enough of these people for ten lifetimes.

And now I've reached my goal—five million.

He chuckled to himself, saved and closed the file, then went back to the e-mails. It took about a half hour to dig through them all. Then he swiveled around to the table behind him and began sifting through an intimidating stack of files that needed to be assigned to other agents. The mere sight of it was depressing, but he thought about the tequila and the marlins again, and suddenly it didn't seem so bad. He grabbed the one on top and flipped it open—a report on a potential terrorist connection with several overseas Internet poker sites. Ironically, the agency's main concern at this point was about the cash the terrorists might be skimming. The previous administration had attempted to clamp down on online gambling in the U.S., but the new laws turned out to be as porous as America's border with Mexico.

No sooner had he reached the bottom of the first page than the computer chimed to let him know a new e-mail had arrived. He would have ignored it had it been the normal chime—but this was one of the others. He had programmed the mail application to use different alerts based on specific criteria like sender address and keywords in the subject line. He hadn't heard this one in over a year.

Rydell spun around and found an auto-forwarded message from his personal address. Getting onto the Internet, he accessed that in-box and found seven messages waiting. All seven appeared to be spam, and six were just that. No one but Rydell would have known the seventh was any different.

It claimed a well-known department store as its point of origin, and the content announced an upcoming sale with special prices on men's shoes and ladies' rainwear. But it was entirely fictional, part of a complex alert system Rydell had personally designed, through which he could be informed of certain important events. He decrypted the message, deleted it, then sat back in his chair and stared fixedly into space as the information hit home.

Margaret Baker was dead.

All thoughts of the Caribbean, the marlins, and the tequila were long gone. The arrogant smile vanished, replaced by an expression of deep contemplation. He sat there for a long while, setting his hands in the familiar church-and-steeple configuration, tapping the forefingers together as he considered what to do. One part of him was tempted to disregard the matter altogether. *Huge odds,* he thought. *Huge. Bigger than huge.* But another part—the cautious and conservative part that remained restless until all contingencies had been accounted for—demanded otherwise. And there was another factor involved now, an unexpected emotion he was not accustomed to dealing with—fear.

He got out of the chair, retrieved a phone from his overcoat, and went into the private bathroom. The phone was connected to a government satellite and used a virtually impenetrable 256-bit encryption formula. It was unavailable to the public and issued only to high-ranking members of the intelligence community.

He locked the door, turned on the exhaust fan, and tapped in a number.

3

EDWARD BIRK lay on his back with the silk sheets pulled up just above his waist. He stared mindlessly at the ceiling, hands tucked behind his head.

The woman lying next to him, a tiny Asian thing with a perfect tan, was on her stomach, head turned the other way. Her black hair fell in sheets over her shoulders and piled up on the pillow. Somehow the posture did not strike Birk as befitting a woman of such natural beauty. Then again, neither did the snoring. She was as light and delicate as a bird, but she snored like a sailor. He found this distasteful and also a bit pathetic when he recalled how she had carried herself with the untouchable air of a starlet the night before.

He got up and pulled on a pair of drawstring pajama pants. The only light in the room came from the vertical crack between a pair of heavy curtains on the opposite side. *Morning sun,* Birk thought. Or was it afternoon? A glance at the digital clock on the dresser resolved the issue—12:44.

He went into the bathroom and switched on the light. The first order of business was a quick self-appraisal in the mirrored shower door. He was unable to pass any reflective surface without taking a glance. He knew he was handsome, and he loved the sight of himself. Excellent build, short brown hair, green eyes, sharp facial contours. The only flaws were the scars on his torso, both front and back. There were several knife wounds, two roughly circular bullet scars, and multiple cigarette burns on his back courtesy of the alcoholic mother who was long dead. His father hadn't left marks; he'd been too smart for that. Only bruises, which would fade. Birk didn't know where the old man was these days and didn't care. The only person he cared about was the one staring back at him now. He put his usual smile on the male-model face—a barely detectable rising of the mouth on one side, designed to taunt, to project arrogance. It said that he was pulling one over on the rest of the world and was pleased about it. He loved that look.

He thought about shaving. Then he decided it wasn't necessary and instead reached behind the vanity light to retrieve a plastic baggie. There were several pills inside, plus a small bottle of clear fluid, a syringe, and a packet of white powder. He took out one of the pills and swallowed it without water. Carefully rewrapping the bag and returning it to its perch, he gave no thought to sharing any more of the stash with his guest. That would be a waste. It had been used as bait to get her here in the first place, and it worked—she came, and she had served her purpose. If she wanted a fix now, she could get her own. He sat on the toilet and closed his eyes.

He emerged fifteen minutes later and was relieved to discover the room dead silent; the snoring had ceased. But then the girl launched into a fresh wave after a combination backfire grunt and full-body jerk. Shaking his head in irritation, Birk shuffled through the dimness toward the vertical light line. He slid the glass door aside and stepped out onto the balcony. It was a calendar-beautiful day, the sky shimmering and cloudless as the ocean washed gently against the beach several stories below.

There was no one else within view, perfect weather notwithstanding. Nor did Birk expect there to be. This wasn't the kind of neighborhood where people brought their dogs to catch Frisbees or where *Brady Bunch* families took their kids on vacation. This was where you came to get narcotics, cheap liquor, or a gun with its serial number sanded off. Half the condos in the complex were empty and would likely remain so until the property owner declared bankruptcy and the place was demolished. It had been built, Birk was told, in a halfhearted attempt at gentrification some years back. When the political landscape shifted, the effort perished. Developers lost their shirts, the outgoing government apologized and meant it, and that was that.

Leaning against the rail with his hands folded, Birk thought about what he would do today. There was no formal plan; he didn't make plans if he didn't have to. *One priority, though, is to get this girl out of here.* He tried to remember her name. Sunni? Suri? Something like that. A fake, he was sure. He'd never met a prostitute willing to give a real one. But then he never gave his, either.

Whatever her name, she had to go. He was hungry and didn't want company while he ate. This evening he would hunt down a new prospect. One for every night of the month was the goal. So far he was on eighteen—more than halfway there.

As he stepped back inside, his cell phone twittered. He found it in the pocket of his faded jeans. At first he didn't recognize the number—maybe a random, computer-generated call from a solicitor. Then he remembered—it was part of an alert system he had set up. He cursed softly.

Grabbing his leather blazer from the back of a chair, he went into the bathroom again, locked the door, and turned on the overhead fan—exactly as he knew the caller would have done only moments before. He removed a second phone from inside a secret pocket in the blazer's lining. It was thinner than most, had no brand name or caller ID, and could only vibrate, not ring. He had been given firm instructions to carry it at all times and make sure it was always fully charged. Two extra batteries had been supplied to make certain of this. He had also been told of the punishment he would receive if he ever failed to answer.

He thumbed the Answer button and brought the phone to his ear.

"Yes."

"Three rings."

"I was in the other room. I'm alone, and the phone was sitting on the bed while I was shaving."

"Try to avoid that in the future."

"Yes, sir."

"This is very important."

"Okay."

"You have to go to Dallas. Get there immediately, and check into the Grand Hyatt, 2337 International Parkway. There will be a room reserved under your operative name."

Birk felt the urge to laugh but held back. *Operative name . . .* In this case, that would be "Brian Clarke." Generic, easily forgotten. The man on the other end had given it to him long ago, and the irony was Birk didn't even know *his* name. In spite of being on his payroll for years, Birk knew virtually nothing about him. But he paid on time, in full, and very well. That was good enough.

"When you get there, you will find a dossier on the

woman, along with all the equipment you'll need. Then you'll receive further instructions."

"Right."

"And you'll get your usual fee once the job is done."

"That's fine."

It was more than fine, but Birk wasn't about to admit that. He had just under half a million left in the Singapore account, which wouldn't last forever considering the lifestyle he was now addicted to. He was in desperate need of replenishment.

"As always, you are to discuss this with no one, and you are to follow all instructions to the letter."

"Of course."

The line went dead.

• • •

Birk moved swiftly. He replaced the phone in its hidden pocket and went back to the bedroom. As he dressed, he shook the still-snoring prostitute awake.

"Time to go," he said matter-of-factly.

"Huh?"

"Come on, get up. You need to get out of here."

She looked around, puzzled, then dropped her head back onto the pillow. "I'll get up later. I'm too ti—"

"Let's *go*," Birk boomed, yanking her out from under the sheets by one arm.

"Oww! What's the matter with you?"

He picked up her outfit, which included a leather miniskirt and bright red heels, and tossed it in her direction. She caught about half of it.

"Get dressed," he said as he continued to do so himself. She didn't obey but instead suggested an action that was physically impossible, and in language that was normally reserved for bathroom graffiti.

His response to this was to grab her with one hand, gather up her remaining clothes with the other, then drag her, screaming obscenities, to the door. He pushed her out into the hallway and dropped the clothes in a heap.

"You owe me five hundred bucks!" she screeched.

"You weren't worth half that," he said before closing the door and locking it.

The pounding began almost immediately, accompanied by more profanity. Birk ignored it and finished dressing. Then he went through the process of removing every piece of evidence that he had been here—the sheets on the bed, soap in the shower, leftovers in the fridge. This was not his unit but rather one of the many in the complex that was officially unoccupied. In spite of that, the water ran and the electricity was always on. Since the owner never bothered checking, Birk used it as a venue for his conquests. He had furnished it sparsely and changed the locks, and he could leave it behind on a moment's notice. It was perfect. The last time the mystery man called, Birk was in Panama for over a month.

He stuffed everything into a paper bag and set it by the door. The pounding had stopped; the girl had finally given up and left.

He checked each room one last time, then went out, locked the door, and tossed the bag into the incinerator chute at the end of the hallway.

• • •

Slipping on his mirrored, wraparound sunglasses, Birk walked the six flights down rather than take the elevator. The garage at the bottom was open-air style, with no walls on the east or west sides. There were very few other cars around. His was a blue Ford Mustang sitting alone near the exit.

As he drew closer, a BMW with mag wheels and smoked windows zoomed off the road and into the lot. Birk was close to one of the cement columns and stayed near it as the vehicle approached. It stopped with a squeal, the decorative chrome discs inside the mags still spinning. The doors flew open.

The driver appeared to be of Italian descent and in his late twenties or early thirties. He was tall and lean and moved with a confident, confrontational stride. He was dressed head to toe in black, the button-down silk shirt open about midway down his hairless, muscular chest and untucked at the waist. Several gold chains ran around his neck, and there were rings on the outer fingers of both hands.

The other person, from the passenger side, wasn't quite so refined. Short, dumpy, dressed in filthy jeans, a gray hoodie, and a skullcap. This was a street punk. His face was ravaged by acne, and the eyes drooped in a way that was both lifeless and unsettling. His big sneakered feet clomped as he came forward, and both hands were kept in the hoodie pockets.

The driver paused, pointed at Birk, and looked back. It was then that Birk noticed the prostitute in the backseat, wrapped in a blanket. She nodded, and the other kid, watching her, said, "Yeah, Romeo, she says that's him."

Romeo started toward Birk again. "Yo, tough guy, c'mere for a second." He snapped his fingers and waved toward himself. "I think we have a problem." The kid came forward too, and Birk noticed his hand moving within the hoodie pocket.

The transformation Birk made could've earned an Academy Award. In a matter of seconds, he went from cool and cocky to squeamish and terrified. His eyes widened, shifting between Romeo and his sidekick, and he took a short step backward while putting his hands up defensively.

"No, please," he said, his voice unsteady. "You don't understand. She wouldn't . . . she wouldn't do—"

Romeo got to him first and pushed him to the ground.

"I don't care what she would or wouldn't do. She was there, she did her thing, and now we get paid. That's how it works."

On his back but up on one elbow, Birk said, "Wait a second. For that kind of money I expect—oh no . . ."

The other punk pulled out a gutting knife. The blade was at least a foot long.

"No, please."

Romeo crouched beside him. "Listen up. I don't have time for this. You can hand over the five hundred now, or my buddy here can fillet your insides and we can take it along with whatever else you got." Romeo hiked up his silk shirt and pulled out the gun that had been tucked in his pants. It was matte black and designed more like a sci-fi prop than a serviceable weapon. Birk recognized it immediately as a 9mm.

"And if you still have trouble deciding, maybe this will help. It'll blow your head into a pink cloud. How's that sound?"

Birk was hyperventilating now. Putting up a hand, he said, "Okay, let me get up. My wallet's in my back pocket."

Romeo rose and took a step back. As Birk got to his feet, he caught a glimpse of the prostitute, who had a triumphant look on her face. She leaned toward the open window on the passenger side and again displayed her fluency with objectionable language.

Struggling to catch his breath, Birk drew a brown leather wallet from the rear pocket of his jeans. He took out five hundred-dollar bills and counted them demonstratively for everyone's benefit. "Here," he said, holding them out.

Romeo, the gun still in his right hand but held slack at his side, came forward. It was the last foolish mistake of his life.

Birk dropped the cash just before the pimp touched it, then spun around and grabbed the wrist of his gun hand while darting an elbow into Romeo's face. Blood spurted from the pimp's nose and he screamed. The street punk lunged with the knife, but Birk sidestepped with the kind of graceful dexterity one acquires only through years of training and experience. The blade went under Romeo's shirt and penetrated his chest on an upward diagonal, slicing into his heart and killing him instantly. His eyes popped open in a darkly comic expression of surprise, then fell shut for good. Birk pivoted while maintaining his hold on the pimp's body in a horror-show pirouette. Raising the lifeless hand still holding the gun, he wrapped his finger around the trigger and fired into the kid's elbow. He screamed in agony and went down. Birk then released his dance partner, who crumpled like a doll on the filthy pavement.

As the kid tried to stanch the flow of blood with his good hand, Birk grabbed him by the hood and dragged him toward the BMW. The prostitute, whose face had gone deathly pale, scrambled from the vehicle and ran off screaming. Birk smashed the punk into the door face-first. Bone and cartilage splintered. Birk then rammed him against the car repeatedly until he lost consciousness.

Blood was everywhere now. Birk opened the door and forced the flaccid body inside. Then he walked casually to Romeo's corpse, dragged it back, and deposited it in the trunk along with the gun; the knife he kept in hand. Getting behind the wheel, he set the BMW in gear and steered it toward the beach. Then he jammed the knife between the gas pedal and the bottom of the dash until it held enough tension to keep the pedal depressed. Once the car was on course, he stepped out and began walking back. He didn't bother to watch as it bumped and rolled its way into the ocean.

Retrieving the five hundred dollars, he got into his own car and drove off.

• • •

He pulled into the entrance of a gated community twenty minutes later. The uniformed guard smiled and waved. He knew "Mr. Tillman" and was always glad to see him; he wasn't obnoxious like many of the residents in Sunrise Harbor. Birk waved back before driving through. An understated but sincere "Have a good day" completed the illusion.

His first task upon entering his home was to disarm the security system. Then he removed his bloodstained clothes and put them in a bag. He showered and shaved quickly, got dressed. Then he slid back a secret panel in the ceiling over the basement water heater and took down a large black suitcase. The lock was an electronic scanner that required a thumbprint. Inside was a variety of weapons and explosives. There was also a flat leather pouch. Birk unzipped this and removed a set of ID cards and passports. He separated all those in the name of Brian Clarke and put them in his shirt pocket. The case was relocked and put back. The last task was to pack and reactivate the alarm.

After putting the bloodstained clothes into the community Dumpster, he got into his car and sped off toward the airport. There was a report on the radio about a possible shooting at the Royale Beach condominium complex.

The smile reappeared on his face.

4

"YOUR MAMA was a wonderful woman," Henry Moore said. He had been the Baker family lawyer for as long as Sheila could remember. He was well into his seventies now with fine white hair and sallow features. And he still had the tiny second-floor office in downtown Dallas overlooking Federal Boulevard. Sheila felt like she'd stepped into the 1960s. Faded wallpaper, sagging and water-stained ceiling tiles, and a radiator that hissed like a huge snake. Fairly pedestrian for a wealthy lawyer, but then Moore had never been the flashy type. No silk suits or gold pinkie rings here.

"She sure was. The best mother anyone could have asked for." Sheila sat on one of the cushioned chairs facing the desk.

The last seventy-two hours had been brutal. First the wake with two viewings, then the funeral. More than fifty people had attended the church service and interment, and at least twenty had come to the house afterward. A caterer had been hired to handle the food, but Sheila had cleaned up the mess herself. She'd wanted to keep busy.

"I knew both of them through five decades," Moore said, stressing the word *five*.

Sheila nodded. "Since 1969, right?"

"That's right. Your daddy came to me looking for help writing his and your mama's will. We settled the matter in less than an hour over two glasses of Scotch. That was when you could do business with a handshake."

"Those days appear to be long gone."

"Tell me about it."

"So how do things look?"

Moore addressed a set of papers and folders that he'd laid out neatly on the desk. "Pretty good, young lady. Pretty good." He picked up a single sheet and peered at it over his bifocals. "The residual medical expenses are fairly heavy, as you know, even with Medicare and all that. But most of it will be covered by life insurance and personal savings. You'll also have enough to take care of the funeral expenses, which is great since they're considerable."

Sheila shook her head. *Vultures.* She found it appalling the way most people started in the world with nothing and ended with nothing. It almost seemed there was a system in place to make sure this happened. Her parents had worked hard all their lives, and in the end they had very little to show for it. It was as if they'd never existed.

"They did have some investments, which you are aware of. I know you've been managing them for the last few months, since your mama gave you control over her assets."

Sheila remembered the conversation, one of the last they'd had in the house. Her mother struggled to get from her bedroom on the first floor—which had originally been a sitting room until she could no longer climb the stairs—to the kitchen. They'd always had money discussions at the kitchen table for some reason. And there, with that accursed oxygen mask strapped to her face, her mother had announced, in a typically straightforward manner, that Sheila was being given control of all her worldly possessions. "You're going to get all of it in the end anyway," she said. "What's the difference?"

"Does this look right to you?" Moore asked, passing over a summary sheet. Sheila studied it briefly and saw that the bottom-line figure matched the one she'd calculated recently. Midrange five digits.

"Yes, this is correct."

"Good. As for the house, I'm sure you also know that the mortgage has been paid in full."

"In November of '92."

One of the proudest days of her parents' lives. Her father had been the first one in his family to own land in America. He was only the second generation born here, his grandparents having come from Europe in the late 1800s. He and Margaret had scrimped, scratched, saved, and sacrificed to cover each payment. When the day finally came to make the last one, he put on his best suit and personally brought the check to the bank. When he left, he was walking on a cloud. The happy couple treated themselves to dinner that night, then a new car—another first in Baker history.

"And you probably realize the house has appreciated considerably since it was first purchased."

"Yes, I figured as much." Sheila was uncomfortable talking about this. It was her parents' home, not hers. She grew up in it, and she had plenty of happy memories. But the idea of profiting from their deaths was difficult to stomach. She knew her parents would want her to have the money and to use it for the betterment of her own life. Still . . .

"Do you think you'd like to sell the property?" Moore asked.

"Hmm? Oh, maybe. I don't know yet."

"Well, don't sit on it too long. You still have to pay the taxes, and they're pretty heavy now. This area has really built up in the last twenty years."

"I know."

"If you sell the property, you could put the money into those gyms of yours." Moore smiled. "You appear to be doing quite well with them already."

"Thanks. We'll see."

"Right now, the house is nothing but a cash drain."

"I know. I'll figure something out."

"I'd be happy to help you with whatever you decide," he went on. "I have some experience with investments and wouldn't want to see you tread those waters without a guide."

"Okay."

She was ready to change the subject again. She looked down at the little notepad she'd brought along. It had a list of things they needed to go over—terms of the will, the stocks and bonds, the house, the remaining debts. It appeared as though everything had been covered. She glanced at her watch and realized nearly an hour had passed. It seemed more like ten minutes. She had no desire to get back to the house—the next project was sorting through Mom's things. That would be painful.

There were plenty of papers for Sheila to sign, which she did after reviewing each one briefly. Nothing new, nothing suspicious. Moore had done an immaculate job of protecting her family from legal nonsense. As she wrote her name over and over, she wondered what the odds were of finding a lawyer of his quality back home in Dearborn, someone she could trust implicitly.

After she signed the last sheet, she handed it back and said, "Well, I guess that's it." She got up and slipped her bag over her shoulder. "Mr. Moore, I want to thank you again for everything. You have really made—"

Moore cut her off by holding up a finger. "Wait . . . there's one other thing."

"One other thing?"

"Yes. Please, sit back down a moment."

As she sank into the chair again, she noticed his manner had changed. Gone was the air of grandfatherly warmth, replaced by a mild unease that appeared as though it could shift into full-blown angst without much provocation.

"Is something wrong?"

He was pulling open the top drawer when he stopped to consider the question. "Well, I don't know." He took out a standard-size envelope that had gone yellow over time but otherwise appeared to be in excellent condition. There was nothing written on the front.

He slit the top with a silver opener and turned it over. A small key dropped into his hand.

"This key has been in this envelope since April of 1976. I know because I was the one who put it in there. I remember the day quite well, in fact. It wasn't particularly cold, and yet when your mama came in that afternoon, she was shivering."

"I don't understand. What does this have to do wi—?"

"The key is hers."

Sheila searched her memory for anything in the house that had a lock but no key. There was a safe in the cellar, but it had a combination dial. There was also a small box of keepsakes in the upstairs bedroom—photos, notes, etc.—but the lock on it hadn't worked in ages.

"I can't think of anything that requires such a key."

"It's for a safe-deposit box."

"A safe-deposit box?"

"Yes, right here in Dallas."

"I didn't even know my parents had one."

"*They* didn't. Just your mama."

"What?"

Moore nodded. "That's right."

Her first thought was that he was mistaken. Her parents did everything together—*everything*. Sheila wasn't so naive to think that married couples, regardless of how devoted they might be to each other, didn't retain a few secrets. But not something like this.

"My dad knew about it, didn't he?"

"I don't believe so."

"Are you sure?"

"As sure as I can be. If he did know, I'm sure he would've said something to me. But he never did. The box was opened and managed by my firm. It still is, technically. But it was for your mama."

"She didn't have it in her name?"

"No, she wanted it in ours. She was very insistent about that."

"Do you know what's in it?"

"No idea." Moore set the key down. "She came in and said she wanted to open a safe-deposit box at Texas First National."

"First National? That's not where they did their banking."

"I know, but I didn't feel it was my place to ask about that. Also, quite honestly, I didn't feel she'd give up much information even if I did ask. Many of my clients have asked my advice on what should be put into a safe-deposit box. You know—wills, stock certificates, things like that. I just assumed it was something of that nature."

Her parents had all that kind of paperwork, but they'd

kept it either in Moore's office or in the basement safe at home. *So what did she need a box for?* Wild, utterly ridiculous ideas began rolling out of her imagination—*Letters from an old lover? The birth certificate of a child given up for adoption?*

Then came the echo of her mother's voice—*"I'm sorry for this burden that I'm leaving you. I'm so sorry. . . ."*

"I did ask her why she didn't just go down and open it herself," Moore continued, "and she said she couldn't tell me. That's when I realized she was scared. I mean, *really* scared. I asked her if she was okay, and she said yes. But she wasn't being honest. Lawyers know how to read people, you know, and your mama had the weight of the world on her shoulders that day. I never saw her like that before."

"Did she have anything with her? Anything that she wanted to put into it?"

"No. She had a coat, gloves, and her bag. That's it. I saw nothing, and she showed me nothing."

Sheila began to experience a feeling of dreamy disorientation. She looked toward the old windows with their cracked paint and smudgy panes. The Piedmont Building was visible on the other side. There was also the usual cacophony of street noise drifting up from below.

"All these years, and she never told anyone."

"It appears that way," Moore said.

"How often did she go to it?"

"Just once."

"Once?"

"Yes. The day after I opened it for her. That was the only time in nearly forty years."

A moment of unearthly quiet hung between them while Sheila tried to find a place for this information in her mind. "Forty years," she repeated.

"This burden . . ."

"Yes. Aside from that, she came here annually to give me the money for the fee. It was always in cash. She asked me not to tell anyone about it until after her death. And when that time came, I was to give this key—" he held it up—"to your father. And if he was gone, then to you."

"This burden that I'm leaving you . . ."

"So now I fulfill this final request." He leaned over and passed it to Sheila, who appraised it as though she'd never seen a key before.

"I'd be lying if I said I haven't been curious about what's in there. Giving that key to you constitutes the longest piece of unfinished business I've had in my practice. I've often wondered if I would even get to do it. I'm not exactly a teenager anymore. And there were days when I thought maybe your mother would just close the box and that would be the end of it. Then again, I'm not all that surprised. You had to see her that day, Sheila. As the saying goes, you had to be there."

She shook her head. *My mother, scared? To the point where she would do something like this without telling anyone? Even Dad?*

". . . probably hidden somewhere in the house," Moore was saying.

"I'm sorry; what was that?"

"I said the other key, *her* key—the bank issues two for each box holder—is probably hidden somewhere in the house."

"Oh . . . yeah, probably."

"Anyway, that takes care of that."

He rose from behind the desk, came around, and sat on the corner of it. "Listen, I don't know what's in there. But whatever it is, if you need me for anything further, I want you to call right away. Okay? Promise?"

Still half-dazed, Sheila nodded. Later, she would barely remember shaking Henry Moore's hand and walking out of his office. By the time she reached her car, an unshakable feeling was beginning to race through her—that whatever was waiting in that box would likely require more than just the services of a lawyer.

5

SHEILA KNEW there were plenty of other pressing matters to attend to, but she also knew she had no hope of focusing on them until she looked into this first.

She found Texas First National on Dearborn Street, just two blocks west of Federal. It was one of Dallas's oldest financial institutions, or so said the motto that ran in gold letters across the front doors. The lobby was all green marble and walnut. The teller windows were on the left, the managers' desks on the right. Only one was occupied—by a heavyset man in a size-too-small navy suit, working at his computer. He had thinning black hair combed in a horizontal sweep over the top, and a doughy, boyish face.

As soon as he spotted Sheila, he smiled and rose. "Good afternoon, ma'am. I'm Jay Gallagher. Can I help you with something?"

An eager beaver. He held his hand out, and Sheila took it. Cold and dry. His eyes ran shamelessly over her body.

She thought about turning around, walking back out, and forgetting about the box. Whatever was in there, she'd lived without it this long.

Instead, she heard herself say, "Yes, I have a safe-deposit box here." She took the key from her pocket and showed it to him.

"Wow, that's one of our older ones," Gallagher said. "How long have you had it?" Before she had a chance to answer, he moved toward his desk and added, "Come on over here; take a seat." He got behind the computer and opened a new screen. "What's your name again?"

"Baker, Sheila Baker. But the box isn't mine—it belonged to my mom."

"Okay, what was her name?"

"It was . . . Well, that doesn't matter either. The box was maintained by the law firm of Henry Moore and Sons." Mr. Moore had added the "and Sons" after his two boys—Louis and Brian—graduated from law school. They had since left to join other firms, in St. Louis and Denver respectively, but Henry had kept the name.

Gallagher continued typing, then stopped. "Did you say Moore and Sons?"

"Yes. Is there a problem?"

"Well . . . are you from the firm?"

"No. Like I said, the box belonged to my mom, but they managed it for her." Then she added, "She passed away recently."

"Do you have any identification with you?"

"Sure." She dug into her bag, found her wallet, and produced a driver's license, Social Security card, and two credit cards.

He looked at each one closely. It struck her as being similar to the way he probably inspected bills that might be counterfeit.

"I also have this," she said, taking out a large manila envelope. She found the form that transferred the box's ownership, with the fresh signatures at the bottom. Gallagher gave it the same meticulous scrutiny.

"Umm . . . are you aware how long this box has been under this ownership?"

"Since April of 1976."

"That's right, that's right. . . . And do you know how many times it has been accessed?"

"Just once." She made a point of saying this as if there were nothing unusual about it.

"Right." He put his hands together and straightened up in a standard concerned-executive gesture. "I have to tell you, Ms. Baker, that we have often pondered the idea of starting an investigation concerning this box."

"An investigation?"

"Yes. We've never had a safe-deposit box sit untouched for such a long period. I've been with this bank sixteen years, and never once have I seen anyone access it. Yes, the Moore firm has paid the fee each year. But no one has touched it."

"I guess my mother never had anything else to put in it."

Gallagher was eyeing her differently now. She felt like a murder suspect.

"No, I suppose not."

"Okay, well . . . can I get in and see it?" Her nerves were frayed enough without this officious little worm complicating matters.

"Sure." He stood and drew a ring of keys from his pocket. "Follow me."

The keys jingled as he crossed out of the managerial pit and into the lobby. "I'm going into the cave," he called out. None of the tellers appeared to notice.

They don't like him, Sheila realized.

The multilayered vault door, with its glass-encased

network of giant gears and polished rods, was already standing open on its massive hinges. That left only the gated inner
door. Gallagher inserted and jiggled one of the keys, and
the barrier swung back with a baritone growl. They passed
through a small antechamber containing several tall cabinets
and long file drawers, then came to a magnificently lit room
that was floor-to-ceiling with boxes. There was also a long
table in the center and two chairs.

"Which one was it again?" Gallagher asked, testing her.

"Number 423."

The box was located in the far right corner, a few feet from
the floor. Gallagher picked out another key and inserted it
into one of the two locks. Each box had two—small circles
with narrow slots.

"This is my master key. Can't open a box without it."
He said this in a singsong way, enthralled by the fact that he
commanded such power.

"I hope the lock still works," Sheila said.

"We maintain them even if they aren't used," Gallagher
told her. "I believe our man squirts a few shots of WD-40
into them once a year."

He was right—the lock turned without any trouble.

"Okay, now yours."

She came forward, thinking that she could still turn back
if she chose. Then she slid the key into the slender cavity.
Like Gallagher's master, hers rotated without resistance.

Gallagher fingered the little door aside, and the box was
exposed. Its looped handle hung down in a huge oval.

"I can manage from here," she said. "Thank you for your
help."

"Sure thing," he said, but he took his time leaving, spinning the keys and whistling as he went.

Sheila took a deep breath. *No turning back now.* She wrapped her fingers around the handle and pulled.

In spite of how long the box had been in there, it cooperated as readily as the locks. This was both a relief and a disappointment. She carried it to the table, making sure to keep it level in case there was something breakable inside. Now there was nothing left to do but open it.

She ran a hand through her short-cropped hair. This allowed her to procrastinate for a few more seconds. Then she decided her bag was getting heavy, so she set it on the table. When that was finished, she wondered if she should check her phone for new text messages or e-mails.

Enough. You can't put this off forever.

She inspected the box from all sides. *What's the right way to open this?* she wondered. There was a narrow lip at the front, just above the handle. It looked as though you set your fingers underneath and pulled up. She saw the rounded hinges on the back and knew this was right.

Crazy . . . This is crazy.

She took a deep breath and let it out, then took hold of the lid and lifted. The dried hinges squealed in protest. She willed herself to look inside.

Nothing.

The interior was almost mirror-shiny. Her stomach dropped when she realized the contents, whatever they had been, were gone.

Then she saw it—another box. Small, square, and flat. It was tucked in the back corner, as if trying to hide from the light. It was school-bus yellow with red letters, which were part of a logo. The brand name was known the world over—Kodachrome.

A film?

She reached in and removed it. The colors were still vibrant, the corners sharp. It was probably worth something to a collector on those points alone.

She opened it. The reel inside was in immaculate condition. This amazed her, as it had to be as old as the yellowed envelope in which Mr. Moore had kept the key.

Then she saw the letter, which had been under the film. This envelope, made of a heavy paper stock, was just beginning to pale. It was sealed only at the tip of the triangular flap—a common practice of her mother's. And then the words written clearly across the front—*For Ronnie or Sheila*.

A chill scurried down her spine. She pulled the flap—it came free fairly easily—and removed the single sheet of paper inside. There were several paragraphs on both sides, written in her mom's distinctive script. As she began to read, one hand moved from the paper to her mouth. Her heart started pounding; breathing became difficult. And when she was finished, she read the whole thing again. Then one more time.

This can't be real. It can't be.

Yet there on the table, undeniable in its physical form, was the film. It had been waiting all these years, like a bomb, in this small room.

I'm so sorry. . . . This burden that I'm leaving you. . . .

Sheila read the note yet again. Then she began to think about the pain her mother had endured—the unimaginable pain of carrying this knowledge for so long, unable to say anything to anyone—to her husband, her daughter, her friends. What must it have been like? *Oh, Mom, if only I'd known. Maybe I could have done something.*

And now she would know for herself, she realized. Now it was her turn to carry it.

The burden . . .

Or she could take her mother's advice, clearly articulated in the note's last line—*Just destroy it and be done with it.* And Sheila could already think of a few good reasons to do this.

The problem was, there were just as many reasons not to.

6

BIRK, DRESSED in a neat gray suit, entered the bank ten minutes after Sheila. He spotted her right away, talking with Gallagher, but kept a safe distance. He lingered by a rack of pamphlets.

One of the tellers, an older woman who was clearly bored and probably thought he looked like a nice young man, came over and asked if he needed help. He smiled and said he was thinking of changing banks—the one he currently used was nickeling-and-diming him to death with fees. A friend had recommended Texas First National, so he thought he'd visit. To support the lie, he'd already taken out a few pamphlets and was reading one about checking accounts. The teller smiled and told him to come to her if he had any further questions.

Knowing the security cameras were recording his every move, Birk worked hard to maintain his cover. It was getting difficult, though, as his subject had been in the vault for a while now. None of the other employees seemed to take any interest in Birk, but they would eventually.

Finally, after nearly forty minutes, Sheila emerged. She had looked worried when she went in, and she was ashen now. Were her eyes swollen? Had she been crying?

She returned to Gallagher. Their conversation was brief, and this time she offered her hand first. Birk tried to move close enough to hear the exchange, but Sheila broke away and headed for the doors. She passed within two feet of him. Yes, her eyes were red and glassy.

He lingered another moment, then followed her out, dumping the pamphlets in the nearest garbage can. He trailed her west down Dearborn, remaining behind a phone pole as she got into her car; he already knew it was a rental. She backed into the street and drove off. To her home, most likely.

And he knew where that was because he'd already been there.

• • •

Sheila was still numb and disoriented when she came through the front door of the house that now belonged to her.

Nothing seemed the same now—the big Asian rug in the living room, the clock on the mantel over the fireplace, the king-size bed in her parents' room . . . Everything had a different cast to it, tainted by the horror of what her mother had endured. Probably an hour hadn't gone by when she didn't think about it. The time they stood in the kitchen and fought over Sheila's first miniskirt, or when she came home late on a school night. Even the happy moments—when Sheila got her driver's license, when she received her acceptance letter to Ohio State. Was her mother thinking about the film through all of this? Did it haunt her every waking moment? For that matter, did it haunt her in her sleep, too?

Sheila went into the kitchen and sat down at the table. With trembling hands, she unfolded the letter and read it again.

April 14, 1976

Dear Ronnie or Sheila,

My heart is so heavy as I write this. Out of love for you both, I have chosen to keep this horrible secret to myself during my lifetime. I have thought a thousand times about destroying this film, but I couldn't. That said, I also chose not to come forward with it, for fear that something might happen to the three of us.

It was taken by me on the afternoon of November 22, 1963, in Dealey Plaza, when President Kennedy was assassinated. Yes, I was there. It was the most horrible thing I have ever seen. He was such an impressive man, with such a beautiful wife and family. For someone to have done something like this, in plain view and in front of all the world, was an unforgivable act. Many have said it was the moment that changed everything. I believe that's true. Nothing in America was ever the same afterward.

Like most people, I watched the reports of Oswald being captured, incarcerated, and then shot by Jack Ruby. I remember when the Warren Commission performed their investigation and published their report. And I've heard dozens of so-called experts make their arguments over whether Oswald really acted alone or was part of a larger conspiracy. I know the truth about that—and the proof is on this film.

I was standing about thirty feet from the president's limousine when the shots were fired. I heard the idea that someone might have been on the area they call the "grassy knoll," behind the fence, with a rifle. That's wrong—in the film, you can see the fence without any trouble, and there's clearly no one there. But there is someone else in a different location—someone who has never been mentioned before. I won't say anything further because I don't want you to know any more than you need to. If you choose to dispose of the film rather than watch it, it's best that you don't know any other details. Believe me when I tell you that knowing too much can be a curse. It's been the story of my life since that terrible day.

I was so scared when I got home that I hid the camera. I still couldn't believe all that I was witness to, and I just wanted to hide. People were asked to come forward with any film or photos—but I didn't. My fear was too great. Soon I began to hear stories—witnesses who were threatened or harassed, cameras that were confiscated and never returned. A few people even died under mysterious circumstances. I had my family, a steady job, and a nice home. I didn't want to put those things at risk.

Most of the other witnesses in Dealey Plaza have been found, and I'm sure they've paid a price for it in one way or another. But I got very lucky—I was never identified. I was afraid of being seen by anyone who knew me, because I wasn't supposed to be there. Dr. Lomax, whom I worked for at the time, was a devout Republican, and he couldn't stand the Kennedys. If I told him I wanted to see the president drive by, he would've said no. So I left work early, saying I was sick, and wore a big scarf over my head and a pair of glasses as a disguise. No one knew it was me. But I have since seen myself in other pictures and films taken that day. Some have called me "the Babushka Lady." I was described as a "person of interest." I knew people were looking for me. I believed I was being followed by men in disguises. I thought the day would come when I'd answer the front door and find them waiting to take me into custody . . . or worse. But it never happened. As time passed, my fears eased—but not much. As I write this now, so many years later, I am still not certain I am safe.

Like I said, I was very lucky. If I hadn't covered myself up, I can't imagine what would have happened. Even so, I know for a fact that there were people searching for me, people who wanted this film. They didn't even know for sure that it existed, but if it did, they'd want to find it—which meant they had to find me. It got to the point where I began to jump at shadows, where every stranger who looked in my direction became a secret agent or a hired killer. I finally decided that if something happened to me, at least this film might end up in the right hands sooner or later.

I know this is part of history, and I also realize it might even help find the president's killers. But I never knew whom I could trust, so I made the decision to keep it hidden. I would do nothing to put the two people I love most in jeopardy. The president is gone, and bringing this film to the public's attention won't change that. But maybe, in the future, the people responsible for committing this heartless act will all be gone, and then the truth can come out without any risk to either of you. This has been my burden to carry, and now it's yours. I apologize a million times over for that.

Watch it if you want to know the truth—believe me, you'll see it. Or just destroy it and be done with it. Do whatever you think is best.

I love you both. Always.

• • •

"Not a sound," Birk said into the cell phone. He was sitting in his own rental car, a nondescript Chevy sedan, across the street and a few doors down from the home that Sheila Baker had recently inherited. Racener Avenue was a sun-dappled, tree-shaded thoroughfare that could have been featured in a coffee-table book titled *America's Most Pleasant Suburbs*. "No visitors, no phone calls, no television or radio. If I didn't know better, I'd say she fell asleep."

"Your opinion is noted," his employer said dryly.

He's on edge, Birk thought. This was of particular curiosity because he had never known the man to lose control of his emotions. Not that they were a significant factor now, but they were present, and that was unique.

Birk had read the dossier on Sheila Baker until it was committed to memory and had done further research on her parents. The family was completely ordinary by all accounts, another uncolored thread in the working-class fabric of the nation. So why the concern from a man who obviously commanded such wealth and power?

There was a small device in Birk's other ear, same make and model as the phone—that is, forged by a team of anonymous government employees in some anonymous building somewhere. It was synchronized to a wireless hub in the trunk, which in turn orchestrated an array of tiny listening devices Birk had planted throughout the Baker home while Sheila was attending her mother's funeral service.

"What exactly am I listening for?" Birk asked.

"Anything unusual."

"Can you be more specific?"

"Not now."

"It would be helpful if I knew—"

"You know as much as you need to know."

"Okay."

"I'll call back shortly," he was told, and the line went dead.

That'll make four calls since the woman got home, Birk noted.

• • •

Rydell emerged from his private bathroom a moment later. He got behind his computer and tried to refocus on his formal duties, but it was proving increasingly difficult. He opened a password-protected file—one of hundreds—stored in a hidden folder that would be automatically deleted if anyone else tried to access it.

The file was an ordinary Microsoft Word document. It contained a simple list of names, all female. There were forty-two in total, and thirty-seven had been crossed out using the strikethrough feature, like completed items on a to-do list. Margaret Baker was one of the remaining five.

Rydell had compiled the list—local women who fit the description and lived in the area—not long after the legend of the Babushka Lady had begun to take shape. He had scrutinized the few photos from Dealey Plaza where she was visible and built up a profile. He had certain advantages that the conspiracists did not, such as images that had been quietly confiscated through the years. As more criteria were applied, the list got smaller.

Of course, the methodology was far from exact; the subject could have been from out of town, for example. But he had to try. He had each of the forty-two women monitored over the years and did not cross out their names until they were dead or until he was absolutely convinced of their noncomplicity. By the time the list had shrunk to five—number six had been a retired schoolteacher from West Plano who died in a head-on collision on Interstate 635 seven months ago—he seriously doubted the mythical Babushka Lady, or her film, would ever be found. And with his escape drawing closer every day, he had found it increasingly harder to care . . . until now.

He scrolled down the list until he got to Baker. The indisputable evidence wasn't there yet, but Rydell could feel it. After more than half a century in this game, his instincts were animal-sharp. *She's the one.*

If this was correct, then she had been clever. She had sensed the potential dangers and had acted accordingly. The safe-deposit box registered to and maintained by the law firm had been a shrewd move, very shrewd. Keeping her mouth shut had been smart too. Rydell knew all about keeping secrets. It required a brand of discipline most people didn't possess. Margaret Baker had known the bad guys were out there, waiting in the shadows. The liberals didn't want to believe that. They bandied the word *paranoid* about like it was a trait of which one should be ashamed. But Rydell knew better. A little paranoia went a long way in this world. Margaret Baker certainly recognized this fact. A part of Rydell admired her for that. But a larger part was irritated at having been outsmarted. There was no way he was going to let this dead woman take him down now.

The Kennedy affair was ancient history in his mind, and he had dealt with it long enough.

7

SHEILA WENT into the basement and found the old projector. It was in a storage area near the furnace, in a cardboard box among dozens of others. There were other reels with it, all in the same little yellow cases. Each one had the subject printed in pen on the spine—*Trip to Organ Pipe Nat'l Park* or *Vegas, 1971.* The one that had been waiting for her at the bank didn't have any such labeling.

There was a room away from the furnace that featured faux-walnut paneling, a ratty carpet, cheap furniture, and fluorescent lights. When Sheila was a child, this had been her playroom. Her parents had given her piles of toys, crayons, markers, paints, coloring books, stuffed animals, and so on and told her to make as much of a mess as she pleased—just leave the rest of the house in order. She remembered having friends down here who thought it was the coolest thing in the world to have a room where you could do anything you wanted. Sheila soon became the most popular kid in the neighborhood. As a teenager, she transformed it into a hangout, replacing the stuffed animals and coloring books with a stereo, black-and-white TV, yard-sale coffee table, and her parents' old couch and love seat. The Eagles and Peter Frampton were favorites, and she had a Paul McCartney & Wings poster on the wall. The poster and TV set were gone now, but the couches, table, and stereo were still there, collecting dust.

She plugged the projector into an extension cord and switched it on. The fan started blowing, and a large rectangle of light appeared on the wall. Satisfied that it was in working order, she turned it off again and, with surgical delicacy, fed the film through the gears.

Maybe it's deteriorated and this'll all be moot, she thought—even hoped a little. Unlikely, but there was always a chance.

She turned the projector on again, and the reel began turning. At first there was nothing but flecks and scratches and a sideways scrawl of benign characters. Then the first images appeared.

• • •

Dealey Plaza on a clear autumn day. People everywhere, lining the streets, creating a human hallway. Some are clapping, pointing, waving flags. They are eager to see their popular young president and his pretty wife. Some female spectators are already wearing their hair like Jackie's. A white pergola is visible in the left side of the frame. A man in a dark suit is standing atop one of its pedestals, holding a movie camera.

The first of three officers on motorcycles appears, hugging the inside curve that connects Houston to Elm. His uniform is navy blue, offset by the white helmet and the white hardware of his bike. Two other officers follow, covering the middle and far side of Elm.

Then the limousine, with a pair of small flags flapping from the front corners. It is crawling along at maybe ten

miles per hour. As it comes into full view, so do the six pas-
sengers. President Kennedy and the First Lady are in the
back. He is wearing a simple gray suit and a blue tie. Her
Chanel outfit is pink wool with a matching pillbox hat. The
president seems relaxed, upbeat. As he and his wife wave to
the crowd, three more motorcycle patrolmen take up the rear.

Up to this point, Sheila had not been able to spot the
evidence her mother had cited as proof that Oswald had not
acted alone. But now she did.

There, in the Elm Street storm drain, the head of a man
appears. He has very dark, bushy hair and eyes that seem
even darker.

For a flicker of an instant, Sheila wondered if perhaps he
was just another Secret Service agent, one who had simply
escaped notice until now. But then . . .

The man's arms come up. He is holding what appears to
be a rifle. He turns once, aware of the limousine's approach.
Then the limo rolls into view and eclipses him. The storm
drain will not be visible again.

Sheila watched the remainder of the film in silent
astonishment.

A firecracker *pop!* pierces the air, and the president lurches
forward and to his left, covering his throat with clenched
fists. His puzzled wife puts an arm around him, perhaps
thinking he is choking. Governor Connally, sitting in front
of the president, turns away from the camera and back to
Kennedy, barely aware that he, too, has been hit. One of the
agents riding on the running board of the car trailing the
limousine is among the first to react. He leaps off and starts
forward.

A second shot comes. The president does not react to it.
The First Lady is leaning down, trying to communicate with

him. At the same time, Nellie Connally is pulling her own husband into her lap. The sprinting agent has yet to reach the vehicle.

The third shot arrives, traveling roughly 1,300 miles per hour and striking the president on the side of his head opposite Margaret Baker's vantage point. A horrid pink spray of blood, bone, and tissue cascades into the air, and Kennedy slumps over.

The First Lady climbs from the backseat and picks a piece of her husband's head off the trunk. She will later claim to have no memory of performing this ghastly act. The Secret Service agent from the car behind the president's finally arrives, stepping up onto the rear bumper and pushing Jackie back while screaming something to the driver. The vehicle's speed increases as it heads beneath the triple overpass.

Many spectators have dropped to the ground, including several parents covering small children. The limousine disappears, and the camera view turns crazily to one side for a moment before the film comes to an end.

* * *

Sheila sat there for a long time, lost in thought as the humming projector cast a bright square on the wall. The unimaginable realities of the situation swam through her mind like tiny, psychotic fish—*My mother really was there. . . . And she captured a second assassin on film . . . a film no one else has ever seen . . . and that some people would probably kill for.*

She had what she considered an average awareness of the assassination. She knew the date, the location, a little bit about Oswald, and the fact that there were about a hundred conspiracy theories. She knew they ranged from reasonable to ridiculous, but she didn't know many of the details. She thought she'd also heard something about a government committee in the seventies declaring that there probably *was* a conspiracy, meaning the government officially believed Oswald hadn't acted alone. But she didn't know much beyond that.

She went upstairs again, to the little room at the back of the house where her parents would sit on Tuesday evenings and pay their bills. It was the closest thing to an office they had. In a temporary spurt of modernistic euphoria, her mother had purchased a computer and tried her best to join the cybergeneration. In the end, she got the hang of e-mail and found a few online games she liked, but she still paid the electric and phone companies by putting a check in an envelope each month.

Sheila went to Google and searched for details about what she'd just seen.

She discovered that the man standing on the pergola was Abraham Zapruder, the guy who'd shot the shaky film of the assassination that everyone had seen in movies, in documentaries, and on YouTube. The younger woman standing behind him was his receptionist, Marilyn Sitzman. She was there to steady him because he suffered from vertigo.

Sheila found another website that had all sorts of information about Kennedy's limousine. It was a customized midnight-blue 1961 Lincoln, and its plastic bubble had been removed and the bulletproof windows rolled down due to the warm weather. The president had been advised not to allow this because the Secret Service considered Dallas a "hot" city—too hostile, too many potential enemies. But he didn't want to appear too much like a royal, separate from and superior to his subjects. The man driving the limousine was agent William Greer, and sitting next to him was fellow agent Roy Kellerman. Sheila already knew former Texas governor John Connally and his wife, Nellie, in the seats behind them.

She next went to Google Images and typed in *babushka lady kennedy assassination*. This produced more than 3,500 results, but there were only six different shots from Dealey Plaza in total. She went numb when she saw the woman in the photos—it was, without question, her mother. In spite of the fact that none of the shots displayed any distinguishing features, Sheila knew it was her. It was those subtleties, recognizable only by those who knew a person best—the way her mom had planted her feet well apart in order to steady herself and, in another photo, how she kept her head slightly bowed as she crossed to the other side of Elm.

Now it all became real—it became *there*. Something right in front of her that could no longer be doubted or denied.

The film was a big thing. *No, more than big—enormous. Evidence of a second shooter . . . the proof conspiracy theorists have been seeking for a generation. A bona fide piece of history.* Just the thought of it made her feel weak and vulnerable. This was miles out of her league, well beyond anything she could handle. She was smart and tough and shrewd, like her mother and father. But this was something on an altogether different level.

Her mother had been right—she couldn't turn to either the media or the government. The former would have a field day. They'd parade her around, expose and stain her mama's memory, and cultivate the story into forty others. They had columns to write and space to fill. People would be knocking on her door around the clock. And the government . . . Sheila still believed there were good people in power, but to disregard the corruption and self-aggrandizement was to be chronically naive. The film would be used as political hay for both sides, serving every purpose but the right one. Maybe the final pieces to the puzzle really were somewhere within those several minutes of celluloid. But would the salient facts ever reach the surface?

Yet she couldn't destroy it. A part of her wanted to. Then it would be gone and no one would be any the wiser—problem solved. But what about the truth? What about *justice*? Some of the people who'd perpetrated this crime might still be out there, enjoying their freedom. Wasn't it about time they received the wages of their sins? And what of the surviving Kennedys? How much suffering had the family endured? How many tragic deaths? What about the president's daughter Caroline, just five years old at the time? What must it have been like for her, being told her father was gone and never coming back? Did she wonder, even now, who was responsible? From her point of view, the politics didn't matter. She was simply another child who'd lost a loving parent. In a strange way, Sheila felt some kind of connection to her at that moment. *I can't destroy the film. It might hold the answer. Something has to be done . . . but what?*

She took a deep breath and forced herself to mentally step back from the situation. It needed to be viewed from a pragmatic and unemotional perspective. *I need help* was the first thought that surfaced. *There's no way I can handle this alone.* Then she followed the same logical pathway her mother had all those years ago. *The government . . . no.* It was just too fraught with uncertainty and danger. Too many variables. Too many people with their own agendas, and the corruption was so out of control these days. *The media . . . also no.* There were so few unbiased journalistic outlets now. When she wanted to keep up with current events, she went to the

Lehrer site on PBS. That was about as close to objective as it got. But even there . . . *This is a trust issue,* she realized. *It's about that one word*—trust. *Whom can I actually trust?*

"I need someone powerful," she said out loud, "yet completely trustworthy." Then she added bitterly, "Yeah, no problem."

She turned back to the computer and started a fresh Google search. She typed in *most trustworthy powerful people.* Ironically, Walter Cronkite came up on the first page. *He would've been perfect,* she thought, *but since he's no longer with us . . .*

Former president Jimmy Carter also appeared on the list, and for a long moment Sheila seriously considered him. He was long out of office now and wouldn't have any political ambitions. He had also, in her opinion, proven himself to be a man of outstanding character; his tireless humanitarian efforts had defined his postpresidential career. *But he's really getting up there in years, and how would I go about contacting him in the first place? Who among his staff would give me the time of day if I approached them with this?* She kept trolling through the search results, discarding one after another.

Then she came to a link that brought her to a halt. It was a young billionaire from New Hampshire. She did a new search with only his name and got more than 4,500 hits. He was considered an adventurer of sorts who specialized in unsolved mysteries. He financed his activities out of his own pocket and, according to one article, never asked for any kind of compensation from those he helped. One blogger referred to him as a "modern-day cross between Robin Hood and Jack Webb from *Dragnet.*" Another site described him in less-than-glowing terms as a bored rich kid who stuck his nose in places where it didn't belong. It wasn't until the fourteenth page—a reprinted article from a CNN archive—that Sheila made up her mind. According to the piece, this man had lost more than a hundred million dollars in assets when a foreign government seized one of his company's factories in retaliation for refusing to reveal the identity of the citizen who had aided him in his search for Michael Rockefeller.

The man's name was Jason Hammond.

8

HAMMOND'S GULFSTREAM G550 soared northward over Pennsylvania, two thousand feet above a cloud field and surrounded by a shimmering blue that stretched into eternity. Inside the cabin, Hammond sat at a tiny table with an executive telephone that had about a hundred buttons on it.

"So you would say the TIGHAR people cooperated with you at every stage?" the caller asked through the speaker. This was Reuters journalist David Weldon, and the acronym referred to The International Group for Historic Aircraft Recovery.

"They were great," Hammond said. "Just terrific. As you might imagine, they wanted to get this mystery solved as much as I did. It really was an honor to be a part of it."

"But they worked on Earhart's disappearance for years, some of them for decades. And here you come along, more or less a stranger, with your money and your connections. Don't you think a little jealousy and resentment are to be expected?" Weldon added quickly, "I'm not trying to be, you know, a jerk or anything. I'm just playing devil's advocate."

"Sure, I understand. I didn't sense any of that. I didn't see

myself as some kind of savior to the project, but rather someone helping to find the last few pieces of the puzzle. They
would've found those pieces whether I was there or not."

"I'm not so sure about that."

"I am. It was funding they lacked most of all, David, and
I was happy to provide it."

David Weldon was the only member of the media
Hammond would speak with. Weldon was in his midtwenties
and technically still just a junior reporter, years away from
veteran status. But Hammond liked the way he approached
his work. He asked good questions, and he didn't waste time
on nonsensical stuff. In Weldon's last position, he was fired
because he refused to dig into the private life of a Hollywood
celebrity to find out if the man's ten-year-old daughter was
really dying of an inoperable brain tumor. Hammond was
impressed by that kind of integrity.

"Incredible. Okay, well, I think I've got everything I need."

"Good. If you have any other questions, feel free to give
me a call. And I'll send you my notes as soon as I've had the
chance to transcribe them out of my indecipherable script
and onto a computer screen."

"Thanks, Jason. Really, thank you."

"Sure."

Hammond tapped the speaker button, and the red light
went out. The only sounds in the cabin now were the steady
hum of the engines and the hiss of the oxygen vents. He
looked toward the flight deck a few feet away, where his
copilot, or at least the back of him, was partially visible.

Hammond rose and went in. "Sorry I took so long with
the call. How's it going up here?" He got back into the pilot's
seat, which was something of a production since he was just
a hair under six foot three.

"Fine, just fine." Noah Gwynn was a smallish man of sixty-two with a round face and wispy white hair sticking out from under his felt cap. Other than a slight belly swell, he was in very good physical shape for his age. "How was the interview?"

Hammond set his headphones into place and positioned the mic in front of his mouth. "No problems. David's great."

"That's why you talk to him, right?"

"You bet." Hammond checked all the gauges, then took a moment to admire the early morning light that was breaking over the horizon. He rubbed his hands together and said, "So I've been looking into the death of Princess Diana. I was researching it pretty heavily before we got involved with the Earhart search, and I think I might have found someone willing to shed some light on—"

"Jason . . ."

"—a few of the inconsistencies in the Paget report."

"Jason."

"Hmm?"

Noah cleared his throat. "We need to talk about some things. Some business things."

Hammond tensed and nodded curtly. "When we get back."

"Of course. I guess I should also mention that Father Outerbridge called to ask if there was any chance maybe this week you'd be willing to come to—"

Noah was cut off by air traffic control asking for their position. Hammond took the chance to respond even though it was normally the copilot's responsibility.

• • •

Hammond kept himself too busy for the remaining fifteen minutes of the flight to revisit the conversation. He was an experienced pilot, making a smooth descent and working the controls confidently, but Noah knew his boss was just going through the motions. When the estate came into view, Noah peered over to gauge Hammond's reaction. There was no longer even a trace of his former enthusiasm. This was a completely different person— one whom, after six very long years, Noah still did not know quite how to handle or help.

Noah hated seeing this transformation—hated it because it was unavoidable. The energetic, enthusiastic Jason Hammond had morphed into the one that was unreachably troubled. On the surface, the conversion manifested itself in simple changes—a faded smile that was now more forced than inspired, eyes that previously held the gleam of excitement thinning with pain and distraction, and a tensed, ready-to-take-on-the-world body loosened by the exhaustion of an interminable struggle.

As they made their approach, more details lensed into view. At the heart of the property was the forty-four-room main house, white with black trimmings except for the dusty red of an enormous chimney. The mansion was surrounded by three guest cottages, a pair of tennis courts, a swimming pool, a greenhouse, and extensive landscaping that included a sizable garden for fruits and vegetables.

To the east, accessible by a brief dirt road that cut through the hardwood forest like a scar, was a house larger than the cottages but smaller than the mansion. It had its own pool and garden and sat a short distance from the edge of a cliff that offered an unfettered view of the Atlantic Ocean. Noah had lived here for much of his adult life. To the west, a longer path led to a modest pond that, in spite of being natural rather than man-made, formed an almost-perfect oval shape and thus bore the name Nearly Oval Pond.

Running south of the main compound, a paved road snaked through the woods for nearly a quarter mile before reaching a security gate and guardhouse at the front of the property. To the north lay the runway, which halted at the base of a gentle hill covered with wildflowers and tall grasses. At the peak of the hill, and farther on about the length of a football field, was a smaller palisade. At the bottom, accessible only by a set of winding steps that were slowly being consumed by thorn tangles, were a small dock and boathouse nestled in the corner of the bay.

Hammond eased the little jet to a landing, retrieved his personal items, and went out. The Ford Expedition was exactly where they had left it the previous month. It started without a fuss when Noah got behind the wheel. As they drew closer to the main house, Hammond said, "Drop me off at the back, would you?"

Noah thought about reopening the discussion, then remembered the old axiom about knowing when and where to pick your battles.

The entrance Hammond wanted was not technically at the back of the house but rather the southeast corner. There was a time when it had been used only by staff. What made it practical in this regard was that it opened to a staircase that led directly to the second and third floors of the east wing and enabled them to conduct their business invisibly.

Hammond climbed out of the Expedition with a quick thank-you, opened the door, and was gone.

• • •

In his bedroom, Hammond dropped his knapsack on the floor and proceeded into the adjoining bathroom, where he took a long, hot shower. Then he got into bed, buried himself under the sheets, and fell into a deep sleep. The dreams came soon thereafter, as he knew they would, and jolted him awake.

He slid up on one elbow, breathing hard. Afternoon sunlight filtered through the tall windows, and it took him a moment to remember where he was. Three orange pill bottles stood between the alarm clock and the lamp on the nightstand—psychotropic medications prescribed by three different physicians. He had never opened them and never would.

He peeled the sheets back and got up. His heart was still pounding as he crossed the room to the walnut bookcase. *Paris-London Connection: The Assassination of Princess Diana* was on the top shelf. Just as he reached for it, he saw his Bible one shelf below. The top and bottom edges of the black spine were frayed, the two bookmark ribbons still buried in the pages. Familiar passages, once trusted and beloved, began surfacing in his mind.

I have set the Lord always before me; because he is at my right hand, I shall not be shaken.

The Lord is my light and my salvation; whom shall I fear?

When the righteous cry for help, the Lord hears and delivers them out of all their troubles.

When I called, you answered me; you made me bold and stouthearted.

After remembering this last, he drove these thoughts violently away, and his jaw tightened as an old, familiar defiance came to life inside. Taking the Princess Diana book down, he returned to bed and began reading.

• • •

Loitering by the bedroom door, Noah couldn't hear any noise coming from inside. He wondered whether Hammond was still asleep. Even if he was, there were things that needed tending to, so he knocked softly.

"Yes?"

"Jason, it's me. Do you have a moment?"

A pause. Then, "Sure, come on in."

When Noah entered, Hammond was holding one hand across his forehead, and the other held a book upright on his chest. Noah saw it was *Paris-London Connection*, the independently published paperback about Princess Diana's possible assassination.

Hammond set the book on the nightstand and moved into a sitting position.

"Did you have a good rest?" Noah asked with a smile. He held a manila folder in his hand, a pen between two fingers.

"It was okay. What about you?"

Noah pulled a chair over and sat down. "I haven't had the chance yet."

"You need some sleep."

"I know. I'll catch up tonight."

"Okay. So what's up?"

"I'd like to go over a few business-related concerns that need your immediate attention. Things that have been waiting a bit too long."

Hammond hesitated, and for a moment, Noah thought he was going to beg off with some kind of manufactured excuse. Then he nodded in resignation. "All right, fire away."

"First, there's the construction of the new fabric plant in Brazil. The workers have been on strike for the past three weeks, and at first we thought it was for the obvious reason—because they wanted more money. As it turns out, the brothers who own the construction company are the ones holding out for more, and they've staged this strike to make their employees out to be the villains."

Hammond laughed, which surprised Noah. Usually he flew into a rage when someone tried to welsh on a deal they'd already signed. "That sounds like the Bouceiro brothers. Okay, if I'm not mistaken, those two scoundrels have been ardent supporters of Miguel Rapoula. Contact Ms. Verdial's people and tell them you're speaking on my behalf. They can call me if they need confir—"

"Hang on a second. You mean *Elana* Verdial? The Brazilian vice president?"

"That's right. Tell her people what's happening. Rapoula really went after her during the last election, particularly with that slash-and-burn story about her son's alcoholism. I'm sure she won't mind shaking the Bouceiros' tree a little bit. They have a couple of major contracts with her government. The threat of losing them should get them back in gear."

Noah scribbled some notes. "Okay. Now, concerning the capital allocation for that green initiative in Texas. They've put up thirty turbines on that wind farm, but they say there's room for at least another twenty. However, they've already used up the money you've loaned them and—"

Hammond put up a hand. "I know what you're going to say. Give them what they need for the other twenty."

"Are you sure?"

"Absolutely. The front-end costs of wind farming are the only significant expense of this particular green technology.

Maintaining them after that is little more than routine housekeeping. As time passes and more people begin to understand the inherent value of wind power, that unused land will increase in value. We'll have people fighting for it, and that's when things will get really ugly. Empty space on a wind farm is valueless space. I'd rather put up the turbines sooner than later. And if it doesn't work out, the materials can be repurposed. The initial debt is already being eroded at an above-average rate, correct?"

"Yes, according to the numbers I've seen."

"Then we'd be foolish not to go forward. We'll never run out of wind, Noah."

"No, I guess not."

"If worst comes to worst, we can always aim the turbines in Washington's direction. One session of Congress will have them spinning so fast you won't be able to see them. But you didn't hear that from me."

"Good point."

"What's next?"

"The tax structure of profits earned through several of our European investments."

"Let me guess—a few of the higher-ups over there are trying to find ways to wrap their greedy little fingers around as much of it as possible so they can help out the E.U. nations who haven't bothered to pay *any* taxes since time out of mind."

"That's one way of putting it."

"No one likes it when the parents come home and the party's over."

"No."

Hammond sighed and shook his head. "Okay. I'm willing to give back a little, but not for free. I start down that road and pretty soon they'll be taking 99 percent and telling us we should be grateful for the remaining one. Call Kip Larson in Switzerland and tell him to ease up on 5 percent. In return, tell him he needs to communicate to the right people that it's about time they softened their tariffs on our exports. Let's get a little quid pro quo going here."

"Do you think they'll go for it?"

"Half the continent is teetering on the brink of insolvency, and the horrors that follow will last for a generation. Yeah, I think they'll be in the mood to bend a little."

"All right."

Noah made more notes and kept going, but it wasn't long before Hammond's attention began fading. This always happened, and it always made Noah nervous. Hammond now had sole control of his father's multibillion-dollar empire. He had inherited much of his father's business genius, but he wasn't as good at focusing it. While some of his decisions had led to significant gains, others had resulted in horrific losses. The only time Noah felt he consistently had Hammond's full attention was when they discussed the handful of humanitarian organizations Hammond had launched on his own. Overall, the businesses were still running strong, but they had definitely declined since the death of the father and the succession of the son. Noah feared the day when the shareholders rose up in rebellion.

He held out a manila envelope, and Hammond took it in his lap. He scanned each document briefly, then jotted his name at the bottom. *Like a teenager doing homework,* Noah thought. *Just get it over with.*

Handing it back, Hammond said, "Is that it?"

"Yes." Noah replaced the chair in its original spot and went to the door. He looked over at the young man he had come to love, whose abandonment of faith concerned him deeply, and whose suffering had become so much Noah's own. Hammond was already lying down again, lost in his book and, Noah knew, the only part of his life that didn't antagonize him.

"Lunch is at two," he said.

"Okay, thanks."

• • •

Hammond read until one thirty, then pulled on cotton slacks and a short-sleeved polo shirt. Stepping into the hallway, he closed the bedroom door and headed toward the servants' staircase.

About halfway there, he came to a halt and turned back. There was still plenty of diffused sunlight coming through the curtains, brightening the pink carpet. One end of the hallway looked the same as the other—a tall window, an accent table, and a vase with fresh flowers. But Hammond fixed on the end farthest from him, staring at it and then away . . . at it and then away.

He began moving in that direction, his breathing heavier. When he got there, he turned again—this time to the right. The hall continued on for only about twenty feet before terminating at a large door, which had been painted white to match the chair rail. He stopped again, heart pounding. A disorganized collection of sounds began playing in his mind, softly at first and then rapidly growing louder—voices in other rooms, music from clock radios, drawers being opened and closed, the whoosh of shoes on carpet. The notes of everyday life.

Each step toward the door seemed longer than the last. He saw his hand reach for the knob as if it were someone else's. The knob turned easily, and then he released it, and the door drifted back. The hallway continued unremarkably, with the pink carpeting and the diffused sunlight and the white chair rail on either side, interrupted occasionally by more doors, each recessed. Nothing unusual to the ordinary observer. To Hammond, however, it felt as though every nerve was coming alive.

He saw ghost images of people going between rooms, could detect a familiar blend of colognes, perfumes, old-house dustiness, and a dozen other aromas. The sights and sounds were phantasmal, he knew. But the faintest trace of that unique odor, even after all these years, remained. That somehow made it all real, as if the accident had never happened. As if it were just another day. *As if they were still here.*

He left his safe zone behind and crossed the border. The first door led to his sister's room. He didn't have to open it; he knew what was in there. As with every other room in this part of the house, it was still, per his orders, exactly as it had been on the day they were taken from him.

A few steps farther, on the right side, was his own room— or at least his former room. It, too, was kept in a museum-like stasis. Very little had been exported to the new one; Hammond bought all new furniture, clothes, and decor. The pictures on the walls were pretty enough: landscapes, mostly. But they were impersonal and generic, like something on the walls of an upscale hotel. Noah once commented that they spoke nothing of the room's occupant. Hammond feared they spoke too much.

He moved on and arrived at the hall's geometric center. This was marked by a set of large double doors on either side. Those on the left led into his parents' bedroom suite, those on the right into his father's four-chambered home office. He had not entered either in six years.

He stood facing the office doors for a long time. More sights and sounds and scents tormented him. He was hyper-ventilating now, his face glistening with perspiration. His hand came up again, reaching for that doorknob a million miles away. He made contact with the cold smoothness of the brass, held there for a moment, then let go again.

The voice of a slightly younger Noah Gwynn echoed in his mind:

"Jason, I've got some very bad news. You'd better sit down."

". . . on the way back from the Caribbean . . ."

". . . They're not sure what happened. . . ."

". . . isn't much hope . . ."

He turned and walked off.

9

THE TRAGEDY that wiped out his family had occurred six years earlier. The Hammonds had been vacationing in the Bahamas at the time, hiding from the brutality of another New England winter. They'd spent the first week on Bimini, then the Abacos, and finally Nassau.

Jason's father, Alan, was known for three things—hard work, a love of family, and an unswerving belief in the Lord. He began in life with nothing and was a member of America's billionaire club by the age of fifty-five. In everything from cable television to software engineering to foreign currencies, he had the Midas touch. "It goes to show you," he reminded his son frequently, "you can be successful without compromising your beliefs. It's not impossible, in spite of what others might try to tell you. Trust in the Lord's way, because it's the only way."

Jason had no trouble following this advice; even as a small boy he had felt a personal connection with God—one that he enjoyed enormously. The relationship with his father, however, was not always so harmonious. Jason had always been aware of his family's wealth, but it was not until his early teens that he began to understand his father had not acquired all of it through ethical means. Early in his career, before he found the Lord, Alan Hammond had a reputation for ruthlessness. He steamrollered anyone who presented an obstacle, skirted any law or regulation that he found inconvenient, and dabbled in businesses that were less than savory. After his spiritual awakening, he abandoned these tactics and made some effort to help those he had exploited. But his son still had difficulty resolving the fact that a percentage of his family's fortune had been acquired in this manner. Fueled by embarrassment, Jason urged his father to do more to help the people he thought of as the man's victims. These discussions sometimes erupted into heated arguments. There was still a core closeness between them, but outwardly their bond was often fraught with discord.

Jason's mother, Linda, played the role of referee during these episodes. A boundlessly patient individual, she was a physician by training who had set her career aside while her children grew up. Once they were old enough, she returned to the medical profession, making missionary trips to developing nations. Her last was a three-week stay in the Democratic Republic of the Congo to treat river blindness with the UFAR organization.

Jason's older sister, Joan—who agreed with most of Jason's positions concerning the family fortune but was not as willing to spar with their father about it—followed her mother's lead into the medical profession and became a pediatric nurse. She, too, decided to devote her life to charity work and had just returned from Burkina Faso when the family left for the islands.

Jason was a postgrad at Harvard at the time, building on his love of history while trying to minimize his lack of talent for mathematics and certain scientific disciplines. He hoped to earn his doctorate and eventually secure a professorship. He also wanted to do some teaching in Senegal, perhaps take part in the planning and construction of schools in areas where there had never been formal learning institutions before.

The Hammonds arrived in the Bahamas together and planned to leave together. Then Jason received word that Pulitzer Prize–winning biographer and historian Doris Kearns Goodwin was due to give a seminar back at Harvard, followed by a Q&A session, so he left four days early. The following Friday, the news came that his family's single-engine Cessna had lost power and fallen into the Atlantic less than a hundred miles from Miami. The search-and-rescue mission found floating debris but little else.

After their deaths, Jason withdrew from the world. He left Harvard, stopped attending church services, and remained within the grounds of the estate, communicating with no one. He did not succumb to the lure of alcohol or drugs or any of the other traditional poisons. He simply turned inward and stayed there. It was rumored that he hired a parade of personal trainers, martial arts experts, combat veterans, and a host of others to develop his physical skills and complement his already-formidable intelligence, even while he remained cut off from the rest of the world.

Then Hammond reemerged. He made headlines a few years later when he launched, with his own money, an investigation into the disappearance of Michael Rockefeller, son of former New York governor and U.S. vice president Nelson Rockefeller. Michael had been studying the Asmat tribe in southwestern New Guinea in the early sixties. While traveling down the Eilanden River, his double-pontoon boat capsized. He tried to swim for shore but was never seen again.

Hammond threw himself into the investigation and eventually found human remains that would be positively identified as those of the missing heir. This brought him international attention, and he dove into other high-profile mysteries. With his considerable family fortune, his father's ongoing business ventures, and his global connections, he was able to succeed where others had failed and became a kind of folk hero. It appeared as though he had found meaning in his life again.

Noah wasn't so sure.

• • •

Lunch included poached salmon and mixed vegetables. Hammond ate, as he always did, in the anteroom just off the kitchen rather than in the formal dining hall where he and his family, in a somewhat dynastic fashion, had taken all of their meals together. The anteroom's furnishings could have come from medieval England—a heavy slab of wood for a table and a pair of long benches.

Aside from Noah, Hammond's dining companions included the few other people who lived on the estate full-time. They had all been close to the family and grieved deeply at their passing, and they now served the sole survivor with the same loyalty and devotion. As with Noah, his pain was their pain.

Hammond said very little, sitting at the end of the table by himself. He was as polite as always, but his emotional demeanor set the tone for the household regardless. The others huddled in a group and spoke quietly. Noah felt a stitch of guilt, wondering whether his earlier comments in the bedroom had triggered this latest bout of melancholy.

Following the meal, Hammond went to the office he

kept for himself on the first floor. It was far too small for its intended purpose; the hulking L-shaped desk barely fit. But it had previously been a sitting room that no one ever used and thus held no memories.

Noah paused at the door, which was open a crack, before knocking. He had received the phone call a few moments earlier, and now the caller was on hold. He considered letting her stay there until impatience drove her to hang up, but he had a feeling she'd just call back. He didn't have a problem with the caller as a person; actually she seemed quite nice. But he did have a problem with the reason for the call in the first place.

He knocked softly.

"Come on in."

He sounds different already, Noah thought, *now that he's in there.*

As the door swung back, a familiar image was revealed— Hammond behind his paper-littered desk, hunched over an open book under the green banker's lamp. This, too, struck Noah as bittersweet. It was the image of What Could Have Been, of Hammond as a university professor had he stayed on track and completed his studies at Harvard. Same man, same scene, but with a very different emotional undercurrent.

"Jason, you have a phone call. She's been on hold for a few minutes."

"Who is it?"

"A woman named Sheila Baker. She's in Dallas, and she says she has some new information about the Kennedy assassination."

The only change in Hammond's expression was a quick raise of one eyebrow. "And you thought it legitimate enough to put the call through?"

"I did."

"What, specifically, is this new information?"

"You really should talk to her."

Hammond's skeptical gaze remained in place as he reached for the phone. "Okay, thanks."

"Sure." Noah closed the door quietly.

• • •

Hammond lifted the receiver and pressed the Hold button. "Ms. Baker?"

"Yes."

"This is Jason Hammond."

"Thank you for taking my call."

"No problem. I understand you might have some new information regarding the assassination of President Kennedy?"

"I do."

"Can I ask the nature of it?"

"I have a film."

"A film?"

"Yes. Taken on the day of the shooting."

"Okay. You mean, like, as the president got off the plane at Love Field? Or on his way down the—?"

"In Dealey Plaza."

Hammond's heart skipped a beat. Even if this turned out to be nonsense, just the thought of it was stimulating.

"Excuse me?"

"In Dealey Plaza, Mr. Hammond. Right there, as it happened."

"You're kidding."

"No, I'm dead serious."

"It's a generally accepted fact that all film taken that day and in that location has been accounted for."

"This one was shot by my mother, who was there when the president was struck, and it's been kept by her in a safe-deposit box ever since."

There was a pause here as Hammond tried to detect any signs of duplicity. She certainly *sounded* truthful.

"Do you mind my asking what, exactly, is on it?"

"Everything, Mr. Hammond."

"Is it all clear? I mean, can you see—?"

"Crystal clear. You can see it all in great detail. The president's limousine, the officers on motorcycles, the people standing on the sidewalks—" she paused before continuing—"and something else."

"I'm sorry?"

"There's more."

"Such as?"

Another pause, and then she said the words he would never forget.

"A second assassin."

Hammond's shoulders sagged. "Ms. Baker, I'm sorry if this sounds rude, but I'm not altogether certain I believe you." He didn't like saying this, but what choice was there? He did get loonies from time to time—practical jokers, nobodies looking to be somebodies, even occasional outright jerks.

"Mr. Hammond, I'm sorry if this also sounds rude, but I really don't care if you believe me or not. *I* know I'm telling the truth. I've got the film *right here*."

"Then why don't you go to the government? I would think they'd be very interested in it."

"I don't trust them. My mother didn't trust them. Would you?"

"Well—"

"She believed she was being followed, watched."

"By whom?"

"She was never sure."

"That's convenient."

"I swear it."

"Then why not go to the media with all this? Tell the papers?"

"I don't trust them, either."

"Okay. Then why me?"

"Because you're the only one who . . ."

"Yes?"

". . . who I think might know what to do." Her voice faltered, finally. Hammond hated himself for putting her through this.

"I'm *scared*," Sheila said. "Very scared, Mr. Hammond. Please . . ."

He lowered his head. "I really want to believe you, Ms. Baker, but . . . a *second assassin*? Also, as I said before, there is very little uncovered evidence of the Kennedy assassination believed to still be—"

"Mr. Hammond, my mother was the person they called the Babushka Lady."

The distance between them seemed endless, the movement of time and space ropy and out of sync. Hammond absorbed this last bit of information and came to the only conclusion possible.

"Ms. Baker, stay where you are and don't tell anyone else about this, okay? Don't tell *anyone*."

"Okay."

"I'm on my way."

10

THE FRONT DOORBELL rang just after six, and Sheila had to stop her current project—going through the kitchen cabinets—to answer it.

She stepped into the hallway and opened the door, and the figure that had been silhouetted against the curtain a moment earlier became a person. The face was familiar—from television, the Internet, and most recently, an issue of *People* she had been browsing through while in her dentist's waiting room.

The first thing she noticed was the smile. *Dazzling* was the word that came to mind; perfect teeth framed by a rugged jaw. Then the eyes, as cheerful as the smile, with a spirited glow that so many people lost over time. He wasn't handsome in the conventional sense, like a movie star. But he had . . . *presence*, she thought.

It reminded her of the time she ran into Dustin Hoffman in New York City. She'd gone into a camera shop to pick up some film, and Hoffman was there with his youngest son. They exchanged brief hellos and no more. She figured he probably got pawed by people all the time, and she didn't want to be one of those types. But she couldn't help sensing a certain power about him, a feeling that the universe just might be revolving around the spot where he stood at any moment. She never thought she'd sense that in anyone again, but Jason Hammond had a touch of it for sure. *But does charisma necessarily make him trustworthy?*

"Hi," he said. "I hope I have the right house. Are you Ms. Baker?"

"Yes."

"Okay, great. I'm Jason." He said this as if he were a door-to-door salesman rather than a minor celebrity.

"Hello, Jason. I'm Sheila."

"Hello, Sheila."

"Please come in."

"Thanks."

He pulled the screen door back and stepped inside. He was nicely dressed, with dark trousers and a pea-green short-sleeved shirt. Both were immaculately pressed and made from some exotic material. The Piaget watch had a black strap and matching face. One of the guys Sheila had dated back home had worn a similar model, but it was an obvious fake. The gold trim had begun to fade, but he kept wearing it instead of having the good sense to buy a new one every few months to maintain the illusion. Sheila didn't have to consult a professional jeweler to know that the one wrapped around Hammond's wrist was genuine. She also noticed the backpack slung over his shoulder, which was bulging and looked very heavy.

"I'm sorry about the short notice," he said. "I hope it isn't too much of an imposition."

"Oh no, that's okay." *At least he's polite,* she thought, and another comparison came to mind—all the stories she'd heard about other people meeting celebrities and coming away with the opinion that they were jerks or full of themselves.

"This is a nice home. It looks like your mom kept it well."

"She was very big on neatness and order." Simple, ice-breaking talk. "So was my dad."

"Then you must be too."

She slipped her hands into the pockets of her jeans. "I try, but I usually don't succeed."

"Ah, well, the fact that you try is good enough."

"Can I get you something to drink?" It felt like a dumb thing to say, but she couldn't think of anything else. *So do you want to go downstairs and watch the film my mother made of our thirty-fifth president being murdered in broad daylight?* She doubted there was proper etiquette for this occasion. "I have Coke, Diet Coke, Sprite, orange juice, bottled water . . ."

"Water would be fine, thank you."

As they went to the kitchen, she opened the fridge and realized that it, too, had to be cleaned out. There were piles of leftovers from the postfuneral reception, and there was no way she'd eat even a fraction of them.

She found a bottle of Poland Spring and held it out. "Here you go."

"Thanks. Looks like you're doing some organizing." The contents of the cabinets were scattered everywhere.

"It needs to be done now that my mother is gone."

"Sure, of course. I'm very sorry for your loss."

"Thank you."

"She had lung cancer; is that correct?"

"Yes."

"How long?"

"She battled it for about three years."

"Brave woman."

"She really was." *You have no idea. . . .*

After a brief and awkward silence, Sheila surprised herself by laughing. "Well, this is a strange situation, isn't it?"

"A little bit, yes."

"I'm guessing you'd like to see the film?"

He took a deep breath. "I just hope I'm ready for it."

"It's pretty harsh."

"Based on your description, I'd say it's pretty *historic*."

"I think you're right. Please don't scare me any more than I already am."

"Sorry."

They went down the basement steps, careful not to trip on more piles of soon-to-be-organized stuff. When they entered what Sheila now thought of as the "film room," Hammond spotted the projector, and she saw the twinkle in his eyes intensify. He moved toward it in a cautious, almost-reverent manner, leaning down to inspect the reel.

"Kodachrome Super 8," he said, "just like Abraham Zapruder used."

"Is that good?"

"Well, it's *correct*. The time frame is right. And it appears to be in great condition. Your mom was smart to keep it at the bank, in a climate-controlled environment. Even some movie studios haven't been so smart. Do you know how many original classics have been lost or almost lost because they were stored improperly?"

"Didn't something like that happen to *My Fair Lady*?"

"Yes, that was one. It was salvaged just in time. A few more years and *poof*—" he accompanied this with a hand gesture—"it would've been gone forever." He moved to the other side of the table, as if the film might look different from that angle. "But that's not the case here. This one's immaculate, which is very fortunate."

"Depends on what you consider good fortune," Sheila said.

Hammond looked at her, his smile disappearing. "This is probably very difficult for you, isn't it."

"Um . . . It's been a bizarre few days for sure."

"Well, please don't worry about this. Everything will be okay."

She wanted to believe it, wanted to be able to set all her fears aside and place her faith in this man. He had a remarkably soothing way about him. But she couldn't shake the feeling that something bad was going to come from all this—if not from him, then from somewhere else. *Maybe I should've followed my first instinct and thrown it in the fireplace.*

She took her mother's letter from her pocket. "I guess you should read this before you watch."

He took the letter and unfolded it. As his eyes moved over each line, his lips parted in astonishment.

"So do you want to see it now?" She wasn't sure if she could stand to watch it a second time herself, but she'd at least get it rolling for him.

"Yes, but before we do that—" He slid off his knapsack, set it on the couch, and removed two large items—a silver laptop with the familiar Apple symbol and a second movie projector. The latter was about the same size as her parents' but with more buttons, meters, and other bells and whistles. It had an expensive look about it. "If you don't mind, I'd like to run it through this projector instead of that one. Okay with you?"

"It won't damage the film in any way, will it?"

"Not a bit. What it will do is transfer it into a digital format. That way we'll have a file to work with. Also, if anything happens to the original, we'll have a backup."

"Oh, okay. Sure."

Hammond found an old table and dragged it over. Then Sheila located an extension cord and plugged it into an outlet by the washing machine. There was a pile of dirty laundry on the floor, which she found embarrassing even though Hammond appeared not to notice.

Another few minutes passed as he connected the devices and got them synced. He detached the film from the old projector with the meticulous care of a professional archivist. Once it was in place, he pulled up two chairs.

"Here, have a seat," he said, getting behind the laptop.

Sheila hesitated—*Do I have to?*—but sat anyway.

He launched a program from the task bar, and a new window opened. Along the top were the words *Avid Technology Digital Transfer*. "This is industrial software. It's designed to do nothing but transfer analog film into digital format. And this laptop is about the best there is for such work."

He opened more screens, made further adjustments. "All right, I think we're ready." Then he turned to her. "Do you mind watching this again?"

"Do I have a choice?"

"I'd be very grateful if you did, just so you could point out the things you saw."

"I'll try."

"I promise—just this one time."

"Okay."

He checked everything once more, then started the projector. When the reels began to rotate, he tapped the touch pad to initiate the transfer.

In a large window, the film that thousands of assassination researchers had sought for decades came to life once more.

"Amazing," Hammond said, his voice barely above a whisper. "Look at the quality, the sharpness."

The advance motorcycles disappeared, and the presidential limousine came into view again. Sheila's throat went dry; she knew what was coming.

"There's Bill Greer," Hammond said, "and Roy Kellerman. They're Secret Service agents. Greer is the driver; Kellerman is the one on the passenger side, up front."

As the limo came closer, the camera panned left to follow it. The handsome president and his beautiful wife waved to the crowd, dazzling and vibrant in their youth and the promises they offered to an America that would remain idealistic and innocent for only a few more moments.

"Zapruder!" Hammond said. "There he is, as plain as—"

"Look down there," Sheila interrupted, pointing.

He followed the imaginary line from her finger to the horizontal gap of the Elm Street storm drain, where the head of a dark-haired man appeared for the briefest instant. And to his right—Margaret Baker's left—was the rifle. The man turned once, facing forward, then to the side again as he lifted the weapon. Hammond strained for a closer look, but the limousine rolled in front of the drain, blocking it. And as Margaret Baker continued panning, it passed out of view.

The president jerked as he absorbed Oswald's second bullet. Then came the third, followed by the hideous explosion of flesh and bone. Sheila made a point of looking away.

Hammond leaned forward as the grassy knoll came into view. "No evidence of a shooter there. That takes care of Ed Hoffman's story," he whispered.

"Who's Ed Hoffman?" Sheila asked.

"A deaf-mute who came to Dealey Plaza to watch the president from the shoulder of the Stemmons Freeway. He claimed he saw a man with a rifle moving in a westward direction along the stockade fence immediately after the shooting. He supposedly tossed the rifle to a second man, dressed in a railroad worker's uniform, who disassembled it and placed the parts in a bag. Both men then moved off in separate directions. When Hoffman went to the FBI with this report, he was largely ignored. Rightly, as it turns out, based on what I'm seeing here."

The crowd scattered as the limousine sped under the bridge on its way to Parkland Memorial Hospital. Then Margaret Baker's film came to an end.

• • •

Hammond continued to stare into the monitor as if something were still there.

"Shouldn't you stop the transfer now?"

"What?"

"The digital transfer."

"Oh . . . yeah." He reached over and tapped the touch pad. "Unbelievable. I don't even know what to say."

"Yeah."

"It's incredible."

"I know."

"Do you understand the magnitude of this?" His tone was in no way accusatory or condescending. "This changes *everything* we know about the assassination. All the theories, all the official reports—this isn't just your mom's film; this could be *the* key piece of evidence."

"Do you have any idea who the man in the storm drain is?"

"No, no clue. There have been plenty of suggestions over the years about who else was involved—the Mafia, European hit men, Cuban soldiers of fortune, CIA operatives, stuff like that—but no one knows for sure." He shook his head. "The mere fact that someone else was there, and with what almost has to be a rifle . . . That's a *very* big deal."

"I don't think he fired a shot."

"No, another shot would've been discovered sooner or later. But I've read a few things about the possibility of a shooter being down there. There were some conspiracy theorists who pushed the point, but they were usually written off as crazies. When I started studying the assassination, however, I thought it made some sense. First, if you look at the layout of Dealey Plaza, you'll see that, from a sniper's perspective, it's actually an excellent position. Chances are you'd have a clear shot at the president at some point. Second, in all the mayhem that followed the shooting, it would be easy for such a person to escape. I don't know where the pipes led, but they obviously went somewhere—maintenance crews had to get in there from time to time, so there were entrance and exit routes. And third, even with Secret Service checking out the site ahead of the president's visit, the shooter could've gone down there a day or two before and simply waited. One quality that's consistent with top assassins, I've learned, is patience. Also, the odds of the person being seen by the crowd were slim to none. Remember—the volume of spectators was much heavier along Main Street than in Dealey Plaza. In fact, on the side where your mother stood, there were no more than a handful of people. So her film is the only piece of visual evidence that even *shows* someone in the storm drain." He checked the screen again. "I don't know everything about the assassination, but I know enough to be sure that this represents a paradigm shift. This is huge *beyond* huge."

The laptop finally finished processing, and the file with the meaningless name WRT0004.mov appeared on the desktop.

"I'm going to take another look at it and try to zoom in closer," he said. "If you don't mind, that is. You don't have to watch."

"Sure."

The transfer was perfect, even slightly improved over the original by enhancement features native to the software. Hammond fast-forwarded to the point just before the second gunman appeared, then paused it. "I'm already thinking of him as Storm-Drain Man, just as so many of the other figures in Dealey Plaza have been similarly anointed. There's Umbrella Man, Black-Dog Man, and of course, your mom, the Babushka Lady." He clicked on the Forward button to move the images one frame at a time.

The storm drain stood empty. Then the gunman's head came up. Dark hair, thick on the top and sides. He also appeared to have heavily rendered eyebrows. "Of Spanish descent?" Hammond wondered aloud. "Latino? Or maybe Italian? Italian might lend credence to the theories of Mafia involvement, although it certainly wouldn't prove it."

The man was initially turned sideways, offering a reasonably good view of his left profile. Then he looked toward the road, which offered a decent shot of the top three-quarters of his face. That was when the man lifted his weapon.

"That has to be a rifle," Hammond said. "No doubt."

The nose of the limousine inched into the right side of the frame, and Storm-Drain Man appeared to follow it. The rifle barrel was still being held at a slight angle, a nonshooting position. Then the storm drain disappeared behind the passing vehicle.

"Is there any way to go back and get a closer look at him?" Sheila asked.

"Exactly what I'm thinking." Hammond returned to the

first frame that offered a clear view of the man—the left profile—and enlarged it. The image pixelated into a blur of meaningless blocks. "No, that's no good." He browsed further, found the spot where the man's face was clearest—the three-quarter shot just after he turned toward the limo—and tried again. The result wasn't much better. "Also no good."

"Is there anything you can do to improve it?"

"Yes and no. Yes, it's possible, but not with the software I have on the machine now. Like I said, this is what they use to make transfers of people's home movies and stuff like that. It cleans them up to a degree, but it's not meant for advanced work."

"So what now?"

"Is there a wireless router in this house?"

Sheila laughed. "Uh, no. . . . My mom had little interest in computers. It was hard enough getting her to use a cell phone."

"That's too bad. I need to get a better image-enhancement program. There are several that will do the job, and I could've downloaded one if I had Internet access. Actually, hang on a second."

With the help of AirPort Extreme's search feature, he discovered that one of Sheila's neighbors had an unprotected router. The signal was weak, however.

"I could probably get the program I need through this, but it would take a while and, by the look of the signal strength, probably cut out a few times."

Sheila closed her eyes and sighed. "Sorry."

"No, that's okay. There's another option—we could go to the nearest Apple Store. There's one about twenty miles away."

"How do you know that?"

"I checked before I came." He stood. "Care to come along for the ride?"

"Yeah, I could use the break."

Hammond smiled. "I had a feeling."

"Let me change, though. I'm not exactly dressed to go out. I've been cleaning out cabinets and closets all day. I don't even *feel* clean."

"All right. I'll hang here and check out the film again."

• • •

Hammond returned to the laptop after she left. He went through the file several times but couldn't get an improved image of Storm-Drain Man, no matter what he tried. It occurred to him that he might want Noah to take a look at it at some point, and that meant posting it on the Internet. While there were security risks to this, they were, he estimated, infinitesimal. He had his own FTP site, password protected and with military-strength encryption. Plus, what were the odds that some hacker would be on the lookout for the Babushka Lady film at this moment?

He opened the Fetch program. Then, by carrying the laptop around the room, he found that the signal strength improved a little by the washer and dryer. He logged in to his storage site, created a new folder called "BLF"—Babushka Lady Film—and started the transfer. A progress box appeared, and he realized the upload was going to take some time. The file was huge. To keep himself occupied, he opened a browser and started going through sites associated with the assassination.

A short time later, he heard Sheila ask, "Everything going okay?" He turned to find her standing on the bottom step, now dressed in faded jeans and a dusty-purple scoop-neck T-shirt.

"Everything's fine. Are you ready?"

"As ready as I'll ever be under the circumstances."

"Okay, let's hit the road."

• • •

Birk's employer didn't react well to the news of Hammond's arrival. While he said it confirmed his suspicions about Margaret Baker, it also meant getting his hands on the film would be considerably more complicated. He also said he knew of Hammond, his reputation—he had recently heard a newscaster refer to him as a "seeker of truth and righter of wrongs"—and the considerable resources at his disposal.

Birk had never heard the man use so much profanity.

"So what do I do?" Birk asked when the storm subsided.

His instructions were brief, explicit, and even by Birk's standards, chilling.

11

THE APPLE STORE was crowded, so Hammond wore glasses and a baseball cap. He found the necessary software and, handing Sheila a folded sheaf of hundreds, asked her to pay for it.

"So tell me about yourself," he said in the rental car on the way back. "I know the last few days have been very hard on you. What do you do when you're not discovering family heirlooms that change how we look at history?"

She laughed. "I own a few fitness centers in the Dearborn area of Michigan."

"Is that right?"

"Yeah. I almost lost them a few years back when a national chain tried to muscle in on my territory."

"And you fought them off?"

"I did."

Hammond looked at her briefly, a look that said, *My opinion of you just went up a notch.* "That's great—good for you. You like running a business, then?"

"Well, it's better than the job I had before that, working in a big corporation. I did that for seven agonizing years after college."

"Not your cup of tea?"

"No, although I thought it was at first. I was so excited when I got it. High-profile organization, good salary, health benefits. It seemed like I was heading in the right direction. Then I got into the actual day-to-day aspects of it, and I was miserable by the end of the first year."

"I've heard stories."

"You sit there from dawn until dusk and spend maybe four hours on actual work. The rest is nonsense. Paperwork, meetings, office politics. Dealing with the bureaucracy is like arm-wrestling an octopus. My department spent so much time talking about work that it never actually did any. I remember one week when I was in meetings every hour of every day. Never even got near my desk. And at the end of all those discussions, nothing was different. Just a bunch of overpaid freeloaders trying to make it look like they were being productive."

"Sounds like big business these days."

"Everything that's bad about the modern workplace could be found in abundance there." She shook her head. "Another big ship sinking slowly, and no one on board cared. Their plan was to scuttle it on the way down, then jump to the next one."

"Why did you stay?"

"Because I thought that's what I was supposed to do with my life. The big important job that would turn you into a big important person. I didn't even consider getting married or having children, and I love children. I have a cousin in Allen Park with three wonderful daughters, and I try to see them as often as I can. But I never had any of my own. I just poured myself into my career. I got the house I couldn't really afford, the car I couldn't really afford, the jewelry, the clothes, the shoes. I bought into the whole spend-now-and-pay-later thing in the early 2000s. The new American dream. Next thing I knew, I was drowning in debt." She sighed. "If you could see one of my old credit card bills, you'd have a heart attack. I still can't believe how much money I blew through."

"But you still managed to start a business?"

"Not right away. A few years into that first job, I began to realize how pointless it all was. I remember sitting in my living room late one night, unable to sleep, surrounded by all my expensive toys, and thinking, *I'm unhappier now than I've ever been.* I couldn't stand the company, couldn't stand most of my coworkers, couldn't stand my neighbors . . . couldn't stand my whole life."

"Sounds awful."

"It was horrible. So I just decided, then and there, that it was time for some big changes. The next day, I sat down and made a plan to get out. I began selling off all my junk, set a strict budget, and slowly crawled out of the financial hole I'd dug. I was nearly back in the black when I learned the local gym where I was a member was about to go bankrupt. It was potentially very profitable, but it was poorly managed. So I talked to a banker friend and got the money to buy the place. It was cheap, too, because the owner was in even more financial trouble than me. He was a drug addict."

Hammond gave a disapproving snort. "Drugs—don't even get me started. One of the greatest evils of our society."

"I agree completely. Anyway, within a year the business was doing great again, and a few years after that I was able to unlock my corporate cage, walk out, and open more locations."

Hammond was smiling. "That's an incredible story. You must be very proud of yourself."

"The gyms were a good opportunity. I figured they'd be

a way to eliminate my remaining debt and build up some savings again. And I'm very nearly there—almost all my debts paid off, including the initial loans for the business itself. But I'm not so sure I want to be running them ten years from now. It's good money, but there's nothing satisfying on a personal level. I'm not passionate about it."

"Then what *are* you passionate about?"

"I don't know. Something where you make a positive difference in the world, I guess. I volunteer at the homeless shelters around Detroit once in a while, but I'm not having any significant impact. They'd survive just fine if I stopped showing up. All I know for certain is that I did the it's-all-about-me thing for years, and it left me feeling as hollow as a rotting log. Expensive home, expensive car, expensive jewelry . . ." She shook her head. "Pretty pathetic, huh?"

"Why do you say that?"

"A love of material things. Sad, right?"

"No. What's sad is that people are programmed from a very early age to do what you did. You can't go anywhere without seeing an advertisement of some kind. You can't turn on the TV without being told you need ten things you really don't. Phone calls from companies trying to sell you all sorts of junk, a thousand pounds of flyers stuffed into your mailbox. Frankly, I'm surprised you weren't *more* in debt."

"Tell me about it. I've definitely learned that money isn't everything, that's for sure. But look who I'm discussing this with—a billionaire. What irony."

"It's not as ironic as you might think. Remember, my fortune was built by my father, not me. It's useful—don't get me wrong. I couldn't do what I do without it. But I don't worship it. I'm not one of these sneering, arrogant types who lives by the motto 'Being rich means never having to say you're sorry.' I know people like that, and they make me sick to my stomach. It's money, but that's all it is."

What he left out here was his ongoing conviction that his family would likely still be alive if they hadn't had the so-called privilege of extreme wealth in the first place. Ordinary people took vacations in ordinary planes, not planes they owned and kept on their estates. Furthermore, Hammond doubted there would have been as much space between him and his father had the latter not been so hard-driven to accumulate such a vast fortune. But he wasn't going to discuss any of this now, not only because he didn't want to expose this part of his soul but also because he had come to understand that people who weren't wealthy found it impossible to believe anyone could resent wealth as much as he did.

Moving back to a more comfortable topic, he said, "So if you're not going to be tending to these fitness centers of yours forever, what's your next big career move?"

"I'm just not sure. It's funny—when you're young, you seem to be able to see the road ahead pretty clearly. You just kind of know what's next. Now that I'm older and my grand plan has been scrambled, I don't have that kind of vision anymore. No obvious career path, no burning ambitions, no significant relationships."

Hammond felt the pull of hesitation here. He'd only known this woman for a few hours and wasn't sure if it would be appropriate to delve into personal topics. He decided to play it lighthearted. "You aren't in a relationship? And here you seem utterly charming."

She laughed again, and he decided her initial apprehension toward him had abated somewhat. "Not that charming, apparently. I was in a serious relationship for more than two years. Then, a few months ago, I caught him with someone else. One of my customers."

"Wow. I'm very sorry."

Staring out the window, she smiled. "What a blow to the ego that was. You really think you know a person, and then . . . I don't mean to ramble on like this. I apologize."

"It's okay."

"No, this can't be making you feel very comfortable."

"It's no problem, really. *I'm* the one who should apologize for prying. I'm just trying to make small talk."

"Yeah, well, long story short, I haven't even thought about having another man in my life since then, and I'm in no rush, either. My heart's still got too many bruises on it."

"That's a good attitude. You need to give yourself time to fully recover."

"From that and from everything else going on lately. It seems I'm at something of a crossroads right now."

"Except the intersection doesn't go four ways—it goes about a hundred, right?"

She thought about this for a moment, then said, "Yes, exactly. That's a perfect way of putting it."

"I'm a regular Ernest Hemingway."

"Yeah, and you sound like you're speaking from experience."

Hammond felt his smile fade away to nothing. Then he said quickly, "Your mom was an amazing woman. I've been thinking about what it must have been like for her all those years, knowing about that film, knowing what was on it."

"Absolutely."

"I'm guessing this has crossed your mind already."

"My heart breaks whenever I think about what she went through. Keeping that secret to herself, living every day in fear."

"I'll bet. Oh, and by the way, I uploaded the digital safety copy of the film onto my online storage site. That's what I was doing when you were getting changed before. I hope that's all right."

"That's fine."

"The first thing I need to do is make sure the file was fully uploaded."

"Aren't you concerned that it's floating around in cyberspace?"

"No. The site has passwords, encryption, all that." Hammond took out his phone and unfolded it. It was fairly large by contemporary standards, and there was no brand name printed anywhere on the case.

"Never saw a phone like that before," Sheila said.

"It's a satellite phone made by Hammond Communications. It's an experimental model, so technically there's no record of its existence."

"Isn't that illegal?"

"The company has a license to develop new technologies. They have to have that kind of freedom or they wouldn't get anything done. Besides, the stuff they're coming up with will be beneficial to everyone. For example, they're putting together a GPS tracking system whereby ordinary cell phones can be located in an instant."

"Isn't there already a technology like that?"

"There is, but it has limitations. We're trying to make significant improvements."

"Some will consider it an invasion of privacy."

"A phone can still be turned off, and I'm sure plenty of third-party hack services will come up with blocking software. Also, phones with advanced encryption and security features—like, say, the one the president keeps in his jacket pocket—will be immune. And of course, you need to know the number of the phone you want to track in the first place. But think of the advantages. For example, parents will be able to locate their children at any time, and *some* criminals will be caught. We're just about finished with the first version of the software, and the results thus far have been very promising."

"Sounds cool."

"It is."

"So what's next with my mom's film?"

"I need to see if I can get a better look at Storm-Drain Man. That's where the image-enhancement software comes in. I have no idea who the guy is, but maybe someone else will. I have a friend in the area who knows more about the assassination than I do, maybe more than anyone in the world. He should be able to offer some insight."

"And let's say you identify the guy. What happens then?"

"Then things could get a little dicey. I don't think I need to tell you how sensitive a subject this is. Remember, for decades more than half the public has believed the assassination was a conspiracy and not the work of Oswald alone. When you were upstairs getting changed before, I did some brushing up on the assassination via the Internet. The Warren Commission's report, which was the official government ruling on the killing released in 1964, concluded that Oswald was the so-called lone gunman. But in 1976, the House of Representatives formed the Select Committee on Assassinations for the purpose of further investigating the murders of both President Kennedy and Dr. Martin Luther King Jr. Their findings on Kennedy were remarkable. They discovered, for example, that the FBI's investigation of the assassination, upon which the Warren Report was largely based, barely touched on the idea that more than one person was involved. They simply didn't want to deal with—or perhaps they were *instructed* not to deal with—the notion of a conspiracy. Also, the CIA gave the commission minimal cooperation. In the committee's mind, that increased suspicion of the CIA's possible involvement. I'm not saying that's conclusive, but it seems highly unusual. Finally, the Warren Commission was under pressure from both the public and many political leaders to issue *some* kind of conclusion, because the general population couldn't deal with the idea of such a heinous crime going unsolved. An answer was needed, so the Warren Commission came up with one."

Sheila shivered. "I can't stand stuff like this. It's terrifying. Dark, sinister figures getting away with dark and sinister things."

"That's not the half of it. The number of people connected with the assassination who have died under mysterious or unusual circumstances over the years is enough to send you diving under the bed. For example, there was a man named Gary Underhill, a Harvard graduate who worked for military intelligence during World War II. After the war, he did some freelance work for the CIA. Shortly after the assassination, he began telling friends that he believed the agency took part in the killing and that he was terrified because they knew *he* knew. In May of '64, he was found dead with a bullet hole behind his right ear. The death was officially ruled a suicide, but Underhill was left-handed, making it extremely difficult for him to have fired that shot.

"Then there was Jim Koethe, a reporter for the *Dallas Times Herald*. He interviewed several people while researching the assassination, including a man named George Senator, who was a friend of Jack Ruby's. Senator visited Ruby in jail after he killed Oswald, but it isn't known what Senator told Koethe about the visit. Senator did, however, allow Koethe to search Ruby's apartment on the evening of November 24, 1963. Eventually, Koethe began writing a book about his findings on the assassination, but he never got the chance to finish it—he was murdered in his home in September of 1964.

"Dr. Mary Sherman's case is particularly interesting. She was an orthopedic surgeon from New Orleans who had apparently been involved in a CIA-funded project under the Kennedy administration to secretly develop biological weapons for the purpose of killing Cuban leader Fidel Castro. As you may know, the Kennedy administration tried several times to eliminate Castro after he overthrew Fulgencio Batista's regime in 1959 and seized all American-owned property, claiming it for his new government and costing its original owners billions. In July of 1964, members of the Warren Commission came to New Orleans to obtain testimony from Dr. Sherman—but she was murdered *the same day*. Quite a coincidence, to say the least. She was stabbed multiple times, and her apartment was set on fire. Her lab was also destroyed, erasing all evidence of the project. To this day, her killing remains unsolved."

Sheila looked at him incredulously. "That's insane."

"I know. The evidence certainly suggests there were some very evil people involved in the president's death. The kind of people we pretend don't exist so we can sleep at night."

"I never should have contacted you about any of this. I should've just burned the film and forgotten about it."

"No, what you did was absolutely right, Sheila. If there's a chance that your mother's film will help to finally solve this case and maybe catch those responsible, then how can it be wrong?"

"But at what cost? How many more lives will be put in danger? Yours? Mine?"

"You won't be involved in any of this—I promise. Your name and your mother's will never come up."

"What if someone asks where the film came from?"

"None of their business."

"Then they won't believe you. They'll think it's a fake."

"I'll prove that it isn't. I'll get historians and film experts involved. I'm not worried about that."

"And what will it matter in the end? Will it bring the president back?"

"No, but maybe figuring out who was behind his murder will finally give the Kennedys—along with a whole generation of Americans—some peace of mind."

"I think that's the only reason my mother kept it. She figured it might help catch the people responsible one day."

"And why you couldn't bring yourself to destroy it either, right?"

"I guess."

As they turned onto her street at last, Hammond said, "Well, let me gather up my things and get out of your hair. I think you need for this day to be over."

"I really do."

12

AS THEY WENT down the basement steps, Hammond said, "If you give me your cell phone number and e-mail address, I'll make sure you get regular updates."

"That'd be great."

The laptop was sitting on the washing machine, the screen blank. Hammond thought this was odd, since he didn't use the automatic standby feature. At most, it should've launched the screen saver.

"How did that get turned off?" he asked aloud. He checked the power cord. *Still plugged in. Maybe the outlet's faulty.* He turned on an old radio that was sitting on the shelf above the dryer. It worked fine. "What the—?" He hit the power button.

Then Sheila said, "What did you do with the film?"

He turned. "Huh?"

She pointed to the bare spindle on the projector. "Wasn't it on here? Or did you move it?"

"I—" he began. Then he froze as he spotted the error message on the laptop's screen.

DISK ERROR. NO DISK FOUND.

Hammond began to understand. "Oh no."

"What's wrong?"

He cut the power, turned the unit over, and took a Swiss Army knife from his pocket. Using the tiny flat-head screwdriver, he removed the bottom panel. There was a rectangular gap where the hard drive should have been.

"The hard drive's been taken out."

"*What?*"

He showed her. "Someone was in here."

"No, don't tell me that."

"Yes. Someone actually came into this house and took it. And the film. They knew what we were doing. Somehow they *knew*."

Hammond ran back up the steps with Sheila close behind. He grabbed a knife in the kitchen from the wooden block by the toaster oven. Then, methodically, they went from room to room. After he was satisfied the intruder had gone, they returned to the basement. As Sheila looked on, he took his phone from his pocket and checked his FTP site.

The file was there, and it was complete.

"Thank goodness."

"Did the file fully upload to your storage si—?"

"Wait, no!" Hammond put a finger to his lips, but he knew it was too late. His shoulders sagged.

"What? What's wrong?"

He leaned in close and whispered in her ear. "This house is probably bugged."

The look she gave him said, *Are you serious?*

He nodded. "I'd bet anything on it, and I've seen it before. Listening devices can be planted anywhere these days. It's the only way they could've known what we've been doing.

That's why I didn't want to say anything about the online file. C'mon, we've got to get moving."

• • •

Out in the street, Birk heard the comment about the file and cursed out loud. He got his employer on the phone, and the old man erupted again. Birk imagined him with veins bulging in his neck like cables.

"Take them out," he said. "And make sure it looks right."

• • •

Back upstairs, Hammond and Sheila went from room to room, turning off lights and pulling down shades.

"Why don't we just get in the car and take off?" she whispered.

"We don't know who's out there. Maybe no one is. But I'm not willing to take that chance. Not yet."

• • •

It would be so much easier to just blow them both away, Birk thought as he moved toward the house. But that wouldn't "look right," as his employer had ordered. That would look like they'd been murdered. He knew the authorities would figure it out in the end regardless. With investigative science being what it was, it was almost impossible to perform a clean homicide anymore. But he was obligated to try.

He moved in the darkness to the side of the property, the earpiece still in place so he could continue monitoring their movements. They were upstairs, hiding in the dark. *That's good,* Birk thought. It would make his job that much easier.

Kneeling along the foundation, he pushed open one of the basement windows. When he was down there earlier, he had unlocked it in case he needed to reenter. This kind of forward thinking was a critical skill in his profession, and those who didn't practice it usually ended up in a body bag. When he was going through the house to plant the bugs earlier in the day, he'd made scores of mental notes. You never knew when something was going to be useful.

He had formulated the method of their execution in the short walk from the car, and now he was excited to see the plan unfold. He passed through the window, his black sneakers barely making a sound as they hit the floor, and found the dryer. There was a flexible hose behind it, which he snapped off. Gas began breathing out, and Birk propped the hose over the dryer's control panel to direct it more efficiently. Then he went to the steps and crept to the top. He grabbed the door along the side rather than at the knob—knobs could be noisy—and pushed it back in one smooth, decisive motion. Opening a door too slowly, he had learned long ago, gave the hinges a chance to groan.

• • •

In the attic, Hammond went to the bare bulb glowing in its ceramic fixture and pulled the string to snuff it. Then he moved to a window and looked out. The landscape was bathed in moon glow.

"Anything?" Sheila asked.

"No, no movement of any kind. Even the trees are still. Just shadows out there."

• • •

Birk went back down to perform the last step. There was an old couch along one wall, and next to it was an end table. Sitting on the table was a rotary telephone. In the home of a modern family, such an item might have been kept around as a novelty. Birk suspected Margaret Baker hadn't thought of it that way.

He picked it up once to check for a dial tone. Then he popped off the case, set that aside, and replaced the receiver in its cradle. *One spark—that's all we need,* he thought. He had already memorized the number.

With the sour scent of natural gas growing thicker, Birk descended the basement stairs and crawled out the window.

• • •

They saw nothing out the other attic window either.

"I really don't think anyone's there," Sheila said.

Hammond continued scanning, then nodded. "Yeah, maybe." But his gut told him otherwise. Something just didn't feel right.

"Should we go downstairs?"

"I guess."

• • •

As Birk approached his car, he took out his cell phone. He did not dial the number but rather checked the time. The gas had been running for about ten minutes. He'd give it a few more to let the place really fill up. *Then the fun begins.*

He got into the car to wait.

• • •

They came down the steps, Hammond in front.

"What now?" Sheila whispered as they reached the first-floor hallway.

"We have to find a place to hide you. I don't think it's safe here anymore." They entered the kitchen. "Then I'm going to—"

Hammond stopped so abruptly that Sheila nearly ran into him.

"What's wrong?"

He held up one finger and sniffed the air. "Do you smell that?"

"What?" She sniffed too. "I don't—"

"Oh no. . . ." Hammond saw the wide-open basement door. Training his hearing in that direction, he detected the hissing from the broken pipe.

He began pushing Sheila back down the hallway. "Out! Quick! *Go!*"

• • •

Birk heard this and cursed again. He jumped from the car and began running toward the house, dialing the number at the same time.

• • •

They passed the enclosed staircase and crossed into a small sunroom. Each of the tall windows had summer screens on the inside and rows of rotating louvered glass on the outside. Hammond prayed the aluminum door, which had matching louvers for consistency, would open.

"HURRY!"

Sheila set her hand on the black lever just as the house phone rang.

• • •

Birk moved closer but made sure to keep a buffer between himself and the three-story bomb he had created—a massive oak tree that stood in a neighbor's front yard. When the gas ignited, the effect was greater than he could have imagined. There was a momentary flash of light in every window, followed by the dusty sparkle of shattering glass. Then walls puffed outward, as if the house suddenly coughed. The explosion was thunderous and epic, tearing through the night with wretched fury. The part that fascinated Birk the most was the pyramidal roof. It went up like a spaceship gently taking off, and for a split second, the bare trusses were visible. Then it eased back down in the same dreamy motion, landing a few degrees off its original position.

• • •

Sheila had opened the back door and taken the first of the three brief stairs down into the yard. The force of the explosion blew them forward, where they tumbled along the lawn like beach balls. Sheila didn't lose consciousness, but she was dazed. Hammond missed smashing into a stone birdbath by inches, and Sheila saw that he had sustained a slanting cut on his forehead from a piece of spinning glass. Blood streamed into his right eye.

Wiping it away, he grabbed Sheila by the elbow and pulled her up. "Come on—follow me," he said.

He had no idea where to go. The yard was dark now; the explosion had blown out the floodlights. Going on nothing but intuition, he led her deeper into the backyard. It was long and rectangular, outlined by rows of dwarf spruces.

"Where will this take us?" he asked, pointing to the northeast corner.

"Into our neighbor's yard," she said. Her voice was groggy. "Mr. Phillips."

"Okay, good. Mr. Phillips will just have to—"

The first muted shot came so close to Hammond that it sounded like a bumblebee flew past his ear.

"What was that?" Sheila cried.

"A gunshot! Keep moving!"

The second round wasn't as accurate, and it ricocheted off something on the other side of the hedgerow. *He can't see us,* Hammond realized. *He's firing blind.*

They reached the corner of the property and disappeared between the spruces.

There was a well-worn path that linked the two yards. It ran alongside Mr. Phillips's large garden shed before terminating at the edge of his lawn. They ducked around the front as the third shot came.

"Get over here and stay down," Hammond said, guiding her under the shed's decorative window.

"What are you doing?"

"You'll see."

There was a wheelbarrow nearby, a hump of dirt in its carriage. A rusty hoe and round-point shovel formed an X on top of it. Hammond grabbed the shovel and went back to the corner of the shed.

"Are you out of your mind?" Sheila asked.

"Very likely."

At first there was only silence, and Hammond wondered if their attacker had given up. Then rapid, lawn-softened footsteps became audible, and a man burst through the spruce wall. Hammond gripped the shovel combat-style, hands underneath and spaced well apart.

The time between their attacker's appearance and Hammond's reaction was infinitesimal. The shovel swung around in a blur and connected with the man's face with both an almost-comical clang and a sickening crunch. The assassin's feet went out from under him, and he fell in a heap. The gun flew away, landing in a patch of Mr. Phillips's marigolds.

To Sheila's astonishment, the man rolled over in spite of

the strike and was on his feet in an instant. Blood poured from his nose and down his mouth, making him look like a wolf at a kill site. Hammond swung the shovel again, but the assailant dodged it with near-inhuman dexterity. He karate-kicked Hammond in the knee, and Hammond cried out as he went down. Another kick sent Hammond sprawling, and a third to the stomach curled him into a fetal position.

The shooter stepped back, wiped the blood from his chin, and muttered a curse. Then he moved in for a fresh blow, but Hammond was expecting this and rolled aside. He got to his feet and turned to face his attacker. The man landed another shot on Hammond's side, an almost-successful attempt at a kidney punch. Then he made his mistake—he tried to strike Hammond in the face with his open palm in a martial-arts style that reminded Sheila of the poorly dubbed Japanese TV shows she and her father used to watch in the seventies. Hammond dodged it, albeit somewhat clumsily, and the attacker, in his overconfidence, lost his balance.

Sheila wondered if Hammond was outmatched as he brought the shovel back up. Flat iron slapped hard against the shooter's lower jaw, driving his teeth together. Hammond swung again as the man staggered back, this time with the handle. Wood met bone at a point on the man's forehead, and he froze as if hit with an alien stun ray. Then he toppled backward and lay still, his arms extended.

Hammond dropped the shovel and was on him instantly, hands swarming around his hips.

"What are you doing?"

"I'm looking for ID, although I don't expect there to be any. See if you can find the g—" But she was already going through the marigold patch. "Okay, good," he said.

Sheila found the weapon at the base of a colorful

pinwheel. She did not pick it up in a pinch between her thumb and forefinger like most who are terrified of firearms. She wrapped her fingers confidently around the butt and kept the barrel pointed downward in the event of accidental discharge. Then she undid the catch at the base of the grip and released the magazine. Finally she worked the slide to see if there was one more round in the chamber. There was, and it popped up in a brassy twirl before falling to the grass. As she bent down to retrieve it, it occurred to her that this bullet could've just as easily ended up in the back of her head.

The frisking of Birk now complete, Hammond got to his feet. "Let's get going. Did you find the—?"

Sheila held out the pieces in two hands. "Some assembly required," she said.

"Wow. Annie Oakley, I presume?"

"Every other Saturday morning with my father at the local firing range."

"Good man. Okay, come on." He took her by the elbow again. "I don't want us here when he wakes up."

They started toward the front of the Phillips property. Then Sheila stopped and looked back. Her mother's house— her childhood home—was blazing. The flames were oddly artful and seemed to be embracing it more than consuming it. Fire engines were fast approaching, their horns and sirens wailing in the distance.

"Sheila, we really can't hang around."

"I know."

"We'll take care of it, I promise."

She lingered another moment, and then the assailant behind them began to stir.

13

THEY TURNED RIGHT at the end of the Phillipses'
driveway.

"Where's the best place to catch a cab?"

"What? Oh . . . Montgomery Avenue."

"And where's that?"

"Four blocks over."

"Okay. We need to get another laptop. Then we have to—"
More blood ran into his eye from the cut on his forehead. He
reached up to feel it, and his fingertips came down bright red.

He put pressure on the wound as best he could, and they
kept moving. Another siren began screaming, and then a
police car zoomed down a bisecting street about a hundred
yards ahead of them.

"As I was saying, we also need a place to stay."

He pulled out his phone and pressed a speed key. Noah
answered on the second ring.

"Yes?"

"I need your help right away, please."

"Okay."

"Book a hotel in the Dallas area. Not downtown—on the
outskirts. Someplace quiet and unassuming."

"What's wrong? What's happening?"

"I'll tell you later—right now we're on the move. Get something nice, but not *too* nice. Two rooms." It occurred to Hammond that whoever had the means to discover Margaret Baker's secret identity, follow Sheila's discovery of her film, and blow their house into splinters very likely also had the ability to access hotel records. "And use one of the aliases." He paused to think about which false IDs he'd brought along. "Use Bartlett."

"Okay."

"Reserve for four people, not two. Tell them there will be two couples. You can make up a name for the other two if you need to. And prepay, okay?"

"All right."

"Please do this right away and call me back with the information."

He severed the connection but kept the phone in hand. It rang when they were one block shy of Montgomery.

"The Royal Crowne in Coppell. Everything's ready."

"Thank you. I appreciate it."

"Don't forget to call me back."

"I won't."

Montgomery Avenue was the closest thing to a business district in the neighborhood. No outlets, superstores, or national chains except for a lone Burger King. Hammond spotted a pay phone outside a convenience store and thought about calling in a tip about the man who had attacked them. The odds of him still being there were slim to none, however. Also, there was no need to risk a horde of police descending upon the area in search of whoever had made the anonymous call.

As Hammond searched for an oncoming taxi, it occurred to him that Sheila hadn't spoken a word in the last twenty minutes. She was leaning against the front window of a jewelry store called the Diamond Den with her arms crossed and her eyes cast downward. She looked like a petulant teenager.

In that expression he saw it all—the fear, the confusion, the despair, the anger—and the tremendous toll it was taking. The death of her mother, the revelation and subsequent encumbrance of her mother's mortal secret, the understanding that she, Sheila, would now be hunted because of it. She had been suffering all along but had been too occupied to feel it. Now the cracks in her facade were beginning to show.

A cab finally stopped, and Hammond took her gently by the arm. She went without resistance.

"To the Royal Crowne in Coppell, please," he said.

"That's twenty-two miles," the driver replied in accented English. "There is a surcharge for any trip more than ten."

"Fine," Hammond said.

• • •

The fare came to just over forty-two dollars. Hammond paid with a fifty and told the driver to keep the change. Sheila did not speak during the trip. At the Royal Crowne, the concierge commented on the nasty cut on "Mr. Bartlett's" forehead. Hammond told her he got it playing baseball earlier in the day. "That's what high school reunions do to a person my age," he said gregariously. "They make you think you're eighteen again." The woman laughed along and got him a small first-aid packet with the hotel's crest on the packaging. It contained two Band-Aids and a handful of antiseptic wipes.

The last of Sheila's resolve crumbled when she got into her room. Hammond handed her a box of tissues from the bedside table as she sat on the edge of the bed. For some reason he found the Beach Boys' "The Warmth of the Sun" going through his mind. Always fascinated by the machinations of the subconscious, he realized that the song's author, Beach Boys' guiding light Brian Wilson, had said in several interviews that he came up with the beautiful but despondent melody after hearing radio reports of Kennedy's assassination.

Sheila hitched and shuddered like a stray dog in a thunderstorm. When she finished off the tissues, he retrieved a fresh box from the bathroom. She apologized for the indignity of the purge, and he told her she was crazy. When the worst of it had passed, he pulled back the sheets, tucked her in, and turned off the lights. She was out in an instant, her face lying against her open palm in a peaceful, childlike fashion.

Hammond closed the adjoining door between their rooms and checked his watch. It was nearly eleven, so he would have to wait until morning to buy another laptop.

"I'll get some new clothes for both of us too," he said to himself. "And food. And she might need a new cell phone. . . ."

He fished through his pockets to find his Bluetooth headset, worked it into his ear, and redialed Noah.

This time, the old man picked up on the first ring. "What's happening?"

"You know the woman who called you? Sheila Baker? Her mother passed away the other day, and she was the Babushka Lady."

"*What?*"

"That's right. And that's not the half of it. She was making a film while she was there. A film that no one else has ever seen. At least not until today, that is."

"Really."

Hammond detected genuine interest, which delighted him.

"She was standing about thirty feet from the president when he was struck, and the images are crystal clear. I'm talking pristine."

"Wow."

"I digitized it and put it on the FTP site. I need you to download the file right away and store it someplace safe."

"Okay."

"Best of all—are you sitting down?"

"Should I be?"

"I would recommend it. Ready?"

"Go ahead."

"There was another gunman."

Noah's immediate response—as Hammond expected—was no response at all. Just the empty silence of the miles between them. Then, "You're kidding."

"Nope."

"Tell me you're kidding."

"I'm not."

"A second gunman."

"A second gunman. He doesn't actually fire a shot, but he's there with what is almost certainly a rifle. I'll know more when I work on the images."

"Where is he positioned?"

"In the storm drain. Remember we talked about that once? You'll see it in the film. It's the one on the side of Elm Street just before the president is hit. No other images from that day show that drain in detail. That's why he's never been noticed before. Remember, he was hiding. And he's only visible in Margaret Baker's film for a few seconds."

There was another long pause while Noah absorbed this heavyweight punch of information.

Hammond, smiling now, went to the wet bar and opened a bottle of water. "Incredible, huh?"

"This changes everything we know about the assassination."

"Tell me about it."

"So she hasn't told anyone else about it? No one else knows?"

The bottle stopped halfway to Hammond's mouth. "I wouldn't go quite that far," he said.

"What does that mean?"

"Someone else knows. At least one person for sure. Besides you, that is."

"Who's that?"

Hammond took a deep breath, then recounted everything—the trip to the Apple Store, the discovery that the film and hard drive had been taken, and the part he dreaded telling Noah the most.

". . . obviously filled the house with natural gas and sparked it by calling the house phone." He could feel the growing absurdity of his attempt to sound casual but plowed ahead anyway. "I have to say, it was pretty clever if you think about it. I never would have—"

"Jason, do you hear yourself? Do you hear what you're saying?"

"Huh?"

"You're in way over your head. I know you've learned a thing or two over the years, but you're not exactly James Bond. And this guy, whoever he is, is a *professional*."

"I know he is."

"Are you aware of the risk involved?"

"Yes."

"I'm not so sure. What about Sheila? Are you aware of the danger *she's* in?"

"Noah, if I hadn't been there, she'd already be dead."

"Sure, I'll give you that. But you're both very lucky to be alive."

"No argument there."

"How much longer do you expect your luck to hold out?"

"I'm hoping luck won't enter into it anymore."

"Don't be ridiculous. You need to come back here, and you need to bring her with you. We can keep her safe."

"No, that's the first place they'll look."

"Jason . . ."

He went into the bathroom and flicked on the light over the mirror. The cut had stopped bleeding and was now just a thin red line. It could've been drawn on with a pen.

"The most obvious places to find her will either be the estate or back at her home in Michigan. For all I know, the people behind this even know who her friends are. We have to remain in hiding."

Noah sighed. "I suppose. But I really don't like any of this."

"I don't like it either. There's nothing to like here."

"You have to be more careful."

"I will—I promise."

"And these people in the shadows—you don't have any idea who they are?"

"The guy who tried to take us out had no ID on him. Nothing."

"I doubt he's the one making the decisions anyway."

"I agree. He's the hired gun, and I'd love to know who did the hiring." Hammond tore open one of the antiseptic wipes from the first-aid packet and pressed it onto the wound. "But more importantly, I have to figure out who's on that film. So let me work on that now and I'll get back to you."

74

FREDERICK RYDELL knew the name Hammond wanted. Sitting in his office the following day with the door locked, he could think of little else.

Birk had sent Margaret Baker's film by overnight delivery to a PO box in the Annapolis suburb of Cape St. Claire. From there it was auto-forwarded to another box in the Washington suburb of Kensington. The first was leased under the false name of an individual, the second by a fictional corporation. Rydell visited the terminus box only when necessary. On this day he had gone over at lunchtime.

The face that appeared for those brief few seconds was the same one that had haunted him in a thousand dreams. Seeing it again unearthed a hoard of memories and details Rydell had tried hard to forget. It also birthed a crawling fear that he bitterly resented.

He had been a careful man all his life, had pored over the minutiae of every operation, examined every possibility, calculated every permutation. He was one of the best in his business at covering his hide—maybe *the* best. But this one man and the singular dealing they'd had . . .

There were factors even Rydell had not foreseen, elements that lay beyond his considerable vision. This man was like none he had ever known. Rydell felt it the day they met, the one and only day. The meeting had lasted no more than an hour, and yet he would never forget it.

He rewound the film and watched it for the fourth time. When the figure appeared this time, a shudder went through him.

Surely, Rydell thought, *he can't still be alive.*

"No chance," he said out loud. When he reached for the can of soda on his desk, however, his hand was trembling.

15

FATHER MICHAEL BREIMAYER stood atop the high ridge on the western side of the village and surveyed the conclusion of another long but satisfying day.

The heat was crushing, as always. Six years on the island of Hispaniola and he still wasn't used to it. He'd grown up in southwestern Alabama, not far from the Gulf shores and a nearly tropical zone in its own right. But nothing compared to this. The humidity lay upon a person like a heavy blanket. Even in his normal outfit of light cotton shorts, a silk shirt, sandals, and a broad Panama hat, he sometimes found it hard to breathe, let alone work. He mopped his forehead with a folded handkerchief.

The site was coming along beautifully. The village had eighteen domestic structures—ten mud huts, six corrugated shacks, one semimodern cottage that acted as a church, and one rickety lean-to that the oldest member of the community refused to upgrade. The cottage had been built in just two weeks through funding from Breimayer's sponsor ministry back in the States. These villagers were still getting used to seeing a white man's face, let alone a power drill. But progress was being made.

The network of PVC pipes ran grid-like in every direction, in grooves dug two feet down into the soft earth. Soon every home would have real plumbing for the first time. That meant fresh water for drinking and bathing, something these people had never known. The main line came from Port-au-Prince, thirteen miles away. Breimayer had also arranged for a feed from a small water tower. It was only for emergency purposes, which might have sounded like overkill in a nation with an average annual rainfall of nearly sixty inches. But they were dealing with a government that was often under the control of different people from month to month. Necessities like clean water had a way of disappearing at a moment's notice. The water tower would be the villagers' ace in the hole.

This was Breimayer's twenty-second year as a missionary and his thirty-fifth as a priest. After high school, he'd done a stint in the military and had spent nine months in Vietnam. That was enough not only to turn him against politics and war but also to persuade him to spend his life making the world a better place. Now, over four decades later, he had gray hair, wore steel-rimmed glasses, and was in remarkably good health for a man in his sixties.

Father Breimayer came down from the ridge to distribute kind words and a few pats on the back. He could offer his people little else, and he often felt the burden of guilt for that. They were all volunteers, some local, others from abroad. They lived nomadically, traveling to whatever location was next on the agenda and setting up a camp a hundred yards or so from the work site. Breimayer insisted on this, not wanting to invade the lives of his beneficiaries any more than necessary. Here, for example, he wanted the villagers to be able to say good-bye to his group at the end of the day, when they would disappear until the following morning. His intent was simply to come in, make as many improvements as possible, and move on.

Standing among the group, he glanced at his watch and announced, "We will be finishing in ten minutes, okay? And tonight after dinner, maybe we should enjoy a little music and dance. Will everyone have enough strength left for that?" There were nods and murmurs of agreement all around. Breimayer rubbed his hands together. "Good. Excellent work today."

The man known as Salvador entered the perimeter from one of the main trails, a stack of narrow pipes under his arm. Breimayer's eyes fell on him and stayed there. Breimayer had met thousands of people in his lifetime—black and white, large and small, good and evil—and none fascinated him more than this one. As hard as he tried, Breimayer was never able to suppress the urge to study him. Even if he had seen him ten minutes earlier, he would still search for . . . well, he wasn't even sure what.

Salvador was smallish, no more than five and a half feet, but stout and muscular. His hair was making the gradual transition from raven's black to pewtery silver, and it was still lush and thick, as were the heavy eyebrows. He had added a beard and mustache in recent years, something Breimayer could not understand given the high temperatures. When he commented on this offhandedly, Salvador smiled but said nothing.

Breimayer had inherited Salvador when he came to the organization eleven years ago, and in that time he had gleaned nothing of a personal nature about the man. As a worker, he was a member of some superhuman subspecies. He rose before everyone else, dove headlong into a task without hesitation or complaint, and possessed machinelike stamina. Observing this each day, Breimayer had built a profile of someone who was highly intelligent, uncommonly focused, and a fast learner.

But that was the "professional" side of the man. The rest was kept in a safe with a lost combination. Salvador spoke only in replies, and even these were economical. Attempts to extract candid information were fruitless, and Breimayer sensed that Salvador knew when someone was trying to do this. Breimayer also no longer believed Salvador was his true name, but he had given up hope of ever learning the real one.

Perhaps most curious of all, Salvador refused to camp with the rest of the group at the end of each day. Even though Breimayer promised him his own quarters and assured him that he would never be disturbed except in the event of an emergency, Salvador maintained his habit of simply disappearing into the night like the specter he seemed to be.

The only other element to the man that Breimayer was certain of—although, again, he was equally certain he would never be able to confirm it—was that Salvador was haunted. The priest had encountered scores of souls who, through unfortunate circumstances or their own lapses in judgment or a toxic combination of both, carried spiritual burdens that were grinding them into oblivion. He recognized the expressions, the mannerisms, and the behavioral patterns, subtle though these traits were in Salvador's case. The merciful side of Breimayer's nature burned to ease the man's pain. He had soothed others, pleading with the Lord to quiet their demons. But he knew he would log no such victory with this man. Salvador was a prisoner of his own dark universe.

Breimayer also knew that people of this stripe had the potential to be thoroughly dangerous. He still wasn't sure if

Salvador was of this variety—nor was he interested in finding out.

"You were a big help today," he said as Salvador passed by,
the PVC pipes bobbing like javelins in his arms.

"Thank you, Father," came the accented reply accompanied by the characteristic smile and nod. The man's voice was
light and scratchy, like that of a washed-up crooner who had
traded his talent for several decades of smoking.

"We may partake in some festivities later, if you'd care to
join us. Just a little song and dance, nothing too elaborate."

"No, no, but thank you."

"Okay. If you change your mind, you know where we'll
be. We'd love to have you."

Another agreeable nod, and then he moved on.

The last of the day's light died away, and torches were lit
to aid in the final bits of work and cleanup. Breimayer kept
watching Salvador, ever hopeful of that momentary glimpse
beneath the surface. When he dissolved unceremoniously
into the darkness, no one else took particular notice; they
had seen it a thousand times. He would return tomorrow,
after all.

Breimayer was never so sure.

16

HAMMOND SHUDDERED AWAKE. The pillow that had been over his head bowled everything off the nightstand before tumbling away. His eyes shifted about like those of a frightened child. There was sunlight slanting through the blinds, casting patterns on the furniture and the carpet. But he didn't recognize the blinds or the furniture or anything else. He was out of breath, his heart hammering.

Then it started coming back—the phone call, the church, the coffins, the sickening emptiness that followed the loss of the most beloved people in his life. He saw it all again in his mind, or at least a vague recollection of it. *It's bad enough I had to live through it once,* he thought bitterly, *but I have to endure repeat showings?* Then he remembered where he was and why he was here.

In the bathroom, he turned on the cold water and splashed his face. He appraised himself in the mirror—pale-gray half-moons had formed under his eyes; any darker and he'd look like a corpse. He remembered Noah's standing offer to fill a prescription for sleeping meds—drugs that would put him into such a deep sleep it would take all the hounds of hell to rouse him. *Forget it—I will* not *give in to this.* When his physician had asked about the nature of his reluctance, Hammond said he was concerned the pills would lose their effectiveness after a while, which was a perfectly valid response. The greater truth, however, was that he loathed the idea of developing a dependency on any type of pharmaceutical. He had a secret goal of going the remainder of his life without ever taking a synthesized substance, regardless of the reason.

He drove away these thoughts in the usual way—by focusing on the day's priorities. *Get some clothes for both of us; get a new laptop; download the file.* The dream images had all but deteriorated now, like the remnants of a chalk drawing on a rain-spattered sidewalk. He pat-dried his face with one of the towels and went out.

He was thinking about calling Noah when he realized the door joining the two rooms was open. Sheila stood half behind it with a ghost of a smile on her lips.

"Good morning," Hammond said.

"Hello."

"Up early, I see."

"Yes."

Hammond immediately sensed something wasn't right. He made a careful study of her face, expecting to see vestiges of the emotional beating she'd taken the day before. What he found instead was a seemingly alert and clear-eyed individual who was scrutinizing *him.*

"Are you okay?" she asked. Hammond found this question somewhat arresting, as he was about to ask the same one.

"Sure, why?"

"I heard you this morning."

"Excuse me?"

"You were yelling in your sleep." She had also heard what sounded like sobbing but decided not to mention that.

"I was? Well, I'm sorry about that. I guess I was having a bad dream."

"It sounded *very* bad."

"That's weird. I don't remember any of it," he said and instantly hated himself for lying. "And what about you? Did you sleep okay?"

"Yeah."

"I'll bet. Feel better?"

"I do. Look, I'm really sorry about my meltdown last n—"

He put a hand up. "Don't apologize. Very, very understandable. Don't give it another thought. I have an idea, if you'd like to hear it."

"Sure."

He pulled out a chair at the small circular table by the window. The heavy drapes were half-open and the gauzy inner curtains fully shut. "Here, have a seat."

"Thanks."

Taking the one across from her, he said, "I know you want to get back to your normal life as soon as possible. And I want that too. But I don't think it's safe for you to go either to your mom's house—"

"What's left of it."

"—right, what's left of it, or to your home in Michigan just yet. Not until I figure out who's behind this. Whoever they are, they're obviously very dangerous people. I'm sure you realize that."

"I do."

"So what we need to do is keep you hidden someplace safe. Someplace where—"

"No."

"What?"

"I'm not hiding. I'm not running." She looked directly at him, challenging him.

"I don't understand. What do you—?"

"I'm not going to sit around waiting for something to happen. I'm going to help you. I'm going to take part in this."

"Sheila, that guy last night was a pro. For all I know there are ten more out there searching for us. Who's to say who's behind this? The Mafia? The NSA? Some foreign government? This is a very delicate situation."

"I realize that."

"You don't know how to do this kind of work. You've never done something like this before. Heck, I've become pretty good at it, and even I admit I might be out of my depth."

"I'm a fast learner."

"I can't be responsible for you."

"I'm not asking you to be. I can make my own decisions. I'm not a little kid."

"What if you get hurt?"

"That's life."

"Or death."

"Right."

"Look, I really don't think—"

"Jason, these people *haunted* my mama. She lived in fear of them every day." Her eyes were beginning to tighten with anger. "Can you even begin to imagine what that must've been like? The effect it had on her mind, on her body? How many bad dreams did *she* have? Or nights when she couldn't even get to sleep in the first place? The constant distraction of it? The constant worry about her safety, about the safety of her family. How much of her livelihood was taken from her? How much of her spirit?" A single tear made a track line down her cheek. "Then these people invade her privacy, blow up her house, and try to kill me, all to continue covering up their crime. These *animals*."

Hammond reached across the table and took her hand. A few more tears came, but her resolve did not waver.

"I don't expect you to understand how personal this is," she said, calmer now. "I know you can't."

"No, you're right. I can't even imagine."

"You say I need to stay here to protect my life. But until this is resolved, I have no life. They're probably waiting for me to use my cell phone right now so they can track my signal. You know all about that. Am I right?"

Hammond nodded. "Probably."

"*Very* probably."

"Yeah."

"And I'll bet they've got people hanging around my mama's neighborhood hoping I'll come back."

"I wouldn't be surprised."

"Sooner or later they'll get to me. If they can get to a president, they can get to anybody. So if I'm going to go down, I'm going to do it fighting. No, of course I don't want to take part in this. But I *need* to."

Hammond studied her another moment, then said, "Are you sure? I mean really sure?"

She nodded. "I'm positive."

17

HAMMOND ASKED Noah to arrange a new rental car and have it delivered to the hotel. Noah insisted on talking to Sheila to ask if she was okay. As they waited for the rental—a nondescript sedan registered under the Bartlett pseudonym—Hammond used the hotel's public computers to locate a mall within reasonable driving distance that had both an Apple Store and several clothing outlets.

They got the clothes first, and Hammond insisted on paying for everything. Just before they reached the Apple Store, Sheila pointed out that the large purchase he was about to make—a new MacBook, a pair of RAM expansion sticks for maximum speed, a color printer, and about a thousand dollars' worth of software—might arouse suspicion if anyone was watching. "The guy at my mama's house knows you were using a Mac, and there aren't that many Mac stores around here," she reasoned, "so it would be pretty easy to monitor them."

Hammond found this logic impenetrable and came up with an idea. Handing her fifteen hundred-dollar bills, he directed her to buy the software and the printer at a different store in the mall while he got the laptop and memory sticks.

The Apple salesman, in his early twenties, looked like he'd overdosed on happy pills when Hammond told him what he wanted. "This makes my commission for the day," he said, his braces shining in the pendant lighting over the register.

Back at the Royal Crowne, they went to their respective rooms to shower and dress, then ordered a room-service lunch—artichoke and olive salad for her, a grilled salmon sandwich for him. Hammond set up the new computer on the table while they ate. It took nearly two hours to bypass all the welcome screens, get the software and extended RAM installed, and download the .mov file from the FTP site.

"Okay," he said, "now let's see if we can figure out what this guy looks like."

He launched the file, watched it once from start to finish, then went back to the first frame he wanted to improve—Storm-Drain Man, turned to the right, offering a strong profile. This was frame 177 according to the counter in the lower right-hand corner. Hammond drew an isolation box around the head and enlarged it. Now it filled most of the screen. The image was blurry and soft, but two clicks of the sharpness filter improved it considerably.

"Wow," Sheila said.

"Latin heritage for sure." Olive skin, dark hair in low, tight curls. He looked rough and rugged, with a scowl that spoke of his grudge against the world. The image still wasn't perfect, but it was the best view they had so far. Hammond saved it as a separate file on the desktop.

"Now for the other angle—straight on."

He advanced the film slowly, and the gunman turned. There would be a split second—Hammond would know it when he saw it—when a certain clarity of character was visible. Something in the eyes, perhaps. It occurred just before the president's limousine came into view. Hammond trapped the face again and brought it forward. Sheila gasped this time—the man seemed to be looking *at* them, the eyes fierce.

"He's just a boy," she said, and Hammond caught a trace of what he thought was compassion in her voice. "Look at how young."

"Yeah. And look at the frame number," Hammond said, pointing.

"232?"

"That's incredible."

"Why incredible?"

"It was also a significant frame in the Zapruder film."

"You're kidding."

"No—it's the one where the president has his hands balled into fists and pressed against his throat with his elbows sticking out, and the First Lady has just turned to see what's wrong. Not *the* most important frame, but still noteworthy."

"Does that mean my mother started filming about the same time that Abraham Zapruder did?"

"It's very possible. Either way, I find it kind of eerie that both films have an important frame 232."

"Tell me about it. This just gets weirder and weirder."

"Maybe it's a sign," Hammond said, smiling. "A *good* sign."

"Let's hope so."

Hammond studied the image more carefully. "The image still isn't *that* good. Even the best software in the world can't perform miracles. The best results come when you view it from about a foot or so away, where you can determine enough native details to fill in the rest with your imagination." Hammond shook his head. "But wow, just look at that face. Those eyes . . ."

"Any ideas?" Sheila asked.

"About what?"

"About who he is?"

Hammond slumped back in the chair and gave it some thought, never taking his eyes off the screen. "No, not a clue. I think I've read every major book on the assassination, and I've scarcely even heard speculation about a possible Latino conspirator."

"Cuban, maybe? Because of the Castro connection?"

"Could be, sure."

"In the storm drain . . . incredible. Who would've thought?"

"Like I said at your mom's house, that possibility has been discussed before. Most of those theories have been dismissed, but think about it from an assassin's perspective. It's actually a very good vantage point."

"How in the world did he even get down there?"

"He could've entered through any nearby manhole. A schematic of the underground pipe network wouldn't have been that hard to find. That kind of information was available to the public. He could've gone down the night before and just waited. A trained assassin would be patient like that."

"It's ridiculous, though. He could've gotten caught so easily."

"Not necessarily. He could've had a silencer, which would have muted the shot. He might have been able to fire without sticking the barrel out that far. One dull thump in a noisy crowd would be nearly impossible to hear. And as soon as the president was hit, all attention would be turned to the limo. The ensuing confusion would have provided the shooter with enough cover to work his way through his arranged escape route."

"Incredible."

"There's another possibility too."

"That he expected to get caught?"

"Exactly. That he was essentially on a suicide mission, so escape wasn't even a factor."

She shook her head. "Insane."

"Tell me about it."

Hammond studied the photos of the gunman again, raking through his memory. There were so many peripheral figures among the numerous outlying theories. But this man was completely new, found along a road few conspiracists had ever traveled.

Perhaps just one, he thought with a smile.

"I know what we can do."

"What's that?"

"Print out the two images, then go see my friend."

"Oh yeah, you mentioned him before. Who is he?"

"I'll show you."

Hammond went to the web and did a Google image search for the name Dr. Benjamin Burdick. The two most common results were a portrait of a bearded, bespectacled, sandy-haired man in his midforties and the cover of a book that looked as though it had been printed at Staples instead of by a formal publishing house. The title was *The Truth behind the Lies: Your Government's Involvement in the Assassination of John F. Kennedy*, with Burdick's name along the bottom.

"It's more than three hundred pages long, but it was self-printed because none of the publishers would touch it."

"Too far out there?"

"Too realistic. I've read it from front to back, and it gave me the shivers. Ben's not one of the crazies, believe me. He's got two PhDs and knows how to research better than anyone I've ever met. And he's very serious about what happened in

Dallas that day. After the public reaction to this first book, he started a second one. It's supposed to be the definitive work on the assassination."

"How do you know him?"

"I found the first book online years ago while I was digging up other sources. Most of the self-published stuff was garbage, but not this. After I read it, I got in touch with him. Within ten minutes we were hitting it off like old friends. He *is* a little crazy, but good crazy. My kind of crazy. He's got the most wicked case of OCD in the world, keeps his house so neat I think he vacuums the lawn. He's a health nut, too. Eats nothing but vegetables and works out three times a day. And he collects Pez dispensers. He has hundreds of 'em. But underneath all that is one of the most brilliant and kind-hearted people you could ever meet."

"Sounds like a fun guy."

"He really is. I came out here a few years ago to meet with several academics who've studied the assassination, and he was one of them."

"You mean he lives in Dallas?"

Hammond nodded. "On the outskirts. He's a professor at Southern Methodist. Here, take a look."

He found the SMU site and navigated to the faculty page, then to Burdick's. One of the photos from the Google image search was in the upper left-hand corner—a smiling Burdick leaning against a loaded bookcase. In the right column was a brief vita, and beneath that was his office phone number and e-mail address.

Hammond took his cell phone out of his pocket. "Let me give him a call and see if he can pull himself away from his Pez dispensers long enough to talk with us."

It rang four times before voice mail took over. Hammond

was surprised to hear a young woman's voice instead of Burdick's. His first reaction was that he had dialed the wrong number. "You have reached the office of Dr. Benjamin Burdick. Dr. Burdick is on extended leave from the university until further notice. If this is an urgent matter, please call Dr. Alma Sentis at . . ."

Hammond flipped the phone shut. "Huh."

"What's wrong?"

"The message said he's on extended leave."

"Is that strange?"

"Very strange. He loves his job, and he's a workaholic. Prime candidate for a stroke."

"I don't mean to sound morbid, but maybe he had one."

"I sure hope not."

Hammond got on the Internet again, this time navigating to Burdick's personal site. What came up took his breath away—

ERROR 404—PAGE NOT FOUND

"That can't be right," he said firmly. "No way." He double-checked the address bar along the top of the browser. The URL was correct—www.drbenjaminburdick.com.

"He had tons of stuff on here—articles, photographs, links. And a lot of stuff about the new book. Teasers and things like that, hints about all the new information it contained. You could also download the first book as a free PDF file. He didn't even care about selling it. He just wanted to get the word out." Hammond shook his head. "Something's definitely wrong."

"You said he lives around here. Do you know where?"

"I do."

"Let's go knock on his door."

• • •

Rydell's secretary tensed when she heard her boss's approaching footsteps in the hallway. He had never caused her to tense before, not even when he interviewed her back in 1991. She had worked for a corporate CFO before Rydell, and that man knotted her stomach every minute of the day. He was a jerk of the highest order who knew how to get to people and loved doing it. When a friend recommended this job, she figured it couldn't be any worse. Frederick Rydell turned out to be the best boss she'd ever had, and that familiar sense of dread gradually withdrew into hibernation. Now it had awoken from its long sleep. He hadn't said anything nasty to her in the last two days, hadn't even raised his voice. But she could sense that his mood was like that of a rabid dog on a frayed leash. After all these years, their relationship was more like a marriage than anything else.

He was frowning when he appeared and walking at an accelerated pace toward his door.

"You received a few messages," she said with a smile, holding out a set of little pink slips. He took them without looking at her and mumbled a thank-you, then opened the door and went inside. On any other day, he would sort through them on the spot and give instructions on each, sometimes with colorful and funny comments thrown in. Not today, though. He still had the good manners to close the door quietly, but under the circumstances he might as well have kicked it shut.

• • •

Rydell dropped the slips on the edge of his desk and sat down. Tapping his keyboard did not clear the screen saver—a CIA logo floating against a black background—but rather caused a password prompt to appear in front of it. Rydell paused a moment, then typed in the eight-key alphanumeric phrase with remarkable speed, his fingers moving over the keys in a chattery blur. The pause came from having to remember it, which both concerned and irritated him; he *never* forgot passwords.

He had always been able to push distractions out of his mind, always been the master of his own concentration. But this Babushka Lady film, and the fact that Jason Hammond and the Baker woman were running around loose . . . He could feel his blood pressure rise every time he thought about it. Sheila Baker would have been easy enough to handle by herself, but Hammond . . . *That could be real trouble,* a voice teased over and over, and then the fear that he hated more than anything else surged into his system.

He had considered prematurely activating his post-retirement escape plan, gaming out the scenario to see if a reasonable conclusion could be reached. But it was simply beyond the realm of the possible. The sudden disappearance of a person in his position would set off alarm bells in every corridor of government. A massive manhunt would be launched, word would leak to the press, and every citizen would become an involuntary de facto agent in the search. Even if he managed to elude capture, every square inch of his life would be scrutinized. No matter how smart you were— and he knew this as well as anyone ever had—you never wanted to find yourself under the magnifying glass of the American intelligence system. Sooner or later, you ended up like a dead frog in a high school biology class, pinned to a dissection tray with your belly sliced open and your guts hanging out.

The screen saver vanished, revealing an Excel spreadsheet

groaning with financial figures. It was the last agency budget he would ever do, and although he had found these rivetingly boring in the past, he found a certain comfort in this one. Just as he was about to turn his full attention to it, however, the phone in his pocket vibrated.

He scowled when he saw Birk's number. He had thought seriously about sending another man out to eliminate and replace Birk. He knew one who was particularly nasty, a true psychopath who made Birk seem saintly by comparison. But that would've been more trouble than it was worth; that operative was too blunt a tool to use for such a delicate mission. Birk, at least, had some finesse. And there was always the chance Birk would survive an attempt on his life, which would further complicate matters.

All that aside, Rydell had still made a point of giving his well-paid employee an epic reaming when he learned of Hammond and Baker's escape. No way the little thug was going to be spared that.

He accepted the call and said, "Wait," then went into the bathroom and turned on the exhaust fan. "Okay, what is it?"

"Hammond made contact with one of them."

"Which one?"

"Benjamin Burdick. He called Burdick's house just a few moments ago."

For the first time in what felt like an eternity, Rydell smiled.

18

HAMMOND FOUND Burdick's book on another JFK assassination site, downloaded it, and brought the laptop along so Sheila could read it in the car.

"There are some pretty serious accusations here," she said, scanning the table of contents. "They didn't stir up any controversy?"

"Oh, they did. They sent ripples through the intelligence community. Most people just never heard about it."

She went to the About the Author page and found the same photo from the SMU faculty site. Burdick looked remarkably ordinary. He could have been an auto mechanic and part-time deer hunter. But a closer look at the eyes revealed a steely awareness, a native intelligence that was easy to miss. This was a careful man, Sheila sensed. A curious and somewhat-skeptical man. Someone who was not easily fooled.

She read through the bio, which was more detailed than the one on the university website.

"He has a doctorate in American history?"

"In American history, yes, and another in world history."

"Married?"

"His wife passed away a while back. They had two children, both of whom are grown and gone. Now he lives alone."

"That's sad."

"He keeps in constant contact with his kids. The three of them are very close. And he manages to keep himself busy the rest of the time."

She went back to the main text. "He makes a very convincing argument that the federal government took part in the assassination."

"He felt he didn't present enough hard proof in that book. But the last time we spoke, he said the new one would take care of that." Hammond made a right turn that took them off the highway and onto a gravel road. "I know a lot of this sounds crazy, but he's not a screwball, believe me. He considers the assassination one of the greatest travesties ever committed against the American public. Even if his accusations have raised some eyebrows, he's famous for the thoroughness of his research, so his conclusions are hard to argue. He covers his bases very well, and he won't open his mouth about something unless he's certain."

"Have you ever discussed my mom's film?"

"Funny you should say that. I was trying to remember. . . . We did have a conversation about it once. He said something like, 'If the Babushka Lady really did shoot a film, she would've had the only good moving picture from that side of the limo when the shots were fired.' He thought it might show something the Zapruder film didn't."

"Good guess."

"He's going to love Storm-Drain Man. This is the kind of thing that really gets him going."

• • •

They rumbled up to an aluminum mailbox with the name Burdick printed on the side. Another right turn brought them down a brief wooded lane, which made a horseshoe in front of a large frame house with a wraparound porch. It was white with black shutters and flower beds on either side of the steps.

Hammond came to a halt but didn't kill the engine. "Uh-oh."

The beds, which had once been vibrant with floral life, were now plots of dried earth crawling with weeds. The paint on the porch was cracked and peeling, and some of the downspouts had broken free of the rain gutters.

"So much for being the neatest guy in the world," Sheila said.

"No, he *is* the neatest guy in the world. If there was a Nobel Prize for tidiness, he'd win it every year."

Hammond shut off the engine and got out, noting other signs of ruination—a rusted lawn mower sitting outside its shed, the grass consuming it in a note of irony. When they went up the front steps, Hammond saw a rip in the screen door, and one corner hung down like a dog's ear.

"Ben would never allow that," he said, pointing. "He'd have fixed it as soon as it happened. You know the saying 'A place for everything, and everything in its place'? That's Ben."

"Maybe he moved."

"I thought about that, but his name's still on the mailbox."

He rang the doorbell—a majestic two-note *bing-bong* that echoed inside—and waited. After a long moment, Hammond pulled the screen door back and knocked hard on the other, causing it to drift forward. Pushing it farther, he took a cautious step forward.

"Ben?"

The furniture and the decor were as Hammond remembered—the polished mahogany table in the dining room, the grandfather clock standing in a corner, and in the hallway, a narrow table with a Tiffany lamp and a collection of framed photos.

"Ben? You home?"

He slipped inside with Sheila in tow. Then the smell hit them.

"Oh, man," he said, waving it away from his nose.

"He apparently hasn't done his laundry in a while."

"Either that or—*oh no!*"

Hammond took off running, going from room to room and shouting Burdick's name while Sheila tried her best to keep up. Finally he reached the den in the back. It had been nice at one time—white brick walls, thick carpet, an expensive home theater system. But like the rest of the property, it exhibited signs of neglect. Dirty plates and empty beer cans were scattered about, and the shades were pulled down. The answering machine by the phone was still blinking from the message Hammond had left on the way over.

Burdick was slumped in the recliner, wearing only gym shorts and a Dallas Cowboys T-shirt. He wasn't moving.

Hammond knelt down and felt for a pulse.

"Is he—?"

"Yeah, he's alive. But, whew, does he reek."

Sheila went to the set of east-facing windows and pulled the shades up, revealing a panoramic view of the expansive backyard and the adjacent woodland beyond. As the room flooded with afternoon light, more details of Burdick's squalor became visible. There was an ashtray overflowing with cigarette butts on an end table and what appeared to be a petrified coffee spill on the table's marble surface.

"Cigarettes and coffee?" Sheila whispered. "I thought you said he was a health nut."

"He is . . . or was. I don't know—Ben? Hey, Ben. Wake up!"

Hammond shook him, then patted the side of his unshaven face. Burdick groaned as his head rolled about.

"Ben, come on. . . ."

At last the eyes opened, the lids peeling apart the crusted organic seal that had formed along the edges. The scleras were red and watery, veins fleeing in every direction.

"What?" he croaked. "Who's that?"

"It's Jason Hammond. Come on, wake up."

Burdick tried to focus. His eyes shuttered in a mechanical manner. He coughed, sending a blast of whiskey in Hammond's direction.

"Thanks a million for that, Ben."

Burdick finally seemed to get a fix on him, a degree of hazy recognition settling in.

Then the change. Even in his diminished state, fear filled his eyes. Burdick tried to move back in the chair as though he thought Hammond had smallpox.

"What do you want?" He said this with more clarity than Hammond would have thought possible.

"Well, I wanted to talk to you about the Kennedy assassin—"

"No, I don't do anything with that anymore." Burdick's head jerked when he noticed Sheila standing there. "Who are you?"

"This is my friend Sheila Baker."

"Hello, Dr. Burdick," she said, smiling.

"Yeah, hi. What do you two want?"

"I'm here to talk to you about something concerning the

assassination. Something very big. You'll want to hear this, believe me."

Burdick shook his head rapidly. "I have nothing to do with it anymore, so no, I *don't* want to hear it."

"What?"

Burdick lifted himself out of the chair, again with greater fluidity than Hammond would have believed. "Just leave me alone," he said, waving his hand.

"Ben—"

"No, Jason. Absolutely n—"

"Ben, it's about the Babushka Lady. We found her film, *and there's a guy with a rifle in the storm drain.*"

This brought Burdick to a halt, his bare feet squealing on the hardwood floor. When he turned back, there was a glimmer in his eyes that reminded Hammond of the old Ben. At first Hammond thought it was a merge of curiosity and fascination. Then he realized what it really was.

Recognition. *He already knows about Storm-Drain Man.*

"No. . . . Don't say any more."

"Ben—"

"I don't want to know. I don't want to know *anything*!"

Burdick spun and continued on his way, taking a pack of Parliaments from his pocket and placing one between his lips.

Hammond shook his head. "I don't get this. One day you're one of the leading authorities on the assassination; the next you're acting like it never happened. What's that all about? And for that matter, what's happened to *you*? You go from Felix Unger to Oscar Madison overnight?"

Burdick lit the cigarette, listening with as much patience as he could muster. Then he walked over until they were face-to-face.

"Listen to me," he said calmly, pointing up. Hammond was at least a half foot taller. "I have absolutely nothing to do with Kennedy anymore, okay? I don't care what evidence you found. I don't care if the conspirators are sitting in your car, waiting to give a videotaped deposition. I'm through with it." He started to walk away, then pivoted back. "And as for what's happened to me, that's . . . none of your business."

He turned away fully this time. Hammond went to say more but Sheila cut him off.

"Jason, maybe we should just let him be."

"Sheila, I don't—"

"Thank you for seeing us, Dr. Burdick," she called out. "We appreciate it very much."

Burdick ignored her and disappeared around a corner.

• • •

They were back on the gravel road, about a mile from the highway, when Sheila said, "You shouldn't have pushed him like that."

"I saw something in his face when I mentioned Storm-Drain Man. I swear, I think he knows something about it. I just don't understand him."

"He's scared."

"Scared?"

"Yeah. He's tormented by something. There's a dark cloud following him around. It would explain everything—his change in personality, his lack of interest in his work and in his own appearance. I get people in my gyms like that all the time. They've had a health scare from their doctor or they're trying to escape drugs or alcohol. I know the look."

Hammond rolled this around in his mind. Burdick was a strong-willed, intelligent man, driven and focused and not the type to give up on anything. What could have occurred to cause the changes? Did it have something to do with the assassination? With his book, perhaps?

"If you're right, then we need to figure out how to help him. Because if we don't, he can't help *us*. And I need his help right now. If anyone knows the identity of the man in the storm drain, it's him."

"So what are you going to do?"

Turning the car around, Hammond said, "I have an idea."

"Jason, you probably shouldn't."

"Just trust me."

• • •

Hammond gave the front door a perfunctory rap this time, more in the spirit of a signal than a request. He didn't bother waiting for a reply before going in.

"Take it easy on him," Sheila said.

"I will. Ben! Hey!"

There were traces of butane in the air, which he took as a sign that Burdick had recently lit yet another cigarette.

"Ben, I'm back! Could you please—?"

Burdick appeared through the dining room archway ahead. The cigarette was dangling from a corner of his mouth, and a beer bottle hung at an angle from the hand that was slack at his side.

"I thought I asked you to leave," he said, his eyebrows touching together in irritation.

Hammond moved forward, Sheila whispering more warnings.

"Ben, look, I need your help." His voice was calm and measured. "We both do."

"No."

Hammond took the color printouts from his back pocket and unfolded them. "Who is this guy? Do you have any idea?"

Sheila watched Burdick's reaction closely. His expression of anger morphed into a blend of rapt fascination and renewed horror.

"Ben, come on, give me *something*."

Burdick's gaze lingered for a moment; then he shook it away. "I'm sorry—I don't know."

"Ben."

"I don't."

"You're lying."

"Jason, I don't know who that is."

"Do you at least have an idea who it *might* be?"

The sheepish little-boy look on his face said it all.

"Tell me," Hammond said.

"No. I don't know anything." He turned and began walking away. "Now please leave."

"Jason," Sheila cut in, "let's go. Come on."

Hammond followed Burdick instead. "Ben—"

"Jason, just go, okay? Do us both a favor."

"Help us, please."

"No, I really can't get invol—"

"Ben!"

This came out like a thunderclap. Burdick whirled around; Sheila jumped. She realized at that moment that she'd had no previous sense of just how intimidating Hammond could be.

"They're *after us*, Ben! I don't know who, but it's someone. They were watching this woman's mother for years, and they blew her house to pieces while trying to kill us. Now, I don't know what's happened to you, and at the moment I don't really care. If you can help us get these people, then you have to do so."

He held the images out again, and Burdick's eyes, now red-rimmed with grief, trained on them once more.

"I can't. I really can't." This was delivered in an adolescent murmur, which Sheila found particularly disturbing coming from a grown man.

"Just what is it you're afraid of, Ben?" Hammond put a hand on his shoulder. "Come on, tell me."

"No."

"Has someone contacted you? Have you been threatened?"

"Jason . . ."

"Come back with me."

"What?"

"To New Hampshire. Come back to the estate with me."

"What for?"

"Protection."

"No."

"Ben, you know Noah and I can protect you. Nothing will happen to you there; you have my word."

"I . . . I just . . ."

Burdick's eyes kept shifting between Hammond and the photos. Sheila thought Hammond's face betrayed a sense of self-disgust, as if he were using them like a piece of meat to lure an animal into a trap.

"We'll protect you—I promise. Just help us get these people. You've spent most of your adult life trying to bring them to justice. Don't you think it's time to close the case? Don't you think they've enjoyed their freedom long enough?"

Burdick was fixated on the images now. His breathing was heavier, his eyes filled with reticent fascination. Sheila thought he looked more alert—more with-it—than ever.

He nodded. "All right," he said in a whisper. "I'll come."

"Great. Thank you, Ben. Thank you so much."

"Let me throw a few things in a bag. I'll be right down."

"Okay."

He was gone no more than five minutes, packing enough for a week and changing into a white button-down shirt, jeans, and leather sandals.

When he returned, Hammond said, "You're doing the right thing, believe me."

"Let's just go. Come on."

"No problem."

Burdick opened the front door and set the lock so it would catch upon closing. Then he pushed the screen door out and stepped into the warm spring air.

POP!

They all heard it. Burdick staggered back, clutching his chest, and blood began to flow between his fingers. Hammond caught him under both arms and dragged him in, easing him to the floor. Sheila shut and locked the doors. Peering through the curtained window, she saw exactly whom she expected to see—the man who had tried to kill them the night before was approaching swiftly, rifle in hand. "He's coming!"

She turned to say more, then lost the words when she saw that Burdick's white shirt was now soaked red. Sheila knelt and began unbuttoning it, but Burdick pushed her away with what little strength he had left.

"Leave it," he said, then turned his head and coughed spasmodically. A flame of blood streaked onto the worn hardwood. "It's better for me like this."

"No, Dr. Burdick. We have to—"

"Get Superman," he told her between hitched breaths. "Downstairs."

"What?"

"The Superman . . . Hurry. . . ."

"He's talking about his Pez dispensers," Hammond said.

Burdick's head rolled again and his eyes slid partly shut in a grimly mechanical manner. Then he lay still.

"Oh no. No, please . . ." Sheila brushed the hair from his face. "No . . ."

Hammond knelt beside her. "We have to get moving," he said. He set a hand on Burdick's chest, closed his eyes, and mumbled something in Latin. It took no more than a few seconds.

They ran to the back of the house, into the den where they had first found him. There was a plain white door in one corner, next to a recessed bookcase.

"That's it over there," Hammond said. Two more shots echoed from the front as the assassin blew through the locks. Sheila surprised herself by not screaming out this time. *I'm getting used to this,* she thought. *That can't be good.*

They took the steps quickly but quietly. Like the rest of the house, the basement's former glory was still discernible in spite of years of disregard. Three baskets of dirty laundry sat on a tan-felted pool table. Several large boxes bearing the SMU logo were piled on the bar alongside more empty booze bottles and overwhelmed ashtrays. And the textured, cream-colored carpeting was in desperate need of a good shampooing.

Along the wall adjacent to the bar was a series of long shelves. Standing in neat rows on each, like lines of soldiers awaiting inspection, were hundreds of colorful Pez dispensers. There were characters from all points around the cultural spectrum, from movie and television icons to sports stars and historical figures.

They scanned the collection like a pair of confused androids, their heads moving about crazily.

"Where is it? Where is it?"

"There," Sheila said, pointing to the lower left-hand corner. The cartridge was bright blue with an armless bust of Superman on top. Hammond grabbed it and pushed the top back with his thumb.

"Oh, wow."

"What?"

Hammond held the contents out for her to see—hidden in the cartridge was a USB flash drive.

Before she had a chance to comment, another muffled report came from upstairs.

"We've got to get out of here," he said, tucking the dispenser and its precious cargo in his pocket. "Come on."

There was a ground-level window above the washing machine. Hammond tried the latch, but it had been painted over too many times and wouldn't budge. When Sheila heard hurried footsteps pass directly overhead, she felt nauseous.

"Jason . . ."

"In there," he whispered, nodding toward a door on the other side of the pool table. Behind it was a small utility area with a slop sink, water heater, and furnace. There was a second window over the sink, but its latch was also the victim of too many lazy painters.

Hammond spotted a cobwebbed broom in the shadows. He grabbed it and climbed into the sink.

"What are you doing?"

"Since our options are obviously quite limited, I'm resorting to extreme force," he said. He aimed the butt end of the broom handle at the latch and began striking it in short jabs.

"Jason! The noise!"

"I know. I'm trying to be as quiet as possible." The latch broke free after a few more shots, and the window came up with a squeal. "Okay, ladies fir—"

Hammond's smile vanished when they both heard a second squeal—the door at the top of the stairs opening.

• • •

Birk still had not heard anything, but he saw the door in the den and had to check it out.

He took the first step carefully, setting his foot down at the extreme edge, where it was least likely to creak. He paused to listen and heard nothing. Part of him didn't believe they were down there, that this was a waste of precious time. Another part, however—the methodical part that had been rammed into place by his masters all those years ago—led him forward.

• • •

Hammond was listening closely, Sheila watching him. Finally he got out of the sink and took her by the hand, leading her to the darkened side of the long room, stopping midway to loosen the bare bulb that hung from the ceiling. When they crouched behind the furnace, he whispered, "Breathe through your nose as calmly as you can." Then he readied both hands on the broom and waited.

A feeling of unreality washed over Sheila. She knew she was frightened, but the fear seemed far away somehow, like a tiny boat moving along a distant horizon. What was inside mostly was nothingness, a bloodless cold that made her feel more machinelike than human. At the same time, she seemed to have a greater awareness of her surroundings than she could ever remember. Every sense was on some kind of physiological high alert. She could hear the man's footsteps as if through headphones. She could smell every dust mote on the floor, every drop of stray heating oil that had dried around the furnace's aging fixtures. She had never known such perception.

When the man opened the utility room door and peered around the corner, Sheila's sensation of surrealism deepened. It was like watching events unfold through a pool of water. The man felt for the light switch and gently lifted it. When the bulb failed to ignite, his eyes went up to it suspiciously, then down again. He took a tentative step into the room, and Sheila saw that he was holding the rifle. *The one he used to kill Dr. Burdick.* The barrel was matte black with a silencer screwed onto the end, and he was holding the weapon low, with the butt against his hip. Death was no more than twenty feet away now. He took another step forward, then paused to listen. The next few seconds were the longest of Sheila's life. To combat the terror that was at last beginning to flow along her every nerve, she tried to focus on Jason's advice—*"Breathe through your nose as calmly as you can."*

After an eternity, the man back-stepped out of the room.

They remained in their crouched positions and listened as he surveyed the rest of basement, then crept back up the stairs.

"I think I just died inside," Sheila said hoarsely as all emotion returned in a wave.

"Me too."

Hammond went over and closed the door, this time twisting the little lock on the knob. Then he returned to the sink. "Let's make like the wind and blow outta here before Chuckles returns." He propped the window open and held out his hand. "After you, madam."

Sheila found herself smiling, amazed again at how casual Hammond could be in a life-and-death situation.

She stepped into the sink with his assistance, like a Gibson Girl being helped into a carriage. Then he guided her through the window.

Once outside, she asked, "How are *you* going to get out?"

"No clue."

He stepped into the sink and paused a moment to think it over. Then the basin collapsed, the front legs bending at the halfway point like a kneeling camel. Hammond grabbed onto the bottom of the window out of reflex, and the sink fell away beneath him, striking the concrete floor with a plastic slap.

"Oh, great."

"*Jason!*"

"Time to wing it," he said. "Look out!"

Sheila was aware of approaching footsteps as Hammond struggled to get through the opening.

"Here he comes," he said when he was halfway out, "right on schedule."

She grabbed his shirt collar and pulled with all the strength she could summon.

• • •

When Birk discovered the door was locked, he let out a frustrated scream. He blew the knob away with two shots.

The assassin paused for a second after kicking the door open, and that cost him his chance—the last portion of his target wiggled through the window and was gone. Birk aimed sloppily and fired once, but the round ricocheted off a cinder block and zoomed away.

He stormed up the steps and hurried to the set of panoramic den windows situated over the area where they had made their escape. He expected to see them running across the lawn toward the woods, which would afford him a gamely hunter's chance. But they were nowhere in sight. He went to the south side of the house, but again there was nothing.

Cursing, he went from window to window for the next ten minutes. When he saw that their rental car was gone, he realized with a sinking feeling that he should've checked there first.

That's when he decided he would lie to his employer.

19

THEY DID NOT SPEAK for the first few miles; the only sound between them was the baseline purr of the rental's V6 engine. Then Sheila said she could tell Ben Burdick was a good guy in spite of the first impressions, and she wondered if they should go to the police. Hammond felt it would be a waste of time, as Ben was dead anyway and the sociopath who killed him would be long gone by now. Also, he didn't want anyone knowing where they were.

Hammond did, however, pull over to a pay phone to report the murder anonymously, covering the mouthpiece to muffle his voice. He couldn't bear the thought of Ben's body lying there, which it might have for days considering the degree of isolation in which the man chose to live his life.

"Are you hungry?" he asked when they got back to the rooms.

"No, I've lost my appetite."

"Thirsty?"

"No."

"Is there anyth—?"

She turned to him, her eyes thinned with rage. "You

should have listened to me, Jason! You should have heeded my warning!"

"Sheila—"

"If you had, Dr. Burdick wouldn't be dead right now!"

"Now hold on a second."

"In your tireless pursuit of the truth, you cost someone his life! Doesn't that bother you? Even a little?"

In his mind, Hammond buried that accusation a million fathoms down in a pool of bubbling blackness that seemed to have grown a little wider every time he checked it.

"Sheila, *calm down*."

She hugged herself and leaned forward.

"That guy was coming to Ben's house whether we were there or not. That wasn't going to change."

"Wrong."

"What?"

"You're wrong. He showed up around the same time you did. Somehow he knew you were going to go there. I don't know how, but he did. Wherever *you* go, *he* goes."

Hammond tried to find a bearable place for this ugly truth in his mental matrix, and when he was unsuccessful, he set it aside.

"What do you care, anyway? Nothing in your perfect little world will change if this all falls apart! What do you lose in any of this?"

Another heart-slicing observation that had to be put in a cage before it bit him too hard. He'd wondered about this point on many occasions over the years and still had not come up with a satisfactory answer. "Look," he said, "I know how upsetting this is."

She wiped her eyes fiercely. "I've never seen anyone get shot before."

"I'm sorry you had to see it today. And if it makes any difference, yes, of course I'm upset about it. But what's keeping me focused is Ben himself. There's no way he'd want us to fall apart now. Getting to the bottom of the assassination was his passion. He dedicated years of his life to it. If we give in to our emotions, then the people who did this get to claim another victory."

More tears came. "I know. I know you're right."

He wrapped his arms around her, and she hugged him back.

"I'm sorry about what I said."

"It's okay." *And if you don't think the guilt is already eating me alive,* he wanted to add, *then you're crazy.*

• • •

Hammond opened the laptop and turned it on, then shook the USB drive out of the Pez dispenser. Once the MacBook's operating system was up and running, he sat down and said heavily, "All right, let's find out what was so important that Ben was willing to dedicate his last words to it." As he plugged the drive into the port, he added grimly, "I think I already have an idea, though."

The icon for the drive appeared on the desktop, and Hammond clicked on it. The new box that opened contained just one file—a Microsoft Word document titled "two.doc."

"As I suspected."

"The second book?"

"I'm sure. Look." He pointed to the columns on the right, where there were more details. "Almost two full megabytes. That's pretty big for a Word document. A normal doc—say, a two-page letter—is only about thirty kilobytes."

"Yeah, it's huge."

"And check this out—the last time the file was modified was less than a week ago." He looked up at her. "He's been working on it the whole time."

"Wow."

"Okay, first things first—making a safety copy." He opened the contextual menu and chose Copy. Then he created a new folder on the desktop and clicked Paste. Once the file was there, he named the folder "Ben" and designated it to be hidden. Then, taking a deep breath, he said, "Now let's have a look."

He opened the document. The title at the top, set entirely in capital letters, hit them like a brick—"AUTHOR'S PREFACE: MY PRIVATE NIGHTMARE."

The opening line was no less startling: "In the time between the publication of my first book on the Kennedy assassination and the writing of this second one, I became the target of a relentless campaign of harassment and manipulation."

Burdick said the threatening phone calls, letters, and e-mails had begun immediately after the first book's release. These were from "the usual crazies, the kind of people you'd expect." That changed, however, after he announced the coming of a second volume, one that would offer new revelations as well as the research to back them up. "As soon as I put teasers on my website to generate some buzz, I started getting phone calls of a very different kind."

It was one man, and his knowledge of Burdick's life was of such depth and detail that Burdick determined, "He had to be connected with the government somehow. I am convinced of this."

Burdick was ordered to take down the site and give up

work on the second book immediately. When he refused, "things began happening that I never dreamed of." Half the money in his personal bank account vanished. His daughter's house mysteriously caught fire while her husband was away on business, nearly killing her and her two daughters. And someone took a shot at his son—the bullet missing him by inches—as he walked through a Home Depot parking lot in suburban Minnesota. "That's when I gave in—and when I started to fall apart both emotionally and physically."

Sheila put a hand to her mouth. "Jason . . ."

"Yeah." He continued reading.

I came to understand that I would never get my life back unless I finished this book. So I worked on it little by little, in secret, each day. Something in here has made these people very nervous, maybe more than one thing. I don't know what that is, but I am willing to risk my life to bring it to the attention of the world and, hopefully, to make those responsible pay for their sins.

Hammond slumped back in his chair and remained in that position, staring at the screen, for a long time.

"I want to read through all of it," he said finally, firmly. "Every word."

"Okay."

"It's going to take some time. See here?" He pointed to the lower left-hand corner of the screen, where the document's status bar was located. "More than seven hundred pages."

"You'd better get started, then."

• • •

The next two and a half hours passed in near silence. Sheila ordered room service for both of them, ate her salad while reading over his shoulder, then lay down on the bed and fell into a deep, dreamless sleep.

Hammond looked like a mad scientist with his face illuminated by the monitor's glow. He barely noticed his food, barely moved. Sometimes he would mumble something to himself. Other times he would make a comment to Sheila, even after she had drifted off.

He reached chapter 32—"A New Pawn in the Game?"—around ten thirty. He read through it once, his attention so fixated that he wouldn't have noticed a bomb blast, then roused his partner.

"Sheila, wake up—I found something."

"Hmm?"

"C'mon, you're going to want to see this."

He got behind the computer again and scrolled to the chapter's opening text. "Okay, check this out—"

I went to the CIA library in May of 2012 to examine some recently declassified files pertaining to the assassination. While reading through them, I came across a single document that was stamped "100-Year Hold," which meant it wasn't supposed to be released to the public until 2064. My best guess was that it had been included with the other material by mistake. This could have happened during the declassification transfer two weeks earlier or on the very day those other files had been originally classified and stored away all those years ago. Whatever the case, I couldn't believe my luck.

Burdick's first instinct, he said, was to take the document into the men's room and photograph it with his cell phone, "but with security cameras and human eyes on me from every angle, I knew this wasn't going to happen." Instead, he kept the document hidden among the legitimate papers and read it a little at a time, making notes as he went along.

It turned out to be the first page of a report about a man he'd never heard of before—a Cuban soldier of fortune named Galeno Clemente. "The image that quickly crystallized was of an utterly terrifying figure with a long history of violence. He started out in Castro's military and fought many battles, surviving through raw natural talent in the ways of warfare. He was soon recruited for more advanced training and was transformed into a killing machine." Burdick said the author of the report believed Clemente might have played a role in the assassination. The report didn't elaborate further, "likely because he didn't know of any details." The author did, however, speculate extensively on Clemente's whereabouts once the assassination had been carried out, "which gave me the impression that there were many people interested in finding him."

Burdick closed the chapter with:

My heart sank when I realized the report had more than one page, but I couldn't find any of the others. I'm sure they were stored in their intended location, along with scores of other documents that continue to hide the truth. I planned to return to the CIA library to research Clemente further. But for obvious reasons, I have not had the opportunity to do so.

When Sheila was finished reading, she looked at Hammond and said, "Do you really think Clemente is the man in my mother's film?"

"It's very possible."

"Did Ben mention him on his website when he put those teasers up?"

"I never saw it, so I have no idea. I wish I had."

"What do you think we should do?"

"I think we should consider—"

Then he was cut off by his phone.

• • •

He took it from his pocket and looked at the caller ID. "It's Noah," he said, bringing the phone to his ear. "Hey, what's going on?"

"I could ask you the same thing," Noah said with a touch of accusation.

"Huh?"

"Turn on CNN."

Hammond was already moving. "What am I looking for?"

"Just turn it on. Hurry."

"Okay." He took the remote from the nightstand and aimed it at the set.

"What is it?" Sheila asked.

Hammond answered by holding up a finger—*Hang on a sec.*

There was a simple four-color map of the Ellis County area on the screen, with Burdick's hometown of Palmer in large letters over a red dot. Along the bottom, the headline read, "Billionaire Wanted in Connection with Murder." Hammond's face was in a small box in the upper right-hand corner. It was a formal portrait he had given to the media a few years earlier to stop them from trying to take pictures while he was at his estate.

"Are you seeing it?" Noah asked.

"Yeah, but there's no sound. Hold on. . . ." He aimed the remote again, and the volume bar appeared over the CNN headline.

". . . preliminary report we're getting now," said the invisible female newsreader, "is that Jason Hammond is wanted for questioning in the shooting death of Dr. Benjamin Burdick. Hammond is well-known as the billionaire sleuth who most recently helped solve the disappearance of Amelia Earhart. Burdick, forty-eight, was a professor of American history at Southern Methodist University before taking extended leave three years ago for personal reasons. It is believed he and Hammond had a casual acquaintance through their mutual interest in the assassination of President John F. Kennedy. Local police have refused further comment. However, a source has told CNN that an anonymous caller who contacted authorities claimed to have seen Hammond and another individual, an as-yet-unidentified woman, leave the property, and that investigators have discovered evidence linking Hammond to the murder site. We will continue to follow this story as it develops."

The map of Ellis County disappeared, replaced briefly by an animated CNN logo before heading into a commercial.

Sheila stared at Hammond, her eyes wide. Hammond hit the Mute button and tossed the remote onto the bed.

"So there it is," Noah said. "A minor crisis to say the least. I've got the phone ringing off the hook here, so could you kindly clue me in on what happened?"

Hammond put the phone on speaker and, with Sheila's help, told him everything.

Noah took the time to repeat Sheila's condemnation that Ben Burdick might still be alive if not for Hammond's myopic determination.

Hammond absorbed this scolding without a word. Then he said, "The shooter had to be the one who called in the tip."

"Why do you think that?"

"Because Ben lived in almost-total seclusion, so it's highly unlikely anyone else would have seen us. Also, we called in a tip too."

"You *what*?"

"I didn't want to leave Ben's body lying there. It could've been there for days."

"It was still a big risk."

"I know, but what if an animal got to him? Ben deserved better, so I went to a pay phone. But according to CNN, the caller saw us fleeing the scene. Obviously we didn't say anything about that."

"Well, you're in an impossible position now. If you go to the police, that's the end of your investigation. They won't release either of you for a while, and when they do, your lunatic friend will most certainly be waiting close by. And if you don't go to the police, you'll have them searching for you day and night."

"Yeah, this is a tight spot."

"Which is exactly what this guy wanted, I'm sure. He's trying to smoke you out, make you show yourself. These are smart people you're dealing with, Jason. Very smart."

"I agree."

"So what are you going to do?"

Hammond looked at the television again. The story now was about another series of floods along the Gulf Coast. "I'm going to turn the tables on them," he said.

"Really? How do you plan to do that?"

"Simple—I'm going to tell David Weldon everything."

"You're going to *what*?"

"Just trust me. Let me get back to you in a few minutes."

He ended the call before Noah had the chance to protest and tapped in another number.

Weldon answered on the first ring.

20

THE MAN known as Salvador always thought of his mother first. Her pretty, smiling face, with red lipstick and elegantly drawn eyebrows, and her satin-black hair tied back with a ribbon.

In this cherished memory, she was wearing an apron and leaning over him with a birthday cake. His father stood behind her, wearing those small round glasses he loved, and kept his own hands stored in the pockets of his slacks.

Even as a child, Galeno Clemente had known his family lived well, better than most in Cuba. They had a beautiful home, a new car, a dog. They always had nice clothes and ate in the best restaurants. His parents appeared to be well liked and respected by everyone, which gave him a warm feeling. Other adults would come to the house to speak with his father because Arturo Clemente was known as a wise man. They would seek his advice on business matters and seemed honored to partake of his wisdom.

The Clementes went to church every Sunday, and the priest adopted a subordinate air when they met after services. His parents were devout, so Galeno's religious education extended well beyond the church walls. Icons hung through-out their home, and a luxurious Bible lay open on a stand in the living room. His parents prayed each night, and Galeno and his brother, Olivero, were expected to kneel with them. A rosary was always woven between his mother's fingers. They thanked God for each other and for their plentiful bounty. Then Mother and Father would take their two sons to their rooms and tuck them in.

And they would be read to, the parents alternating between the two boys so neither would seem favored over the other. And when the stories ended, their hair would be stroked and their cheeks kissed. Neither could imagine a greater love in the universe. Their father would speak of wondrous days to come, of days spent hard at work in a place called "university" and of taking over his businesses together, as brothers, to continue amassing the family riches. The present was glory and the future unlimited, and the burden of worry was an unknown quantity.

Neither boy took much notice of Fulgencio Batista's rise to power at first. It was the early fifties, and they were too young to be concerned with such matters. They heard his name spoken among the adults, and they got the impres-sion he was not well regarded. Their father once called him a "feckless punk." Nevertheless, their prosperity continued. A second car appeared in the driveway, making their mother one of the only women in the community who had her own. She was given a small safe for her best jewelry. There was also talk of buying land purely for investment purposes, maybe leasing it to tenant farmers.

And then, with the swiftness of an ax blade, it all changed. Even now, Clemente could remember the date—August 11, 1956.

It began with a knock on the front door. The boys were in their rooms, changing to play baseball in an empty lot down the street. It was a Saturday afternoon, and their mother was baking a cake for dinner that evening. She wiped her hands on her apron before answering.

The brothers, thinking it was their friends growing impatient, ran down the steps to greet them. Instead they found two bullish-looking men in dark suits. They had the hard faces of street brawlers, but the suits were tailor-made. They also wore gold rings and watches. They were both gangsters; Galeno was a smart kid and could see through the slick packaging. You could put them in suits, but it changed nothing.

The men seemed to have little interest in his mother. She was frightened, Galeno could tell, and this angered him. He watched the men carefully, promising himself he would act if necessary. He was still small and was no match for either of them, but the thought of his mother being harmed made his blood boil. She retreated to her bedroom, and her husband came out bleary-eyed and shoeless; he had been resting.

When the men asked him to come outside to speak, he seemed hesitant. But he went, closing the front door quietly. Galeno and Olivero understood that he did this so they would not hear the conversation. There was something sinister about all of it, and they knew real fear for the first time in their lives. They were genuinely unsure if their father would come back.

When he did, he looked dazed.

By collecting small bits of conversation between their parents over the next few days, the brothers pieced together a general sense of what was happening: new businesses called "casinos" were being opened on the orders of President Batista. These new casinos, they heard, were to be stocked with the finest foods and liquor Cuba had to offer, for they would attract visitors from all over the world, especially America. Galeno knew America was the richest country in the world, but this idea of catering to their tourists made him feel dirty, as if they were royalty and the Cuban people were merely their servants. His father produced some of the best wines, sherries, and rums on the island. He had labored for years to formulate his blends. Now Batista was demanding that he increase his output in order to please these foreign customers. And he wanted the supply at a cut-rate price. Other distributors had made similar demands of Arturo in the past, and Galeno remembered his father always politely refusing. He had never compromised where his product was concerned. But this time he was being given no choice in the matter.

As time passed, other Batista agents came to the home, always unannounced, always with a new twist on the deal. More product, lower prices, a free delivery here and there, privately labeled bottles for friends of the president, and then, inevitably, the demand for exclusivity. The life Galeno and Olivero had known slipped away in stages. The second car disappeared, then the jewelry in their mother's safe. Restaurant visits became less frequent; clothes were handed down.

Once the luxuries were gone, the essentials began to diminish. Their father worked longer hours, and he sometimes wasn't home when they went to bed. His parents fought from time to time, something they had never done before. Young Galeno found his mother crying a few times, and he vowed to find the cause of her grief and destroy it.

Then came the night of June 10, 1958.

● ● ●

"Ou vle yon lòt?" the shirtless bartender asked in his native Creole. *Do you want another?*

This pulled Clemente out of his reverie and back to the present. He looked at the man, who was as thin as a whip and as dark as coal. *"Wi, tanpri." Yes, please.*

The bartender nodded and whisked away the empty glass. The ramshackle hut in which Clemente sat passed for a drinking establishment in this forgotten corner of the world. The beer was usually warm, the roof leaked when it rained, and the air reeked of rotting vegetation from a nearby compost pile. But there was also running water, cable television, and even an ancient computer with Internet access. Getting here might have required a two-mile walk from the encampment, but it was the way Clemente kept in touch with the rest of the planet.

The bartender, whose name was Seydou, set down the second rum and waited. Clemente removed a bill from his pocket and handed it over. Seydou nodded reverently and withdrew.

Alone now in the gathering afternoon heat, Clemente turned his attention back to the television: a tiny CRT on a platform that hung from the corrugated ceiling. CNN was running through a sports segment; celebrity news would be next.

Father Breimayer had a hundred questions for him, he knew. The priest was a good and decent man, one of the most admirable Clemente had ever met. Breimayer had been through his own share of hardship, Clemente had learned. He had seen things that would have devastated the spirits of other men. But he was a follower of the Lord, and the Lord had delivered him. Breimayer drew his strength from his faith, the kind of faith Clemente had known at one time, a time so far back that it seemed a part of someone else's life rather than his own.

And what of forgiveness? That, too, had been promised in the Holy Book, taught to him by his parents. The Lord understood the frailties of the human condition, accepted the errors and misjudgments of his brood. Through his divine mercy, he released them from the crushing burden of their sins. And in his Kingdom, when their time in the prison of mortality drew to a close, they would be welcomed with open arms.

Clemente had wondered endlessly about this over the years. What would be his final judgment when he stood before the Lord and the ledger of his life was opened? Even with God's capacity for compassion, was time now the only barrier between himself and eternal damnation? How could anyone forgive such sins? How was one spared such suffering? Would genuine remorse coupled with decades of good works be sufficient? Clemente had come to suspect it would not. For any hope of reconciliation, he felt he had to make some effort to balance the specific injustice of his transgressions. Even if he failed, maybe the sincerity of the effort would be sufficient. Was that the policy? Was that what God was waiting for? The search for this answer had been his obsession. *Please, Lord, present me with the opportunity to redeem myself.*

When CNN returned to the story on billionaire Jason Hammond, Clemente thought perhaps that opportunity had arrived. The mention of the American city of Dallas sent a familiar charge through every bone. The mention of the dead president sent another. But it was the face of the woman that gripped his heart with an icy hand. He had never forgotten it. She was the daughter, yes, but her eyes were so like her mother's.

He knew Margaret Baker's lens had found him that afternoon, in spite of his meticulous precautions. Now a strange feeling filled him—a mixture of great relief, sadness, and a dozen other emotions that had been hibernating in some cavernous corner of his soul.

And something else came to the surface then, as certain as anything he had ever known.

The time had come to leave this place.

21

FREDERICK RYDELL stood by the French doors in his den and watched the sprinklers twirl over his surgically perfect lawn. Some of the spray dotted the flagstone pavers on the patio—a patio where he had stood with the most influential intelligence figures in the nation. Conversation had ranged from state secrets to dirty jokes and was stage-propped with the usual brandishments of male ritual—a pipe or cigar, a ceaselessly ringing cell phone, and a rocks glass of straight whiskey or vodka or whatever.

He had one of those drinks in hand now and was mindlessly rotating it in such a way that the ice jingled along the sides. When he had poured it ten minutes earlier, he tried but could not recall the last time he had indulged in alcohol during daylight hours, much less working hours. The latter was irrelevant, however, as he would not be a part of America's workforce today. He had already left a message on Theresa's machine saying he was feeling a little under the weather and wanted to get some rest. He could not recall the last time he had done that, either.

Deep concern continued to press upon his mind. It had started the day before, following the realization that Hammond had not only dodged his attempt to put pressure on him but had managed to turn the situation around in his own favor simply by using the media to provide a measure of protection for himself. *He turned half the people in the nation into his personal security force by leveraging the public's fondness for him. Now how did I not foresee that possibility?* This was the question that had plagued him until finally, reluctantly, he'd swallowed the harsh truth that he had badly underestimated the man. Hammond was nothing like the bored rich kid some in the media made him out to be. Not even close.

Once Rydell accepted this, he dug deeper to study his adversary. A former Harvard student with a sterling academic record. Not someone whose parents had bought his way in but rather someone who had earned it. And his other record, his "professional" record—success with nearly everything he touched, including many instances where others had failed before. Hammond wasn't just another spoiled legacy brat. He was legitimate, and he was formidable.

But there was even more to it than that. Rydell couldn't assemble a sharp-edged image of Hammond because the man was also a study in contrasts. He had a natural, easy brilliance in many subjects, yet he seemed genuinely humble. He had been handed an empire he'd played no role in building, yet he appeared to be managing it with remarkable efficiency. He had tremendous resources at his command, yet he exercised phenomenal self-control. No record of drug use or excessive drinking, no tabloid photos of Hammond with prostitutes or controversial celebrities. And he was apparently a religious man as well. Sincere, compassionate, and moral. *That's a problem,* Rydell thought.

Now Hammond had the public on his side as well. They loved his reaction to the frame attempt Rydell had orchestrated. Another David-versus-Goliath scenario, and the

American people never tired of those. Hammond had known exactly what to do, had manipulated the media perfectly.

Now we're *the ones who need to be careful,* Rydell thought bitterly. *Particularly that idiot Birk.* Taking out Burdick had been good—something that should've been done ages ago. But to let Hammond and the girl get away again . . . Rydell felt the urge to choke Birk to death with his bare hands. *How much did Burdick tell them? How much do they know?*

He brought the drink up and took another sip. This time the ice jingled because his hand shook, which only served to make him angrier. There were few things he hated more than losing control of a situation. The enemy was out there, methodically chipping away at the wall that had protected him for half a century, and he wasn't able to do a thing about it. *"Just find them and take them out,"* he had told Birk. Birk had countered with an argument about logistics, about how it would be nearly impossible to get to them with the public's attention fixed in their direction. Rydell knew this was true, but he wasn't interested in excuses. *"Find a way,"* he had said. *"That's why you're being paid so much."* He had let his emotions get away from him during the call—another source of irritation. Ultimately, however, he didn't care what Birk thought. He owned the man.

One sprinkler zone quit, and another squirted to life. Rydell put his free hand gingerly on his chest and took several measured breaths. There was a tightness inside, the kind that always accompanied the feeling that danger was closing in. If Hammond and the girl did learn too much, what then? He wondered again about disappearing sooner than planned. Was that possible? Realistic? *Maybe.* . . . Most of the pieces were in place now. Even his sick-day call had inadvertently created an advantage. He could do another tomorrow, tell Theresa he wanted to go to the doctor, just as a precaution.

Ever faithful, she would cover for him. That would buy forty-eight hours, maybe seventy-two.

But it wouldn't be enough, not in the long run.

What would happen if Hammond learned about Clemente and got the word out? And what if Clemente was still alive? Rydell wanted to tell himself there was no chance of this, but he didn't fully believe it. Galeno Clemente was another one he had tragically underestimated. Even if he really was dead, if the public found out about him, the investigation would begin anew, and this time the media would be relentless. *It was bad enough in years past, but now, with the power of the Internet and all regard for privacy relegated to history . . .*

And even if he did manage to escape, the fact that a high-ranking intelligence officer had suddenly disappeared would send the government into pandemonium. They would have no choice but to launch a massive investigation. *And if they discovered my connection to the assassination . . .*

His phone twittered, jolting him out of his thoughts. He yanked it resentfully from his pocket, expecting to see Birk's number on the caller ID. More whining, more excuses. This time Rydell wouldn't worry so much about decorum. He would give Birk a tongue-lashing he'd never forget.

All emotions came to a standstill when he found a different number on the tiny screen. It produced only a faint memory at first. Then he noted the location—New Jersey—and the pieces of the puzzle came together. The color drained from his face until he really did look ill. He closed his eyes and shook his head. *Please tell me this is a wrong number.*

But it wasn't, of course. Rydell mumbled a short run of profanities and considered letting the call go to voice mail. But that would only prolong the inevitable. This particular individual would keep trying until he got through.

Rydell took a deep breath and unfolded the phone. "Yes."

There was no greeting from the other end, no "Hello" or "How are you?" The caller launched immediately into his own profanity-laced tirade, and he did so with such rage that Rydell was forced to hold the phone a few inches from his ear.

"I have the situation under control," Rydell replied. "Don't be con—"

"I *am* concerned. I am very concerned. The situation does not appear to be under control at all."

"I have someone on it right now. The problem will be taken ca—"

"Your confidence is not being felt on this end. Not by any of us."

"It'll be fine, believe m—"

"It had better be, or you'll have more trouble than you'll know what to do with. Am I clear?"

Rydell's body stiffened. There was no instrument in existence that could measure how much he hated this man.

"You're clear," he replied.

The line went dead.

He stood there, phone in hand, for a long time. He thought more about his hatred for the man and for the way they were inextricably fused together. This bond would haunt him into eternity. He would pay for it forever, for something the four of them had done as very young men so many years ago—him, the man he had just spoken with, and two others. Four men who had craved power all their lives and yet were utterly powerless when it came to dissolving their baleful union. Through them, he was as trapped as it was possible to be.

Or am I?

For the first time, he began to wonder if this was irreversibly true.

22

HAMMOND SAT on the edge of the hotel bed with his eyes locked on the television, where a female MSNBC newsreader was reporting the latest with a photo of him in the corner of the screen. Noah was talking at the same time through the speaker of Hammond's phone. Sheila, in a chair by the table, was reading a text message on her own phone and looking particularly distressed.

". . . Weldon of Reuters, the only journalist Jason Hammond will speak with, confirmed yesterday that the billionaire was, in fact, investigating the assassination of President John Kennedy based on new evidence he claims to have in his possession. Hammond admitted to Weldon that he was at the home of Professor Benjamin Burdick at the time of Burdick's murder but said he had nothing to do with the shooting. In spite of this, he is still wanted by the authorities for questioning. Hammond stated that the killer was an unidentified assassin who also tried to kill him as well as a female friend whose involvement is still unclear. Based on an anonymous tip received by major news services earlier today, the woman is believed to be Michigan resident

Sheila Marie Baker—" a second photo, a head shot of Sheila taken from her Facebook page, slid into the frame alongside Hammond's—"who owns two gyms in her current hometown of Dearborn but spent her childhood in the Dallas suburb of Addison. . . ."

Sheila glanced briefly at the photo of herself, shook her head, then went back to the text messages. Hammond switched to CNN, where another newsreader was replaying the phoned-in report by David Weldon from the previous day.

". . . said that he was following a lead stemming from a new piece of evidence, one that has never been seen before. And from it, he has learned of a new person who was likely involved in the assassination. During his investigation on these leads, he twice encountered an individual who not only tried to kill him and his female companion but also shot and killed Dr. Benjamin Burdick. Hammond said that this alone lends tremendous credence not only to the possibility that he may be getting closer to the heart of what really happened on that dark day in American history but that some of the people involved might still be alive and well—and quite worried."

And on Fox News there was an unsteady helicopter view of the New Hampshire estate with the camera trained on the main house. As soon as Hammond saw it, he began to feel nauseous.

". . . and neither Hammond nor his family's longtime assistant, Noah Gwynn, has responded to repeated phone calls from Fox. We do know that Gwynn is here at the family compound, and it is believed Hammond and his sidekick, gym owner Sheila Baker, are still somewhere in the Dallas area. . . ."

Hammond switched back to CNN—more to remove the

image of his home than anything else—and thumbed down the volume.

"I don't know how much longer I'll be able to hold them off," Noah said through the tiny speaker. "The phone is ringing around the clock, and there are about ten news vans parked at the gate. Can you believe Fox has a *helicopter* out here?"

"I'm getting all kinds of text messages and voice mails," Sheila said and began massaging her temples. "Everyone wants to know what's going on. I'm hearing from people who haven't contacted me in years. And I've got urgent business questions from Vicki to answer, but I'm afraid to send any replies because they might pick up the signal and find us."

"Jason, you can't stay there," Noah said.

Hammond, his attention still possessed by CNN, nodded. "I know."

"There are reporters swarming the Dallas area too," Noah said.

"I figured as much," Hammond replied.

"Then what's your plan?"

Hammond switched to one of the local stations and found a reporter on the sidewalk randomly interviewing people. "How do you feel about the possibility of the assassination of President Kennedy finally being solved?" One was a black girl who appeared to be about college age. Another was a thirtysomething woman carrying an infant. The third was a well-groomed older man in a gray business suit. All three shared the sentiment that it was long past time to close the case and bring those responsible to justice.

"We'll go early tomorrow morning," he said finally, "while it's still dark."

"Oh?" Noah said. "And where will you go?"

"Back east."

"You mean here? Home?"

"No, to the CIA library in Washington."

A few seconds passed without a word from his audience. "You're kidding me," Noah said finally.

"No."

"You can't be serious."

"I'm very serious." He glanced at Sheila, who was staring with both eyebrows raised. "It has to be done, Noah. Sheila and I have explored just about every conceivable sector of the Internet and come up with nothing on Clemente. You said you went through every book and paper we've got in the home library and couldn't find anything either. This guy's been invisible since the day of the assassination, and I'm sure that's because a lot of people want it that way. But there's one place where we know there's information, and that's this one building in D.C. And since we can't exactly make a formal request for it, we've got to go there in person."

"Okay, it sounds good in principle. But what do you do at the library once you get there?"

"I've got some ideas."

"I'm sure."

"What if we're seen, Jason?" Sheila asked, resignedly powering down her phone and putting it in her pocket. "There's a pretty good chance of it."

"We'll just have to reduce that chance."

"You have ideas about that, too?"

"I do," he said.

•   •   •

They waited until after midnight for the trip to the drugstore. Hammond stayed in the car while Sheila went inside with the list he'd made in his careful print. She kept her head down and avoided security cameras. When they returned to the hotel, she used her key card to open a door facing the back lot. The hallway was deathly silent.

Hammond dumped the contents of the two bags onto the bed—lipstick, rouge, skin toner, eye shadow, grease pencils, a variety of powders and hair dyes, a do-it-yourself haircutting kit, two pairs of low-magnification reading glasses, and two baseball caps.

"You really think this is all it's going to take?" Sheila asked. "Some makeup, glasses, and hats?"

"Oh no," Hammond said, ripping things out of their packaging. "It's just the starting point. I'll show you the rest."

"You know about this stuff?"

"I did some acting at Harvard. Freshman theater program, American Repertory, like that. Stage presentation was required learning. The art of changing one's appearance has been around for centuries. Did you know that actors in ancient Greece and Rome covered their faces with flour and wine? They also used animal fur to make beards."

"I recommend we not try that."

"No, I think we'll stick with what we've got here." He lined up the hair dyes in a neat row. "Pick one you can live with, at least for a while."

She studied her choices and settled on a light blonde. "This should be sufficiently different, yes?"

Hammond inspected her natural color, which was a deep brown. "Yeah, that'll be okay. Much lighter, but not so much that it'll attract attention. Or worse, look fake."

She raked her fingers through it. Each little piece flopped right back into place. "Too short to cut, right?"

"Yeah, no cutting. You'll look like Mr. Clean. Or Mr. Clean's wife."

She sniffed out a little laugh, her first in a while, noting that Hammond seemed pleased by this. "What about you? What'll be your new color of choice?"

"I don't know." He stroked his chin and appraised the boxes. "I've got this wicked midnight black now."

"With some light touches of gray, I see."

"I'll pretend I didn't hear that. Umm . . . okay, how about this one?" He picked up a medium chestnut, which bore the more marketable name of "ash brown."

"That should work. Are you going to cut it too?"

"A little bit. Maybe lose the sweepback that makes me look like a college boy and go for something more modern. Frankly I like the Julius Caesar thing you've got going on."

"Oh, thank you."

"I'll be a regular George Clooney."

"Right, that's what you'll be."

"I'll meet you back here after the metamorphosis is complete."

It took about an hour, and Hammond looked anything but pleased with the results.

Sheila said, "You don't like it?"

"Not particularly. My head looks like it got caught in a blender."

"Well, you didn't cut it very straight."

"I don't do this every day."

"Here, give me those."

She took the scissors, led him into the bathroom, and patiently fixed it. Hammond, wearing fresh clothes and covered with a bath towel around his neck and torso, frowned like a disgruntled schoolboy being primped for a class picture.

After they cleaned up both bathrooms, they returned to his suite.

"Okay," he said, "now for step two—the basics of acting."

He began by explaining that every person already had a method of his or her own—that is, normal, everyday mannerisms. The key to true acting was to learn how to alter those mannerisms in order to adopt the manifestations of someone else. "We communicate more information with our body language and our appearance than we do with our words," he said. "People get about 90 percent of their impression of you long before you open your mouth. The way you walk, the way you sit, the way you dress, whether you make eye contact or not, what you do with your hands, your general posture . . . everything. People who move with good posture, keep their head up, and look straight ahead as they're walking, for example, project confidence. Those who shuffle along hunched forward with their head down, on the other hand, display—and thus inspire—very little confidence. What you therefore need to do is decide on a subtle persona that won't be too difficult for you to emulate, then learn the little traits that project it."

Hammond demonstrated a few examples—an old man, a street punk, a wino, a narcissistic game-show host.

After an hour of practice plus the application of some basic makeup, Sheila saw a stranger in the mirror over the dresser.

"I look like I'm sixty!" she said with mild horror. The rectangular-framed glasses gave her a measure of affluent dignity, but the delicately applied age lines added a decade or two.

"I certainly hope so," Hammond said, sitting with his arms crossed on the bed. "We don't want anyone going, 'Hey, isn't that the girl we've been seeing on CNN?'"

"No, definitely not." She moved closer to the glass and

touched her face lightly. "I wonder if this is how I'll really look someday."

"As long as you get to that age in the first place," Hammond said. "That's my main concern at the moment."

The comment didn't register with her at first, but when it did, it opened a floodgate of affection that, she realized, had been culturing for a while. She turned her mirrored gaze in his direction—he was cleaning up the room now—and smiled.

Her initial caution toward the man had melted completely away. She had tried at several moments to fit him with her stereotype of the rich—arrogant, aloof, etc. But it just never worked. Hammond exhibited the natural tendencies of one who had lived in splendor all his life, one who simply did not know any other way. And the detachment was not aloofness but shyness. He only made eye contact when speaking to her; the rest of the time his eyes were kept respectfully away. Further, he never made even the faintest implication that she owed him anything. She had wrestled—sometimes literally—with men who expected quite a bit for something as simple as dinner and a movie. Hammond had not demonstrated so much as a hint of this mentality. Furthermore, he had been concerned with her welfare from the moment they met. He had done so at great expense to himself and with no regard for his own safety. *The fact is, he's one of the most genuinely decent people I've ever met—and I was right to trust him.*

A short time later, she drifted off to sleep.

23

HAMMOND SLID UP onto his elbows, his chest heaving and slicked with sweat. His eyes, wide and wild, darted about the room, taking in the shadows and the scattered moonlight that danced along one wall courtesy of a muscular north wind blowing through the ornamental trees outside the window. It was just after two thirty.

Throwing the covers back, he got into a sitting position and yanked open the nightstand drawer. There was nothing inside except a small, maroon-covered Bible. Stamped in gold foil along the bottom edge was the legend *Placed by the Gideons*. He took it out and flipped until he found Matthew 5:4:

> Blessed are those who mourn, for they will be comforted.

Then he located John 6:39-40:

> And this is the will of him who sent me, that I shall lose none of all that he has given me, but raise

them up at the last day. For my Father's will is that everyone who looks to the Son and believes in him shall have eternal life.

He mumbled the passages to himself as images from the dream began to reinvade his conscious thoughts. He closed his eyes tight and shook his head like a wet dog. He murmured both passages again, chanting them like incantations. *"I shall lose none of all that he has given me. . . . Everyone who looks to the Son and believes in him . . . they will be comforted. . . . They will be comforted."*

But the dream images would not abate, and soon more began to slip through.

"No!" he screeched with naked rage. *"No! How could you let this happen?"*

In one fluid motion he got to his feet, took the book in hand, and readied to throw it against the wall. He stopped himself when he realized Sheila was standing in the doorway that separated their rooms—and had likely been there for some time.

• • •

They engaged in a silent staring match for a long time. Hammond's chest was still heaving, and crystal beads ran down the sides of his face. Sheila knew she must look every bit as petrified as she truly was.

"I'm sorry," he said finally. "I woke you up again." He looked down at the Bible that was still in his hand, regarding it with a distinctly skeptical expression before tossing it onto the little writing desk against the wall. "I guess I had another bad dream."

"I guess so."

He smiled and looked away. "Well, nevertheless, we should try to get back to sleep. It's going to be a long—"

"You have them all the time, don't you." This wasn't really a question.

"What?"

"The nightmares. They come all the time." She moved closer.

"No, not really."

"Yes, they do."

"No. I mean, I don't want them at *all*, of course. But hey, what can I do, right?"

"They're about your family, aren't they? About what happened to them?"

All expression fell from his face.

"I read something about it on the Internet when you were on your way to my mom's house. The plane crash in the Caribbean. It was awful, Jason. Just awful." She was very close now. "That's what the nightmares are about, right? I heard you talking when you had them. Screaming."

His breathing was becoming labored again. "Sometimes. Not always." He swallowed hard and willed himself back to reality. "It's not a big deal, really. Please, go back to bed so you can—"

"And that long period of depression afterward. All those years. You never really got out of it, did you?"

"No, that's all behind me now. Well behi—"

"Jason."

"I'm fine."

"You're *not* fine. You need to talk to someone. You need help."

"No."

"You need to get this out of your system before it eats up everything inside."

"It only comes once in a while, and I can control it when it does."

"You're only telling yourself that." She set a hand gently on his back. "You're not controlling it. It's controlling you."

He appeared to consider this for a moment—she saw a flash of resigned acknowledgment there—then began to turn away. She moved to follow him, however, to maintain eye contact. "Jason, look at me. Jason? Hey, look at me."

At first he wouldn't give in, turning farther and farther away. Then he relented. Sheila was momentarily stunned by his expression—that of a frightened child rather than a grown man.

"It's okay," she said with exquisite delicacy.

Hammond nodded after a brief pause, again with the countenance of a little boy.

"Jason," she said firmly, just to get his attention. Then, mouthing the words without sound, she repeated herself. *"It's okay."*

They remained in a benign stare for what felt like an age. Then Hammond came unglued all at once. It was as if his resolve had been supported by a machine whose plug had suddenly been pulled. He collapsed against the side of the bed, weeping more powerfully than anyone Sheila had ever seen.

When she knelt down and pulled him to her, he did not resist.

24

IT WAS a very old photograph, black-and-white and creased and edgeworn. Nevertheless, Clemente, sitting on a cot inside the canvas tent he had called home for so long, held it with the utmost reverence, suspended like a plank between his thumb and forefinger. A hurricane lamp burned on a small table nearby.

The picture showed a happy family standing alongside a 1950s Chevy Bel Air convertible. They were resplendent in their Sunday outfits, the father looking every inch the respectable businessman, the mother as beautiful as ever. The two boys, one in his early teens and the other approaching fast, had the first flickers of mischief in their eyes.

Clemente remembered that the photo had not, in fact, been taken on a Sunday but rather a Monday, at the start of a weeklong vacation to their uncle Hugo and aunt Mariela's coastal home in San Cristóbal. He always thought of the trip as a significant historical marker along the timeline of his life—the last of the Good Days. A week of swimming in the warm Caribbean while the women drank sweet *garapa* on the porch and the men smoked cigars, played chess and checkers, and drank rum that they said tasted like liquid gold and ushered them into a stone-dead sleep, often on the patio furniture in the backyard and still fully dressed. During the day, when they were free of alcoholic influences, they discussed plans to combine their businesses. The boys were too young to understand the details, but they could grasp the elementary concept that their father had lost much in the last few years and was growing increasingly worried. Forming a partnership with Uncle Hugo was a survival tactic.

The plan never got off the ground. Four days after the family returned from San Cristóbal, Batista's guerrillas came in the middle of the night and hauled the Clemente parents away. Olivero tried to fight them off and ended up bleeding and unconscious in the kitchen. Galeno fared a little better, breaking one man's arm and another's nose. Ultimately, though, he had to flee through the back door to narrowly avoid what the gunfighters of America's Old West called "a sudden case of lead poisoning."

The boys spent the next two years simply trying to survive, which was nearly impossible as their parents' bank accounts had been mysteriously cleaned out and their father's business interests seized. They were forced to sell their family home, which had sustained six generations, and live like gypsies. They also found it impossible to obtain information about their parents' fate. One government official referred them to the next, but none had any answers.

While the younger Olivero was consumed by depression, Galeno became consumed by anger. Then he heard of Fidel Castro's revolutionary movement to dethrone Batista and saw an outlet for his bitterness. When Castro rolled his tanks victoriously into Havana in January of 1959, Galeno was marching at his side. Less than a year later, as a loyal member of Cuba's

Revolutionary Armed Forces, he finally learned the details of his parents' tragic end—just weeks after they had been detained, they were shot and killed. The report filed by the Batista official claimed they had attacked a prison guard, who then fired upon them in self-defense. Galeno wasn't fooled; his parents had been lifelong pacifists who despised violence.

With his anger now converted into a euphoric, full-bodied rage, he decided to allocate himself entirely to Castro's cause. In the years that followed, he worked tirelessly, both physically and mentally, to join the ranks of the fighting elite. When his superiors suggested finding more suitable work for one so young, talented, and motivated, he was only too eager to comply. New assignments began soon thereafter, first at home and then overseas. He pursued his objectives without question, hesitation, or mercy.

Clemente slipped the old photo between the pages of a little Bible. The Bible was then placed in a backpack, which he slung over his shoulder as he rose. He turned back to make sure the note he had left for Father Breimayer was on the pillow and to blow out the lamp. Then he took one final look around before exiting. The dusky glow of morning was beginning to spread over the canopy.

No sooner had he stepped from between the flaps than he stopped again. Breimayer was waiting just a few yards away, clad in shorts, sandals, and an untucked linen shirt modified at the collar to denote his office.

"You're up early, even by your standards." Breimayer said this with his usual top-of-the-morning gaiety, but it was tempered by an unmistakable note of curiosity.

"That is true."

Breimayer nodded toward the backpack. "You're leaving us, then?"

"Yes, Father, I am."

A smile appeared on the priest's face. "Heading anyplace special?"

Clemente didn't offer a reply, and surely Breimayer didn't really expect one. The priest had, after all, been gently probing him for years with nothing to show for it. There was no reason to believe today would be any different, but Clemente supposed the priest had to try.

"The work you've done here has been remarkable and is very much appreciated by myself, the people of this village, and the Lord our God." His voice had already changed. Gone was the passive interrogator, replaced by the gentle holy man.

"I was glad to be of service, Father."

A silence fell between them, each man grappling with a hundred thoughts but unsure of which to follow.

"For what it's worth," Breimayer said finally, "you are going to be dearly missed. And I want you to know that you can return whenever you wish. You are always welcome with us." Before Clemente had a chance to respond, Breimayer drew a cross in the air with two fingers and incanted a traditional blessing.

"Thank you, Father," Clemente said. "For everything." A lump had formed in his throat, one that he hoped wasn't evident in his tone. "I must go now."

Breimayer nodded. "Farewell, my friend."

"Yes . . . good-bye."

Clemente had taken just a few steps when Breimayer decided to gamble just once more.

"Salvador?" he called out softly. Clemente was certain the priest knew that this was not his real name, but he had no other at his disposal.

Clemente came to a dead halt and stood with his back hunched up defensively, as if he were awaiting execution.

"Never forget—the Lord grants forgiveness to all those who truly seek it."

More quiet followed, punctuated only by the sounds of the awakening wild. Clemente turned back, but in the end he did not speak, did not gesture, did not in any way acknowledge the sentiment upon which the fate of his eternal soul rested. Instead he began forward again, moving deeper into the lush jungle growth until it enveloped him completely.

25

"THE CIA LIBRARY opened its doors more than a half century ago," Hammond said as their taxi sped through downtown Washington, "and yet most people don't even know it exists. It's actually three libraries in one because there are three separate collections—circulating, reference, and historical. There are more than 1,500 magazines, 100,000 books, and millions of individual documents."

"And anyone can just walk in off the street? That can't be right."

"Some items are available to the public, but most aren't. Even people with high clearance need special permission to access certain things. And it's not like a traditional library, where you can take something off the premises and return it later. You go, you see what you need to see, and you leave."

"Security is pretty tight, then, I'm guessing."

"Skintight."

"So how do we get in there?"

"I'm still working on that," he said, smiling. She smiled back for reasons of her own.

He had wept for a long time. When the tears dried up,

he had said, "Okay, we need to get some sleep, both of us. We've got a lot to do today."

She'd nodded and left him there, swallowing all the questions she wanted to ask. The last image she caught before entering her own room was of him, still fully dressed, climbing into bed and pulling the sheets over his head.

She slept for only a few hours, but her exhaustion had been such that she awoke feeling fully refreshed. She went back to the partition door and could hear him moving about busily on the other side. When she knocked, she was surprised to hear an enthusiastic voice inviting her in. He had showered and put on new clothes and was in the last stages of packing. He had also contacted Noah to arrange a flight to Washington for them. "As soon as you're ready," he'd said, "we'll apply our makeup and disappear into our new identities."

He seemed more energized than ever, and she thought his earlier catharsis must be the reason for it. She knew such purges served to wash emotional contaminants from the system, allowing the individual to think more clearly and feel with heightened sensitivity. The effect was always temporary, but she was still happy to see him unburdened for a while.

Once they were in their disguises—she continued to be amazed at how effective these were—they left through the hotel's rear door and got into a waiting taxi that Hammond had called ahead for. At the airport they went into the restrooms to remove their makeup so their faces would match their IDs.

Sitting on the plane, Sheila began to feel uneasy about how smoothly their little operation was going. She was convinced they would be arrested the moment they arrived in D.C. They got off the plane along with everyone else and began down a crowded corridor. Then an unsmiling, thick-necked policeman stepped in front of them and held a hand up. Her heart seized like an old engine before she realized the officer was simply pointing out that the magazine she had bought in the Dallas airport had just fallen out of her bag. They went into the public restrooms again and reapplied their false faces. Then they were in another cab, heading toward the heart of the nation's capital.

The driver slowed to a halt in front of McCormick & Schmick's on F Street as instructed. Hammond got out and paid the driver, then slung his knapsack over his shoulder and began walking. One block over, he stopped at the corner and nodded to a building about a hundred feet farther on. "There it is."

It was as plain and unassuming as any urban location could possibly be—six narrow stories of white sandstone with the blinds drawn in every window and no clues on the facade as to the occupants or their purpose. To the left was a dry-cleaning and tailoring shop; to the right a driveway that appeared to have been recently repaved.

"Looks inviting," Sheila said.

"Doesn't it?"

"Any ideas yet on how we get in there?"

"Possibly."

He started forward again, his eyes moving back and forth as he absorbed everything around him. Motivated by the desire to be helpful, Sheila began doing the same. She had no idea, however, what she was supposed to be looking for.

When they reached the paired glass doors at the front, Hammond turned abruptly and went inside.

"Jason!"

"Relax," he whispered.

They entered a small foyer, then went through a second set of doors. Just beyond them was a circular reception desk commanded by a middle-aged woman wearing a uniform of indistinct patronage.

"Good morning; may I help you?" she asked. Sheila was surprised by her congeniality. She could've been a greeter at a department store.

"We have an appointment," Hammond said. He checked his watch, then added, "At eleven o'clock."

"An appointment? I don't understand."

Hammond took out a pocket-size notepad with spiral binding along the top. Flipping up the cover, he pretended to read the first page. Sheila saw over his shoulder that it was blank.

"With a Mr. Keller. Brett Keller."

The receptionist, now clearly perplexed, shook her head. "There's no one here by that name."

"There's no Brett Keller? Physical trainer?"

"Oh, you must be thinking of the gym. The Iron Pit."

"That's correct. This isn't it?"

The guard laughed. "No, it's a few more doors farther down." She lifted herself an inch out of her chair and gestured with a ballpoint pen. "That way."

"Oh, jeez. I'm sorry."

"That's all right."

Hammond turned away with a wave. "Thanks very much. Have a nice day."

"You too."

As soon as they were back outside, he went left and then left again—down the freshly paved driveway that lay between the library and what appeared to be a very busy Starbucks.

"What was that all about?"

"Did you see the registry book?"

"You mean the binder on her desk?"

"Yeah. Everyone has to sign in. That means they've got to show some form of ID."

"So? You've got a few falsies, don't you?"

"This is the CIA. How long do you think it'll take before they figure it out?"

"About two seconds?"

"Yeah."

"So what now?"

"I don't know. Let's see. . . ."

They crossed into the library's rear parking lot. It was only half-filled with vehicles and surrounded on three sides by scraggly, stunted trees. A Dumpster stood at the far end with one rubber flap up and the other hanging down.

"Looking for the back door?"

"Uh-huh."

"You don't think they've already considered that?"

"I'm sure they have, but there's always . . . Ah, there it is."

The door stood atop a short run of concrete steps. It was battleship gray with a small caged light above it and—most importantly—no knob, bar, handle, or any other mechanism that allowed access from the outside. A few feet away, tucked in a corner of the aluminum handrails, was a long-necked cigarette receptacle.

"A fire door," Hammond said. "I knew there'd be one. It's the law, after all."

"Terrific, so how do we—?"

It opened as if on cue, and a young black man in a tie and short-sleeved shirt came hustling down the steps. He nodded as he breezed past them, then climbed into a Honda compact and sped away.

"Did you see his ID?"

"Yeah."

"It was bouncing and flipping off his chest. There was a photo and text on one side, but the other side was blank."

"So?"

Hammond smiled. "So let's go get a pack of smokes."

"Excuse me?"

• • •

They went to a convenience store Hammond had noticed when they first got out of the cab. When he announced that he wanted a pack of cigarettes, the girl behind the counter—barely old enough to smoke herself—asked which brand he wanted. This stifled him, and he stared at the myriad selection with his mouth half-open. Sheila snorted; evidently she found this amusing.

"You don't know which brand you like?" the girl asked with more than a trifle of derision. She was resplendent in a red apron with large pockets along the bottom and a tiny name tag that read *Billi Jo*.

Without missing a beat, Hammond said conversationally, "I was just released on parole, and I don't see the one I used to get when I was in the joint." The girl's face drained of all color, and Hammond could feel Sheila struggling to keep from laughing. He settled on a pack of Marlboros because that was the only brand he'd heard of. After he paid and got his change, Sheila grabbed a folder of matches from a plastic bowl by the register.

"Now what?" she asked when they were back on the street.

"You'll see."

He went into a Staples farther down and followed the aisle signs to the construction paper. He bought a ream that was pale green—the same base color as the library employee's ID—and a pair of scissors. He took out one sheet and cut two rectangles that were roughly the size of baseball cards. Then he scribbled a decent facsimile of the president's signature on each.

"What's that for?"

"Motivation."

"Huh?"

They went to the store's copy center. The lord of this particular fiefdom was a young man, roughly the same age as Billi Jo, who appeared to possess no greater interest in his duties.

"Excuse me; you do laminating here, don't you?"

The kid seemed put out by the question, as if the very idea of having to perform this function was almost unbearable. "Yeah."

Hammond produced the two cards from his shirt pocket and fanned them between his thumb and forefinger.

"My wife and I saw the president during a White House tour yesterday afternoon, and he signed these for us."

The attendant's manner changed immediately. "Whoa, cool!"

"Cool indeed. I would like to have them laminated to preserve them for posterity, please."

"Sure!"

The attendant took the holy relics in hand with exquisite reverence. After they were sealed in the laminate, he removed the excess around the edges with a swing-arm paper trimmer, taking great pains to assure that each border was cut equidistantly. He set the finished products in a flat paper bag, then returned them to Hammond along with an in-store receipt and instructions to pay at one of the front registers. Before doing so, Hammond also grabbed a pair of lanyards from aisle 6 and a manual hole-puncher from aisle 8.

• • •

As they walked briskly down the library driveway again, Sheila said, "You had that poor kid thinking he was touching the Shroud of Turin."

"Good thing he didn't know the president has been in the Pacific Northwest all week."

She shook her head and took the fake ID out of her pocket. "So I'm assuming we'll be wearing these with the blank side facing out? Is that the idea?"

"You will, but I'm putting mine here." He slipped the lanyard over his head and tucked the laminated card into his shirt pocket so that only a narrow strip of green was visible along the top. "I just hope some gung ho type doesn't insist on seeing the whole thing."

"This is crazy, y'know."

"Oh yeah, I know."

As they climbed the three steps to the little landing by the back door, Sheila's remaining courage began to fade. Even if they did manage to get inside, there would still probably be cameras everywhere. What if someone in the security room took particular notice of them? What if it seemed unusual that there were two people walking around together who had IDs that weren't fully visible? Her imagination began pumping out follow-up scenarios in the event they got caught. Arrest, incarceration, indictment . . . *Wouldn't that be the irony of ironies,* she thought, *to blow all of my parents' money on a team of lawyers just because I was trying to protect myself from—*

She was yanked out of this toxic daydream by the sound of Hammond smacking the pack of cigarettes into his palm.

He was obviously trying to copy what he'd seen other smokers do, but he was performing the act incorrectly, using the full length of the box rather than the end.

"Here, give it to me."

"That's not right?"

"No, you have to hit the top, not the front. Like this." She gave it three quick whacks, then unwound the cellophane in a way that was so fluid it looked like a magic trick.

"Wow, you're good."

"Nothing I'm proud of, believe me."

"You still smoke?"

"No, I did for one year, back when I was in corporate purgatory. I never developed the addiction, thank goodness. I freely confess I did it for the image. I thought it made me look older and more with-it."

"Ah, well, no harm done."

"No, hopefully not." She was troubled, though, by the way her hands recalled the motions so effortlessly. This was further evident in the way she flipped up the lid with her thumb, then shook the pack just hard enough to make a few cigarettes stick out above the others.

Hammond paused before taking one, looking at them like a child being told by a zookeeper that it was perfectly fine to touch the giant snake he was holding. When he finally drew one out, he didn't put it in his mouth but rather held it like a pretzel rod.

"Would you like me to light it for you too?"

"Yes, please."

She put both in her mouth and lit them simultaneously— again, the ready expertise—then handed one back to him, filter first.

"What do I do now?"

"Set it between your lips and draw."

Following these instructions, he took in a lungful of smoke before succumbing to a coughing jag that almost brought him to his knees.

Ripping the cigarette from his mouth, he said severely, "People really do this to themselves?"

"Every day."

"You know what? I think I'll just hold it. At least that'll make it *look* like I'm smoking."

"Good idea." For her own part, Sheila was not only drawing on hers but finding the experience disturbingly pleasurable.

It took almost a half hour—two more worrisome smokes for her, one more loathsome prop for him—before the door opened again. A man and a woman emerged, the former in his midfifties, the latter about ten years younger. They both wore glasses, were smartly dressed, and carried themselves with an air of self-importance. As they took note of the two strangers standing there, the man's eyes went straight for their IDs. Hammond, meanwhile, had abruptly shifted the conversation they were having about Sheila's own knowledge about the assassination to something with a more casual tone.

". . . been rough for them the last few seasons, but I have a feeling the Nationals will pull it together this year. Their roster's starting to gel. I see them breaking .500 with no problem."

Sheila was astonished by how utterly convincing he sounded; she nearly believed it herself. Her heart, meanwhile, was trip-hammering with such force it felt like it might explode.

The pair that had exited the building reached the bottom

of the steps and turned toward the parking lot. *They bought it,* Sheila thought. *Wow!*

But just as Hammond slipped his foot in front of the door to prevent it from closing, the man stopped and turned back. "Excuse me." His tone was demanding and unfriendly. Whoever he was, he was used to giving orders. "Sir? Excuse me?"

Hammond glanced at him, maintaining a perfect aura of calm. "Yes?"

Following a brief pause that constituted the longest few seconds of Sheila's life, the man said, "Their relief pitching still stinks, and they can't hit the long ball to save their lives."

Hammond sniffed out a laugh. "No, but they can still pile up the singles and doubles, plus they can draw walks like nobody's business."

"That won't be enough."

"I disagree, and I stand by my prediction." Then, with the most disarming smile Sheila had ever seen, Hammond added, "Care to put a fiver on it?"

His new friend snapped his fingers and pointed. "You got it."

"Okay then."

And with that, the man returned to his original course and was gone.

• • •

As they slipped inside, she said, "How on earth do you do that?"

Hammond rapidly took stock of his surroundings—a zig-zag set of fire stairs painted the same flat gray as the door, enclosed in a column of echoey cinder-block walls.

"Do what?"

"Act so . . . *normal* in that kind of situation."

He chuckled as he started up the steps. "I guess I'm just good at hiding it."

"Hiding what?"

"How terrified I am on the inside."

Sheila smiled. "That makes me feel better."

"I'm so glad."

When they reached the door, he consulted a diagram of the building's floor plan, which had been helpfully posted on the wall by order of the local fire marshal. The computers were one story farther up. As they reached that door, Hammond said quietly, "Stay behind me and remember to act casual. Big Brother will not only be watching; he'll probably be listening, too. That said, please keep your own eyes and ears wide open. You have to watch my back while I dig through the dirty laundry."

Sheila took a deep breath. "Sure, no problem."

The door opened into a short hallway. This led to a brightly lit room with several rows of cubicles, each with its own computer terminal. On the far side was a panoramic window covered by hanging blinds. Beyond the computer area was a long run of freestanding bookshelves, and behind those stood another set of stairs. The decor was spare and somewhat predictable—agency citations and awards along with framed photos of notable figures both past and present. Hammond recognized all the presidents and vice presidents plus some agency heads, but other faces were unfamiliar. He also noted with some relief that there weren't too many other visitors around.

He sat at the terminal closest to the little hallway and shook the mouse, which cleared the floating CIA logo. Next was a search screen—an empty bar in the center with the phrase *Search Words* on the left and another CIA logo above it. Hammond set his fingers on the keyboard, then paused. It occurred to him that typing *Galeno Clemente* might pop a red flag somewhere in the system. He guessed that Clemente was about as deeply classified as it was possible for someone to be. *I need to find him by digging* around *him,* Hammond realized.

He started with the three words *Clemente, soldier,* and *missing.* This produced 462 results. Based on the information given in the first few snippets, however, none seemed to have anything to do with his subject. He then tried *Clemente* and *1963,* but that also produced nothing of value. He did note one interesting citation that had to do with baseball great Roberto Clemente and his stint with the Marine Corps Reserve but reminded himself that this wasn't the time to indulge random curiosities.

After several other dead-end combos, he hit pay dirt with *Clemente, Cuba,* and *military.* This led not only to two mentions of Galeno—although the snippet blocks were covered by an arresting red moiré with the words "Authorized Access Only" stamped over it at an angle—but three others that mentioned a brother, Olivero.

"Whoa," Hammond whispered. "What have we here?"

Keeping her eyes on everyone and everything in their vicinity, Sheila said, "Find something?"

"Maybe. . . ."

He clicked on the first result and learned that Olivero Clemente was born in the El Cano section of Havana in May of 1942 and that he served in the Cuban Revolutionary Armed Forces from April of 1960 until January of 1964. The second result outlined his attendance at the University of Havana following his military service, with a major in civil engineering and a minor in unspecified foreign languages. The third and final result, a PDF of a brief report that appeared to have been hastily written by a low-level operative just two years earlier, read like some kind of "Whatever Happened To . . . ?" featurette in *People* magazine. Although built mostly from assumptions culled through secondhand information, the report did provide a singular nugget of information that made Hammond's heart jump—Olivero's current whereabouts were believed to be "the Old Havana section of the city, possibly somewhere on the north side."

Another search, this time using *Olivero Clemente* directly, merely produced the same three results Hammond had just read. He then backed up a page to the previous list. Those three were still demoted under the tantalizing two where Galeno's name was visibly nestled inside a larger paragraph whose full contents remained maddeningly out of view.

"Okay, keep your eyes peeled."

"I have been."

"Good."

He clicked on the first one, which took him to a flashing screen with two blank bars—one marked "User Name" and the other "Authorization Code." He hadn't expected anything less and figured he had nothing to lose if he hit such a wall. Then he saw something else—beneath the log-on area was a digital timer, rapidly counting backward:

:10

:09

:08

:07

"I think perhaps it's time we hit the road," he said, rising slowly and keeping his voice low.

"Huh? Why?"

:03

:02

:01

"Because I think I just goofed."

:00

The screen didn't just go blank—the monitor turned off. Then Hammond saw them: two men in suits and ties coming up the steps beyond the bookcases. They weren't wearing sunglasses like the CIA guys in the movies, but they were rugged, rough-hewn types who, he suspected, probably possessed the authority to use deadly force whenever they pleased.

"Time to be on our merry way," he said, guiding Sheila firmly toward the fire door. Just before it shut, he turned back and saw their pursuers—the one in the lead was white, his partner black—break into a run.

"*Go! Quick!*" His voice echoed throughout the corridor. He did not follow her down, however. On the side of the fire alarm box was a small steel hammer, which served the sole function of breaking the glass so the alarm's handle could be pulled. What interested Hammond most was the long chain that dissuaded people from stealing it.

Sheila didn't realize he was still up there until she reached the first landing.

"Jason!"

"In a sec—"

"What are you doing?"

He snatched the hammer from its hook with trembling hands, wrapped it around the door's access bar as many times as the chain would allow, and inserted the head through one of the links. "Saw that in a movie once. I think it might slow them down," he said as he took off again.

They were already past the first landing when the agents tried to get through. There was a pause as confusion took hold following this first attempt. The second was more forceful but still cautious. The third, a hard kick, snapped the chain and sent the door slamming against the wall. Broken links jingled along the polished floor.

Sheila reached the bottom first and went out.

"To the back!" Hammond said. "Where the trees are. Hurry!"

She raced down the steps and turned while Hammond stopped again, this time to move the cigarette receptacle from the corner of the landing to the first step. It was filled with sand and weighed considerably more than he expected, causing him to groan when he lifted it.

Once beyond the tree-lined border, he stopped and waited. The door swung open and the two agents, in their haste, failed to see the receptacle. As the white one tried to halt himself, the black one plowed into him. This propelled them both forward, where they engaged in an ungraceful swan dive that terminated in a painful crash on the pavement below.

"Sorry, guys," Hammond mumbled. Then, more audibly, "Okay, let's get out of here."

26

RYDELL SAT behind his desk in downtown D.C., working through one more insipid report, his hands paused on the keyboard as he tried to recall the correct spelling of the word *rhythm*. In spite of his vast intelligence, he, like everyone else, had blind spots, and this was one of them.

"Two *h*'s and two *y*'s?" he mumbled, then tried it— *rhythym*. It didn't look right.

"Just one *h*, then," he said, typing again—*rhytym*. That wasn't right either.

When he tried it a third way, his aging fingers accidentally inserted a *u* and then a *g*—*rhuytgym*—and when he went to delete these, he inadvertently eliminated several of the correct letters as well. He cursed and smacked the keys with his balled fist.

It's getting harder, he realized. Harder to maintain the pretense of normalcy, the facade of all being well and good in his increasingly nebulous world. His anger toward Birk was becoming impossible to contain. He found himself checking his cell phone frequently, on the off chance he hadn't felt the vibrations or had somehow, accidentally, turned the ringer volume all the way down. But neither of these things ever really happened, of course, and he knew that.

Birk's lack of progress was infuriating. *"Find them—kill them"* were the last orders Rydell had given him, delivered in a tone that left no room for interpretation. *"I don't care how."* It was true that Birk had successfully tracked down their previous location and that his investigative methodology had been impressive. He had determined that they had given the hotel false names, that the staff swore to seeing only two guests during their stay even though four had been registered, that they had suddenly vacated the rooms without formally checking out, and that there had been hair samples found on each of the pillows that, Rydell was certain, would be a spot-on match if he bothered to run the necessary tests. But this was all after-the-fact information.

Where were they now?

Since their exit from the Royal Crowne, they had fallen off the radar screen—and that made Rydell very nervous indeed. Hammond wasn't the type of person you wanted running around loose. And the Baker woman was becoming irritatingly resourceful in her own right. There had been no sightings on any of the security cameras in the Dallas area, no further media reports, and no electronic contact—phone, text, or e-mail—with any of the people in their lives. This included several other Kennedy experts under Rydell's surveillance, members of Baker's extended family, her many business contacts, and the handful of friends he knew about.

They've fallen off the face of the earth.

But he knew better than that. The intuitive touch of genius that had carried him to the greatest heights of his profession while enabling him to become a master criminal could feel them out there, closing in. He began to wonder what needed to change in the equation to tilt the numbers back in his favor.

He was about to check his phone again when a small flashing alert appeared in the corner of the monitor. His eyebrows rose as he read the text. Then he clicked on a movie player application and watched a grainy fish-eye video of Hammond and Baker as they fled from their computer terminal at the CIA library. He took note of the time stamp and realized the incident had occurred less than two hours ago. Fear branched through him, and his hand seemed to reach for the cell phone on its own. Stepping into the bathroom and shutting the door, he got Birk on the first ring.

"I need you here, immediately," he said, making a conscious effort to keep his voice steady.

There was a pause on the other end. "And where is that?" Birk asked.

Rydell's stomach began to churn as he realized his mistake. In all the years he had dealt with the many Birks in his employ, he had never, not even once, revealed any details about his identity. The need for anonymity was paramount; the problems that could stem from a compromise were too numerous to contemplate.

Rydell caught a glimpse of himself in the small mirror over the sink. The man who stared back was haggard and worn, an adaptation of himself he had never seen before. It was someone on the losing side of whatever battle he was fighting—also unfamiliar. *You've got to get yourself under control,* the survivalist part of him said firmly. *Right now.*

He cleared his throat. "Chicago. You need to come to Chicago. Get a flight into O'Hare and call me when you land. You'll receive further instructions at that time."

"I understand," Birk replied. His tone was flat, obedient.

But Rydell detected something else, something just below the surface. Was it doubt? Had Birk also sensed the error?

It doesn't matter, Rydell told himself. *Soon, none of this will be relevant.*

He ended the call and replaced the phone in his pocket. He would call back in twenty minutes and say the destination had been changed to D.C. instead. That should take care of the gaffe. *No problem.*

He took one last look at himself before going back out.

• • •

Events following their escape from the CIA library unfolded at breakneck speed. Beyond the tree-lined border, they found themselves in the grimy rear driveway of an Italian restaurant. Running past a reeking, fly-clouded Dumpster, they reached the next street over and slowed to a stroll so as not to attract attention. The sidewalk teemed with moving bodies. Hammond flagged down a taxi and told the driver to go to the National Zoo, then shut the partition between them.

When Sheila questioned this choice of destination, Hammond said he needed a moment to think. He googled what he felt was an appropriate hotel on his cell phone and was about to call Noah to arrange the reservation when Sheila pointed out that most local hotels were likely to have security cameras that could be accessed by intelligence authorities. She suggested they seek a bed-and-breakfast in one of the outlying suburbs instead, as most of these were privatized and less likely to feature any high-tech gadgetry. Hammond found this an excellent suggestion and, after another brief Google search, apologetically gave the driver new instructions.

The Rosewood Inn turned out to be a well-kept antebellum set on a shaded street in Gaithersburg. The woman behind the desk, a spinsterish old thing with yellowing hair and a tiny mouth, sized up her latest visitors with unabashed disapproval. Sheila could almost read her mind—*young, attractive, no wedding rings . . . I wonder if his wife knows about her.* Hammond requested a menu, then ordered two meals and asked that they be brought to the room as soon as possible.

The room in question—called "The Plover's Nest," which Sheila found a little kitschy—was actually a spare, modest efficiency that included a kitchen, deck, washer-dryer combo, and full bath. Hammond sat down at the round table in the main living area and returned to the Internet. Sheila watched with mild envy from the chair across from him. She still could not risk using her own phone, which now held 129 text messages, 47 e-mails, and 26 voice-mail messages. Hammond apologized again for the inconvenience and promised to think of some way of resolving the problem. Then their food arrived, wheeled in by a tiny man of considerable age. He transferred the meals—broiled filet of sole for him, a chicken Caesar salad for her—onto the table without a word. When Hammond tipped him, he took the folded bill without glancing at it and bowed before withdrawing. Twenty minutes later, Hammond called home.

"What's going on?" Noah asked through the speaker. "I've been waiting to hear from you."

"We're in a B and B on the outskirts of Washington."

"Did you make it to the CIA library?"

"We did."

"And?"

Hammond retold the story from beginning to end, leaving out nothing. When he was finished, Noah said sharply, "You're going to get yourself killed, Jason. Either that or incarcerated. Sheila, too."

"I've been giving a lot of thought to what needs to happen next, and I keep arriving at the same conclusion—I have to go to Cuba and find Olivero Clemente."

Sheila, who was taking her time with her meal, was about to jab a fork into a pile of romaine when she came to a halt.

"Are you out of your blessed mind?" Noah asked. "Americans aren't even *allowed* into Cuba. Not without special permission from the American government."

"I know, Noah."

"The odds of them granting it to you are pretty slim at the moment, considering you're a wanted man."

Hammond reached beside the corded phone on the desk and retrieved a notepad bearing the Rosewood's letterhead. "But I should be able to get by on humanitarian grounds, right?"

"What do you mean, 'humanitarian grounds'?"

"In connection with all the food, clothing, and medicine we send down there. I believe we gave $1.3 million last year alone, through our organization in Spain. Isn't that correct?"

"I believe so."

"Okay, so that should cover me on legal grounds, assuming I need such coverage at all."

"Assuming? I don't understand."

"I'm not going to apply for the travel license from the Treasury Department, Noah. They're not going to give it to me. As you say, I'm a wanted man."

"So what are you saying? You . . . you're not actually thinking of—"

"Going down there without one, yes. Traveling *incognito*."

Sheila jumped into the fray. "We'll be breaking federal law. Even I know that."

"Jason," Noah said patiently, "think about this. Really

think about it. Do you know how much trouble you can get into?"

"Yes, but there's really no choice. I'll take the first available seat on a flight to Miami in the morning. I'll have to use one of the false identities too, unfortunately. I hate doing that, but I don't see a choice. From there I'll charter a boat and sail the remaining ninety miles. I'll need you to arrange everything, please. Right away."

"'I'?" Sheila interjected. "Don't you mean 'we'?"

"Jason, I really have to protest. Come back home for a while. Straighten things out with the government, and let the situation cool down. If Olivero Clemente has been down there all this time, he'll still be there when you get the proper permission."

"No," Hammond said, "that won't work. I agree with you that it would be safer to come home first and do this properly. But if Galeno Clemente really was involved in the assassination and his brother is still down there, then the people trying to stop me now know that *I* know about him. If they don't think they can get to me, they might just try to go after him instead. He's my only link, my only solid lead. We all know what happened to Ben. Now is the time to act on this, not later."

In a whisper, Sheila said, "Jason?"

Hammond looked up, startled, as if he'd forgotten she was there. "Yes?"

"What's this 'I' stuff? Don't you mean 'we'?"

He shook his head. "I'm sorry, but I can't risk bringing you along."

"What are you talking about?"

"I know how personal this is for you, but Cuba is big-league stuff. If something happens, it's not like America, where you call the police or your lawyer. It's essentially law-less in many areas. It's no place for someone like you."

Before she could protest further, Hammond said into the speaker, "Noah, would you be willing to accommodate our dear friend here for a while? Keep her safe at the estate?"

"Of course."

"Then please make the necessary arrangements for her as well. She can take a train out of Union Station, maybe into Boston, and you can meet her with the boat in Boston Harbor or something like that. Can you do it?"

"I can."

"Good. Oh, and one more thing—once she's there, please figure out some secure way for her to start digging into all her messages."

"I will."

"Great." He looked at her and smiled warmly. The smile he received in return was superficial at best. "Okay, Noah, we've got to do another clandestine shopping run, then get some rest. Call me back when you've got the travel details."

"I will."

• • •

It was still dark outside when Hammond shook her awake. He had asked Noah to book Sheila's train as early as possible so they could leave before sunrise. It took less than an hour for them to shower and dress, put on their new faces, and erase all evidence of their presence. They had the taxi driver pull through a Dunkin' Donuts for an on-the-fly breakfast of orange juice and wheat bagels. At Union Station, they avoided as many security cameras as possible, retrieved Sheila's ticket from the first available window, and went straight to the platform.

Sheila's train—which would deposit her in Boston in approximately seven hours—was scheduled to depart at 8 a.m. As its headlight appeared in the distance, Hammond said, "Okay, this looks like your—"

She turned abruptly to face him. "Jason, don't do this. Come to the estate with me."

"No, I appreciate your concern, but—"

"You were talking again in your sleep last night. I heard you out there." He had given her the bed while he slept on the living room sofa. "The nightmares are back, aren't they?"

"No."

"Jason."

"Okay, yeah," he said, "but it's nothing I haven't dealt with before. I can handle it."

"You need *help*," she said.

"This really isn't the time to discuss—"

"Come with me. We'll figure it all out. Everything."

He took her by the hand. "Not yet. Maybe later, but not yet. Try to understand—I have to do this."

The train rumbled up, blasting its horn.

"Go ahead," he said. "I'll be back in a few days."

"You can't be certain of that."

"Yes . . . *yes*." He guided her gently to the steps. "I want to see how this turns out too."

"And then you'll get some help?"

"We'll see. Now get going. Noah's dying to meet you."

She started up, then turned. "Take care of yourself, please."

He nodded. "I will."

A conductor appeared and politely asked her to go inside and sit down. Hammond waved a final good-bye.

• • •

Sheila went past the conductor and found a seat in the rear. Her last image of Hammond was of him walking away, his broad figure weaving through the thick of the crowd on the platform until it disappeared. A sadness overwhelmed her then, and she struggled to hold the tears back. As the train jerked forward, she slid down into the seat and closed her eyes. Sleep came quickly, mercifully.

Meanwhile, the call she had accidentally placed on her cell phone, which was in her back pocket when she sat down, sent out a signal that was received by two people—a very confused aunt in Jackson, Mississippi, and the assistant deputy director of the CIA.

27

NO SOONER had Sheila closed her eyes, it seemed, than she found herself lying on a surfboard, rising and falling with the gentle respiration of a nameless sea. The day could not have been more perfect—the sky shimmered without end, the sun was shining gloriously, and the water was as clear as liquid glass. Only dimly aware that she was dreaming, she looked back along the beach for other signs of life. There were none.

A wave—not particularly large, but it caught her by surprise—rolled in and pushed her off the board. She tumbled over the side and went under, a million tiny bubbles boiling up around her. She knew how to swim—her mother had taken her to lessons every summer from third to sixth grade—but those skills abandoned her now. She flailed about in a spasmodic attempt at the breaststroke, yet the surface of the water, though only a few feet overhead, never seemed to come any closer.

A tiny flicker of light caught her eye, no more than a glint in the distance. Then she saw it—a metal rod of some kind, moving through the water in a hurry. *A spear,* she realized.

Not black and rusty like the one her uncle Brian, a lifelong enthusiast of deep-sea fishing, had mounted over the mantel in his den. This one was chromed from head to tail.

She tried to move out from its path, but her body refused to obey. The spear surged past her face and buried itself in her right arm. She tensed, expecting the pain to be extraordinary. It turned out to be nothing more than a muted sting, as if she had been poked with a freshly sharpened pencil. Then came a most magnificent sensation—warmth, pure and sweet and fine, flowing down every physiological pathway. *No,* she thought, *not warmth—at least not physical. Emotional warmth. Happiness . . . elation . . . euphoria.* It was the most blessed and blissful state of mind she had ever known.

She looked to the surface again. Sunbeams were splayed out playfully around their brilliant core, which only served to heighten the ecstasy. Getting back there no longer seemed imperative. It was too wonderful down here, too perfect. *Yes, perfect,* she told herself. *It is perfect here. Perfect everywhere. The world could not be a more perfect place right now.*

A hand plunged through the water and went to her shoulder. She was jerked back and forth dazedly, in slow motion. Then the watery kingdom that surrounded her began to evaporate. The sunbeams retreated, although the bright core remained. She was shaken again, and a voice, murky and far-off but still intelligible—*Come on, honey, we need to get off here. Honey . . . wake up.*

Her eyes fluttered open. The ocean was nothing but a memory now, replaced by the bowels of the train. The cheerful sun had become a recessed light in the ceiling.

The voice spoke again, this time with greater clarity. "Honey? Let's get going, okay? We don't want to miss our stop."

She found a person sitting across from her. The image was hazy at first; then it improved. It was a man, young and handsome. Dark hair, rugged features, fashionably unshaven. At first she didn't recognize him. Then she thought she did, and a flame of fear alighted. In a peculiar way, she sensed that it should be greater, more intense. But the notion could not fully form because she was unable to access the rationale behind it.

"Come on, babe. We've got to get off now."

She realized she was on her side, curled in a fetal position. When she went to sit upright, the effort was surprisingly difficult. Then she felt a soreness in her right arm. Pulling up the sleeve, she saw a circular area about the size of a silver dollar that had become pink and puffy. In the center was a little red dot. *How did that get there?*

Her companion leaned over and pulled the sleeve down. "This is our stop," he said. "Let's go."

He rose, slid a backpack up his arm, and took her by the hand. She still felt that initial twinge of caution, but it seemed halfhearted and unconvincing now. This man meant her no harm; he was a friend who could be trusted. Her earlier concerns had been unfounded, even silly. Whatever he wanted to do, it was fine with her.

• • •

Birk smiled as he led her off the train and through the thickening crowd of morning commuters. As he passed a trash can, he disposed of the brown paper bag containing both the syringe and the unlabeled bottle.

28

HAMMOND'S BOAT cut a foamy scar through the waterway that linked the Caribbean Sea with the Atlantic Ocean while also separating the United States from one of its closest neighbors, the island nation of Cuba. Relations between the two had been strained from the moment Fidel Castro overthrew the American-friendly regime of Fulgencio Batista in January of 1959, then sunk to a nadir when Castro invited the Soviet Union to park a few boatloads of ballistic armaments along their northern shores. This led to the infamous Cuban Missile Crisis in October of 1962—thirteen nail-biting days in which the world came within a hair's width of nuclear war. President Kennedy and Soviet leader Nikita Khrushchev engaged in the greatest game of chicken in human history while citizens on both sides dug fallout shelters and cleared grocery aisles of all canned goods. In spite of Kennedy's eventual success, diplomatic relations between the U.S. and Cuba never resumed.

Having traveled the bulk of the ninety-mile journey from the Florida coast, Hammond could now see the island's hulking form in the distance beneath the tropical sky. The boat, which rented at five grand a week, was a forty-foot, fully modernized cabin cruiser that slept six and could effortlessly maintain the twenty-two knots required to cover the trip in about four hours. Her name was *Wind Dancer*.

Standing at the helm and staring through the bridge's split window while the engines groaned away, Hammond concentrated on his objective. Finding Olivero Clemente would not be easy. Like his brother Galeno, Olivero was a specter. Beyond the three records at the CIA library, Hammond had found no further mention of him. The man had gone out of his way—or at least *someone* had—to erase all evidence of his existence. This meant a grassroots investigation would be required—knocking on doors, talking to strangers, spreading cash around. Hammond knew American money went far in Cuba. The exchange rate favored the dollar to begin with, but on the street it held even greater value. He had learned this through the travel guides he bought at a bookstore back in Miami. Several of the more unsettling tips about Castro's Communist paradise included the fact that his American health insurance would be invalid, his credit cards were useless, and any U.S. citizens who ventured out of the traditional tourist zones would be, at least from a security standpoint, "on their own." One of the guides also urged travelers not to be alarmed by the apparently common sight of uniformed soldiers, armed with machine guns, on virtually every street corner.

As the island drew closer, Hammond decided his first order of business was to set up headquarters in the Old Havana neighborhood. It offered a broad selection of hotels, most of which were run jointly by the Cuban government and a variety of private European firms. *I'll get something to eat,* he decided, *and then—*

His phone rang before he could complete the thought. He removed it from its belt case and checked the ID before answering. "Hello, Noah. How is our new guest do—?"

"Jason, there's a problem. A big problem." He was out of breath.

Hammond tensed. "Tell me."

"Sheila never showed up."

"*What?*"

"I'm sitting in a cab just outside the station in Boston. Her train arrived an hour ago, but she never got off. I waited on the platform, watched every passenger. Then I got on and took a quick look around in case she'd fallen asleep or was in the bathroom or something. I talked to two different conductors, and neither even remembered her."

"Oh no. . . ."

"Are you sure she got on in D.C.?"

"Yes, I watched her. And I watched the train pull away. You need to use the GPS tracking system that we're devel—"

"I did. In fact, I did that first. Her phone must be off."

"Or it was turned off *for* her."

"I also checked to make sure I had the right train. Number 4674 northbound from Washington."

"That's right," Hammond said. His voice had reduced to a hoarse whisper.

He spun the wheel and gunned the motor, and the boat listed so severely that he nearly fell over. The phone flew out of his hand, bounced on the deck, and missed going over the wall by a hair before he managed to retrieve it.

"What was that?" Noah demanded.

"Nothing. I'm coming back."

"Huh?"

"I'm coming home, right now."

"Jason, no. There's no point in that."

"No point?"

"You won't get here for hours, and we need to act on this right now. It's a *missing person*. Besides, the authorities will pick you up the moment they see you. You know that."

Hammond dropped the clutch and slowed the boat to a powerless drift. Now the only sound was the gentle waves slapping against the bow.

"What do you suggest, then?"

"We have to get the police involved. They're the only ones equipped to handle this. They can mobilize immediately. If we try to do it privately, it'll take too much time."

"The media will find out. It'll leak."

"That could be to our advantage. And hers. It might put more pressure on whoever took her." He added quickly, "Assuming that's what happened."

"That's what happened," Hammond said angrily. "It was the little slug who's been trailing us all along, I'm sure. The one who tried to kill us before, the one who killed Ben."

"If you're right, then every second counts. We've got to stop discussing and start acting."

Hammond let out a deep breath. There on a hunk of fiberglass bobbing like a cork in the open sea, he had never felt so helpless.

"Okay, go ahead. But I still think I should come back."

"No, finish what you've started."

"I thought you were the one who wanted me to come home."

"You're too far into it now. What happened to Sheila is proof of that. Whoever's still hiding in the shadows, you've riled them. They'll never let you rest regardless of where you go. Your only choice is to see this through."

Hammond's considered reply was delivered in a whisper—"But at what price?"

"You should've thought of that a while ago, my friend."

Hammond said nothing, but the bubbling pool of black grew just a little bit wider.

"Go on," Noah said. "Get down there and try to find Clemente. I'll take care of this."

"Keep me updated, no matter what happens."

"I will."

Hammond put the phone back in its case. He continued considering and reconsidering the notion of heading back. But Noah was right—they'd nail him in short order, and those who had been hiding underground would go even deeper. This opportunity would never come again.

Then he heard Sheila's voice in his mind—*"Think about what they did, Jason. To my mother, to the president, to his family, and to the country. If you give up, they win. Hasn't that been their objective all along—to get you to give up? To stop you before you found out too much? Before you found out the truth?"*

Hammond heard all of this as clearly as if she were standing right beside him. And that was what he wished at that moment—for her to be beside him, as she had been since the beginning. Now he didn't know *where* she was or if she was okay or if she was even alive. *Maybe that's why I'm hearing her so clearly—maybe she's speaking to me from above, urging me to go forward. Not just to avenge Kennedy, but now to avenge her as well.* His blood boiled at the thought. His breathing became rapid, and every muscle tightened like a steel cable. *If they've hurt her, may the Lord have mercy on their souls— because I won't.*

29

SHEILA'S EYES fluttered open as she emerged from one of the deepest sleeps she had ever known. There had been no dreams or interruptions, just a lost gap in the timeline of her life. She felt slightly loopy, like she did back in the stress-laden corporate days after taking a hit of NyQuil when she absolutely had to get a good night's rest.

She lay on a brown leather couch with her head on a small pillow, her hands and feet bound by repeated coils of nylon rope. The room was relatively small and, in spite of being essentially a prison, tastefully furnished and decorated. Aside from the couch, there were a pair of matching chairs on either side of an accent table, two chrome floor lamps, a large area rug that covered all but a narrow margin of the hardwood floor, a selection of framed landscape prints, and a large potted plant of some leafy, semitropical variety. There were no windows, and the only door was shut tight. There was also no clock or any other way to tell the time.

She trained on the ceiling—plain white, with a dome fix-ture in the center—and tried to figure out where she was. No answers came, and fear began to trickle in. She lifted her head and saw a man sitting at a small round table on the other side of the room, smoking a cigar and reading a magazine. Then the recognition struck, and several disturbing facts jelled into one horrific realization—he was not only the person who had led her off the train but was also the man who had tried to kill her by blowing her childhood home to pieces, the man who had successfully erased the life of Dr. Benjamin Burdick.

The remaining pieces of the puzzle whirled into place in her mind. After they got off the train, he took her to a car in the parking lot. *A white sedan,* she remembered. Then he handed her something to drink . . . *a water bottle, with the cap already off.* Under normal circumstances, she wouldn't even consider drinking something that had already been opened. But she had taken this without hesitation and downed it like she'd just crawled out of the desert. *Because he told me to . . . just because he told me to.* The world around her had begun to spin away and she had plunged into pure darkness, pure nothingness. *Drugs,* she realized. *He drugged me. First on the train with a needle, then with something else in the car.* She could not conjure any memories after that, and the fear blossomed into breathing terror. *Has he raped me? When I was out cold, did he actually—?*

This chilling notion was cut off when her captor looked up from the magazine and took note of the fact that his prisoner was awake. "It's about time."

"Let me go," Sheila said, using the no-room-for-debate voice she unleashed on her employees when she wanted them to jump. It always worked back home, but she doubted its effectiveness here. "Right now."

The man set down the magazine and rose, unhurriedly. He strolled over, leaned down, and reached for one of the nautical knots he'd tied. For a flicker of an instant, Sheila thought he was actually going to obey her. Instead, he simply gave his handiwork a tug to make sure it was tight.

"Sorry; I can't help you," he said, moseying back to the table. "Orders from the boss."

"And who's that?"

"I can't help you there, either."

"Then who are you? What's your name?"

He was standing at the table now with his back to her. "Mickey Mouse," he said and picked up something she couldn't see.

"Yeah, well, let me out of here, Mickey, or I swear I'll—"

He turned, and when she saw the gun, her mouth clamped shut. It wasn't so much the weapon itself that blew fresh fear into her—at no time did she expect that he wouldn't have one—but rather that he was casually screwing a silencer onto the end of it.

He came back over and sat down next to her on the middle cushion. Then he gently placed the rounded end of the silencer under her chin and moved it slowly southward, all the while with one finger around the trigger. She was barely breathing now, every inch of her body as cold as if it had developed a layer of frost. She had never known such fear.

"I'm afraid you are not in a position to give orders this evening," he said emotionlessly. "On the contrary, tonight you're going to do everything I decree."

"Don't bet on it," she heard herself say, although she had no idea where she was summoning the nerve.

"Oh, I don't need to bet on it—I know it. Here's how it's going to work: I'm going to ask you some questions, and you're going to give me the answers. All of them."

"Yeah? And why would I do that? Are you gonna shoot more drugs into me? Is that it?"

"Regrettably not. Truth serums such as sodium thiopental and amobarbital are notoriously unreliable. What I gave you on the train was simply designed to make you more docile and cooperative, and what I gave you in the car was meant to put you to sleep. What I need now is a way to make you talk."

Sheila snorted a laugh. "I'm not telling you jack." She nodded toward the gun. "And you don't scare me with that thing, because I don't care if I die."

He leaned in close to her—their noses were just inches apart—and said, "Frankly I don't care if you die either. But you'll talk anyway because there are so many things worse than death."

He pulled away from her panic-stricken face, set the gun on her stomach, and removed something from the breast pocket of his linen shirt. "For example, this."

It was a standard-size piece of paper that had been folded into quarters. He opened it and showed her a list of seemingly random numbers. Some were broken up by hyphens; others had dollar signs and decimal points.

"See this one?" He pointed to the figure of $8,534.01. "Does it look familiar?"

Sheila felt her face turn white. "No," she said, already knowing it was pointless to lie.

"Of course it does. That's exactly how much you have in your savings account as of this morning. And this one here—" he singled out the nine digits below it—"is the account itself. This is my favorite, though." It was a four-digit code that Sheila knew all too well, as it was the day and month of her birthday in reverse. "The secret code for your bank card. Not much of a secret anymore."

He went on to the other figures, many of which were unfamiliar to her. They turned out to be PINs, balances, and accounts belonging to close friends, home addresses and unlisted phone numbers of extended family members, even Social Security numbers for their children.

When he was finished, he smiled and said curtly, "You wouldn't want me to make use of any of this information, right?"

In a final gesture of defiance, Sheila refused to respond. It was a decision she would quickly regret. Her captor's arrogant grin vanished, the muscles in his face tightened, and the eyes darkened with a sadism that eclipsed whatever remaining fragments of humanity he possessed. In that instant, the smooth operator fell away, and the sociopath that dwelled beneath was exposed.

His hand shot forward like a striking cobra and clutched her throat. Then he was in her face again, his lips twisted in a horrific snarl. *"Right?"*

She gasped, her eyes bulging. *"Yes, yes! Whatever you want to know, I'll tell you!"* The tears came in a rush as the last of her emotional resolve disintegrated.

He watched her for a long moment as if savoring his victory. The smile returned. He got to his feet, retrieving the gun from her stomach as he turned away. Even through her grief, albeit in a far-distant corner of her mind, she wondered what chain of events led someone to become such a monster. Then she did what so many do in times of extreme crisis— she promised God anything he wanted if he would just get her out of this alive and in one piece.

"I'm glad you've decided to be cooperative," her captor said. "That'll make things much easier for both of us."

He dropped the gun on the table and fished something else out of his shirt pocket. It was a Bluetooth headset, which he set in his ear. Then he took out his cell phone and tapped in a number. The call was answered right away on the other end.

"She's ready," he said.

• • •

Noah walked into the kitchen of the main house, still fully dressed in spite of the late hour. He carried an empty plate and a tall, milk-stained glass to the sink. Under normal circumstances he would have put them in the basin and walked away, as Rosetta would be there in the morning to clean up. But tonight he went about washing both by hand, using a little Palmolive and a scrub pad, then setting them in the drainer. After that he scrubbed the sink and rinsed away the soap bubbles with the sprayer. Finally he dried the sink with a hand towel, then hung the towel over the back of a chair.

It occurred to him that his behavior was bordering on OCD; then it occurred to him that he really didn't care. He had been distracting himself with busywork all night—laundry, dusting, vacuuming. The staff would be puzzled tomorrow, but he would tell them he had been unable to sleep. This wouldn't be a lie, but it wouldn't be the full truth, either. Then again, intentionally offering half-truths had become something of a habit of late, and his conscience acknowledged this with growing concern.

The police had grilled him for information about Sheila. Then, as he expected, they had turned their attention to Jason. He answered all questions honestly but volunteered no more than necessary. This intentional sin of omission weighed heavily on his conscience. He heard back from the authorities only once, when they acquired two security videos—one on the station platform in Wilmington, Delaware, and another in the parking lot. They had not yet been able to identify the man who had apprehended Sheila. They did, however, make the determination that the plates on the white sedan had been stolen, which led them to conclude that the kidnapper was fairly clever. When they sent still photos from both videos to Noah, he immediately forwarded them to Hammond, who confirmed that it was the man who had tried to kill them at Sheila's mother's house and who had killed Ben. Hammond grew increasingly agitated on the phone and again had to be talked out of coming home. Police had since spoken with Sheila's family and friends, but no one had heard from her.

When the media inevitably caught wind of this latest turn of events, they ran with it. The same video stills accompanied lead stories on countless news channels and across the Internet. It was sensationalism at its finest—one member of this underdog team kidnapped, the other valiantly carrying on, and the Hammond estate officially taking the classic "no comment" position. Theories abounded from all fronts, most on the basis that sinister figures in the government must be at work.

Noah followed the broadcasts until he could take no more. He kept both the house and satellite phones clipped to the back of his belt and repeatedly thanked the Lord for the miracle of caller ID.

He stood by the sink, his mind in neutral as he stared at a dim circle of moonlight on the countertop. Then one of the two phones—the house phone—rang. It was a Dallas phone number he did not recognize. The name read *Private Caller*. His first inclination was to ignore it, let it go to voice mail. If Sheila had been with him, safe and sound in the guest room he'd prepared for her, he would've done so without hesitation. Current circumstances demanded otherwise, however.

"Hello?"

"Jason Hammond, please." It was an elderly male, but his voice had a surprisingly energetic, even forceful quality. It also possessed a gentle Southern accent that was not altogether unpleasant.

"I'm sorry; Mr. Hammond isn't here at the moment. May I—?"

"Then I'd like to speak with Noah Gwynn."

"This is he. How—?"

"My name is Henry Moore. I'm Sheila Baker's attorney."

Noah scanned his memory but could recall no mention of such a person by either Sheila or Jason. It was entirely plausible that she had retained legal counsel following her mother's death. But anyone could have learned about that. It was not beyond imagination that the caller was another reporter sniffing around for details. Noah had experienced enough of their odious tactics in the last few days to believe anything was possible.

". . . concerning my client."

"I'm sorry," Noah said. "What was that?"

"I need all the information you have concerning my client."

"Unfortunately I can't say I have any recollection of Sheila mentioning—"

"Do not stonewall me, Mr. Gwynn," Moore said, firing it back so rapidly that it was obvious he had anticipated resistance. "I have known Sheila Baker since the day she was born, and I knew her folks long before that. I helped her daddy set up his first business. I managed the fund that put Sheila through college. And I was the executor for her mama's estate after she passed. One of the tasks I performed in that capacity—" this came out particularly inflected: *cuh-paa-sih-TEE*—"was to give Sheila the key to a safe-deposit box that

272

her mama opened in 1976. Now I see on the news that my girl has disappeared and is possibly the victim of a kidnapping. And this after romping around the country with your Mr. Hammond. Can I assume all this has to do with what she found in that box?"

"Well, I—"

"I want to be clear here, Mr. Gwynn. I will not hesitate to open litigation if I feel it warranted. And make no mistake, I know more about the law than any of your high-priced hotshots. Now, I'll ask you again—does this have anything to do with what she found in that safe-deposit box?"

"Yes, it does."

"And would you kindly give me all the information you have so I can begin making inquiries on my end? Time is not to be wasted here."

Noah tried to find further reason to be doubtful, but nothing came. If this person was in fact a reporter, he would've served humanity better in the movie business. But he wasn't, and Noah knew it. Time and age and the wisdom of experience had taught him to recognize the ring of truth when he heard it. *And he's right—time is not to be wasted. On that point there can be no argument.*

He took a deep breath and began at the beginning. And this time, he left out nothing.

30

THE OLD WORLD colonization of Cuba began in the early 1500s with the Spanish, who built villages around the natural inlet that is known today as Havana Harbor. It soon became a stopping point for weary travelers sailing under Spain's flag, as well as a shipbuilding center and something of a treasury.

As this original configuration of Havana—redubbed "Old" Havana centuries later—grew and prospered, so did its immigrant population. These early settlers then bore a generation that were not immigrants at all, that generation was eventually buried by its own kin, and Cuba was off and running. Villages became towns, and towns became cities, and the majority of new construction was fashioned after Spain's interpretation of architectural baroque. Facades featured bold and striking projections rendered in towers, colonnades, and balconies. There were high domes and ornate naves and sprawling courtyards. Civic planners often began a neighborhood with a central square, then moved outward in radiating lines via narrow cobbled pathways. The latter were intended to be traveled on foot, and thus most that remain are impassable by modern forms of transport.

These early influences remain in Old Havana to this day, although the years have exacted a heavy toll. Some of the original structures have collapsed and, with no serious inclination or available funds to rebuild them, exist now as piles of rubble. Others have enjoyed the benefits of renovation to varying degrees. This has occurred not only because of a love of their beauty and respect for their heritage but also to make them safe for continued use. Many have been recast in the pastel colors so loved by the Cuban people. But even these have succumbed to harsh weather and lack of vigilance, making them appear like the ruins of a more prosperous time.

Perhaps the most curious facet of Old Havana's urban landscape, one that seems to stand in unresolved contrast to its beautiful if crumbling architecture, is the ubiquitous presence of preembargo U.S. vehicles—swollen old Chevys, fin-tailed Fords, and sturdy, confident Oldsmobiles. These stand as evidence of an age when Cuba was viewed by a generation of Americans as a vacationer's paradise, a Caribbean pearl gleaming with the lure of cheap liquor, exotic women, postcard beaches, and a bustling casino industry run by unseen entities who made sure everyone had a good time while keeping the proper authorities fat and happy on a clandestine payroll. In the decades since the feud between Kennedy and Castro, a few of these vintage vehicles have been lovingly maintained in a near-pristine state. Most, however, are faded and pitiable relics, held together by body filler, random household items, and the irresistible force of economic necessity.

Walking down an uneven sidewalk lit by weak sodium lights, Hammond passed one of these exhausted classics, a '52 Chevy Deluxe badly in need of a paint job. A young couple in the front seat doing what young couples have done since time immemorial took no notice of him. He strode wearily by and turned down an alleyway that had a stream of water running down its spine. Some of the doors and windows on either side were shuttered by iron gates as if to confirm after-hours criminal activity in this narrow corridor. Others gave no such evidence—a few of the windows stood open and had colorful flower boxes attached to the sills, and clothes had been hung out to dry on poles secured by electrical wire. One dwelling appeared to be freshly painted, whereas another had been gutted so completely that the doorways and window frames looked like empty eye sockets.

Hammond took no more interest in these details than he had the amorous couple in the car. Every muscle ached, every joint was sore, and his head throbbed with frustration and anger. He had spoken to nearly forty people so far, yet the amount of solid information he had gathered on Olivero Clemente wasn't enough to fill one side of an index card. He had been polite, had spread some money around, but no one was talking.

These people knew who Clemente was; of that he was certain. But they were feeling protective, like they were all members of the man's personal security detail. Hammond was keeping notes and had already encountered several examples of blatant misinformation. The lead he was following now had sounded promising, as they all did at first—a tip from a punky-looking kid who said he knew a bartender who could tell Hammond everything he wanted to know. The bartender's name was disseminated for twenty dollars. It cost Hammond another ten for directions to his place of employment.

He emerged from the alleyway into a tiny courtyard. Several structures surrounded it, all in apparently operable condition. There was a neoclassical fountain in the center that looked as though it hadn't functioned in ages. There were more people here too. A middle-aged couple enjoyed each other's company at a candlelit café table under an archway, the man leaning back smoking a cigar, the woman holding a glass of wine. On the opposite side of the courtyard, two sun-leathered men sat on upturned crates, hunched over a game of chess, the board on a crate of its own. And there were children, in spite of the lateness of the hour, running around the fountain clad only in ratty cargo shorts, the outlines of their ribs clearly visible against the smooth brown of their skin.

It took Hammond several moments to figure out which of the buildings housed the bar. The absence of posted address numbers only heightened his irritation, as did the fact that advertising of any kind was forbidden in this country. The only way you really knew what was where was by living here. Since he didn't meet that criteria, logistics made even the most basic tasks tiresome. He wondered how a person could hope to accomplish anything in such a deliberately halting society.

His destination, he finally determined, was a three-story building that looked like something out of an old spaghetti western. The triple-arched front porch supported a large balcony occupied by more café tables and more young couples unafraid to display their affections in public. The women wore bright salsa dresses, the men tight black pants and white silk shirts with broad-wing collars. Behind them stood a pair of open doors, and beyond that a formerly elegant dance hall now served as a discotheque. Hammond could not see this, but he could hear the pounding beat of Latin-flavored hip-hop and could see the swirling lights.

As he approached, one of the young men began hurling expletives down. The girlfriend, perched on his lap, giggled and kissed him on the cheek. Hammond heard and understood every word but offered no response. The idiot was still crowing when Hammond went up the three brief steps and pulled the screen door open.

The bar's interior possessed as much character as the town around it. The carpet, still beautifully patterned in spite of being worn shiny, led to a long bar built from a dark and handsome wood of some exotic variety. The mirror behind it had become so aged that it offered no more than a pensive reflection. Crystal chandeliers hung from a high ceiling that had been smoke-cured to an inconsistent light brown. In the back, a spiral staircase ran up to the discotheque. Hammond could still hear the music through the ceiling, albeit in a mercifully muted form. It was further smothered by the more civilized *danzón* music that drifted through a handful of large and strategically spaced speakers on this floor.

The crowd here was older than the adolescent herd upstairs. The men wore Panama hats to conceal their retreating hairlines; the women wore dresses that wrapped around their increasingly plump frames and makeup that, along with the poor lighting, made them almost desirable again. Some patrons were already thoroughly drunk, others well on their way. A few heads turned when Hammond entered, but most paid him no mind. The fact that there were other customers of Caucasian lineage was a contributing factor. This was something Hammond had also read about in his guides—American citizens who visited Cuba illegally, traveling through third-party countries and making sure their passports weren't stamped by Cuban authorities, all to take advantage of the tropical clime, easy companionship, and perpetually desperate economy.

Hammond found an unoccupied sliver of space at the bar and wedged himself in. A very young bartender, looking more respectable than any of his kin with slicked-back hair and a smart red vest, approached.

"Qué se le ofrece?" What would you like?

"Una Coca-Cola, por favor."

Some heads turned, and the boy paused. The confusion printed on his face seemed to say, *You mean, without alcohol?*

As if to clarify, Hammond added, *"En una lata o una botella, no abierta."* In a can or bottle, unopened. He didn't particularly like soda, but he liked alcohol even less and had no intention of drinking anything that required tap water.

The bartender gave a stoic nod and squidged off down the rubber mat. While he was gone, Hammond spotted the person he was looking for. At the other end, leaning on one elbow and chatting with customers, was a man in his early sixties. He was heavy around the waist and had dark hair that was too fine to control in such a humid environment; it ran in every direction. Like his young coworker, he was clad almost regally in pressed black pants, a white shirt, and a red vest with gold buttons. But the most arresting feature by far was the dark patch that covered his right eye.

His younger colleague reappeared and set down the Coke, which came in a frosted can, along with a ridiculously small glass half-filled with ice.

"How much?" Hammond asked, continuing with his excellent Spanish.

"One," came the reply, along with a raised finger.

Hammond removed a five from his pocket and set it down, watching the boy's face. There was an instant—fleeting but detectable—when the kid's eyes widened at the sight of American currency.

"You can keep the rest," Hammond said, "but please do me one favor. The gentleman down there, with the eye patch. Would you ask him to come over here?"

The boy nodded and snatched up the bill. When the

older bartender turned to appraise Hammond, the person he'd been speaking with—a man of remarkable bulk—leaned over to get a look at Hammond for himself. Neither of them projected a particularly welcoming deportment. The bartender tossed one last remark to his friend, then pushed himself away and came forward at a leisurely pace.

Upon his arrival, he set his hands well apart on the bar and said, *"Qué quiere?" What do you want?*

"Information," Hammond said. He had reached into his pocket and taken out another folded bill—a ten this time.

The bartender's good eye gave the note only the briefest acknowledgment. It was an impressive display of self-control when one considered the average salary in Cuba was about less than twenty dollars per month. "What information, exactly?"

Hammond reached in again and took out a third bill—a twenty. This was shown in a flash, almost like a magician's trick, then laid over the ten and kept under his palm.

Again, the man seemed unmoved.

"I'm looking for someone."

The bartender smiled. All the teeth were there, but it had been many years since they possessed their original color or positioning.

"Many people come in here looking for someone," he said.

"I doubt many come looking for this one. His name is Olivero Clemente."

This time there was a reaction, one that managed to be subtle and dramatic at the same time. The man's one eye narrowed while the eyebrow rose. The smile vanished, the mouth re-forming into a twisted expression of revulsion.

And the man leaned back slightly, as if he'd just detected an unpleasant odor.

Hammond had seen similar reactions earlier in the night. *He knows,* he thought. *The kid I paid was right—he knows Clemente, and he knows him well.*

"I have nothing to tell you."

"You're lying," Hammond said. It came out too quickly and with too much acid, but he was past the point of caring.

"What was that?"

"I know you know him. I was told by others that you would know about him, know where I could find him. I insist that you tell me."

There was a brief pause in their volley, during which the bartender gave Hammond a look of incredulity that said, *Are you serious?* Then he smiled again. "Good-bye, *señor,*" he said and began to turn away.

Hammond reached over and grabbed him, a move so abrupt that several people gasped. The bartender turned back, clearly shocked, looking first at the hand holding him and then at its owner. The mountainous figure of a man that he had been speaking with earlier rose from his stool at the other end of the bar. Hammond was aware of this and of the fact that he was even larger than originally estimated.

"It is most important that I speak with him," Hammond said in a low, steady tone. "It may be a matter of life and death."

He released the bartender and went yet again to his pocket. His hand revealed five twenties this time, all neatly folded into little rectangles. It had occurred to him on the trip down that he should also bring a supply of fifties and hundreds, feeling they would be dazzling enough in their mere appearance to loosen even the tightest lips. But the guides had corrected his instincts—it was nearly impossible to change out American bills of such denominations.

He pressed the twenties into the bartender's hand. "Please, *señor*, whatever information you can give me . . ."

The recipient stared at the money for a moment, almost as if unable to believe it was really there, then deposited it in his own pocket and leaned in close.

Hammond's heart began pounding. *Here it comes.*

"It is you who may find yourself in a life-and-death situation," the bartender whispered, "if you do not forget about this man."

Hammond's face darkened with fury; he struggled against an instant, blinding-hot desire to physically harm another human being. Then a hand fell on his shoulder. He fully expected to find the monstrosity from the other side of the bar behind him. When he looked back, however, he found another kid, early twenties, with peach fuzz around his mouth and a lean, muscular body that was kept well displayed in a tank top one size too small.

The ten-ton beast was there too, standing just behind the kid. "It's time for you to go," he said. There were others, too. *An insta-gang,* Hammond thought, and he noticed that the rest of the patrons were giving them a wide berth.

He looked back at the bartender and said, *"No disimule."* *Stop pretending.* Then he felt the tip of a blade poke into the flesh of his lower back.

"Vamos," the kid said. *Let's go.* The rum on his hot breath blended pungently with the reek of his unwashed body.

"Desaparécete," Hammond replied without turning. *Get lost.*

He was jerked away from the bar, arms slithering around him like tentacles. People began moving back, clearing a space for what would come next. Some lingered, eager to see. Others went off to find new stations, indifferent to what was obviously a common occurrence here.

Amid the growing cheers, the ten-ton beast came forward and swung his cannonball fist into Hammond's gut. Hammond doubled over with a groan, but since he was being held tight, he did not go down. His attacker moved in again and used a knee to deliver the second shot—to his face. Stars exploded in Hammond's brain, and blood began running warmly out his nose and down his chin. The third blow, a punch to the jaw, felt like a cinder block. Hammond was released and allowed to drop to the floor. Dazed and breathless, he remained flat on his stomach as the crowd laughed and pelted him with obscenities. He struggled onto all fours and watched the blood drip onto the carpet. Finally he got to his feet. The bartender with the eye patch was still there, his face impassive.

The kid with the knife came behind once again. "Now, let me show you to the door."

"I know where it is," Hammond shot back, grabbing a pile of napkins from the bar and pressing them against his nose. He pushed his way out and cut through the courtyard with long strides as the delinquents on the balcony began berating him again. One took a lime from his drink and tossed it down, where it missed its target by no more than a foot and bounced away.

* * *

On the floor above the balcony, through the louvered shade of a private room, a pair of eyes followed Hammond as he went around the dead fountain, reached the mouth of the alley, and disappeared.

31

STANDING IN FRONT of his dresser mirror, Rydell tried again to get his tie just right. This was the third attempt, and after feeding it through the knot and pulling it down, he felt his blood pressure surge as the front flap fell two inches short of the narrow strip in the back.

He undid it in a mad flurry and whipped it onto the floor, cursing vividly. Then he took several deep breaths and sat on the edge of the bed. The sheets were in a swirled mess behind him. It was a rare morning when Rydell left his bed unmade, but then it was rare for the sheets to have been twisted into such a state in the first place. He was a sound sleeper who barely moved during the night. He'd had mornings when he literally peeled the sheets back, got up, and with a single motion returned them to a made position.

Last night had been a very different affair, maybe one of the least restful nights of his life. He'd lain there for hours, eyes aimed at the ceiling, replaying Sheila Baker's answers over and over in his mind. Each was more chilling than the last, thrusting lancets of fear into his eroding psyche. *They have all the pieces of the puzzle now. All they need to do is locate the man who can put them together.* He wondered again if

Galeno Clemente was really still alive, still out there some-where. Even if he wasn't, what about the brother? Surely Hammond would find him. How much did *he* know? Some of it? All of it? *Hammond is the key. You have to act, and you know what needs to be done. There are no remaining options.*

He rose from the bed and scooped up the tie, and his thoughts flowed back to the woman. He was deeply relieved he had retracted the green light for Birk to eliminate her. The man had all but begged, but Rydell had said to hold off and simply mind her for a while. Rydell's intuition had told him she might still have some value. That had turned out to be most prescient, as half the nation was now trying to figure out where she was. If Birk had slipped up and Baker's body had been found somewhere . . . that could've been a problem.

Rydell began working on the tie again. *Take care of Hammond,* the voice in his mind pressed, *and you'll be in the clear.* He wasn't even certain he wholeheartedly believed this, but what else was there to do?

When the tie came together at last, he relocated to the kitchen and made a pot of coffee. He had never been particu-larly fond of it, but he knew he'd have no chance of getting through this day without at least one cup. He checked his watch—7:04. *Still plenty of time.* He downed the cup in three gulps, then went into his den and got behind his desk. The e-mail address he needed was on his personal computer, buried in an invisible folder and then a password-protected file. He hadn't used it or even thought about the owner of it in years.

He prayed it was still valid.

* * *

Police Chief Gilberto Diaz sat behind his antique desk fill-ing out paperwork when a knock came at the door. He was dressed impeccably, as always, in his Policía Nacional Revolucionaria uniform—short-sleeved gray shirt with epaulets, dark cotton trousers, and patent-leather jackboots. A matching black beret with insignia sat off to the side of his desk, along with his sidearm. He looked starched and clear-eyed, every hair in place. He was only four years shy of sixty, yet his stately gray mane was thick and lush and exhibited no signs of diminishing. It seemed the perfect metaphor for everything else about the man, whose unblemished complexion and full frame seemed to radiate health and vigor.

He called out, and the door opened. The two men who walked in were junior officers, each on the force less than a year. They patrolled the central region of Matanzas, in the area around the Palacio de Junco. It was not uncommon for writers, musicians, painters, and other creative types to gather there and commiserate about the government's limitations on their respective crafts. One individual in particular, a homeless and streetwise poet named Enrique Sardina, had crystallized into a natural agitator, stirring up the kind of passions the Cuban government worked so hard to smother. Diaz had sent these two officers to bring him in for questioning and, his answers notwithstanding, incarceration.

Diaz stood and walked around to the front of his desk, a sheaf of papers and a pen held in the same hand. *"En qué puedo ayudarlos?"* he asked, smiling. *What can I help you with?*

The men exchanged nervous glances. Then one said balefully, *"Lo localizaron hace una hora."* *He was spotted an hour ago.*

"And?"

"And we pursued him . . . but he got away."

Diaz looked from one to the other, his eyes giving no indication as to the thoughts that lay behind them.

"We apologize," the second officer said sheepishly. They

bowed their heads toward the checkerboard-tile floor, the shame like a rash on their faces.

"Well, it is disappointing," Diaz told them, his smile retreating only slightly, "but it is the way it goes sometimes. I have every confidence you will secure his capture tomorrow or the next day."

Their astonishment was as plain as the fear had been a moment earlier. The younger of the two, an adolescent-looking boy named Javier whom Diaz had recruited personally, stared at the man with worshipful adoration.

"We will, sir," he said, snapping to attention. "You will be pleased."

"I'm sure I will. All right, you are both dismissed."

"Thank you, sir," they said in unison, then strode out with military stiffness.

They are in awe of me, Diaz thought as he walked back to his chair. *All of the boys.* And this was the truth—all the officers under his direct command, most of them still in their twenties, treated him with the kind of easy, willful respect that only came from true affection. The secret, he had told himself a thousand times, was to give a little every now and then, loosen the leash. So many of his equals did not understand this. Cracking the whip every moment of the day might be an alternative method of harvesting respect, but it was respect of the anemic, fear-based variety, and that usually came back to haunt you. If you made the effort to show a little kindness, you never had to worry about having your throat cut. Even with those above him, from his bosses at the Ministry of the Interior to friends he had made through the years at the Council of State, he had always known when to push forward and when to pull back. The real key to his survival, however, had been the simple fact that he went out of his way not to make enemies.

He got behind his desk, spent another half hour on paperwork, then turned to his computer. It was a somewhat-outdated system, at least five years behind the latest models in offices across America. Still, having one of his own made him part of a very tiny Cuban minority. He opened his e-mail program and waited. All messages would be filtered through the ministry even though most were part of the nation's Intranet; very few came from outside. Eleven appeared on the screen, most from senders he immediately recognized. One did not look familiar but, judging by the subject line, was part of a mass mailing from some ambitious bureaucrat in the ministry trying to splash his name around.

It was the last one that gave him a jolt. It appeared to be spam—*American* spam—from a furniture store that was going out of business. *Impossible.* Such a thing would never clear the government's filters. Then Diaz realized what it truly was, and his large mouth dropped open.

"No," he mumbled, guiding the cursor toward it. "It can't be. . . ." He clicked on the message, read it from top to bottom, and said, "No" one more time. Every function in his body felt as though it had ceased.

There was a phone number embedded in the ad. Diaz was amazed that he remembered how to decode it after all these years. He did not write it down but rather committed it to memory in his reeling, overwhelmed mind.

Then he rose and hurried out.

• • •

The tiny white Peugeot—standard issue among Cuban police—zipped through the rain-soaked Matanzas streets, its blue light turned off but its radio antenna waving crazily. Diaz went down a narrow corridor to a construction site that had been abandoned two years earlier. The crude wooden fence that surrounded it was covered with political graffiti, including a DayGlo rendering of Che Guevara over the motto *"Hasta la Victoria, Siempre!" Until the Victory, Always!*

Diaz parked between the fence and a rusting Dumpster on the south side, well out of view. Removing his cell phone, he licked his lips and dialed the number. It was answered immediately.

"Tardó mucho en llamar," the voice on the other end told him. *You took too long to call.*

"Estaba en mi oficina y tuve que salir," Diaz replied. *I was in my office and had to leave.* "What is it you want?"

"Your services are required."

A shudder went through him—this was precisely what he didn't want to hear. *No, please. . . .* He was still having trouble believing the conversation was even taking place. It had been more than eight years since he last heard from this man, whose name was still unknown to him. He had prayed—literally, on his knees, alongside his wife and children during their own entreaties—that the man had died somewhere along the way. The fact that he was there now, alive and well, was the manifestation of a thousand nightmares. "I thought we agreed last time that my services were no longer available. I thought it was understood that the last time would, in fact, be the last time."

"We dictate the rules where your services are concerned," the man replied. "We do not have them dictated to us."

"And if I don't cooperate?"

"This is a waste of time. You will cooperate because you want to keep your home, your family, and your job. A job that you would not possess if not for us. Have you forgotten that the position only became open because the man who occupied it before you—a man who, if memory serves, passionately disliked you—conveniently died of a heart attack in spite of having a clean bill of health? You owe us on that alone, wouldn't you agree?"

Diaz did not reply.

"Today you are the revered head of one of your nation's most able police forces. The men under you would follow you off a cliff, and those over you believe your dedication to the revolution is absolute. I wonder, then, what would result if word got out about your past efforts to bring that same cause to ruin? If they knew, for example, of your part in the plot to assassinate three of your leader's most trusted ministers in the spring of 1992? Or your facilitation of domestic protests two years later? Or, for that matter, the sheer volume of intelligence you have provided to my country over the course of—"

"All right, all right," Diaz said, undoing the top button of his shirt. "You have made your point. I was a different man then. I was trying to survive."

"Don't insult me. You were selling yourself to the highest bidder. You know nothing about loyalty. Whoever provides you with the means to reach the next step on the ladder is your master."

Diaz felt sick to his stomach. So much about this man was coming back to him. *He can see straight into a person's soul.* "Just tell me what you want," he said in a whisper.

"You will get in touch with some of your friends in Old Havana. Some of your friends from . . . your earlier days."

Breathing was becoming difficult now. Diaz put a hand on his chest. "For what purpose?"

• • •

Rydell told him.

32

DAVID VOIGHT stepped out of a conference room in the U.S. Department of Justice and closed the door gently so as not to disturb those who remained inside. An anonymous woman who worked elsewhere in the vast universe of this million-plus-square-foot building walked by. Voight mouthed a silent hello, then set off down the long corridor. He was in his early fifties, of slight frame, with steel-rimmed glasses and dark hair combed in the same respectable style he'd had since prep school. He wore his usual dark suit and tie and carried a leather portfolio in the crook of his arm.

He moved in a measured, purposeful stride, his leather shoes squeaking on the polished marble floor. When he started here six years ago, the noisy steps reminded him of his beloved basketball games at Cornell. But he was a veteran of the job now and barely noticed anymore. Like the hundreds of other federal prosecutors who worked in D.C., he had too much on his mind every day.

He turned left and started down a ridiculously wide staircase; his office was three floors below. He never took the elevator; the steps were healthier. He was in terrific shape for his age and had every intention of staying that way. His father had been a boozer and a smoker and cashed out at the age of sixty-two, leaving David, his sister, and his mother nearly destitute. There was no way he was going to pass that legacy to his own wife and children. He felt great and never failed to thank God for it.

He reached the last step and turned right, down a carpeted hallway. At the far end, in front of his door, he spotted a man sitting on the sofa in the waiting area. At this distance, he could only determine that the man had gray hair and was wearing a tan overcoat. His first thought was that it was someone from the U.S. Immigration and Customs Enforcement office. He'd been going several rounds with them lately, and they'd been sending people nonstop. Most came without an appointment, and his secretary had been making them wait in the hall as a kind of punishment.

As Voight drew closer, however, something about the stranger seemed familiar. Full recognition struck when the man realized he was being approached and turned.

"Oh, my goodness," Voight said, a smile spreading across his face. "Can it really be?"

Henry Moore stood, wiped the wrinkles off his coat, and held out a hand. "Hello, David."

"Mr. Moore . . ." Voight still could not bring himself to refer to the man by his first name in spite of Moore's repeated urgings over the years. It just didn't seem appropriate where former teachers were concerned. "I can't believe this," he said. "My secretary gave me your message, and I was going to get back to you this evening, from home. I didn't know you were in the area."

"I wasn't," Moore replied. "I flew in this morning. I haven't even been to my hotel yet."

Voight's brow furrowed. "I'm sorry; you . . . you weren't in town when you called?"

Moore shook his head. "No. Look, David, I need your help, and I need it very quickly."

Voight suddenly realized something—Moore hadn't smiled back, hadn't asked him how his folks were doing, hadn't cracked one of his characteristically lame jokes. There was no geniality to the man. True, there were times when he could be bearish, particularly when he went into one of his tirades about the eroding ethics of the legal profession, tirades that Voight secretly held dear to his heart when he had been formulating his own career. But there was always that underlying paternalistic kindness that endeared him not only to the much younger David Voight but to just about every one of David's classmates as well. That warmth was absent now, replaced by an unsettling nervousness that Voight had never seen before. "Is there something wrong?"

"Yes, there is." Moore looked up and down the hallway. Then, evidently estimating that there were just too many people coming and going, he took Voight by the crook of the arm and led him gently forward. "Have you been following the stories in the news about this Jason Hammond fellow and the Kennedy assassination?"

"I've heard about it, although I haven't been watching closely. Someone independently reinvestigates that case every week or so, and the government always ends up the bad guy. If I took the time to address every single accusation in that regard, I'd never—"

"It's all true," Moore said, turning to face him. They had reached an elevator atrium where there was no one else in sight. "Every word of it. This Hammond is onto something."

Voight stared at his old teacher with a touch of concern.

"I'm not losing my mind, David, if that's what you're wondering. Don't think all this snow on the roof means I've gone soft up there too."

The tiniest hint of a smile returned to Voight's mouth. It wasn't that he was reassured by the comment but rather that he found the folksy metaphor amusing. It was a welcome glimpse of the Henry Moore he had always known.

A herd of young lawyers, all without jackets, ambled by. They glanced curiously at the conversation taking place between Counselor Voight and some guy none of them recognized.

Moore waited until they passed, then led Voight into one of the waiting elevators. Once the doors closed, he said, "You know the girl Hammond is with? Sheila Baker?"

"I knew there was a woman involved. I didn't know her name."

"She's a client of mine."

"No."

"She is. I was her parents' attorney for years, long before she was even around."

"Okay . . . ?"

"When her mother passed away, she left behind a key to a safe-deposit box that she opened in 1976. And do you know what was in it? A film she made of the shooting while she was standing in Dealey Plaza."

"You . . . No. Mr. Moore, tell me you're not serious."

"Dead serious. She kept it a secret for the better part of half a century. Thousands of people have been looking for it. She was known as the Babushka Lady. I went on my computer and looked at the pictures of her standing there. It's her, all right. I'm positive."

Voight struggled to get his mind around the massive

reality of this. "Well . . . okay. That's incredible. I mean, I won't argue that that's incredible. But why are you telling *me*?"

"Because Sheila Baker has been kidnapped, and someone in the government is behind it."

"Excuse me?"

"I've talked to Hammond's people in New Hampshire. I had to threaten them with a lawsuit, but they told me everything. When Sheila first discovered the film, she contacted Hammond because she was scared and didn't know what else to do. She wanted to give it to Hammond and have him take care of it. But then someone else found out she had it too—someone who was able to keep her mama under surveillance all these years just in case the film turned up in her possession. As soon as it did, a gunman was hired to try to eliminate the daughter."

"That doesn't necessarily mean—"

"The killer blew Sheila's mother's house apart by staging a gas leak. I saw the wreckage myself. And then the guy murdered a professor from Southern Methodist, an expert on the Kennedy assassination, who'd been helping Hammond. Apparently he had also been under surveillance for some time. Now this same lunatic has kidnapped Sheila. He grabbed her while she was on a train from D.C. to Boston. I've seen the security film from the station in Delaware. That's where he got her."

Voight was shaking his head. "I . . . I just don't know what to say."

"Who else could coordinate such an effort, David? Who else would have the power, the resources, or the motive?"

"What's on the film that could've triggered all this?"

"A second gunman."

Voight would remember the moment—Moore's simple delivery of information that would send a tremor across the world when it became public—for the rest of his life. "That's unbelievable."

"I said the same thing until I saw the images myself. Hammond converted the film into a digital file some time ago. The second gunman doesn't actually fire a shot. But he's plainly visible with his weapon."

"Where?"

"In the storm drain on Elm Street. Margaret Baker's camera was the only one that caught him."

Voight's mind was swirling now. The enormity of it all, the implications . . .

". . . on this."

"What? I'm sorry."

"I'm asking you to act on this and to do it immediately. Sheila Baker is being held against her will by someone in this government. I'd bet my reputation on it. I'm asking you to launch an investigation right away. She has to be found."

The residue of doubt still clung to Voight's thoughts, but it was eroding rapidly. He had known Henry Moore too long, had become too convinced of his thoroughness and seriousness, to go on thinking this was folly. If Moore believed some hidden entity in the government was involved, then Voight would treat it as fact. "Do you have the film with you? Or at least do you have access to it?"

"It's on my cell phone."

Voight reached over and poked the button that would take the elevator to the top floor.

"Where are we headed?" Moore asked.

"To see the attorney general."

33

HAMMOND LEFT the sidewalk and turned down a quiet corridor between two small apartment buildings. His untucked silk shirt fluttered as a welcome breeze blew through the crushingly hot morning. Stopping at the steps of a service entrance, he guided himself into a sitting position like an arthritic old man. His eyes were red and watery, the lids impossibly heavy. He was badly in need of a shave. And he could not halt the tremor in his hands—a sign that he was short on both nutrition and rest. His nose had not been broken the night before, but it had swollen a bit and still throbbed like mad. Two teeth had been loosened. Above all else, though, he prayed he hadn't suffered a concussion. His head was still pounding, but it was hard to take particular notice of it when everything else ached too.

He leaned against the wall even though it was filthy, as were the steps, the tiny landing at the top, and the weather-beaten door. He took several deep breaths, staring forward with a dead man's gaze. A child's inflatable ball, strikingly red in contrast to the dull tones of its surroundings, rolled by. It was chased by a boy of no more than five or six, deeply tanned with a cherubic grin. Neither the child nor Hammond took much notice of the other.

Hammond removed a notepad from his breast pocket. He flipped to the first page and reviewed the entries. Each one, rendered in his careful print, had been crossed out. Same with those on the next page and the next. The cancellation lines had become progressively darker and deeper as his frustration grew. He'd spoken with nearly sixty people, given out more than five hundred dollars, and believed he was no closer to finding Olivero Clemente than before. He hadn't paid for information, he now realized. He had paid for *mis*information. Every person with whom he'd spoken had been deceptive. For all he knew, he had already walked past Clemente's home, maybe more than once. He was becoming familiar with the area through sheer repetition, learning the lay of the land. But he wasn't learning what he needed to know most.

He put the pad away, pulled up his knees, and set his head down on his arms. Everything ached: every bone, every muscle, every tendon. He had never felt so used up. He'd had trouble sleeping again, and not just because of the physical pain or the dreams. The call and ensuing legal threats from Henry Moore had rattled him. Moore, Noah reported, clearly did not think much of what he called Hammond's "reckless hobby." That hurt for reasons Hammond still didn't fully understand, although it nagged at him. No progress had been made where Sheila was concerned either.

Every time Hammond thought about this, he felt sick to his stomach. No, he rationalized, he wasn't the one who kidnapped her. Nor was he the one who blew her house to pieces or tried to shoot them both. *But am I responsible for all of it nevertheless?* It was this moral question that plagued him, and when he finally felt as though he was approaching an answer, he backed away from it simply because it wasn't one he could live with. *Yes, you are. If you had insisted she go to New Hampshire on the first day, she would still be there and still be safe.* And what of Ben Burdick? Every time the guilt started eating into him about Sheila, thoughts of Ben came in tandem. *Gone forever. And before you reentered his life . . . maybe he was a wreck of his former self, but at least he was alive.*

He tried to drive it all out of his mind. He'd done this many times before but could never sustain it. The guilt kept hammering away. *Maybe it really is time to give up,* he thought. He was coming unglued both physically and emotionally. Sheila was missing; Ben was dead. There were people in government, both good and bad, ready to pounce on him as soon as they had the chance. There was also Sheila's lawyer, who had him in his crosshairs and was madder than a rattlesnake.

And he was no longer making progress. The trail—if it could really be called that, in light of Moore's opinion of his pursuits—had gone cold.

Hammond closed his eyes and began to piece together an exit strategy. The first step would be to go back to the hotel, pack his belongings, and wait until sundown. *Then I'll call Noah and make my way back to the boat. After that, I'll have to—*

The church bells that suddenly began ringing in the distance caught his attention not because of their ethereal beauty but because they sounded hauntingly similar to those in the church where he used to attend services less than a mile from his family estate. In fact, Hammond realized with a chill, they were identical.

His head came up, the eyelids peeling apart, and he tried to pinpoint the source. It certainly wasn't far. He got to his feet somewhat clumsily and resumed his route down the alley. By the time he reached the end, the bells had stopped. Two blocks farther on, however, he saw a tiny cathedral that stood alone at the end of a weedy, spider-cracked parking lot. It was a boxlike structure made of white sandstone that had become grimed by age and neglect. There were two red doors set into a broad archway and a three-segmented bell tower with a gold crucifix on top. He stopped at the front, wondering if the place hadn't been altogether abandoned. Then he saw that the door on the right was open a crack. He pulled it the rest of the way open, the hinges groaning, and stepped inside. The door eased to a close, enveloping him in darkness.

The odors came first—ancient dust, tired wood, rotting books, and incense. Then, as his eyes adjusted, familiar shapes began to emerge. There was a pile of fraying hymnals stacked on a table. A once-beautiful tempera painting of Jesus hung at a forward angle, rippled by the tropical heat and discolored along the bottom by what appeared to be water damage.

He crossed slowly into the nave. The velvet carpet was worn to near transparency. Pews no longer possessed the luxury of uniformity, as many had undergone repairs of varying skill. Some of the chandeliers had broken shades, and most of the stained-glass windows had mismatching or altogether-colorless patch spots.

As he moved down the aisle, he thought about some of the people he'd seen since his arrival—not just those he'd spoken with but others he'd noted in passing. There was a group of boys playing volleyball in a street, the "net" nothing more than a length of rope. They were all alarmingly skinny, even for young boys. A tiny woman of great but indeterminate age had shuffled up to him, her withered features like the skin of a dried apple, and openly begged for money.

When Hammond gave her a twenty, she rubbed her cheek against the back of his hand like a servile dog. And his sadness toward the countless prostitutes who seemed to populate every street mellowed into pity when he was told by one of the taxi drivers that most of them were, in fact, college students in need of extra money—not for drugs or liquor, but for school supplies that the government failed to provide.

As he drew closer to the front of the church, he began to see things that weren't really there. The three polished caskets, lids still closed, resting on their wooden biers and surrounded by candles. In the far reaches of his mind, he wondered if he would ever be able to enter a church again without conjuring this image. In spite of it, he willed himself forward. Just like in the dreams, the lids began to open slowly, and the waterlogged corpses sat up and reached out to take hold of him. . . .

Then he was there, in front of the altar, in the precise spot where he stood each time the nightmare came to its violent end. He looked up at the huge crucifix suspended on two thin wires, gazed into the eyes of the suffering-Christ effigy.

Then a voice broke the silence. *"Puedo ayudarlo?" Can I help you?*

Hammond turned like a trapped thief. The man who stood there was small but well built and dressed in a priest's casual vestments. He was older but still appeared to possess much vitality. The cleric came forward, studying Hammond with benevolent curiosity.

"I apologize, Father," Hammond replied in Spanish. "I didn't mean to trespass."

"That is okay," the man said. His voice was so powerful and resonant that it seemed odd coming from someone of his size. "All are welcome here. I am Father Núñez."

He held out his hand, and Hammond took it. "I'm Jason Hammond."

Núñez nodded. "You are American."

"Yes. I am . . . visiting. I heard the bells and wanted to see what the church looked like inside."

Núñez's bushy eyebrows came together in puzzlement. "Bells? What do you mean?"

"The bells in the tower, I heard them just before. That's what led me here."

The priest seemed to consider the idea for a moment, then shook his head. "No bells have been rung today. They are only rung on Sundays, before mass."

Hammond couldn't decide if this man, whom he had never met before, was kidding or not. But Núñez's expression did not change, and Hammond intuited that he was not the type of person to joke about such things.

"The bells weren't ringing just a short time ago?"

"No. I would know this. I am the bell ringer here."

Hammond watched him for another moment in a final search for signs of trickery, then turned his eyes back to the massive wooden crucifix. "Is there another church in this area?"

Núñez laughed. "No, *señor*. It is hard enough keeping this one. My country's government is not exactly sympathetic, you understand."

Hammond nodded absently.

"Are you okay?"

"Hmm? Oh . . . sure."

"Why don't you sit down, and I will get you something cold to dr—"

"No, no. Thank you." Hammond turned and began walking away. "I'm sorry to have bothered you."

"Mr. Hammond, please," Núñez called out. "You do not need to go."

But Hammond did not turn around. He went out the door and crossed the parking lot without looking back.

• • •

He called Noah as soon as he left the church property to let him know the search was over. The older man tried to talk him into carrying on, but it was a halfhearted attempt, and they both knew it. The news from home hadn't changed. Still no word from the police, no word from Sheila herself—when Hammond finally conceded the fact she might already be dead, he had to struggle to keep from vomiting—and Henry Moore yelling into the phone every time Noah tried to talk to him.

Hammond took a few bites of a room-service sandwich, then slept until the dreams forced him awake. As soon as darkness fell, he jammed everything into his bag and went out. Thinking about the real-life nightmare that awaited him back in the States numbed him. After paying his bill in cash, he traversed the lobby of the Hotel Parque Central and exited through one of the side doors. He paused to make sure his phone was on and fully charged, then tucked it in his pocket and started toward the rear of the building, away from the traffic-clogged Neptuno Prado y Zulueta.

He reached the corner and crossed into a quiet residential neighborhood; the street noise from the heart of the city grew fainter with each step. Then, seemingly from nowhere, a stranger appeared. It was a young man of perhaps twenty-two or -three, dressed in dirty jeans and a plain T-shirt. He had a cigar box in his hands and was holding it up to Hammond, smiling eagerly.

"*Americano rico, mire, por favor. Esto es lo que quiere.*" *Please, wealthy American, look here. This is what you want.* He said this quietly and was being watchful of his surroundings.

Hammond had been offered contraband cigars several times before, along with a variety of liquor, narcotics, weapons, and cheaply pirated pressings of popular CDs and DVDs.

Without breaking his stride, Hammond tried to wave the kid away. "*No, no—déjeme en paz.*" *Leave me alone.*

"*No, esto es lo que quiere,*" his antagonist insisted. *This is what you want.* Then he added, "*Mire, por favor.*" *Please look.*

Hammond took a deep breath, stopped, and glanced at the box as the lid was lifted.

There were no cigars inside, but rather a note cast in fairly legible print—*I can take you to Olivero Clemente.*

Hammond studied the boy for a moment. "How much?" he asked, still in Spanish.

"One hundred," came the quick reply.

"How do I know you're not lying?"

The kid closed the box and held it at his side like a book. His eyes kept shifting about. "My mother and I live in the same apartment building. He rarely goes out, but we see him sometimes."

This had a ring of reality to it. But Hammond was still hesitant; he'd been fooled too many times. And he'd made a plan that he was in the process of executing; his mind was already moving in that direction. *On the other hand, the worst that can happen is the guy is lying and I'm out another hundred. No great loss.* If that turned out to be the case, he'd view it as nothing more than an annoying detour on the way back to the boat. *And there's always the chance he's not lying.*

Hammond had learned through experience that sooner or later, you usually encountered someone willing to talk.

He unbuttoned the back pocket of his cotton pants and pulled out a hundred-dollar bill. The kid's eyes just about sparkled when he saw it. While he paused to admire it, Hammond wondered where he'd be able to break it into smaller bills. The kid stuffed it into his own pocket and gestured with his finger. *"Vamos!"*

As they moved farther from the city center, the neighborhoods became increasingly run-down and depressing. The roads lost their pavement and became rutted trails of packed earth. Streetlights were dimmer and spaced at greater intervals. Most homes appeared to be unoccupied, many collapsed or just about to. Particularly unsettling was the fact that Hammond's guide seemed to be growing more nervous. Sometimes he would jerk his head left or right, but Hammond never saw anyone or anything to justify these reactions. He felt increasingly isolated, thoroughly detached from civilization. It occurred to him that he was walking through a completely forgotten section of the world. *And no one knows I'm here.*

They came to what appeared to be a park of sorts. There were dozens of dwarf trees arranged in concentric circles, their hanging fruit dried and rotting. Benches had been set in select locations, but they were badly dilapidated and unsuitable for use. There was also a statue in the center of the property—a generic Cuban farmer with a sickle on his shoulder and a proud, determined look on his face. *From the days when Cuba was floated by Russian welfare,* Hammond thought, making a point not to share this political commentary with his companion. *Another Communist experiment that didn't pan out.* The kid did not appear to take notice of the memorial, as if he'd been through here a million times.

Then he took off running. Hammond, instantly furious at being deceived again, shouted and began to pursue. Then the other two appeared—young men of about the same age but much greater size. In fact, Hammond saw with skyrocketing alarm, they were massive. They had been hiding behind two of the trees and were on him in an instant. Then the cigar salesman returned, emerging from the darkness as silently as he had the first time. The box was no longer in his hand but rather a long stiletto with a crude wooden handle.

He came forward and brought the blade up quick, stopping just as the tip pressed into the soft of Hammond's throat.

"Si te mueves estás muerto," he breathed into Hammond's face. *You move and you're dead.*

Hammond swore at him in English. The very thought that his audience couldn't understand him was satisfying in itself.

One of the muscle heads responded to this obstinacy by driving a fist into Hammond's stomach. He folded and went down. Then they were on him, their hands swarming greedily over his body. Stiletto man was on his knees a few feet away, digging through Hammond's bag. When they were certain his pockets had been emptied, all three began kicking him viciously. He tried to crawl away several times, only to be struck harder for his temerity. Then came a hard, metallic click, a sound he knew all too well.

He looked up to find one of the two monsters—he wasn't sure which—holding a gun inches from his head.

"I think we'll leave you here," the brute said, licking his lips with nervous pleasure.

Hammond stared hard at him, refusing to show any sign

of fear. He even smiled a little. There followed a moment, no more than a flicker, when the gunman first looked confused, then enraged. In that instant, Hammond knew he would at least be able to claim one small victory before his life came to an end.

The thug's mouth twisted into an animalistic snarl. Then a shot pierced the night air.

• • •

Hammond flinched at the sound of the report. What happened next surprised him—there was no pain, no suffering, no agony. Nothing at all. *So why do I hear screaming?*

When he looked around, two facts immediately presented themselves—the first was that he hadn't been struck, and the second was that the soulless beast who'd been holding the gun had. He now lay on the ground just inches away, writhing like a worm and screeching at the top of his lungs. Both hands were clamped to his thigh, blood flowing between the fingers.

The other two punks stood in a frozen panic, searching for the sniper. Another shot came, ripping into the upper part of the arm holding the stiletto. Hammond expected the skinny kid to start squawking like his colleague, but something else happened—he took one dazed look at the blood turning his sleeve red and fainted dead away.

The third delinquent wasn't interested in waiting around to discover what the shooter had in store for him; he turned and fled into the night. Then Hammond heard soft footsteps and saw the figure of a man develop from the darkness.

He was tall and lithe, moving with an almost-feminine grace. His garb was oddly formal—gray slacks and matching jacket and a black shirt open at the throat. It was the face, however, that commanded attention—a sailor's gray-flecked beard, the deeply carved lines that come only from decades of hard living, and the large, faultless eyes of a man not easily conned. One who saw everything and found most of it unworthy of further consideration.

He walked to the scene of the carnage he had created and stopped. The weapon he'd used—a Walther PPK—was held slack in his hand. When the thug who'd been shot through the thigh noticed him, he pushed himself halfway up and said something unrepeatable. The man responded by swinging the Walther under the kid's chin in one vicious blow, causing the punk to snap back, his arms flying almost comically over his head, before coming to rest in a jumbled heap. He did not move again.

The gunman went about the seemingly menial task of gathering up Hammond's belongings, placing them gingerly into his bag. Then he slung the bag over his shoulder and stood before its speechless owner.

"I am Olivero Clemente," he said plainly.

An electric charge went through Hammond; he hoped he didn't look as dumbfounded as he felt.

Clemente held out a hand to help him up. "Come," he said. "We cannot stay here long. Follow me."

34

FREDERICK RYDELL stood by the panoramic window in his office, hands deep in his pockets. He watched the busy evening activity on the street below with detachment. His office door was still closed even though Theresa had gone home hours ago and there was no one else out there. It was quiet now, almost peaceful; the only noise in the room came from the computer's exhaust fan. This serenity stood in stark contrast to the fact that he was experiencing one of the most miserable days of his life.

It began just minutes after his morning arrival, when he and nine others were called into an emergency meeting with Director Vallick. Rydell had never seen him so angry. *Apoplectic* was the word that came to mind, like the man was trying to push himself to a stroke. He had a pile of newspapers on his desk, each with a front-page story about how Hammond had new evidence in the Kennedy assassination and how Sheila Baker had been kidnapped as a result and how the government—supposedly the CIA in particular, most said—had something to do with her disappearance.

That's right, Vallick had said as the veins in his neck

bulged; the media was running with it now. And this attorney from Texas, Henry Moore, was stomping around like a madman. He had a friend in the Justice Department, and this friend had seen the evidence and felt justified calling in the attorney general of the United States. "One step below the president," Vallick raged, holding up a finger. *"One step!"* Now the FBI was involved. That meant a full-scale investigation into the CIA's role in the affair.

This was the point in the meeting where Vallick had gone cardiac. He took great pride in the way he had gradually but traceably improved the agency's reputation during his tenure. No more draconian tactics, no more arrogant disregard for legal boundaries, no more public embarrassments. He insisted that his people could do their jobs within honorable limits. He was realistic enough to know that ethical standards had to be softened from time to time, but he was determined to prove to the American populace that the agency's outlaw days were over. "I want full transparency and *total* cooperation from each of your departments," he barked. "If I hear so much as a peep from the bureau that someone is putting up roadblocks, I'm going to eat that person alive. Am I perfectly clear on this point?"

He finished by saying he planned to direct Justice to open a lawsuit against Jason Hammond if his accusations proved baseless—which, he added, he fully expected them to. "I will ruin that man," he screamed. He was throwing things when the attendees filed out of the office.

Just a few hours later, another dreaded call came from the other hothead in Rydell's life: the faceless phone screamer. He had been expecting it for days. He sat wordlessly in his chair and endured a historic tongue-lashing. They had lost faith in him, the caller said, believing he had now become more of a liability than an asset. Rydell stiffened as though caught in a cold wind. *A threat—an actual death threat from that madman.*

When the caller finally paused to take a breath, Rydell curtly informed him that Hammond and Baker had both been eliminated. This produced the most satisfying response imaginable—silence. Rydell then added another layer to the lie by saying the FBI investigation was nothing more than window dressing on Vallick's part to keep the public and the media placated. "He's throwing them a bone to chew on," Rydell said, amazed by the calm confidence of his tone. The man at the other end seemed to be buying all of it, and that was good. But it was only a temporary respite, Rydell knew. As much as he hated the man, he had never lied to him. But he'd had no choice this time; he needed the breathing room. The moment the call ended, however, he knew a clock had started ticking.

A full reevaluation of the situation was required then. The fundamental paradigm had changed. No—it was much more than that. *Everything* had changed, and all factors were working against him. As soon as his lie was noticed, he would become a target—and that was presuming the FBI didn't figure things out first. They hadn't come knocking yet, but they were on their way.

That made the situation with Sheila Baker a much bigger problem than before. He couldn't just set her free . . . but he couldn't just kill her either. There'd be a body. Even if Birk successfully disposed of it, there'd be a *missing* body.

And Birk was causing problems of his own. He was growing impatient, tired of his babysitting duties. He had no more narcotics to pump into his captive, and she kept making his life difficult. And then there was Hammond himself, the one who had caused all of this. America's "folk hero," valiant crusader of truth and justice . . . Rydell could not think of a person he hated more passionately. How the little slime ever got the best of him, he simply could not understand. Rydell's heart had sunk when he learned that the hit squad deployed by his Cuban contact, Diaz, had failed to take Hammond out, that some "mystery figure" had appeared at the last moment and thwarted the attempt. Now Hammond would go deeper underground than ever. He'd jump at every sound, dodge every shadow. And how much did he know now? Had he found the man he was looking for? And had that man named names? *Am I already living on borrowed time?*

On the street below, a middle-aged couple dressed as though they were attending the Academy Awards hailed a taxi. The man said something to the woman, and she laughed uproariously. Happy, everyday citizens on their way to dinner or the theater or wherever.

At that moment, Rydell experienced something for the first time in his life—the desire to trade places with an ordinary person. He would've given anything to be that man, young and handsome and probably wealthy, with an attractive woman at his side, on his way to some interesting place for a night of pleasure. Rydell had never been moved by life's conventional joys. Having dominion over people like that couple had always been his drug of choice. The ability to use them like chess pieces, to overthrow someone's existence with the stroke of a pen or a single command delivered through a telephone, to play the role of a deity from the safety of his office . . . that had been his oxygen.

His thoughts wandered again to his earliest years in the agency, when his elders regarded him as one of their brightest recruits and the future stretched out gloriously before him.

So young, so eager, so devoted—*and so clean. So very clean.*
Then he arrived at the same question that had been coming
to him for hours—*How did it come to this?*

A taxi arrived and whisked the couple off into the
night. Rydell watched the red taillights until they dwindled
to nothingness. Then he went about calculating all of his
options again. There was only one left, and he knew it. What
he was really doing was trying desperately to find another,
no matter how radical. But he could not, not anymore. The
developments of the day had forced him into a corner. And
like any other animal in that position, he had only one priority now—survival.

He took out his cell phone and went to his desk. The
hidden file he opened contained classified information that
was already known to several others in the agency. Rydell,
however, was not supposed to be one of them.

He dialed the number and waited. It wasn't answered until
the third ring, but Rydell did not dare scold the person on
the other end. He didn't know the man's name, background,
or location. He only knew his professional affiliation—leader
of a black-project team, more commonly known as "black
ops." This was the agency's ugliest stepchild, a living manifestation of plausible deniability. Extortion, espionage, traf-
ficking . . . and assassination. Vallick rarely spoke of them
and only utilized their services as a last resort. They were the
tool you kept in the back of the bottom drawer.

"Commander, this is Silver Shield." Rydell prayed the
name was still valid. The person to whom it had been
assigned was still actively employed, but the pseudonyms
changed from time to time.

After a pause that felt like hours, the voice on the other
end said, "Confirmation."

Rydell read off the twenty-digit alphanumeric code slowly and precisely.

"Accepted," came the machinelike response. "Mission summary."

Rydell swallowed into a throat that had suddenly gone very dry. "You will have multiple targets, in three separate locations," he said, "which will require the activation of other units. And you will have to complete your objective in less than twenty-four hours."

"Understood." This was said without the slightest hesitation. "Details."

"They are as follows. . . ."

Rydell spelled them out and repeated them once for clarity. Rolled into those details were three names, people who had been part of his life for what felt like an eternity. When he was finished, he was asked for final confirmation—the "go" code. Now it was his turn to pause. This was not because he did not have the sequence in front of him; it was there in plain black characters on the screen. But the magnitude of what he was about to do eclipsed all other thoughts. The illegality alone was staggering.

"Final confirmation," the faceless killer said one more time. There was a hint of impatience in his voice. If he had to make the request one more time, Rydell knew, the impatience would transform into suspicion.

Rydell took a deep breath as silently as possible, then methodically recited what he saw on the screen. It was one of the most surrealistic moments he would ever experience.

"Accepted," came the zombielike response. There was a single click and the line went dead.

No stopping it now, Rydell thought, his heart beating like a drum.

He put his phone away and closed the document. It was summarily discarded and the recycle bin emptied.

The next two hours were spent deleting similar files, then shredding physical documents that had been stored for years in a small safe by his refrigerator.

35

HAMMOND FOLLOWED Clemente for over an hour. In spite of his earlier conviction that he had already covered every inch of Old Havana, he did not recognize any of the routes they traversed. At times he felt like a mouse in a maze, moving along cramped cobblestoned roads and turning down narrow alleyways. He wasn't even certain they were still *in* Old Havana. One certainty that was unimpeachable, though, was that he should continue to exercise caution where his guide was concerned. Throughout the journey, he was careful to remain several paces behind him. Clemente, who had not uttered a single word since the park, did not seem worried.

They arrived at a soldierly line of low-rise apartment buildings, all of identically antiquated design and delineated only by color. Clemente went up the steps of the first, which was sky blue, and held the door open. "To the top," he instructed. The fluorescent bulbs in the stairwell buzzed mutedly, and the air reeked of plaster dust and wood varnish. On the top floor—the fifth—Hammond stood back to let Clemente pass. Clemente opened the first door on the right and again invited his guest to enter before him.

There were multiple rooms, each weakly lit and sparsely furnished. Very Old World, Hammond thought, very European. It was also kept astringently neat, with an agreeably sweet odor. Olivero Clemente was nothing if not fastidious.

Clemente brushed past and gestured for Hammond to follow. The kitchen was small but serviceable, with painted cabinets, a gas stove, a ballooning Philco refrigerator that could've been taken from the set of *Leave It to Beaver*, and an equally nostalgic boomerang-laminate table bathed in the glow of an aluminum pendant lamp.

Clemente motioned for Hammond to sit. Then he laid his gun on the counter as unceremoniously as if he were setting down his keys and wallet at the end of the day. He filled an enamel kettle with water and placed it on the stove, igniting the gas flame with a wooden match.

"Do you like tea?"

"Uh, sure. That'd be fine. Thank you."

Now that Hammond could study his host in a better light, he noticed that a subtle metamorphosis of sorts had taken place. Clemente no longer appeared to be the fierce warrior from the park but rather an ordinary man upon whom the specter of age was steadily gaining. His posture was slightly swaybacked, and there was a hint of gout in his knuckles, a few of which appeared to be swollen. His skin, while generally free of the manifold discolorations common to the geriatric set, sagged in places, as if it were about a half size too large for his modest frame.

What also struck Hammond as noteworthy was Clemente's resemblance to the man who had been hiding in the Dealey Plaza storm drain. The broad nose and small, closely spaced eyes, in particular, left no room for doubt about the relationship between the two. Either unaware that he was being evaluated or simply disinterested, Clemente took two saucered cups and a small box of tea bags from the cabinet. After that, and without any kind of preamble, he said, "How did you learn of my brother's participation in the plot to assassinate your president?"

Hammond felt as though he'd been struck by a sledgehammer. *And there it is,* he thought, *just like that.* He wished he had a recorder going, and for a moment he thought about using his phone. He had a feeling, however, that Clemente was the sort of man who always knew what was going on behind his back.

"I saw a film of the assassination, and he was in it."

"The film of the woman called the Babushka Lady?"

A second jolt—*He knows about her?* Hammond was beginning to feel like he'd undergone one too many sessions of shock therapy.

"You've heard of—?"

"Yes. So he was in the film?"

Hammond nodded. "In the storm drain on Elm Street."

If Clemente felt any emotion toward this information, he kept it to himself. When the kettle began to whistle, he moved it to a dormant burner and killed the flame. Then he dropped a bag of tea in each cup and poured in the water.

The host set one cup in front of his guest, the other just across from it, and pulled out a chair for himself. Once seated, he paid no attention to Hammond for a time. And in spite of the tea still being well above comfortable drinking temperature, he took long sips with no apparent effect.

"I didn't know who he was at first," Hammond went on. "I had to see an assassination expert named Ben Burdick, a professor at Southern Methodist University in Texas. His book gave me a pretty good idea of the man's identity. Incidentally, Ben was murdered for helping me."

Clemente closed his eyes and shook his head as if Burdick had been an old friend.

"From there I went to the CIA library in Washington, D.C. That's when I first saw your brother's name officially recorded somewhere."

Clemente took another sip of tea. "I thought those files were sealed for a hundred years."

Here was another missile strike to Hammond's sensibilities. This one, however, did not pack the punch of the previous two, for he was beginning to understand something—*There are people in the world who know the whole story.* They were, by simple virtue of either having been on the inside of the conspiracy or very close to it, one crucial level above the thousands of enthusiasts who had spent thousands of hours agonizing over thousands of details. He imagined this to be a very tiny group, maybe only a handful now. And he wondered what they thought when they watched the assassination documentaries on television, listened to the so-called experts spew forth their manifold theories on countless talk shows, or read books like those written by Ben Burdick and others.

"Dr. Burdick found a page from one of those sealed files that had been mislaid. That's where he first encountered your brother's name. When I went to the CIA library to learn more, I couldn't get past the security filters. But I did find *your* name in multiple places. That's why I came to Cuba—to see if I could locate you. And to find out if that really was your brother in that film."

Hammond watched Clemente and waited. As he expected, there was no immediate reaction. The man drummed his fingers contemplatively on the table and stared into his cup.

Then he said, "My brother led a long and interesting life, to say the least." He sighed. "A long and interesting life."

Hammond felt something drop in his stomach. "You say 'led' as if it were over. Does that mean . . . he's dead?"

The tiniest of smiles materialized on Clemente's mouth, and his head rocked back as if he found this amusing. "Oh no, he's not dead," he said, his tone suggesting that the fact was a great burden to him. "He's still very much alive."

Hammond was unable to keep his own smile from forming. "Okay. . . . So is there any chance I could speak with him? Would you be willing to tell me where he is?"

He figured another long silence was coming, followed by a polite rejection of the request. He was barely able to believe his eyes, then, when Clemente pursed his lips and began nodding.

"I will tell you that, yes. It is no problem, Mr. Hammond. He is standing right behind you."

Hammond's expression shifted from ebullient to bewildered. His first thought was that Clemente spoke metaphorically, although the meaning wasn't immediately clear. He also considered the idea that the man was joking. Olivero Clemente, however, didn't strike him as the humorous type.

Then Hammond saw that Clemente was no longer looking directly at him but rather at a spot just over his shoulder. And when he turned, he found the man from Margaret Baker's film—older, but inarguably the same person—standing in the doorway between the kitchen and the living room. He was dressed in black jeans and a gray T-shirt, the latter matching both his mustache and the thick hair that covered his smallish head. The eyes still held the same fierce glimmer they had on that day in 1963. Hammond also noticed that Galeno Clemente had a silenced revolver in hand and was pointing it in his direction.

"Some things in this world are better left unrevealed, Mr. Hammond," he said. "Don't you think?"

36

IT WAS A LONG, frozen moment. No one spoke; no one moved. Even with a gun pointed in his face, Hammond felt no fear. He kept his eyes locked on Galeno Clemente's.

Then Clemente brought the weapon down and held it limp at his side. "The human desire to kill . . . it should be buried deep down and forgotten. Don't you agree, Mr. Hammond?"

"As a matter of fact I do, yes."

The weapon came up again, but only so Clemente could give it a cursory appraisal. "We have made it so easy, though. So very easy. We build the tools, then convince ourselves to use them. If we don't have the reasons, we find them." He shook his head. "We justify it."

He came into the kitchen and put the gun down alongside Olivero's, kind of dropping it there as if contemptuous of it. Then he pulled out the chair next to his brother's, sat down, and massaged his face the way someone does when exhausted. What was particularly fascinating to Hammond was how *ordinary* this made him seem. At that moment, he was not a historical figure but a flesh-and-blood man.

"You did not come to Cuba to listen to my philosophies, though. Am I correct?"

"No," Olivero cut in, "he did not. And I'm not interested in hearing them either."

Hammond felt the insane urge to laugh. Another human moment—typical sibling tension. He thought he caught a glimpse of their core personalities then—Olivero, the commonsense one, grounded and calculating, somewhat machinelike in his black-and-white thinking. And Galeno, passionate and opinionated—the philosopher—given to outbursts from all points across the emotional spectrum. A touch melodramatic perhaps, but sincere. He probably kept a journal, wrote poetry. And yet . . . *A killer. A man willing to take the lives of other men, who was ready to shoot the American president. How does that resolve itself?*

"I came here to learn the facts," Hammond said firmly. "To solve this mystery once and for all. To bring the answers to the American people."

Galeno was nodding. "Yes, I know of this, of your crusades to expose truth. Truth can be a dangerous thing, but in the end it is a good thing. The only thing. I have seen you on television, read about you in newspapers and on the Internet. And I can tell you the truth in this case, Mr. Hammond, for I was indeed there that day. That was me you saw in the woman's film, sitting in the sewer like the rat that I was."

"You *knew*!" Hammond said, incredulous. "You knew she captured you with her camera?"

"Yes. I saw the lens, like a black eyeball, aimed in my direction. I had a feeling."

"Yet you didn't consider killing her, too, just to eliminate the possibility of her film becoming public?"

"No. I could not have killed anyone at that point."

Hammond's eyebrows rose. "I'm sorry? I don't underst—"

"I know you don't," Galeno said. "I know that. But you will. If you are to know the full truth, then you must be told everything."

"And why would you do that? Why tell *me*? And why now?"

"In part because of reasons you yourself have touched upon. But also for reasons of my own. Reasons that I will explain later. So are you ready to hear this?"

Hammond looked to Olivero, who had finished his tea and was staring at nothing in particular. *He's heard it all before, probably many times, and is weary of it now.* It made Hammond remember the realization that had struck earlier—*There are some people who have always known.*

"Yes, I'm ready," he replied.

• • •

"My brother and I were very happy when we were small boys," Galeno Clemente began. "My father made a good living, and my mother took care of our home. We always had good food, wore nice clothes, went on trips. . . . It was a wonderful way for two children to grow up."

"And then came Batista?"

"That is correct. He took everything my father had worked for. First his businesses, then his house and his land. Then he took our parents from *us*." Clemente waved a finger between himself and his brother, his voice rising. "His men came one day and simply took them. We never saw them again."

"I'm sorry," Hammond said. "I can well imagine how difficult that must've been."

"We had no place to go and no money. We knew nothing

of that kind of life. We lived in the streets and picked our food out of garbage cans. We begged, too. Some friends helped us, but most were afraid to. They were afraid of what would be done to them if they did. So we were left to fend for ourselves. The things we had to do . . . the things we saw out there . . . we lived this way for *years*. It changed both of us. Our innocence disappeared. We became hard men. Not boys, playing soccer with our friends like we should have been. Do you know what happens to vulnerable young boys? You do not, nor should you ever. *No* boy should ever have to know this."

Olivero moved his hand up and down—*Take it easy; take it easy.* Galeno leaned back, palms flat on the table, and took a deep breath. Then he came forward again.

"We didn't know how long we could survive, but it probably would not have been much longer. Then Fidel Castro came, and he changed everything for us. He was an avowed enemy of Batista, so we supported him. We wanted to be part of his movement, join his army of revolutionaries. We were given training, new uniforms, food, and a place to live. You must understand, Mr. Hammond; to us, this was like winning one of your American lotteries."

"I can imagine."

"When Castro came to Havana in 1959 and drove Batista out, it was one of the greatest days of my life. We had won! We had beaten the man who had taken everything from us! I had become a very good soldier by this time. Practicing in the hills, and all the guerrilla warfare . . . I discovered I had natural skill with a gun. I could hit targets others could barely see. I never missed." He sat up proudly upon making this announcement. Then, just as suddenly, he sagged again. "Yes, I never missed. That was when it all began to go bad. After one term in the military, my brother got out. He went to school and became an engineer. But I stayed in. I was being treated like a prince for my talent. I was given extra rations, better quarters. Officers who were my superiors treated me with respect. Several of the medals I received were given to me by Castro himself. I felt like the world was in my hand. From living on the streets to receiving medals in just a few years. Do you know what this does to a young man, Mr. Hammond? It develops a sense of loyalty that goes beyond what is rational. I would've done anything for my leader. I would've walked off a cliff if he'd asked. If he had said it was for the good of the revolution, I would have done it like *that*!" He snapped his fingers. "And Castro knew this. He was a master of human psychology. He knew exactly how to work a person like a puppet. It wasn't long before he was sending me all over the world to do his killing for him. I thought it was romantic and exciting. It was all for the cause, you understand. The great and noble *cause*."

He dropped his head and took several deep breaths. At first Hammond thought it was because he had become winded. Upon further reflection, he realized Clemente simply found the memories unbearable and needed to clear his mind temporarily.

"Then Castro began loaning my services out. I've killed for other politicians, for wealthy businessmen, even for his family and friends. As I said, I would've done anything for the man. I viewed him as my savior, remember." Clemente leveled his gaze at Hammond. "And that's how I became involved in the plot against your president."

Hammond's eyes popped wide in surprise. "Are you saying that Fidel *Castro* was responsible for—?"

Clemente put a hand up. "No, no—let me finish. It was

late October of 1963. I was told I would be part of a secret operation that was to take place in the United States. I had never been to the States before, and this was exciting to me. I would not receive any information about the operation until just before it began, but I was assured—as I always was—that my target was an enemy of the revolution. On November 20, I was flown to Dallas and put in a hotel room. I was told not to speak with anyone and not to leave until I received further instructions. The weapon—a bolt-action European Mauser M59 with a side-mounted sight, if you are interested in such details—was already in the room, along with a box of ammunition. The next day, a man came. He was young but very confident in himself."

"Do you know who it was?"

"No, he did not give a name, and I never saw him again. He had two maps with him—one showing Dealey Plaza and the route your president would be taking, and another showing the plaza's sewer pipes. I was required to memorize these maps while he waited because he did not want to leave them behind. He showed me where I was to go and what I was to do. Then he told me who the target was. . . ." Clemente trailed off here, head cocked slightly and one eyebrow raised. "You should know, Mr. Hammond, that I would not have hesitated to fire if Lee Harvey Oswald had not. Your president had humiliated my leader during the Cuban Missile Crisis. He had imposed an embargo on my country that crushed our economy. He was Castro's enemy, which meant he was my enemy." Clemente shook his head sadly, ashamedly. "That was the state of my mind at the time."

"So Oswald *was* the man who hit the president?"

"Oh yes, of that there is no doubt." Clemente surprised Hammond with a chuckle here. "It is amazing to me that

there has been so much debate about this. I have heard arguments, for example, that he was a poor marksman who could
not have possibly hit such a target from such a distance.
Ridiculous. Mr. Oswald was a very good marksman, and
with his weapon of choice—a single-action Carcano M91—
he would have had no problem hitting his target from the
sixth-floor window of the book depository. What *is* amazing
is that he missed on the first try. With the element of surprise
in his favor, that should have easily been the fatal strike."

"Then how did he miss?"

"Nerves, I'm sure. He was probably very nervous. I never
met him, but I have done much reading about him in the
years since. He has always seemed to me the type of man
whose ambitions greatly surpassed his abilities. The kind of
man who, when put in critical situations, finds it hard to
quiet his feelings and focus on the task at hand. A far, far too
emotional individual."

"So there really were two gunmen," Hammond said,
mostly to himself. "Incredi—"

"No."

"Hmm?"

"Not two. Four."

"*What?*"

"There were four snipers hired to hit your president that
day."

"No . . . there's no way. I don't believe you."

"I was in the storm drain. That's one. The emotional
Lee Harvey Oswald was in the book depository. That's two.
Another was in the Mercantile Building on Main Street.
That's three. And the last one, number four, was in the tex-
tile building next to the book depository. What they called
the Dal-Tex Building. It was on Elm Street right before Elm

turned into Dealey Plaza. In fact, the man who shot the famous film, Abraham Zapruder, had an office there."

"But . . . no one has ever suggested that there were four, ever. It's impossible."

"Is it? Think about it, Mr. Hammond—Mr. Jason Hammond, who always seeks the truth. Think about the importance of the target. This operation could not fail. It had to work. It would have only taken one shot to get it done. The more gunmen hired, the greater the chance of success."

Hammond was shaking his head. "That's *incredible*."

"Not if you look at it through the eyes of the people who wanted to do this. It was very smart."

"Then who was behind all this? Who was it that hired you and the others?"

"Ah, well, that is a good question."

"And do you have the answer?"

"It was everyone, Mr. Hammond."

"Excuse me?"

Clemente surprised him again with a chuckle, so casual and matter-of-fact he might as well have been discussing a pleasant afternoon he'd spent at the beach. "It was your military and your Mafia and your Central Intelligence Agency and my government and others. It was all of them."

"That's . . . No, that just can't be."

"Of course it can. Do not think of the situation dramatically. Don't think of it like a myth or a legend. Strip away all of that and look at it like reality. Your president made a lot of enemies, and many of them would have benefited from his death. For example, what did he say about the CIA that time? Something like—"

"'I want to shred the CIA into a thousand pieces and scatter them to the four winds.'"

"That's right. And the Mafia. All those stories about how they helped him get ahead in politics, rigging elections for him. But then after he became president, his brother Bobby, as attorney general, went after them. How much of that is now fact? And Fidel Castro . . . how many ways did President Kennedy antagonize him?"

Hammond was shaking his head. "Still, there couldn't have been that many people involved. To keep a secret among just two or three is nearly impossible in the corridors of power. You're saying—"

"You are not understanding—there *were* no secrets to keep."

"That doesn't make any sense."

Clemente leaned in to get closer. "What secrets are we talking about? There was no 'official' assassination plan, no drawings on blackboards or signed paperwork or midnight meetings. Nothing was recorded. At some point in time, someone suggested killing your president. It was that simple. Other people heard about it, so it became something of a rumor. But rumors like that, even in your United States, come and go every day. A few people—I would be surprised if it was more than four or five—talked about how it would be done. Others may have known about it, but they said nothing. They let it happen. There may have been another twenty or thirty people like this. But only a few would have been needed to organize the operation and keep it quiet until the last minute. Those two other gunmen? They were probably loaned out like I was. Maybe one from your American military, another from your CIA."

"Then how come neither of them fired? Based on what you're saying, they both would've had their chances before the president even reached Dealey Plaza."

"The one in the textile building never got a clear shot, and the other—the one in the mercantile—lost his guts. He couldn't go through with it." Clemente smiled here. "You know what's amazing about the gunman in the textile building? He was caught by police shortly after the assassination and then let go. He was just a boy, really. Even younger than me at the time. He played the role perfectly, wearing a black leather jacket and looking like what Americans called a 'greaser.' The police thought he was a nobody. They never even took down his name. But check the records; you'll see. They had him."

"How do you know all this? How *could* you?"

"Because I was supposed to die," Clemente said.

"Excuse me?"

"We were all supposed to die, the four of us. And three of us did."

"I . . . I'm not following. What does that have to do with—?"

"We were told about each other. We knew. The man who came to my hotel room, he told me about the others. Not names, of course, but he showed me their positions on the map and said I had to fire if they did not. I should've realized then that he revealed this information because we were all going to be eliminated afterward."

"Then what about—?" Hammond stopped dead and looked away, his mouth hanging open stupidly. "Jack Ruby," he said in a whisper. "Oswald was killed by Jack Ruby two days after the assassination."

Clemente was nodding. "Oswald was killed by Ruby, and Ruby never got the chance to give a full confession. If you remember, he wanted to talk to the Warren Commission, but they weren't interested. What was never revealed was that one of the other gunmen was found dead in a hotel room in Montreal with a pistol shot to the head, and the third—the kid—was found hanging in an apartment in Paris. Both deaths occurred less than a week after the assassination. Quite coincidental, don't you think? They were ruled suicides, but I can assure you they were not."

Hammond's head felt like a balloon being inflated beyond its capacity. "So why weren't *you* killed?"

Clemente tapped the side of his nose. "Because of this, my survivalist's instinct. A gift from the heavens. It has kept me alive many times. After Oswald was shot, I began to worry that it wasn't just the work of an enraged patriot. Then I learned of the other two deaths."

"How?"

"Because I knew people who worked in that level of society. Do you understand? It is like a community. An underground community, yes, but still a community. People know other people, and they talk. I found it unusual that these two experienced gunmen had died in the same week. It became obvious that I would be next. It started to make sense to me—once the president was dead, the people who had done the dirty work would have to go too."

"So you just took off?"

"Not at first. I was supposed to meet the man who had been in my hotel room a second time, in San Antonio. There I was to be paid—$100,000 for taking part in the shooting, and another $250,000 if I had been the one who made the hit—and given a passport into Mexico. From there I would fly home to Cuba."

"But none of that happened?"

"No. I escaped Dealey Plaza in the confusion the same way I entered it—through a manhole near the corner of

Houston and Pacific. I took a cab back to my hotel. I waited five days, as instructed, then took another cab to a parking lot in Waxahachie. There was supposed to be a car waiting there for me. And there was. But something was not right. There were no other vehicles around, no other people. I became very suspicious. Instead of going to the car like I had been told, I took a shot at it from a distance—and it went off like a bomb."

"Explosives?"

"Yes. Rigged to the door handle. A fairly common method of elimination, really."

"So what did you do?"

"I still had most of the money I'd been given at the beginning of the operation, so I took a bus to another town. Do you know what the name of the town was, Mr. Hammond?"

"What?"

"Trinity. And that was ironic, because in Trinity, sitting in yet another hotel room, I became a different man. I finally got off the road I'd been traveling since Fulgencio Batista came and took my father and mother."

Hammond shook his head. "I'm sorry; I don't understand."

"I know, but this part of our conversation will have to wait until later because we have to get going now."

"Going?"

"Yes—back to the United States."

"You want to come back with me?"

"I do. I want to tell what I know. There is more, more than I have said here. I have learned much in the years since. As you say, the American people have a right to know the truth. The whole world should know. It is long past time."

"You'll be locked up afterward, possibly even executed."

"I am aware of this."

"And you still want to do it?"

"Yes."

Silence fell between the three of them. The Clementes were watching Hammond intently, waiting for his response. The casual looks on their faces were somehow maddening.

"I'm thrilled at the idea of you coming back, of course, but . . . *why*? What is your reason for—?"

"We will discuss that on the way." Galeno rose, his chair groaning on the wooden floor. "I think you will be most interested."

"And how do I know you won't kill me on the boat and dump my body in the Caribbean?"

Clemente shook his head. "I do not kill anymore. I would not even kill a fly if it landed on this table right now. I kill nothing."

"If we had wanted you dead," Olivero added, "I could have taken you down when you left the Café Cantante or when you were walking back from the Cathedral of Santa Catalina. Or, for that matter, while you were sleeping in your room at the Hotel Parque Central." He held his hands out, palms up, as if to say, *See how easy it would have been?*

Galeno, amused by Hammond's stunned expression, chuckled and said, "Come; we need to begin."

37

THE PALATIAL HOME of retired Mafia boss Bernesco Magliocci sat atop a forested hill on the outskirts of Chicago, surrounded by high walls, a laser security system, and a staff of thick-necked guards who roamed the property with pistols and machine guns. Magliocci sat in his bedroom—the furnishings and decor so gaudy in their faux regality that the space looked like an ill-advised fusion of Egyptian noble and Las Vegas antique—in an upholstered chair with a snack tray in front of him. His large, deep-set eyes were trained on the flat-screen television across the room, his lips pulled back in a skeletal grin. On the screen, a young couple engaged in the kind of amorous activity that was far from appropriate for a noncable channel, even at this late hour.

In spite of his geriatric state, Magliocci still found the images irresistible. He had not participated in such things in quite some time, although not as long ago as most would imagine. Watching it helped him to remember. Some of the women had been his wives, others disposable lovers who had come before, during, and after. Not all had been willing partners, but they had cooperated nonetheless. He held no regrets about that, for Magliocci was never one to waste energy on regret. Not for the women he had consumed, not for the millions he had accumulated through narcotics, extortion, racketeering, influence, and protection, and not for the dozens of brutal murders in which he had participated either directly or indirectly to further his interests, including the assassination of a young and handsome American president in the fall of 1963. He had no capacity for remorse and no tolerance for those who did. Humanity could be neatly cleaved between the winners and the losers, and he considered himself one of the biggest winners he'd ever known.

The scene came to a close and was replaced by a commercial for toothpaste. Magliocci grunted something profane before calling out to his manservant. A young Italian boy with a long face opened the door and stepped into the room. He was clad in a waiter's uniform, white on top and black on the bottom, the former replete with a buttoned waistcoat. He kept a respectful distance and awaited orders.

"I need more," Magliocci said, pointing to the crumb-peppered plate before him. The boy nodded and withdrew, returning moments later with a sterling-silver tray and a towel hanging from his forearm. On the tray was another plate of tea biscuits, along with a full glass of sherry. Magliocci had not gestured toward his empty glass, but had the boy neglected to refill it, he would have berated him for his ignorance.

The boy brought the tray over and switched the old with the new. Magliocci watched him the whole time, a habit he knew the boy found unnerving. Even at the age of eighty-six, Magliocci could still frost a person's innards with his glare. He derived great pleasure from keeping people on edge. He had decided long ago that this was a common trait among the successful, so he had integrated it into his persona until it functioned from the subconscious. He could not treat the boy benevolently if he tried.

The run of commercials ended, and the movie returned. The boy left the room; Magliocci took no notice of his exit. His attention was fixated again, waiting for the next racy scene to unfold as he lifted a fresh biscuit from the plate. He became irritated when another round of commercials arrived. This annoyance was further compounded by the fact that a chilly breeze had begun to blow through the open windows. When Magliocci called out this time, the boy did not appear. In a huff, he moved the tray aside and got into his slippers. As he padded across the carpet, he fantasized about the boy's punishment.

The paired windows that stood open by the burnished bureau were diamond leaded, the glass arranged in a cheerfully haphazard variety of colors. The twinkling city was beautiful beneath the clear and starry sky, though Magliocci took no notice of this. Another gust billowed in as if aware it was about to be terminated and wishing to menace him one last time. Magliocci cursed the boy again and raised his hands to grasp both parts of the window lock at the same time. In doing so, his body formed a large capital Y and fully exposed his torso. For the black-ops team nestled in the hedgerow 160 yards away, this was an unexpected gift.

A tiny flash appeared in the dark, as if someone were trying to signal Magliocci with a penlight. He noticed this and looked in that general direction, but there was no time for anything else. The last sound his mortal ears ever caught was the distinctive thump of a silenced round. The bullet entered his chest just to the left of center, ripped through his heart, continued out his back, and became lodged in the baseboard of his tasseled four-poster bed, where it would be discovered by investigators the following morning. Magliocci's final thought was to wonder how "they"—the list was far too long for specifics—had managed to get past his carefully considered defenses. He would never know that his assassins had already taken down the guards and cut the power to the laser system. Magliocci gasped once, then fell back like a tree.

The team packed up their gear rapidly and methodically, then melted into nonexistence.

The boy found his master some fifteen minutes later. When he realized what had happened, a smile began on one side of his face.

38

HAMMOND STOOD at the wheel of the *Wind Dancer*, wide awake in spite of the late hour. Galeno Clemente, seated on the starboard side with one elbow propped on the railing, appeared relaxed as he watched the miles go by. Havana was still visible in the distance, barely.

The brief walk from the apartment to the dock had been uneventful. Hammond had feared his attackers might return, perhaps with reinforcements, to exact vengeance. But Olivero once again negotiated a route that kept them in the shadows and, Hammond was sure, didn't exist on any tourist map. Hammond overheard bits and pieces of the Clementes' conversation as he readied the boat. Olivero said he would abandon his apartment, what with the storm of media attention that was surely headed his way, and move to Santa Clara to live with friends for a while. Then, he said, he would try to slip into America for a visit. When the two brothers embraced, it was the younger Olivero who struggled to maintain his composure.

Now Hammond repeatedly shifted his gaze from the open sea to his guest, doing his best to keep his wariness discreet.

Eventually, however, Clemente said, "You don't need to do that, Mr. Hammond. I am not going to harm you. I told you before, my days of violence are long behind me and have been for a very long time."

"Sorry," Hammond said. "I just . . . It's hard for me to imagine how someone can go from one extreme to another. I know people can change, but you're talking about change of an amazing degree."

Clemente nodded. "Yes, that is true. It did happen, though, and it happened like *that*." He snapped his fingers as he had in his brother's apartment. "In just a few days, sitting in that hotel room in Trinity, Texas."

"How?"

"This might be hard for you to understand, but it was the death of your president that did it. That was the breaking point. I could not get the pictures out of my mind. I had seen so many deaths, but this one was very harsh, very . . . messy. And his wife, too. Such a beautiful woman. To see her on the back of the car, crawling to pick up the pieces of . . . It was truly horrible. I could not sleep, could not eat. I kept hearing the sounds of people screaming on the sidewalk above me, their feet as they ran in all directions. The hits I carried out were always done in secret, at night and in darkness. But this was done in the day, when everyone could see. Why did it have to be this way? I wondered about the children who were there. What did they think about it? What about *his* children? What must it have been like for them? Sooner or later, I am sure, they saw the film that the dressmaker Mr. Zapruder took. I cannot even imagine what they felt. And then to think that I would have fired myself if I had to, if Oswald had not. I was supposed to hit him just before he reached that highway bridge, the one they call the triple underpass. I would have had a clear shot, and I would have taken it."

He closed his eyes and took a deep breath.

"Sitting in that room," Clemente went on, "I thought of something else too. Fidel Castro, my very beloved leader, must have known that I was not coming back. He must have known that I was to be eliminated after the hit. That surprised me and made me angry. All that I had done for him, all the other killings. All, I thought, for his great cause. I was young enough and foolish enough to believe that I would be treated differently, that I was special to him. But I was just another piece in his game to be moved about. I realized that then. I saw the man for the egomaniac that he really was. His revolution—nonsense. Castro did not change Cuba to Communism; he changed it to Castroism. *He* was the political system and the legal system and the economic system. The Cuban people were there to serve him and not any grand political or ideological philosophy."

Clemente was becoming more animated now, more passionate. Hammond watched with rapt fascination.

"Who benefited most from his policies? *He* did. He and his friends and his family. He promised everything for the working class. And yes, yes, he did make some improvements for ordinary people. But for the most part, there were only two classes in Cuba—Castro and his circle at the very top, and everyone else on the bottom. The well-fed and the starving. And I had to live with the fact that I had helped build that system. I had played a part in its creation. I had fought for it, killed for it. But the worst part, Mr. Hammond, is that I killed *myself*, too."

This was one of the most fascinating monologues Hammond had ever heard. He could not have torn his eyes from Clemente at that moment if the moon had dropped out of the sky and splashed into the sea.

Clemente smiled. "I'm sure you won't believe this, Mr. Hammond, but did you know what one of my ambitions was as a boy? I wanted to be a holy man. I thought about being many things, but that was one of them. My parents were devout believers who prayed every night and took us to church every Sunday. My brother and I did not resist this. Each night I would thank God for all the good things we had. I told him I would do anything to keep my family healthy and make my father richer and all of that. I obeyed my parents. I did my schoolwork. I was like an angel. But when our life started to fall apart, I felt as though God had betrayed me. I became very, very angry. I blamed him for everything that happened." Clemente paused here to make sure he had his listener's full attention, then said, "Just like you have been doing."

Hammond's reaction was slow, a dawning kind of comprehension that the conversation had, in just one sentence, taken a hard about-turn and was now focused squarely on him. "I don't know what you m—"

"Yes, you do. I have seen it in your eyes. I know the look all too well. Your eyes held no fear when I was pointing the gun at you. Do you not think I know what this means? The fearless way you have acted since you came to Cuba? And your adventures all over the world. Seeking truth? Yes, I believe you seek truth. I believe you to be an honest man who wants to see justice done, yes. But there are other reasons as well. Am I right?"

Before, Hammond had not been able to pull his gaze away from the man. Now he found it impossible to keep it there.

"Yes," Clemente continued, "I know something of this. You cannot do the deed yourself, so you put yourself in danger in the hope of having someone else do it."

"I'm sorry, but I have no idea what you're talking about."

Clemente delivered the next proclamation with chilling confidence. "You want to be with your family again, Mr. Hammond."

Hammond was left speechless. Even Noah had never penetrated his psyche at such depth. And yet this man—this *stranger*—had done so, though they'd met only a few hours ago.

"Let me tell you, Mr. Hammond, the path you are traveling might not be exactly the same as mine, but it is similar enough. They run side by side. You have not yet destroyed yourself as I did, but you will in time. Do not doubt me on this. Remember that time is one of the most precious gifts the Lord gives us. Mine is almost used up, but you still have much of yours left. And you have received many other gifts as well. You are intelligent; you are healthy; you are rich. You can do so much good in this world. Do not waste your opportunities. Do not waste *yourself*, like I did, by letting anger get ahold of you. It is not too late."

Hammond slid his hands into his pockets and feigned a concerned glance at the boat's control panel.

"You seek truth? Well, here is a truth I learned while sitting in that hotel room—God was not responsible for putting Batista in power, taking my parents away, or ruining my childhood. Men did that. Ordinary men like you and me. Men who had more power than they should have. Men who had evil in their hearts and the means to use it. I have come to believe that God has given us this world as one gift, and the chance to live in it as another. But what we do with it

342

is up to us. If he did not want us to think for ourselves, we would not be able to. Misfortune is part of life, and evil is part of humanity. It is sad, yes, and it is angering. But it is not God. God did not take my parents from me, Mr. Hammond. And he did not take your family from you."

"Maybe, maybe not."

"He did not. Your greatest mistake was to turn away from God when you lost your family. In such times, your faith needs to become your refuge. You need to trust that he has a greater plan for you. Let him be your strength; let him lead you to the next chapter in your life. You have left no opening in your heart for this because your life has become empty. In many ways, it has stopped."

"Maybe it's my faith that's stopped."

Clemente grinned. "Do not try to fool an old man, Mr. Hammond. If you did not still believe, you would not be having this battle inside yourself."

Hammond started to reply, then stopped. It occurred to him once again that the depth of this man's insight into his soul was staggering—and unsettling.

"If you do not trust in the Lord, then who, Mr. Hammond? In television celebrities? Professional athletes? Politicians? I put my faith into politicians, and look where it took me. Replacing God with someone else or with something else is the path to destruction. Life without God is not living; it is only existing. And that is the path you are on. What have you done since your family's tragic death? Think about this."

"Are you saying I shouldn't be trying to get to the bottom of all these mysteries? I'm wasting my time trying to provide closure for the families involved? And bringing criminals to justice?"

"I do not know the answer to that. Perhaps you *are*

supposed to be doing this. Perhaps that is part of God's plan. But how can you know when you've shut him out? How can you find the true answers? You focus on the terrible things that have happened. Look at all the gifts he has given you. You have so many opportunities, and you are a strong and courageous man who has been through much suffering. But you have stopped *listening*."

Hammond turned away, setting his hands on the wheel.

After a while, he cleared his throat and said, "So what did you do after you left Trinity?"

"Well, I decided it was time to begin making up for my sins. That was the only way forward. In my head I believed I had already been forgiven and my soul saved by grace alone. But for me personally, that was not enough. I could not bring any of my victims back from the grave, but I could right my wrongs in other ways. I changed my name several times so the people who wanted me dead would think that I really was. Only my brother knew the truth. I eventually settled on the name Salvador Romero. Salvador means 'savior,' and Romero means 'one who seeks enlightenment.' I liked that. This new identity would, indeed, save me, and the person that I had been before really did die. I traveled around the world doing charity work with missionary groups. I went to many countries, Mr. Hammond, just as when I was killing for Castro. Only this time I was helping to preserve life rather than take it away. I have been in Haiti for the last few years, helping to modernize villages."

"Then why did you come back? Why now?"

"You were one reason. When I saw you on television and saw that you had the woman's film, I knew it was time. I felt this very strongly inside. But I had also come to believe that all my charity work had not been enough. I need to do things that will have a direct effect on the sins I committed. Coming back to America to reveal my part in your president's assassination might change history for some, Mr. Hammond, but for me it is just one step. I would also like to give information about the others who were involved. Maybe it will help provide some measure of peace. So this is where it begins for me. And, I am guessing, where it will end as well."

Hammond had no response to that.

39

BERNARD KANTER awoke with a start. He was a huge man with a beefy, Germanic face framed by waves of white hair that had remained thick despite his age. He looked around the room confusedly, almost fearfully, until the last of the transitional sleeping-waking residue had evaporated and the recall machinery could fire up—*the town house in Florida, the factory disputes* . . . His eyelids sagged to a close as he expelled a long breath.

The factory was one of sixty-two manufacturing plants around the world that operated under his ownership. This particular facility produced aftermarket automotive parts, and it was one of his most profitable. However, human resources had been remiss in their interpretation of the hiring guidelines he had set out for all his enterprises, and a few rabble-rousers had slipped through the net. Now they were pushing for unionization for the third straight year. Kanter would not permit one of his factories to unionize if the future of humanity depended upon it. The fact that he knew the complaints were fully justified—he was working them half to death while subtly maintaining layoff threats to smother the possibility of raise requests—was immaterial. If they successfully voted to unionize, he would pack up the show and move it to a site in the Philippines. One of the rabble-rousers had told him the day before that they'd sue if he tried that. He'd nodded mindfully, feigning deep concern, but he was laughing inside. Billionaires didn't worry about lawsuits from blue-collar bozos who could barely afford to make their minimum credit card payments, or from loosely organized unions that had been rendered impotent by their own corrupt and incestuous behavior.

Kanter peered at the clock on the nightstand—4:22. He swore into the dimness with a chicken-like thrust of the head. Staying asleep had never been a problem until recently— more to the point, until his prostate had decided to start acting up. He'd enjoyed good health all his life and hated the idea of having to submit to surgery at the age of eighty-six. But three months of random waking, which left him feeling heavy-headed during the day, was gradually recalibrating this opinion.

He peeled the sheets back in a huff. This did not disturb anyone on the other side because there was no one there. He'd had three wives, but the last one had been ushered out of the picture almost fifteen years ago. He didn't speak with any of them now and had scant contact with only two of his eight children. He had been an indifferent husband and father at best and did not feel the least bit guilty about it. As with most selfish people, Kanter was solitary by nature and, in fact, felt distinctly uncomfortable in the company of others. The dollar would always be his one true love, and he had no trouble living with the things he'd done in pursuit of it.

Including the funding of a presidential assassination in late 1963.

Kanter had not viewed Kennedy as his nation's leader but rather as someone standing in his way. The very notion of reducing American involvement in the Vietnam War while Kanter was trying to secure multibillion-dollar defense contracts was simply unacceptable. Kanter knew the military-industrial complex that had been ushered in by Eisenhower and others during World War II would never have tolerated such a policy. So, when approached with the idea of lending a hand with the finances, he had not hesitated.

When his secretary came running into his Manhattan office on the afternoon of November 22 with tears running down her cheeks, Kanter had feigned concern as well—a shake of the head and a mumbled comment about what a shame it was. Then he had gone back to his paperwork. In the years since, he had scarcely given the incident a thought. Kings and queens were removed from power all the time, after all.

He went into the adjoining bathroom, cursing bitterly, then returned to bed. Before he lay back down, however, he felt the call of his only other vice—food. There were leftovers in the refrigerator from an excellent Thai meal he'd had the night before. He shuffled into the kitchen, which was luminescent with moonlight, and opened the fridge door. This bathed him in a different kind of light: a spotlight of sorts. He stood there in his boxer shorts and crew-neck T-shirt searching for the Styrofoam box. It was on the top shelf, right side, with its lid open a crack.

He heard the sharp pop as he reached for it, and he turned. There was a small and perfectly round hole in the window over the sink. Kanter had time to wonder what had caused it; a bullet never entered his mind, figuratively speaking. Then his perspective continued rotating—albeit involuntarily—first to the recessed light over the window, then the ceiling, and finally the etched-glass dome. Then the world began to spin away in a reverse cascade, higher and higher until it zoomed out of existence and all became dark and silent.

The cleaning woman found his body, stuck to the floor due to the coagulated blood, shortly after sunrise. Her screams awoke several people in the complex.

40

GALENO CLEMENTE sat alone in *Wind Dancer*'s cabin, in the cushioned booth that looked like something out of a fifties diner, holding Hammond's iPad in both hands. He used his index finger to brush aside one web page and move to another. Every major news site had a story about Hammond's ongoing activities. Certain details were common to each—the status of Sheila Baker was still unknown, as were Hammond's whereabouts; one man had already been murdered, and there was a possible government connection to all of it. The facts were followed by a plethora of speculative editorializing. No one had yet made any mention of Margaret Baker's film or the Babushka Lady pseudonym. Clemente had a feeling that would change very soon.

Hammond came down, leaning awkwardly to fit through the passageway. "We'll be there shortly."

Clemente nodded without taking his eyes off the screen.

"Incredible what makes the news these days, isn't it?" Hammond added.

"What is more incredible is this device that brings it to you."

"Yes, the iPad. A great little toy."

"I can work with a computer, but I am still somewhat inexperienced with related devices."

"It's been around a while."

"I know, but I have not held one before. It is wonderful. Your Steve Jobs was truly a man who saw into the future."

"You've heard of him?"

"Is there anyone who has not?"

Hammond laughed. "I guess not. The Thomas Edison of our time, they called him. Very apt."

"I would agree."

"Okay, well, just to let you know, the plan is to get ashore, then drive to my home up north. Hopefully no one will recognize us along the way. If we can find a drugstore in Florida, I can put together some disguises for us."

"I can help with that too."

"Good. Once we're in New Hampshire, I can introduce you to a few attorneys I know. They can help you do whatever you wish."

"That would be fine. Thank you."

• • •

Hammond got a bottle of water from the mini fridge. He turned to ask if Clemente wanted one, then stopped. Appearing relaxed a moment earlier, his guest now looked sickly pale.

"What's wrong?"

When Clemente didn't respond, Hammond moved behind him to see what was on the iPad's screen. It was an article about the CIA's response to the media's charges that someone in their ranks was responsible for Sheila Baker's abduction. In the accompanying lead photo, an angry

Director Peter Vallick stood at a podium with several sober-looking men behind him. There was one in particular, far left and almost in the shadows, who seemed to be distinctly uneasy.

"Do you know this man?" Clemente asked, pointing to him.

Hammond squinted. "Umm, I don't believe so. Why? What's the—?"

"Is there any way to make this picture bigger?"

"Sure." Hammond pressed his thumb and forefinger to the screen, then spread them apart. This time, Clemente did not pause to marvel at the technology.

"That's him."

"Excuse me?"

"That's the man who was in my hotel room in Dallas, the one with the maps of Dealey Plaza."

"You're not serious."

"Yes."

"That was fifty years ago. How can you—?"

"I am sure of it. The eyes, the nose. He even keeps his hair the same way. He is much older, of course, but it is him. I would bet my life on it."

"Okay, hang on. Let me take a look at something." He slid in beside Clemente and took the iPad, keeping it angled in such a way that they could both view it comfortably.

He scrolled down to the caption, which inventoried everyone in the photo.

"Rydell, Frederick Rydell. Sound familiar?"

"No."

"All right, let's try this. . . ."

He navigated to Google Images and launched a new search. There were only two photos, both from articles about the agency's attempts to promote Rydell to the director's post at the CIA. The most recent was from 1999, the other 1988.

When Hammond enlarged the latter to fill the entire screen, Clemente nodded. "That is him; I swear it."

Hammond now did a regular Google web search and found just one site with biographical information. This in itself, Hammond felt, was notable given the fact that the Internet had all but eviscerated the concept of privacy. Rydell was born in Indiana in 1941, attended military schools, then served briefly in the Navy before his career as a hot new CIA recruit began in 1961.

"He would've been—"

"Twenty-one or -two when we met," Clemente said. "That is exactly right."

Hammond shook his head. "I can't believe it," he whispered.

"It is him. Trust me. I have never forgotten that face."

The final line in the bio grabbed Hammond like a hand around the throat—*He continues his duties today as the agency's assistant deputy director.*

Hammond got to his feet and took out his phone, then went to the deck to assure the best reception. Clemente followed.

"I was just about to call you," Noah said upon answering.

"Noah, we've found the man."

"Jason—"

"The operational leader from 1963. The one who was in Galeno's Dallas hotel room."

"Jason, lis—"

"Galeno is sure of it. Absolutely certain. And I'm sure he's sure."

"*Jason.*"

"Noah, please, are you hearing what I'm saying?"

An exasperated sigh. Then, "Okay, who is it?"

"His name is Frederick Rydell, and he's the assistant deputy director of the CIA. That's who the FBI needs to look for."

"Okay, good. That's great. I'll get on it right away."

"Tell Henry Moore, too, please."

"I will."

There was an awkward pause. "I don't understand," Hammond said. "You don't find this amazing?"

"I do, Jason. But there have been some other developments that are also quite amazing."

"More amazing than this?"

"Well, I didn't know we were having a contest. But yes, I'd say so. Maybe more so. However . . . they're not good developments. Not good at all."

"Okay, tell me."

"First, I received a call from Chip Frazier. He said he was contacted by the Justice Department. It seems CIA director Peter Vallick is thinking of having you sued for implying that the agency was somehow involved not only in President Kennedy's assassination but also Sheila's disappearance."

"They were and are. The connection to Rydell proves that."

"Yeah, well, he obviously doesn't know that yet. And if you don't come up with proof to back up those claims, he's planning to throw the full weight of the government at you. If that happens, Jason, it could really hurt you. Bad."

Hammond closed his eyes and shook his head. "Great. And what else?"

"I received another phone call just a few moments ago, and you won't believe who it was from."

"Who?"

Noah told him. Hammond stood motionless, his mouth hanging open.

"You're *kidding*."

"No."

"Noah . . ."

"I swear it."

The conversation continued for a few more moments, but Hammond barely heard a word of it. When the call ended, he turned to Clemente and said, "You won't believe this."

Before he had the chance to say more, a brilliant white light spilled over them. They turned like two convicts caught trying to scale the prison wall. Next came a voice through a loudspeaker, ordering them to stop.

"The Coast Guard," Hammond said sharply. "Wonderful."

He made his decision about what to do next—a calculated risk to be sure—in a millisecond.

47

RETIRED GENERAL Arnold Shevalek sat on a military field stool, his breath visible in the frosty morning air, and broke kindling over his knee before tossing it into the growing fire. After several minutes of gentle prodding, it was finally reaching a reliable burn. The satisfying crackle provided an organic tune to the steady, white-noise harmony of the narrow river that flowed around the northwestern curve of the campsite.

Across the water stood a small palisade of jagged shale, the foundation for the forested ridge that ran along the top. Shevalek peered beyond the neat row of A-frame tents and scanned the ridge judiciously. He was clad in a camouflage jumpsuit and bright-orange vest, his hunter's permit pinned to the back of his fur-lined cap. He was an unusually severe-looking man, unsmiling and intense, the kind who stirred discomfort in others simply by standing in their proximity. His facial features were sharply drawn, the pinkish skin making it appear as though he were perpetually on the verge of an eruption. In spite of being in his late seventies, he still telegraphed the impression that he could kill with his bare hands.

Detecting no movement along the ridgeline, he broke up the rest of the sticks and tossed them into the flames. He pulled his sleeve back to check his watch—5:27 a.m. Three more minutes to work on the fire; then it was time to wake the others and get breakfast going. Shevalek referenced his watch several dozen times a day, for he was a man who believed in schedules. It was part and parcel of living an organized and efficient life, which had always been his passion.

He had spent fifty-two years in the military, starting as a second lieutenant fresh out of ROTC in 1959, and loved every moment. He had pulled every string, tried every trick, and bent every regulation in an unsuccessful attempt to dodge retirement two years ago. He was given a second star as a parting gift from the Pentagon but gladly would have given it back to return to active duty. He sorely missed the discipline, the orderliness, and—of course—the fighting in the name of the red, white, and blue. He believed the United States was the greatest civilization in human history, well beyond the Mesopotamians, the Romans, the Aztecs, and all the other reputed big leaguers.

He had eagerly signed up for stints in Vietnam, Lebanon, the Persian Gulf, Somalia, Afghanistan, and finally, Iraq. And while he held no love for his foreign adversaries, he at least felt a token empathy for them, for patriotism was admirable in any form. What he loathed with a white-hot intensity was anti-Americanism among America's own citizens—people who did not hesitate to embrace the nation's many privileges and luxuries while participating in activities designed to stifle them. John Kennedy had been one of these people, with his liberal foreign policies and dangerous talk of disassembling America's military-industrial complex. It had been one of Shevalek's greatest honors as a young officer to take part in the operation to remove that closet Commie from power. He would go to his grave believing he had done his country a great service.

He took his long poker stick in hand and pushed the embers around to encourage oxygenation. Frederick Rydell entered his thoughts at this moment, and his jaw tightened. Since Shevalek was the one in the trio who had been tacitly assigned to contact Rydell when necessary, he had also been granted the honorary role of de facto decision maker. The other two, Bernesco Magliocci and Bernard Kanter, could not be bothered with the whole affair any longer. Shevalek held no ill will toward either of his partners, for he frankly wasn't interested in dealing with it any more than they were and therefore understood their point of view. But he had never cared much for Rydell personally, either, which was why he didn't exercise decorum during their phone calls. Now he had to figure out what to do about the man. The little runt had made a royal mess of the situation, missing the chance to grab the film this woman's mother took, allowing Jason Hammond to enter the equation, and sitting by stupidly while the media whipped up a fresh round of public interest in the assassination. It gave Shevalek the kind of headaches that felt like razor blades were cutting into his brain tissue.

He set all thoughts of Rydell aside for now and focused on the priorities of the day. There were three dead bucks in the back of his truck, and he wanted to score at least another two before the end of the trip. He turned his mind, inevitably, to The Daily Schedule—at 5:30 he would wake the others and have breakfast, and at 6:00 they would take the western trail to stand number seven. They had built eleven blinds in this area since the start of the previous season—little more than large boxes on stilts with horizontal slots in the walls through which prey could be targeted. They were also using a scented lure that was illegal in the state of Pennsylvania. But the land they were on was privately owned by a friend, and Shevalek was secretly delighted by this display of defiance. He placed the "sea-turtle police," as he called them, in the same league as the Kennedys.

At precisely 5:29, he rose to get a coffee kettle from his kit bag. As he did, he glanced at the ridge again. This time his eyes caught some movement in a run of scraggly under-brush. He froze in midstride, looking like the generic figure in street-crossing signs around the world. Then there was more movement over there, just enough to make him believe it wasn't a lousy squirrel or a groundhog. He reached for his rifle, which lay fully loaded on the picnic table next to the kit bag, and began creeping toward the river.

There was a crashing sound in the brush, followed by a flame-shaped flash of white—a deer tail! The animal was moving away from him now, to the southeast. He went in that direction as swiftly as possible without making too much of a racket, following a worn trail that paralleled the river's stony shoreline. He estimated his target to be no more than fifty feet ahead. That was fine, he thought. *All I need is a clear shot.* He was an excellent marksman and had no doubt he could take the creature down with one squeeze of the trigger.

Unfortunately the shrub movement had ceased. This could have meant that the deer had sensed the danger and turned inland. If that was the case, it could be two hundred yards away by now. But it could also mean the animal had simply been spooked and was now waiting for more informa-tion. Shevalek knew patience often paid off in these situa-tions. If Bambi was still there, she'd stick her head up sooner or later.

He found a grassy niche in front of a cluster of boulders and nestled down to wait. He also used this intermission to remove a pair of Zeiss binoculars from one of the large pockets of his vest. He studied the ridge inch by inch but found nothing. Not a good sign, but not definitively bad, either. He set the strap over his head and let the binoculars hang in front of his chest. Then he checked his watch again and decided to wait it out for precisely five minutes.

Halfway through the first, he heard a brief, singular sound, like that of a nut or a twig falling from a tree and landing in a pile of dried leaves. His hands went automatically to the binoculars, but they never got there. A second sound came, like someone punching a bag of laundry. Then he felt a sharp pain in the center of his chest, and all the breath left him in a single, hitched gasp. When he looked down, he found the binoculars cleaved neatly in two and bright-red fluid pumping out of what appeared to be a gunshot wound. He could not take his eyes off the sight of it, the same thought looping through his flabbergasted mind—*How can I be hit? How can I be hit?*

Every operation in his traumatized body went haywire. The desire to reach up to the wound, maybe plug it with one of his fingers, was there, but his hands wouldn't move. He could not have known that the black-ops bullet had not only sliced away the bottom third of his heart but also neatly severed his spine. His thinking became disjointed and syrupy. He wondered if perhaps the deer he was tracking had shot him. *Are the sea-turtle police arming them now?* Then his strength began to go like water spinning around a drain. The edges of his world grew fuzzy, fading to a brownish gray, until they closed in and consumed him. Then there was silence, until even that devolved into nothingness.

42

RYDELL WAS ON I-95, halfway between his home and his office, nursing a fierce headache as he continued to hyper-focus on an escape plan that now had to be plucked from its tree well before it was fully ripened. Not all the money was tucked safely away yet. Not all the travel tickets had been purchased. For that matter, the itinerary hadn't even been finalized. There were no bags packed, no disguises assembled. *I have to buy more time,* he thought, barely aware of the thickening traffic around him. *Somehow . . . maybe with Theresa's unknowing cooperation . . .*

What jarred him out of this trance was the mention of Hammond's name on the radio.

"Billionaire Jason Hammond has finally reappeared on public radar, spotted when his rental boat encountered a Coast Guard vessel near Key West during the early morning hours. And while a Coast Guard spokesman is refusing further comment on the matter, Hammond is believed to have slipped through their fingers, and his whereabouts are once again unknown. A report filed by the Associated Press also states that Hammond was traveling with one other passenger, an older Latino man whose identity is unknown at this time. . . ."

Rydell whispered one word—*"Clemente"*—then took out his cell phone.

Theresa answered on the first ring. "Where are you?" she asked, clearly shaken.

"I'm on my way right now, but there's traffic. Why? What's going—?"

"Director Vallick has been asking for you. He's called three times and come by twice. I can't hold him off forever."

"Okay, okay. I'll be there shortly," he said.

He got into the left lane to take the first available U-turn.

• • •

Exactly forty-two minutes later, an enraged Peter Vallick burst into Rydell's empty office with four FBI agents close on his heels and Theresa peering through the doorway with tears in her eyes. It would take another seventeen for this impromptu team to establish that many of Rydell's most sensitive papers had been dumped into the building's basement incinerator, and that a large and now-irretrievable portion of his computer's hard drive had recently been erased. Both operations had been carried out without authorization.

Red-faced and screaming, Vallick ordered an immediate manhunt, and the FBI formally issued an arrest warrant for J. Frederick Rydell.

• • •

Rydell was already in his home, having entered through the back door so he wouldn't be seen by his neighbors. He had a list of needed escape items on the computer in the den, but it was unfinished. He would now have to complete it on the fly. He passed through the kitchen and went into the living room, where he turned on CNN. There were no reports that concerned him yet.

First—cash. Leaving the TV on, he went into the bedroom, parted the louvered closet doors, and knelt in front of the small safe. There were several stacks of banded bills on the top shelf, resting on a large envelope containing his Social Security card and birth certificate. A similar envelope on the middle shelf held a variety of agency papers that he was required to keep in the event of his death. There was also a DNA sample in a small vial. On the bottom was a handgun and a magazine, the latter separated from the former but fully stocked. Rydell grabbed the cash, the gun, and the magazine and slipped them into various pockets around his blazer. Then he shut the door and gave the dial a spin.

The next item on the list rolled out of his memory as effortlessly as the first—*clothes.* He retrieved a large duffel bag from under the bed and began loading in handfuls of socks, undershirts, and underwear from the dresser. He went back to the closet for several pairs of pants, shirts, shoes, and belts. Then into the bathroom, where he gathered toiletries and several over-the-counter medications.

Next, disguises. The bag, which was nearly full already, had to be carried into the basement. The space was unremarkable, with unpainted cinder-block walls, a maze of copper piping, and a single bare bulb in the center of the ceiling. There were several dozen cardboard boxes stacked by the water heater. Rydell moved box after box until he reached one with *Tax Receipts—Nondeductible* written on the front with Magic Marker. He set the box down beside the duffel and unfolded the flaps.

He froze when he heard the screech of tires on dry

pavement outside. *They can't be here already.* He took the gun out, rammed in the magazine, and went back up the steps. He made sure to stay low at the top, out of view.

Then the question presented itself: *If this does turn into a shoot-out, will you really fight to the death? Will you be able to take your own life, if it comes to that?* He didn't know. An unpleasant mental image followed—his bloody, bullet-riddled body, lying half on the living room couch and half on the floor, arms extended, one eye partially open, tie running down his shoulder. They'd take pictures for their official files, but a few would mysteriously make it to the newspapers and the Internet. It would be his fifteen minutes of fame, which was fairly ironic given that he had worked all his life to remain invisible.

He was surprised to hear the tires a second time, preambled by another uniquely automotive signature—an engine being revved over and over, in progressively higher tones. He went to the front window and parted the blinds with one finger. The tires on the vehicle in question had drawn a long equal sign, wavy and dark, on the macadam. Farther up the street, two boys of no more than nineteen or twenty stepped out of a '68 Plymouth Barracuda. Rich kids with too much free time and parents who couldn't be bothered watching them. They went around to the rear of the car, inspected their handiwork, and traded enthusiastic high fives. Rydell fantasized about shooting them dead where they stood. *How much precious time did I just lose?* He slipped the gun into his jacket and went back downstairs.

There actually was some tax paperwork at the top of the box, but this was a diversion in and of itself. He tossed it aside and turned the box over, shaking the contents into the bag—wigs and other false body parts, hats, eyeglasses, hair coloring, skin toner, all of professional grade. Like everything else, though, this kit was incomplete, and he'd had no time to study up on how best to use it.

Identity. Sliding back a tile in the drop ceiling, he groped about with one hand until he came upon another large envelope, this one containing a collection of false passports, birth certificates, Social Security cards, credit cards, and driver's licenses. It would be difficult to travel without these and impossible to leave the country. Two of the personas were already active, tied to bank accounts in Switzerland, Singapore, and Morocco. He had made some progress with this aspect of his strategy, knowing it was the most delicate. Creating a fictional character who functioned in the real world required time and patience, which he'd had in abundance until recently.

Returning to the first floor, he made a conscious attempt to calm himself. What happened next did little to fertilize this effort—CNN broke in with an alert about early reports of a trio of murders that had occurred overnight in different parts of the nation. Then another story—possibly connected to the murders, according to the newsreader—about a manhunt that had been ordered by the FBI for the assistant deputy director of the CIA. When Rydell saw his official agency photo appear on the screen—not off in the corner but rather front and center, along with a phone number that "anyone with information that might be helpful" was urged to use—he felt like he'd been hit in the chest with a railroad tie.

He slung the bag over his shoulder and went into the garage. It was as astringently bare as the basement, save for a car that was covered stem to stern with a blue tarp. He went to the front and peeled the tarp away in dramatic fashion, revealing a stone-gray 2004 Chevy Malibu. Rust bubbles were beginning to form around the lower edges of the body, there was a soft dent in the front passenger's door, and the previous owner had put a Washington Redskins sticker on the rear bumper. In other words, it was remarkably unremarkable, which was exactly why Rydell had bought it, with cash, three months earlier.

He threw the duffel into the backseat and got behind the wheel. The key was still in its hiding place above the visor, and the engine turned over without a fuss. Realizing he would need a disguise immediately, he stepped back out, removed his jacket and tie, and took a baseball cap and a pair of glasses out of the bag. He used the remote on his other set of keys to open the garage door. As it lifted, his heart began thumping again. He imagined a fleet of government vehicles screaming up the street to intercept him.

But the road was empty, so much so that it was downright eerie. Even the two motor heads had disappeared.

He pulled out and pressed the remote again, sending the door back down. As he navigated through the development, his eyes darted from place to place. He reached the exit gate, which was mercifully raised, and cruised out.

Once in the flow of traffic, he allowed himself to relax a little. *Still a long way to go,* he told himself, but he was pleased by his progress so far. What he required now was a diversion of some kind, something to throw the Feds off his trail for a while. The inspiration came to him, as so many had before, virtually on command. He leaned over and removed the cell phone from his pants pocket.

Birk answered immediately. Rydell felt him out first, trying to determine if he had seen any of the news reports and perhaps put the pieces together for himself. He hadn't.

Then Rydell gave him his new orders. These would be the last, Rydell promised; then he could return to his gigolo's life on the Gulf Coast—and with an extra $100,000 to boot. That caught Birk's attention, as Rydell knew it would. Unfortunately for the employee, the employer had no intention of carrying through on this part of the proposal.

Mere seconds after the call ended, two black Chevy Suburbans—smoked windows all around and FBI without question—appeared ahead, approaching with frightening speed. Rydell knew the rest of the script—one would spin to a sideways halt in front of him, the other along the driver's side. Then a dozen or so agents, weapons drawn, would jump out and surround him. The options at that point were fairly obvious, and the choice would be his alone: give up or go down in a blaze of glory.

But nothing of the sort happened. The Suburbans zoomed past, their engines roaring, and kept on going. It didn't take an MIT graduate to figure out their destination. Rydell watched them vanish in the rearview mirror and exhaled deeply.

If his attention hadn't been trained so pointedly on the Suburbans, he might have noticed the white Lexus SUV three cars back that had been on his tail since he pulled out of his development.

43

HAMMOND KEPT his speed at the legal limit as he drove the rental car—secured under the same false identity as the southbound flight to Miami—north on Interstate 95. He was still shaking from the Coast Guard encounter. They had ordered him to stop, and he had evaded them through a combination of raw speed and strategic maneuvering. It had been a risky decision, but it was one he would make again under the circumstances. Still, he regretted breaking the law and knew beyond any doubt that some unpleasant punishment would be part of his future.

Beside him in the passenger seat, Clemente seemed largely unaffected. If anything, he struck Hammond as energized by the recent excitement. He also continued his love affair with the iPad, his face like that of an enthused child.

Hammond looked at the old man and was unable to suppress a smile. "I'm glad you're enjoying that so much."

"It really is most remarkable. When I was a boy, we played dominoes or chess for fun. Now there is this."

"Both those games are on there, along with checkers, cribbage, blackjack, poker, and others. You can also read books, listen to music, draw pictures, send e-mail, take photos, watch television . . ."

Clemente shook his head. "It is unbelievable. But I worry about children. If they have these, they will not leave their homes. They need to go outside and play in the fresh air."

Hammond nodded. "That's a problem, no doubt about it." When he saw that Clemente was paging through the Internet with his forefinger again, he said, "What are you looking at now?"

"More stories about Rydell and these other killings. I would not be surprised if, as some of these sites are suggesting, they are all connected. The three victims—Shevalek, Magliocci, and Kanter—are of the right age and from the right places. One Mafia, one military, one business. Their hits were very professional. The Mafia man, for example— his guards were taken down without a fight, and his alarm system got turned off. Then the killers just disappeared— *swoosh!*—like smoke in the wind."

"Now Rydell is gone too," Hammond said bitterly, "also like smoke in the wind."

"He is an old man like me, but I would not be surprised if they never caught him. He would have to be very smart to go so far in the CIA. I'm sure he knows many tricks."

Hammond felt real anger begin to bloom. All the suffering Rydell had spread around during his career, including the death of a president that he was supposed to have served . . . *Look at what he's done in the brief time since Margaret Baker's film was found.* This made him think about Sheila again, and the nimble fingers of depression began reaching out. "I hope they do catch him. And then I hope they . . ." He trailed off, not wanting to give in to the kind of hatred that manufactured the Rydells of the world.

Clemente looked up. "Don't feel bad, Mr. Hammond. He would deserve such a fate."

For a brief moment there was a formless yet undeniable brand of understanding between them. And in spite of Clemente's many sins, Hammond could not help but feel some benevolence toward him. It had been there all along, he realized, waiting for the cue to surface. "You know, you can call me Jason. You are twice my age, after all. No offense."

Clemente laughed. "No offense taken. But only if you will call me Galeno."

"I think I can manage that."

"We are friends then, yes?"

"Sure."

"Okay. Friends." He went back to the Internet and soon thereafter laughed out loud.

"What's funny?"

"I am reading something now about the hill in Dealey Plaza by the fence, the one they call the grassy knoll."

It occurred to Hammond that they hadn't discussed the assassination since they left Cuba. It seemed like too sensitive a topic. But now that Clemente had introduced it, Hammond found himself eager to engage this soon-to-be-historic figure before he was in the clutches of federal prosecutors.

"That theory has been around for ages," Hammond said.

"I know this, and it is what we in Cuba call *tonterías*— nonsense. The fence above the knoll was very tall. Did they think the shooter would stand on a box? There were also people there who would have seen him. No professional assassin would want to be seen. There were people in that big parking lot on the other side of the fence too."

"But a sewer grate was there."

"Yes, I know. I saw that on the map in my hotel room."

"Did it also go to your storm drain?"

"No, to the river."

"Well, that would have allowed a grassy knoll shooter to escape quietly in the confusion, no?"

"Maybe, maybe not. As I said, a smart assassin does not want to be seen regardless of his escape route. Of the four of us, only Oswald made a mistake there."

"He did?"

"Yes, he stuck his rifle too far out the window. There were people on the sidewalk in front of the book depository who looked up and saw it. That was stupidity on his part. If he had brought it back farther, the shots would not have been any harder for him to make."

"That's interesting."

"He also left the shells on the floor. How long would it have taken to pick them up and put them in his pocket? He did a terrible job of hiding the weapon too. His planning was very poor. If he had done everything right, he might have gotten away with it. And then killing that police officer, Mr. Tippit." Clemente shook his head sadly. "Why did he have to do that? He could have just pointed his gun at the man and run off. Foolish . . . foolish."

Hammond nodded. "Do you think Oswald was going to—?" His phone cut him off. "It's Noah," he said, then answered it. "Hello, how are—?"

"Jason." Noah's voice was unsteady. "I've got a call on hold here that I'm passing to you."

"Who is it?"

"He wouldn't give me his name, but . . . he's got Sheila."

"What?"

"I'm sure it's the same nut who's been tailing you all along, the one who shot Ben."

"Haven't you received several other calls from people claiming—?"

"I *talked* to her, Jason. She's with him right now."

"How did she sound?"

"Upset, very upset. But . . . he wants you. I need to transfer the call."

"Was there any caller ID?"

"No."

Hammond took a deep breath. "Okay, go ahead."

Clemente, noticing his strained expression, said, "What is wrong?"

Just before switching to speakerphone, Hammond said, "It's the man who kidnapped Sheila Baker. He's got her with him now."

There were two clicks followed by silence, and for a bone-freezing moment, Hammond thought the call had been lost. Then—"Mr. Hammond?"

The voice was exactly how Hammond always imagined it would be—on the surface, calm, even polite. The sound of a man capable of producing the illusion of decorum and etiquette whenever he chose. But even this well-used talent could not entirely eclipse the corruption beneath, the sadism and irrational self-love that lay at the core of his being. "I'm here."

"Good; very good."

"And what should I call you?"

"You can call me Birk, but we really don't need to get into names, Mr. Hammond. We're not going to become friendly."

Hammond could not have agreed more. The notion that this was actually Rydell flashed briefly through his mind. *No, too young. This is Rydell's lapdog. The asylum inmate who's been after us all along.*

"Then what *are* we going to do?" Hammond asked.

"We're going to make a deal."

"Can I assume it involves my friend? The one you kidnapped?"

"That's right."

"And what are the terms?"

"Well, I'm all finished with her. She has served her purpose."

The implications made Hammond feel murderous. He forced himself to ease up on the accelerator. "If you have harmed her in any way, I will make you regret it."

This came out in a calm, measured tone and without a trace of humanity. Even Clemente looked stunned.

Birk immediately tried to regain the upper hand. "Do not threaten me, Mr. Hammond."

"Let me speak to her."

"You are not calling the—"

"Let me speak to her." Hammond enunciated each word as if teaching a primer class in the English language.

There was a long pause, during which he inwardly prayed he had not gone too far.

Then Sheila spoke, her voice wobbly. "Hello?"

"Sheila? It's Jason."

"Hi."

"How are you holding up?"

"I'm okay, for the most part."

She sounded weak, feeble. *Broken,* Hammond thought, then forced the word down until it was out of his mind.

"Has he hurt you in . . . in any particularly bad way?" He couldn't bring himself to name specifics.

She sniffled. "No, no, he hasn't."

"Okay. I'm going to do everything in my power to get you back, all right?"

"Sure."

Then Birk's voice again—"Now you know your little damsel is fine."

Hammond's fist tightened on the steering wheel. "And what is it you want? What's our 'deal'?"

"As I said, I am finished with her now. I could so very easily kill her and put her body someplace where it would never be found. But upon further consideration, I believe she would be more valuable to me alive, to be used as a bargaining chip."

"To bargain for . . . ?"

"Half a million dollars."

Hammond said nothing.

"Are you still there, Hammond?"

"Yes."

"And you heard the amount?"

"I heard it."

"I want it all in cash, naturally. And in bills no smaller than fifties. Can you do that?"

"Yes."

In the background, Sheila yelled, "Jason, no! Don't give him the satis—"

"*SHUT YOUR MOUTH!*" Birk screamed, away from the phone. Hammond tensed, waiting for the follow-up sound of a physical strike. When it didn't come, he let out a long breath.

"Half a million," Birk continued, "in fifties and hundreds."

"Where and when?"

"There is an abandoned shipyard in D.C. on the Anacostia

River at the end of Third Street. Go to the main building tonight at eleven. Use the side entrance, white door. You will bring the money inside and leave it on the floor. And make sure your other friend comes along too."

"Other friend?"

"The one you're currently traveling with. I know who he is, and I know *what* he is."

"Why does he have to be there at all?"

"So I can see both of you in plain sight. I don't trust you—or him."

Hammond looked at Clemente, who nodded.

"Okay, we will both be there."

"Once you drop off the money, you can take the girl and go."

"Just like that, huh?"

"That's up to you. Again, I'm done with her. Now I'm looking for a payoff. So if you want this to be simple, then it will be simple. But let me be clear on one very important point."

"What's that?"

"If you deviate from this plan in any way—if you come armed, if you alert the authorities, if you make any attempt to trip me up, I *will* kill her. I have done this before, and I am very good at it. Don't think of trying to be a hero, because I will make sure you don't get that chance. Am I perfectly clear, Hammond?"

"You're clear."

"Do we have a deal?"

"Yeah."

And Birk was gone.

• • •

The money was Birk's idea. His handler had been unspecific in his instructions. "Just get all three of them together in the same place," he had said. "I don't care how. Get them together, and kill them all."

Birk had every intention of carrying out his orders, but he wasn't going to toss away a golden opportunity to indulge in a little extortion at the same time.

He had thought carefully about the amount. He decided that something outrageous—say, $5 million—could cause several problems. First, Hammond might not be able to come up with the money quickly enough. Second, for that kind of number, he might resist. But half a million, Birk figured, was nothing to a guy like him.

Five hundred thousand, plus the hundred grand he was getting for this job from his employer, would be more than enough to set Birk up for quite a while. Very soon, this whole business would be over.

44

BARRY WHYTNER, the veteran FBI agent who had been put in charge of examining every inch of Rydell's home with a microscope, removed his glasses and rubbed his eyes. He stood in the kitchen, which was stage-brightened by a pair of droplights, and watched as two members of his team crawled around the linoleum floor wearing rubber gloves and dust masks.

It had been an unbearably long day; getting out of bed this morning seemed like a week ago. And what did Whytner have to show for his team's hard work? Not much—zillions of useless fingerprints and DNA samples, bags of innocuous trash, a safe that had recently been opened, and an upturned cardboard box in the basement whose contents had obviously been important to Rydell but were now impossible to determine. A glimmer of hope was doused when it turned out Rydell's personal computer was missing its hard drive. Whytner was further inflamed by the fact that he had been forced to post several of his men outside, where their time and talents were wasted fending off pesky reporters and curious neighbors. A few of the residents had already been interviewed, also without result. No one had seen the fugitive arrive or leave.

Whytner checked his watch—9:42 p.m.—and sent a silent thank-you to the heavens. *Eighteen more minutes.* When his relief man arrived, he would go home, take a shower, and fall into bed. Now three years into his fifties, he found he slept fewer hours each night, but the need for those hours was greater than ever. Covering a yawn with his wrist, he thought he certainly needed it on this particular night.

His personal cell phone issued the two soft tones that indicated a text message had arrived. He removed the phone from inside his jacket and opened the text.

Mr. Whytner—This is Jason Hammond. I am texting you because I am desperate for the FBI's help. I am supposed to meet the man who kidnapped Sheila Baker tonight, at the old Walton shipyard at 11:00. I am under the impression that Frederick Rydell will be there as well. I was told Sheila would be killed if I contacted the authorities, but I now believe we will both be killed regardless. Please send agents to the scene. Whatever happens to us happens, but you may not have the chance to catch either of these men again.

Whytner had to read the message twice to make sure he wasn't imagining it. He checked the incoming log and saw that there was no ID or point of origin. The agency had already established that Hammond's phone had that capability.

"Oh, man . . . ," he breathed.

• • •

As soon as Rydell was certain the message to Whytner—whom he had recognized in one of the Suburbans—was sent, he closed his eyes and took a deep breath. *That should take care of them,* he thought. He knew how Birk worked, how the agents worked, and, he believed, how Jason Hammond worked. *With a little luck, I'll kill all the birds with the same stone.*

He chuckled at his choice of platitude. Then he checked his rearview mirror for oncoming traffic, pulled off the shoulder, and continued onward.

The driver of the white Lexus, still keeping a discreet distance, did likewise.

• • •

At exactly 10:44 p.m., the rental car that had been carrying Hammond and Clemente for most of the day turned off Tingey Street and took Third until it terminated at a small parking lot formerly used by the employees of Walton Boat Works. The plant had been idle since February of 1996, when the owner and family patriarch, Ellis Walton IV, died of a massive stroke at the age of eighty-one while sitting behind his desk eating a Big Mac. His relatives fought one another for control of the business until they reached a stalemate, due more to concern over exorbitant lawyers' fees than anything else. Since then, the property had sat like a ruin, trapped in a legal stasis while the Waltons played a protracted game of chicken and waited for someone to blink.

Hammond pulled up to the side entrance as instructed, and he and Clemente got out. Although they were not aware of the fact, they were being observed by FBI teams in four different positions. None had seen anyone else arrive to this point, making them highly skeptical that the text Whytner received was genuine. Now they scrambled to report that Hammond was, in fact, on the scene, accompanied by an older man of Latino descent and unknown identity. There were a total of sixteen agents in the area, all under the same orders—keep a safe distance for the time being. They watched Hammond open the back door of the car and remove a brown leather bag containing what they correctly assumed was ransom money. They had traced recent bank activity in the area and found just one large withdrawal—half a million in cash from Virginia Commerce Bancorp shortly after eight thirty. The account was held by a retired invest-ment pro who, as it turned out, had been a close friend of Hammond's late father.

A chill breeze rolled off the waterfront, but Hammond ignored it and slid the bag containing the ransom money over his shoulder.

Clemente was on Hammond's side of the car now, watch-ing him. "Are you ready?"

Hammond nodded. "I guess so. Listen, this guy's obvi-ously out of his mind, so . . . in case anything unfortunate happens, I just want to thank you now for what you did during the drive."

Clemente smiled. "It was no problem."

At Clemente's urging, Hammond had showed the older man how to use the iPad to video-record what amounted to a detailed deposition concerning the Cuban's role in the assassi-nation. Hammond, driving, had been spellbound, marveling that he was the only person in the world aside from Clemente himself to have all the details of this information and to watch as the missing pieces to the most tantalizing puzzle of the modern age were set into place at last. Later, Hammond had uploaded the video to the same FTP site he'd used for the digitized copy of Margaret Baker's film. Then he'd instructed Noah to download it at home. Noah was to release it publicly if the meeting with Sheila's captor went afoul.

Through the door, they found themselves in what appeared to be a small receiving office. Some basic furniture was still there: a desk with a blotter, a cheap couch framed by mismatched end tables, and several straight-back chairs, as well as a large artificial plant in a cheap plastic pot. Everything was finely powdered with dust.

There was another doorway on the opposite side, the door itself removed long ago. This led into an employees' anteroom. Although details were scarce in the dark, Hammond could make out a bank of cubbyholes and a long bench bolted to a tile floor. The scratching of their shoes echoed expansively, suggesting much greater space than was visible. Hammond's heart jumped when he spotted a face in the dimness, then realized it was his reflection in a cracked mirror.

Moving forward again, he and Clemente came to yet another door. This one had a large rectangular window, through which Hammond could see the vast, cathedral-like hall where the Walton company had built its wares. A light, too high to be seen through the window, sent a cone of radiance to the concrete floor. Hammond pulled the door open and was immediately struck by the sour pungency of the Anacostia River. Then he could hear it, and he quickly located the source—a framed opening in the floor where the finished vessels had been lowered. To the right of this was a pair of bay doors that slid apart to mark the launch of each boat's maiden voyage. Each door was at least thirty feet tall and looked strangely magnificent in the distance.

But the sight of the doors was not what caught and held Hammond's attention with electromagnetic force—it was Sheila, hanging by a rope from the ceiling.

"No!"

He rushed in, ignoring Clemente's shouted warnings and caring not a whit if Sheila's killer took him down right then and there. As he drew closer, he made a sobering realization—she wasn't dead. The psycho who put her there had gagged her and tied her to one of the straight-back chairs from the receiving office, then suspended the chair over the rectangular maw that led to the river beneath. The rope ran up to a large pulley wheel, then angled down to a battleship-sized eye screw in the concrete floor. The fact that the wheel was rusted completely brown was heart-stopping enough, but what Hammond found more alarming was that a cement block dangled from the bottom of the chair on a few more feet of rope. Both Sheila and the block were rotating in an unhurried manner that was somehow grotesque, like huge Christmas decorations on display in the overhead light.

Hammond slowed to a walk and continued closer. Sheila was facing away from him for the moment, but he could hear her crying softly. Then came a metallic click, which he immediately recognized as the hammer of a pistol being thumbed into place.

The man called Birk stepped from the shadows, smiling confidently. He was lean and handsome, slightly unshaven, clad in jeans and a white dress shirt unbuttoned toward the top and untucked at the bottom. He appeared to be the kind of man who would not be out of place in a trendy nightclub, would maybe make some extra money doing magazine ads for cologne or liquor. But Hammond could also sense the disturbance behind those eyes, the peripatetic psychosis that would always keep him a few steps behind the march of normalcy.

"So you really did show up to save the girl." Birk put a curled hand to his mouth and performed a melodramatically triumphal horn signature, then laughed like a drunken hyena. When he noticed that neither of his guests were amused, he said, "Let me guess. Now you're going to exercise your solemn Christian duty and try to talk me out of my sinner's ways, right?"

"No," Hammond said without a trace of inflection, "I don't waste my time on hopeless cases."

Birk's smiled faded, and he brought the gun up until the barrel was aligned with Hammond's face. "Don't press me. You can make this quick and easy or slow and painful."

Hammond didn't flinch; neither, for that matter, did Clemente. Birk looked like he found this irritating.

"Is that the money?" Birk asked, nodding toward the bag.

"Yeah."

"Open it. 'Show me the money,' as they say."

Hammond took it off his shoulder and began unzipping.

"Dump it on the floor," Birk amended.

"On the floor?"

"Yeah, all of it. I want to see that there's no dye pack or wireless transmitter inside."

Hammond shrugged and followed his instructions. He actually had considered using an exploding dye pack, then decided not to take the chance. As he turned the bag over and began shaking out the neatly banded stacks, he cursed himself for not considering the transmitter idea. *It could've been sewn into the bag itself. . . .*

After the last stack fell, Birk motioned for Hammond and

Clemente to move away from the pile, then came over and kicked it around.

"Okay, now put it all back in again. Get down on your *knees*, big shot."

Hammond obeyed without comment.

When he was finished, Birk said, "Now slide it over to me."

Hammond did so while still on his knees. He got back up while Birk relocated the bag just outside the circle of light. Birk never once took his eyes off either of them.

"Okay," Hammond said, "you got what you want. Now please leave so I can get her down."

Birk wagged his finger. "No."

"Excuse me?"

"You won't be getting anything you want tonight. No girl, no riding in on your white horse to save the day. You get nothing."

"We had a deal."

"And I have another deal with another party. And that deal is contingent upon my wasting the three of you. It's one of the great laws of the universe—when someone gains, someone else loses. Today, you three are the losers."

"Rydell must be very proud," Hammond said.

"What?"

"Rydell."

"Who's that?"

Hammond traded a look with Clemente, the unspoken sentiment being, *His confusion really is most convincing. This guy is some actor.*

"Your boss, Frederick Rydell. I know all about him." When Birk's puzzled expression deepened, Hammond continued with, "You can't honestly expect me to believe you don't kn—"

Then he saw it all, the amazing truth of the matter coming to him in a wide, grand vision. *Of course he wouldn't know. Rydell would have to remain anonymous. Not only because it's his standard MO, but also because he could never run the risk of revealing his identity to crazies like this who work for him. The blackmail potential alone . . .* "The man who's pulling your strings is named Jasper Frederick Rydell, and he's the assistant deputy director of the CIA. He's been part of that agency since 1961. He also played a small but operational role in the assassination of President Kennedy."

Birk's eyebrows rose in surprised admiration. "Really?"

"—and it is likely he arranged the three murders from last night, each victim also having taken part in the conspiracy. As of this morning, however, he has been exposed and is on the run. Your assignment here is him getting you to do his last bit of dirty work."

"Yeah, so? It's nice to know who you're working for, but what does it change?"

Hammond could only stare in fascination. *How can anyone be this far removed from rationality? How does a person reach this point?* Shaking his head in disgust, he said, "Birds of a feather, I guess."

Once again Birk's smile fled. He walked over, gun out, and delivered a vicious kick to Hammond's stomach. Hammond dropped to all fours, gagging.

"I've got my money from you and plenty more coming when I send you and your friends to the afterlife. How I choose to do it is my business, so you might want to think about showing me a little respect." Birk motioned toward Sheila. "See that little sweetheart of yours? She didn't know how to show respect. One of the nastiest pieces of work I've ever met. Scratched my face and kicked me where it hurts the most."

Hammond, still trying to catch his breath, peered up at Sheila and found she was at a point in her rotation where she could return the glance.

He smiled and winked. "Good girl."

Birk kicked him again, harder this time. Hammond rolled onto his side and struggled to keep from crying out.

"Yeah, and now you get to see your good girl die. Try to smile about that."

Hammond shook his head and tried to say no but was unable to summon the breath. Clemente, kneeling at his side, held out a pleading hand. Birk ignored them both and swung his arm up, taking careful aim at the rope over Sheila's head.

"Have a nice swim," he said.

Then the lights went out.

• • •

Nothing happened for a brief moment as each character in the play tried to make sense of this unexpected change in the script.

Then Birk cursed and started firing. Each shot produced a flash, creating a silent-movie strobe effect. Hammond and Clemente instinctively dove away from their current positions—where Birk would expect them to be—and dropped to the ground with hands over their heads. More shots went off, and at first Hammond thought, *He can't have that many left.* Then he realized more than one person was firing. Two more reports were issued from close range—from Birk—then Hammond heard a mighty splash.

Sheila . . .

Disregarding the gunfire, Hammond got to his feet and took several blind steps until his foot found the edge of the frame that outlined the boat launch. He took the deepest breath of his life and dove in.

The frigid water attacked him with a million tiny needles. He growled in pain, the sound fragmenting like tissue paper in the greenish, murky darkness. He groped wildly for the chair, the rope, Sheila herself, but nothing was there. He did a split-second calculation, estimating where he had been in proximity to Sheila when the lights went out, then adjusted for where he had relocated to avoid taking a bullet from the enraged gunman. *I need to go left,* he decided. *Left and down.*

He cut a diagonal path in that direction, flailing his arms after each muscular stroke. Precious seconds burned away, and alarm began flooding in. His lungs began to tighten, then burn. He kept moving but still found nothing. He screamed out—"*SHEILAAAAA!*"—knowing the effort was futile. Now his lungs felt like they were about to explode. *God, please . . . Please help me.* He moved farther down, the pain in his chest unbearable. He reached out, swirled his arms around madly. Still nothing . . . nothing at all . . .

Then his foot struck something solid.

He turned, reached out, and grabbed onto the corner of the chair. He felt farther and found the contour of her face. He moved in close, wanting to let her know he was there. Then he saw that her eyes were closed.

Oh no. . . . Jesus, no. . . . Please. . . .

In spite of the adrenaline and the rage and the overwhelming desire to save her, he simply could not go another second without oxygen. He rocketed up and found he had been only four or five feet beneath the surface.

Breaking through, he produced a sound that eclipsed all others in the vicinity. Then he saw them—several men in dark suits and ties.

"SHE'S HERE! RIGHT DOWN BELOW ME! HELP ME, PLEASE!"

When he went under this time, he could hear others diving in. Then there were hands and faces everywhere, taking hold of different things, lifting Sheila and moving her toward the shore as the others hurried over to help them. Hammond saw her face again, kept screaming, *"HURRY! HURRY!"*

The next minute would be forever burned in his mind as a blur. They reached the muddy shore and eased her down. Someone produced a flashlight, someone else a knife. Once Sheila was cut free, Hammond began performing CPR. She did not respond at first, and her head rolled hideously to one side. Some of the suited men took a step back, their faces grim.

"Come on," Hammond said, tears rolling down his face. "Come *ON!*"

Then she jerked forward in a fierce belly crunch, filthy river water exploding from her mouth. Hammond cradled her in his arms, slipping one leg behind her back for support. She continued to cough and sputter for a time before her eyes fluttered open. There was enough fear and confusion there to last ten lifetimes.

When she looked up and saw who was holding her, a smile began to form. Then, abruptly, it vanished again. "What took you so long?" she demanded.

Hammond had never laughed so hard.

45

RYDELL NAVIGATED through the darkened suburb until he reached Pitney Avenue. The street was lined with massive sycamores and transversed the neighborhood's grid of right angles in a broad southwesterly curve. He was pleased to see no late-night stragglers about, no fortysomethings taking health walks or teenagers cruising around on bicycles. Everyone was tucked into bed and sleeping the just and noble sleep of America's working class.

He desperately needed sleep as well; the stress of the day had drained him. He had spent the last several hours in the multistory parking lot of a busy shopping mall, tucked in a corner with the driver's seat fully reclined as he waited for nightfall. Since the car was unknown to authorities, he judged that the odds of being discovered were virtually nil. He collected his thoughts, calmed his nerves, and ate two power bars—and never once noticed that the Lexus that had been tailing him earlier was parked about a hundred yards away. Just as Rydell required darkness to move forward with his plan, so did his pursuer.

As Rydell approached his destination—house number 194—he turned off the headlights and allowed the vehicle to roll quietly into the driveway. The house was an unremarkable ranch, cream yellow with black shutters and a great belly of a bay window next to the front door. The agency kept the property as a third-tier safe house but was now considering selling it due to lack of use. The story they had circulated through the area was that it was owned by a wealthy developer in North Carolina who was considering razing it in favor of a split-level prefab. That seemed to satisfy the local gossips, who so helpfully made sure to spread the word even further. In the meantime, good taxpayer dollars went to its upkeep, including basic landscaping in the spring and summer, snow removal in the winter, and minor repairs as needed.

Rydell got out, fished the keys from his pocket, and entered the garage through a side door. He lifted the bay door as quietly as possible and pulled in the car. Then he went through the house to make sure all blinds and curtains were closed. He returned to the car and retrieved the duffel bag, groaning as he picked it up. He took it into the basement, which was finished with Sheetrock and carpeting and, most importantly, a small bathroom with no windows.

• • •

Outside the house, the white Lexus sat under one of the sycamores, lights off but engine still idling. The driver, now wide awake with a mixture of both excitement and apprehension, watched and waited.

• • •

Hammond sat on the rear fender of the ambulance with Sheila huddled next to him and a heavy woolen blanket wrapped around them both. They had been given fresh clothes and strong black coffee. Red lights swirled around them, agents moved about in every direction, voices on radios cut in and out. They, in the center of it all, seemed to have been forgotten.

"No, she's okay, Noah," Hammond said into his phone. "They're taking her to the hospital to run some tests, but she told me she feels fine."

"I'm fine, Noah," she said into the mouthpiece.

"Okay," the older man replied, still sounding unconvinced. "What about Mr. Clemente?"

"They've taken him into custody," Hammond told him.

"You didn't—?"

"He wanted to go. He was eager to. I called Chip Frazier, and he's already agreed to represent." Frazier had been Hammond's attorney and friend for years.

"You're not worried about . . . you know? Something *happening* to him while in the government's hands?"

"I'm not. I think Vallick is a good and decent man who is making a real effort to scrub the CIA's reputation wherever he can. But just in case, I made sure to let it slip that I had Clemente's deposition on video."

"That must've had them jumping."

"It was suggested that I turn the files over as evidence. Chip told them to get stuffed."

"Very good. And what about this mental case who almost killed all of you?"

Hammond sighed. "No sign of him."

"He got away? With all those agents around?"

"Yeah. They think he had an escape route planned out. That would make sense if you think about it from his perspective. There were other openings in the floor that led to the river, and they think he just dove in."

"Too bad."

"Tell me about it. However, some blood was found inside that has to be his. We assume he was wounded because no one else was."

"Oh, well, they can use the samples and maybe make an ID on him."

"Exactly. And he left the money behind."

"You're kidding."

"No. When you're running for your life, I guess you don't stop to pick up heavy bags. That's what he gets for asking for so much. If it had been fifty grand, he might have been able to stick it in his pockets."

"Incredible. By the way, how did the agents know to go there in the first place?"

"They received a text message."

"From whom?"

"Me."

"Excuse me?"

"No, I'm kidding. One of them told me he received a text from someone *pretending* to be me."

"Rydell, I take it?"

"I don't know for sure, but I'm willing to bet on it."

"Yeah, it sounds about right. Does anyone know where he is?"

"No, no sign of him, nor did I expect there to be. When the heat's on, the man's a coward. That's the bottom line."

"Who knows where he could be by now."

"Smart guy, but still human. Maybe they'll pick him up."

"I hope so."

"Yeah. So let me get going. I have to call our curious friend and give him an update."

"I'm very relieved you're both all right."

"Thanks."

"Keep me updated too."

"Always."

Hammond replaced the phone in his pocket, checked to make sure no one was within earshot, then took Sheila by the shoulders. "You're sure he didn't . . . you know?"

She smiled. "No. As strange as this might sound, I would rather have died fighting him off than let him get away with anything."

Hammond shuddered. "Nutcase."

"And a half."

One of the EMTs appeared. "We should bring you to the hospital now, Ms. Baker."

She looked to Hammond. "Coming along?"

"I'll be there shortly."

"Okay." She reached up and kissed him on the cheek. "Thanks for saving my life, by the way."

"My pleasure."

"Mine, too."

After she was gone, he took out the phone again and dialed a number with a Dallas area code. It rang seven times before going to voice mail, which Hammond found highly unusual. *If the phone was turned off, or if he was already talking to someone, it would've gone right to voice mail. So why isn't he picking up?*

He tried a text instead.

Hey—A lot has just happened. Are you there?

He waited a few minutes, as the recipient in question was always prompt with his responses. When none came, he went to plan C—the home number. It was picked up on the second ring.

"Hello?" The voice belonged to a woman, late twenties or early thirties.

"Hi, Crystal. It's Jason."

"Hello there."

"Can I speak to the old man, please?"

"Excuse me?"

"Your dad—can I please speak to him? There have been some interesting developments in the last half hour, and I want to give him—"

"Isn't he with you?"

"With me?"

"Yeah."

"I don't understand."

"He got on a plane right after you called the first time."

"What are you talking ab—?"

Then he understood, and the nightmare scenario rapidly unfolded in his mind. There had, in fact, been one or two moments when he'd envisioned the possibility, but he never believed it would actually happen.

Crystal was speaking again, but Hammond didn't hear a word of it.

"You're sure he left?" he said, cutting her off. "You're absolutely certain he came here?"

"Yes. I made the travel arrangements while he packed his bag. And he called me when he arrived."

"Oh no. . . ."

"What, Jason? What's happening?"

"I'm not sure. Maybe it's nothing. Let me call you right back."

He launched the phone's GPS tracking software and entered the unresponsive cell number. Nothing happened for several moments. Then a street map appeared on the screen, a red dot blinking in the center. He didn't recognize the neighborhood, but the town—Lake Barcroft, Virginia— was less than thirty minutes away.

Hammond brought the phone to the agent standing closest to him. "Excuse me, does this area look familiar to you?"

The agent, a young guy who looked like he still had parties in his dorm room every Friday night, studied the map and shook his head. "Lake Barcroft? No, I don't—"

"Barcroft?" someone else cut in. "What about it?"

This was an older individual, silver-haired and serious. An in-charge type of guy.

Hammond brought the phone to him, and the map was appraised again.

"What's this red dot?"

"It's a friend of mine," Hammond said. "He apparently has some interest in this particular area. Can you think of a reason why?"

The agent seemed hesitant to answer. His eyes went over Hammond, scrutinizing him. Then, "The CIA has a safe house there, an old one that hasn't been used in a long time."

"On . . . ?"

"Pitney Avenue, yes. Right where your friend is." In-Charge Guy looked at the screen again to double-check. "Do you mind telling me how he would know about it?"

Hammond did, leaving out nothing. Then they were on Route 395, heading southwest at galactic speed.

46

RYDELL STARED into the mirror of the basement bathroom, and a stranger stared back.

It was a most remarkable job, he thought. Particularly gratifying considering his lack of expertise. He had known hundreds who lived and died with their ability to alter their appearance, but he had never conversed with any of them on the subject. No casual lunches in the agency cafeteria to pick their brains, no invitations to dinner and drinks on a Friday evening. He got his information, as so many did these days, off the Internet. As such, he'd been forced to absorb and apply it far too rapidly. And yet . . .

I can barely recognize myself, he thought with a satisfied grin, turning his head back and forth.

His hair, formerly in the transitioning-from-black-to-silver phase, was now uniformly iron gray. And the respectable combed-back style was gone, replaced by a more unkempt, almost-frazzled look. The false mustache was particularly effective—he had been concerned that it would look ridiculously bogus, like something attached to a set of the plastic Groucho nose and glasses found in every gag shop in the world. But this one was so convincing, it looked like it might start growing. Best of all, it matched the new hair perfectly.

Of the six alternate personas he'd created over the last two years, the one he decided to go with was named Louis Cooper. Cooper was what he thought of as "an old man who worked with his hands all his life." Lower income, minimal education, generally ignorant toward world affairs, and not too concerned about his appearance. To that end, Rydell decided the most appropriate costume would be a pair of work boots, jeans, and a plaid fleece coat. He'd also keep the glasses and hat he'd been wearing since he left the house. He liked that the aging Chevy Malibu seemed a credible choice for the character. Best of all, this alter ego was far enough removed from his actual self that it would just about eliminate any chance of his being spotted as he carried out the crucial next phase of the escape.

That phase had but one objective—to get out of America. This would be accomplished by road travel, he'd decided, on a southwesterly route that could cut through Virginia, Tennessee, Alabama, Mississippi, Louisiana, and then Texas. The newly minted Mr. Cooper had a birth certificate, driver's license, and passport, so a border crossing wouldn't be a problem. Besides, Rydell thought, it was a rare occasion indeed when anyone cared if you went from America *to* Mexico.

At first he thought it might be best to travel only at night. But that could cause problems, like attracting the attention of some bored cop on an otherwise-empty stretch of highway. So he would drive during the day, mostly while the rest of the country was hard at work, and maybe some evening hours as well. He would get his food at drive-throughs, go to the bathroom at rest stops and gas stations, sleep in small, out-of-the-way motels, and pay for everything in cash.

When he reached Monterrey in Nuevo León, he could begin the next phase of the plan. This was his favorite by far—taking a flight to the Caribbean island of St. Eustatius, buying a villa, and spending the rest of his days with a straw hat propped over his face while he snoozed under the afternoon sun.

He stepped out of the bathroom and into the small sitting area. This included a couch, CRT television, faux fireplace, and coffee table. He had set the duffel bag on the couch and taken out only those items required to become Louis Cooper. But now he noticed that something was different. Many items were scattered around the bag helter-skelter, as if a small bomb had gone off inside it. Then came the sound, instantly familiar and doubly chilling.

Click.

He turned slowly, already knowing someone was there holding a gun. What he did not expect was *who*. With a sickening acceptance, he figured it would be someone from the agency, maybe some wet-behind-the-ears kid who took a chance on this largely forgotten safe house and could now expect a citation for his brilliance, maybe even a promotion. Or perhaps it would be Vallick himself, mad as a hornet and ready to parade his catch in front of every camera in town. Neither guess was correct, and a hundred more would not have made any difference.

Ben Burdick's face was a study in murderous hatred. The eyes, deep set under a tightly furrowed brow, were locked on his prey. His lips were pressed together hard. And there was a slight tremor in the cheeks, which Rydell recognized as the burbling of loosely controlled rage.

Fear blew through him like hot gas. "But . . . you're *dead*."

"Sorry to disappoint you, but no."

"That's impossible. You were shot."

Burdick undid the second and third buttons of his shirt with his free hand and pulled the placket aside. The large gauze pad taped there was spotted with blood. "But not killed. A broken rib and a punctured lung. Your hired thug could have easily finished the job, but he didn't. What should've been the last day of my life turned out to be the luckiest because it gave me the chance to hunt you down."

"The press . . . The stories about your death . . ."

"My kids helped with that, and a doctor friend who came through when I needed him most. All misinformation. The bit about my being cremated and my ashes scattered in a private location? That was their idea. Brilliant, just brilliant. You remember my kids, right, you sniveling little worm? If memory serves, you threatened to kill *them* on several occasions too."

The look on Burdick's face was truly terrible now, and Rydell's fear was rapidly morphing into unadorned terror.

"Maybe we can make a deal," he said unevenly, his throat as dry as a chimney flue. "I have two hundred thousand in cash with me. You take half of it for yourself." That amount would be covered by the fee he had no intention of paying Birk. "In return, you let me leave th—"

• • •

Burdick strode briskly forward and backhanded him across the face. Rydell spun around like a ballet dancer, blood flying, and crashed to the floor. The false mustache that had so impressed him dangled ridiculously from one side. The hat and glasses had also been jarred into new and awkward positions.

"You think you can buy your way out of this?" Burdick screamed, leaning down as if scolding a dog. "Are you out

of your *mind*? YOU RUINED MY LIFE! YOU DROVE ME OUT OF A PROFESSION I LOVED! *YOU ENDANGERED MY FAMILY!*"

Burdick delivered a soccer-style kick to the stomach, and Rydell twisted into a fetal position.

"If I get a hundred thousand, then how much do you suppose you owe the *Kennedys*? What's the going price for a dead son or a murdered father in your book? And for that matter, how much will it take to repay the American people for their *lost president*?"

Burdick kicked again, this time in a location where no man likes to be struck, and Rydell cried out.

"No," Burdick said, shaking his head, "there's no out for you this time, you heartless monster. This time you pay your bill, and I get to be the collector."

He wound up for another shot, but Rydell surprised him by swinging his own foot up and connecting at the point where he'd seen the gauze pad. The pain was impossibly radiant, snatching the breath from Burdick's throat and causing him to take several staggering, robot-like steps backward. Then he lost his balance and went down, clutching at the site of the blow as the gun bounced away on the cheap Berber carpet.

Rydell got sluggishly to all fours and began crawling for it. Burdick wrapped his arms around Rydell's thigh. Rydell responded by using his open palm to piston Burdick's head into the floor several times. Burdick released his grip, and Rydell started forward again.

But Burdick wouldn't quit, grabbing him around the ankle this time. When he pulled, Rydell fell flat. Cursing, Rydell sat up more quickly than Burdick had thought possible and drove a fist into the wound site. Burdick screamed and rolled over, a burst of blood exiting his mouth. Then, with a strength fueled by absolute hatred, he lunged forward just as Rydell reached for the weapon.

They both let out guttural moans and crashed to the floor together. Burdick scrambled over him and got his hands around the butt of the pistol. He wasn't even certain how good a grip he had, but it would have to do. He rolled over, swung the gun around, and with trembling hands fired off a single round.

Rydell was on his knees at that moment, about to pounce on him. When he froze like an image in a photograph instead, Burdick thought he'd killed him. Then he realized the bullet had in fact gone up and to the left, through the ceiling to who knew where. What he found encouraging, however, was the fresh overlay of dread on Rydell's face.

Burdick rose slowly and with great effort. He was aware of the warm flow coming from the reopened wounds in his chest and the matching one on his back. The pain was like nothing he ever imagined a human being could endure. Worse, it was beginning to make him feel light-headed again. He had experienced this many times since the shooting. It was normal, he had been told, and would pass in time. Meanwhile, it was relatively harmless as long as he didn't engage in any stressful activity. The adrenaline was compensating for now, but he knew that wouldn't last forever. If he grew dizzy in front of this man, if he began to lose consciousness . . .

Get on with it.

"Okay," he said with labored breaths, "now . . . for all that you've done to me and my family, for what you helped do to the president you swore an oath to serve, and for every other crime you have committed in direct violation of the laws and ideals of this country . . ."

Burdick pulled the hammer back and took careful aim.

Then a familiar voice said softly, "No, Ben."

The two battle-weary men turned at the same time and found Jason Hammond standing there with three agents behind him. Several more could be heard thundering down the steps out of view. The trio had their own weapons drawn but not raised, as Hammond had one hand open to signal that they should hold their fire.

"Ben, if you pull that trigger, he will never stand trial, never be held accountable for his crimes. At least not in his mortal life. Is that what you want? Is that what you *really* want?"

Burdick gave this some thought but did not lower the gun. "The things he did . . . to me, to Kennedy . . ."

"No one's doubting that. And no one's doubting that he'll be made to pay for his sins."

"Who knows how many other victims there are? How much more suffering has he caused?"

Hammond walked toward Burdick slowly, hands raised. "I know. Everyone knows. But if you pull that trigger, you become like him. You *become* him. You are a man of peace and justice, whereas he is a murderer. He possesses no regard for human life, no sensitivity toward the effect his actions have on others and on the world at large. He only understands his own wants. Remember when you and I talked about how America changed after the assassination, how you thought it marked the beginning of the end of America's innocence? That's exactly what the Rydells of the world want. They have no innocence of their own, no humanity, so they devote their energies to shattering whatever beauty they encounter. Their selfishness, their ego, their arrogance . . . when these things are empowered, they act like poison, infecting and polluting every good thing in their path. It is his *willingness* to kill in the first place that makes him what he is. Yes, he should be held accountable for what he has done. Yes, he deserves to be punished. But do you want to sacrifice yourself just to expedite his sentence?"

No one moved or spoke. Burdick maintained his lethal gaze and kept the gun at the pale expanse of Rydell's forehead.

Hammond took another step closer; now they were inches apart. "He's been trying to destroy you for years, Ben. Are you really going to hand him that victory now?"

Another moment unwound slowly. Then Burdick brought the weapon down, his shoulders fell, and all the strength went out of his body.

Hammond stepped in to catch him while a team of agents descended upon Rydell, who was cuffed behind the back and led away.

47

A BLUE SEDAN pulled into the lot behind the infamous picket fence and rolled into one of the empty spots. Ben Burdick got out first, camera in hand. Then Hammond, who had taken out his cell phone and was reading something on the screen. Sheila emerged from the backseat and slipped on a pair of sunglasses to shield against the late-morning sunlight. Then Noah, looking as affable as ever in his ubiquitous felt cap. He had already been here for three days, readying Jason's private plane for the return flight to New Hampshire. The other three had landed at Dallas/Fort Worth International just a few hours earlier.

"This was a stockyard in November of '63," Burdick said as they moved southeast toward the triple underpass. "Nothing but dirt and gravel. Now it's a parking lot for the Sixth Floor Museum."

"The railroad tower's still there," Hammond said, nodding toward the tiny structure behind them, "where Lee Bowers was when he saw two unidentified men."

"When he testified for the Warren Commission, he claimed they were near the underpass. A few years later, however, he said they were closer to the fence."

Hammond shook his head. "Everyone had a story to tell. Everyone but the people who knew the truth." He sighed. "Well, at least that'll be taken care of now."

They walked down the hill to the mouth of the underpass. All the major landmarks in Dealey Plaza could be viewed from here—the grassy knoll, from which countless conspiracy theorists insisted the fatal shot was fired; the concrete pergola where Zapruder filmed the assassination; and the former Texas School Book Depository, since sold to Dallas County in 1977. The first five floors had been repurposed as administrative offices. The sixth, from which Lee Harvey Oswald finally satisfied his obsessive desire to write his name into the pages of history, eventually became a memorial center to the president whose future he stole.

"In so many ways," Burdick said, "it seems like nothing's changed. I can still feel it."

Hammond nodded. "I was thinking the same thing. The ghosts of that day, the emotions . . . it's like they linger here, trapped forever."

Sheila slipped her hands into the pockets of her jeans and shuddered. "That's eerie."

"It certainly is."

As they began walking, Sheila asked, "Do you think they'll bring Galeno Clemente back here? As part of his testimony?"

"Chip thinks there's a chance of that," Hammond said. "They might ask him to reenact what he did, not just for the case but to fill the gaps in the historical record."

"How's he holding up?" This question came from Noah.

"He's fine. He's so at peace with everything it's scary. Lawyers are coming out of the woodwork in droves, trying to get involved in either side of the case so they can get their names attached to it. What case is there, though? He wants to confess everything." Hammond smiled. "He said he's going to start a prison ministry once he's permanently incarcerated. He mentioned getting help with it from someone he knew when he was doing missionary work. Father Breimayer, the name was."

Sheila said, "I know this is going to sound strange, but did Galeno technically commit a crime? I mean, he didn't fire, after all."

"No," Burdick replied, "but you're still not allowed to take part in an assassination plot against the president—or anyone else, for that matter. Actually, that reminds me of an interesting point. A lot of people don't know this, but in 1963, there *was* no specific law against assassinating the president. Oswald was charged with ordinary murder."

"He killed that police officer too," Noah said.

"Yes, but I mean where the president was concerned. That murder charge was the same as the one for Officer Tippit. Can you believe it?"

"A murder's a murder, I guess," Sheila said.

"I suppose."

"And how are you feeling now? Any better?"

"Yeah, a little bit. When I told my doctor what happened, he went ballistic. Actually yelled at me through the phone."

"Ben, if this is an uncomfortable topic," Noah said, "just tell me to go jump in a lake. But what actually happened after you were shot?"

"Well, when I regained consciousness, my first instinct was to call 911. That's what most people would do, right? But then it hit me—*if I let them think I'm dead, maybe I can work that to my advantage.* Remember, this Rydell guy was on my back for years, but if he thought I was out of the picture, he'd finally leave me alone. So I called my doctor, whom I've become pretty good friends with, and told him what had happened. He came right over and treated me on the spot. He wanted me to go to the hospital, but I wouldn't. I told him the whole story at that point—about how I was being threatened because of the book, how my kids had been threatened, all of it. Finally he agreed to keep everything quiet. He came and checked on me every day. Then my daughter, Crystal, got involved. She was the one who came up with the idea of leaking the story to the press, and man, did they run with it. She said she had me cremated and all that. Brilliant. She's always been the smartest kid in the class."

"Had us fooled," Hammond said.

"I had to do it, Jason. I needed the cover. Crystal and I began researching all the guys in the intel community to see if we could find the person or persons who might be responsible. We eventually came up with a list of twenty-two names—people who had high clearance, who had been around since '63, things like that. Rydell was on it, and when I got that call from you confirming him, I knew then . . ."

"Knew what?" Sheila asked.

"That I had to come to D.C. to face him. Yeah, the Feds might've caught up with him sooner or later. But it was more personal to me. Too personal to not at least take a shot at it—no pun intended. That's why I didn't tell anyone when I went there. I knew you'd try to talk me out of it."

"You could've been killed," Noah said. "He was one sly character."

"I know; I know. I got very lucky. I admit that."

"So are you going to publish the second book?" Hammond asked.

"Of course. But I need to add a bit more now, obviously."

"Good," Hammond said. "Somebody should certainly write all this down."

"I'm going to head back to D.C. once I'm fully healed. I want to follow both trials—Rydell's and Clemente's. And can you believe I've already been contacted by two publishers? They're offering big advances too. I can finally get the house in order, maybe start seeing a personal trainer and get some of this weight off."

"No word on the lunatic, though?" This was Sheila's question. "Birk?"

With the help of the blood samples found at the abandoned boat works, Birk's identity had been confirmed. Ex-military, with a long disciplinary record culminating in a dishonorable discharge following an altercation that left a superior officer with a shattered jaw. Worked as a soldier of fortune for many years afterward, building something of a reputation. Held no national loyalties, always willing to sell his services to the highest bidder.

Hammond shook his head. "No, no word yet. But the FBI is searching hard for him."

He took Sheila by the hand and crossed to the other side of Elm, stopping at a point about fifteen feet from the curb, just across from the storm drain. There were other people walking around, on the pergola and the knoll and the sidewalk by the former book depository, taking their own photos and making their own observations. Dealey Plaza had become more of a tourist attraction now than anything else, as if the events of that day had been part of a popular movie rather than reality.

"This is where your mom stood that day," he said.

Sheila nodded. "I know." She tried to imagine what it must have been like for her. Margaret Baker had been just another citizen, excited at the prospect of seeing the handsome young president and his beautiful wife. What promise the future held for America! The bustling economy . . . the civil rights movement . . . the Peace Corps . . . the Space Race . . . New ideas were pouring forth from his White House as the nation moved toward a future that seemed unlimited with possibilities. Margaret had never given much thought to politics one way or the other, but Sheila knew her mother had genuinely liked John Kennedy of Massachusetts.

"And there's where Galeno Clemente sat waiting," she said. Ben was over by the drain, kneeling down in the road taking pictures.

"That's right. There's too much asphalt built up now to try something like that again." Hammond nodded toward a spot in the road, in the middle lane a bit north of center, where a simple X had been applied with the same luminescent paint as the traffic lines. "And that's where it ended for the president."

"But for my mama and me," Sheila added, "it was just beginning."

• • •

When it was just the two of them in the car on the way back to the hotel, Hammond said, "So are you sorry? Sorry you didn't destroy the film instead?"

"There hasn't been an hour since you first came to the house that I haven't asked myself that question. I've tried to weigh both the good and the bad. Getting kidnapped versus exposing Rydell and putting Birk on the run. Nearly getting killed a few times while having one of the most unforgettable experiences of my life. Losing my childhood home but helping to complete one of the greatest unfinished chapters in history. It's tough." She shook her head. "I'm just glad my mama didn't have to go through it."

Hammond thought she might start crying then. But no tears came. She was all cried out—or so he imagined. "And what's next for you?"

"When I was sitting there in captivity, wondering if I would ever see sunlight again, I got to do some serious thinking. When your life's on the line, you suddenly see things very clearly. I made a promise to God that I intend to keep. I asked him to save my life, and here I am. It's funny—so many of us have it so good when we're young, but then we abandon certain things because we feel we've outgrown them or because we think it's time for a change or we *have* to change or whatever. One of the things I really liked as a kid was when I went to church with my parents. And I have to admit, I've been pretty inspired by Galeno Clemente's story too."

"No doubt," Hammond said, nodding.

"There's a pastor in my complex back home, and he's asked me a few times if I'd be interested in attending services on Sundays. Maybe it's time I took him up on his offer."

"And what about your fitness centers?"

"I'm just about out of debt, like I said before. Once that's out of the way, I'm going to sell the—"

"It *is* out of the way."

"Hmm?"

Hammond turned to her and smiled. "It's already out of the way. The debt's been satisfied."

"What do you mean?"

"Noah and I took care of it this morning."

At first she seemed confused; then her eyes widened and her mouth fell open. "No . . . Jason!"

"Yes, Sheila."

"Jason, no . . . seriously. I can't allow you to—"

"It's already done. Can't undo it; sorry."

The smile that was spreading across her face gave him boundless pleasure.

"Jason!" She reached over and slapped him on the shoulder. "How could you do something like that!"

"It wasn't a big deal, really."

"I can't believe you!" A few more whacks, and then she settled back into her seat and started shaking her head. "I'm going to pay you back. Every penny."

"You absolutely are not. You are going to go on with your life without this millstone around your neck anymore. You've been through enough in the last few years, don't you think? Sell the property where your mom's house used to stand, then take the money and run."

Now the tears did come, but Hammond was reasonably sure they weren't the by-product of grief.

"I can't believe it. I just can't believe it."

"Also, I think you said you had a love of children?"

"Yes . . . ?"

"And a passion to give rather than take?"

"Yes?"

"And to make a meaningful difference?"

"Yes?"

"Well, if you want it, there's a job waiting for you in the Hammond Guiding Light Organization. I set it up three years ago to provide basic necessities and medicine for youngsters in the most impoverished areas of the world. We have twenty-two locations, but we'd like to have a few more. That said, we could use someone who knows how to get a business up and running." He pulled into the hotel parking lot and turned off the engine. "So what do you say? Do you think charity work would be your—?"

As he turned to face her, she gave him a hug with such force it almost drove him against the door.

Laughing and hugging her back, he said, "I'll take that as another yes."

As they began walking toward the hotel, Hammond said, "You realize, of course, this means I'll be your boss."

Sheila made a face. "Dream on."

"Mmm . . . I didn't think so."

"No."

48

NOAH THOUGHT David Weldon might just be the happiest man in the world. Hammond gave the reporter as many details as possible during the flight back to New Hampshire, avoiding only those topic areas that had been forbidden by Chip Frazier. "I might be called in to testify," Hammond said. "At some point, though, I'll fill in all the gaps for you." Weldon said he was plenty satisfied with the information he already had. Every major journalist wanted the exclusive, after all, and he was having it handed to him.

Noah expected Hammond to have his customary emotional meltdown as soon as he got behind the controls of the plane, but it didn't happen. *There's something different this time,* Noah thought. *He's more pensive, more meditative. He's withdrawn, yes. But he doesn't seem like a caged animal.* Noah wasn't sure what to make of this. "We have some matters to tend to when we get back," he said.

"I know," Hammond replied with a nod. Before Noah even had time to register his shock at what sounded like willingness, Hammond continued with "And what's the damage?"

"Damage?"

"For everything I've done. I'm sure I've got some trouble coming my way. I evaded the Coast Guard; I didn't go to the police after Ben was shot; I went to Cuba without written permission from the Treasury Department. . . ."

"Are you sure you want to discuss it now?"

"Now, later, no real difference. Let me have it, minus any candy coating."

"Well, the Dallas police are willing to forget about the issue with Ben since he wasn't actually killed. You voluntarily left a crime scene, but I don't think they'll pursue that. I can talk to Chip to make s—"

"No, don't do that. If they decide to come after me, let them. I'm guilty. What else?"

"You're going to have to appear in court concerning the Coast Guard evasion. It's unlikely that incarceration will even be considered, mainly since they were looking for drug smugglers and not you. But you're still going to get a fine for not stopping. That's pretty much guaranteed."

"And?"

"And you'll probably lose your boating license for a year, maybe two."

"I figured as much. What about the lawsuit Vallick was going to launch?"

"All things considered, Chip doesn't think they'll bother now. Not with Rydell in custody."

"And what about Cuba?"

"Well, that's pretty serious. That's federal. You can count on a fine there, too. A big one, reaching into six figures. And if you ever want to go down there again, regardless of the reason, it'll take a miracle for the government to give you the green light."

"Is that all?"

Noah took a deep breath and let it out. "No. They're going to review possible revocation of your company's humanitarian license. Even if they don't take it away, you just slid the company way down the list for early consideration when the Cuban market reopens to American businesses. Your father worked like mad to get a head start on those opportunities. In the long run, that'll hit us pretty hard. And you'll be lucky if they allow you to keep your passport too."

Hammond sat quiet for a long time. The engines droned and the oxygen hissed. Then he nodded again. "Yeah, okay."

∙ ∙ ∙

They landed on the estate shortly after ten and took the Ford Expedition to the main house. Hammond made sandwiches for both of them, and they ate in silence. When Noah went back to the kitchen to set his plate in the sink, he considered opening the conversation that neither wanted to have—once again, certain business matters were reaching a critical point and required decisions. He opted to wait until morning, as that was the time of day when Hammond seemed happiest. He said good night and left for his cottage.

∙ ∙ ∙

Hammond took a quick shower and got into bed. The book he'd been reading before Sheila's call, *Paris-London Connection: The Assassination of Princess Diana*, was still on the nightstand. He picked it up and continued where he'd left off, as if the events of the last few weeks hadn't even occurred. A few pages in, however, he found he was having trouble concentrating. He set the book on his sheet-covered chest and stared aimlessly forward for a time. In this powered-down mental mode, he heard a voice in his head—Galeno Clemente, in a rewind of the conversation they'd had on the boat ride from Cuba. Bits and pieces had been echoing all along—

"You cannot do the deed yourself, so you put yourself in danger in the hope of having someone else do it."

"You have not yet destroyed yourself as I did, but you will in time."

"Do not waste your opportunities. Do not waste yourself."

And finally:

"God did not take my parents from me, Mr. Hammond. And he did not take your family from you."

He looked to the little Bible on the bookshelf, and his gaze remained there for a while. He closed the Princess Diana book, set it aside, and got up. The Bible felt cool in his hand—a comforting kind of cool that comes from a book for which one has genuine affection.

He sat down on the edge of the bed and began to read. This time, he found he had no trouble concentrating at all.

• • •

The hallway was soundless, the sconce lights dim. When he reached the door that led to his family's suite of rooms, he opened it. It was like opening the door on a carnival scene, except these sights and sounds, vivid though they were, existed only in his mind.

There was Joanie in one of her long nightshirts, in this case the one with the black-and-white stripes that he thought of as her "burglar's uniform." And his mother, resplendent in her baby-blue robe and matching slippers, on her way to the sitting room to watch reruns of *Frasier* or *Designing Women*. And there was his father, shoeless and tieless but still in his wool trousers and dress shirt—his definition of "casual"—striding between his bedroom and his office as more ideas dropped into his tireless brain in a never-ending hailstorm of business wizardry. No matter how busy the man was, though, he found time every night to stop in and have a brief end-of-the-day chat with each of his children. He wanted them to know that they were important to him, that their *lives* were important to him. Hammond would have given anything to have just one more of those talks. And one more kiss on the cheek from his mother. And one more hug from Joanie. And to feel the warmth of simply knowing that they were there.

He moved forward until he came to the paired office doors. Every emotion was in play now. He reached for the knob as he had weeks earlier, sliding his fingers around its cool surface. The urge to let go was powerful, but he turned it and pushed the door open. Then another voice spoke up in his mind, this time his own from a verse he had memorized in his teenage years: *"For if our heart condemn us, God is greater than our heart, and knoweth all things."*

There was no light inside the office, only formless shadows and the suggestion of things unseen. He came alongside his father's desk and turned on the lamp. The shadows fled, and the shapes became things—the antique furniture, the framed family photos, the telephone, the stacks of books and newspapers. He could still smell his father's cologne and his beloved hazelnut coffee. One of his navy blazers hung from the back of the chair, and a silver pen—his favorite—lay on the blotter exactly where he had left it. Hammond could see him there, doing paperwork with his sleeves rolled up. And his mother coming into the room to fill her cup at the water cooler. And he could hear Joanie's radio going in her bedroom down the hall.

He took a deep breath, and all the ghost images vanished. Now only the reality remained.

49

NOAH WAS lying on his side and snoring like a longshore-man when the phone on the nightstand rang. He jerked awake, confused, and waited to see if more would come; perhaps he had only dreamed it. The second ring dashed this notion, and he snatched the handset from its base. He checked the caller ID—the main house—and then the clock radio—2:33 a.m. *This can't be good,* he thought.

The anxious voice of Valeria, the housekeeper, chattered through the line. Noah became more awake with every word.

He dressed quickly and went out.

• • •

When he reached the hallway intersection, he found Val in the same outfit he was wearing—a robe and slippers—standing a few cautious paces back from the entrance to Alan Hammond's office. The doors were open, and the light inside spilled across the pink carpeting.

As Noah came forward, he saw the fearful look on the woman's face. His instinct was to be comforting, to tell her not to panic, everything was going to be fine. But that might not be the truth here.

When he reached the open doors, he was confronted by a scene that he never, in a billion centuries, would have thought possible—Jason sitting behind his father's desk, going through paperwork. Two filing cabinet drawers were open, and folders were stacked around him in sloppy piles.

Noah could only stare, fascinated. He felt like a child watching a magic trick, seeing it clearly but still unable to believe it.

"Jason?"

There was no response. Hammond was reviewing a spreadsheet, working his way down the columns with his father's silver pen.

Again—"Jason?"

This time Hammond, shaken out of his concentration, looked up. "Huh? Oh, hi, Noah."

"Hi. Er . . . are you all right?"

The question seemed to baffle him, and a few moments ticked away without a sound. Noah didn't mind; he was willing to wait all night.

Hammond let out a breath that seemed to carry all the strength from his body. "No, not really," he said. Then he did something else Noah would not have expected in an eternity—he smiled.

"But I think it's time I tried to be."

Afterword

THIS IS A TALE of fantasy, of course. The core concept came in a bright moment of inspiration in November of 2003 while I was watching a documentary about the Kennedy assassination on—what else?—the History Channel. Long before then, however, and certainly many times since, I have been asked the pivotal question: "Do you think Oswald acted alone?" My answer is an unequivocal *yes*. Of this I no longer possess a shred of doubt.

For those of you who are already steadfast disciples of the lone-gunman theory, this should come as a welcome admission, as you now have one more member among your flock.

For those who are determinedly fixated on the notion that the shooting was, in fact, the work of surreptitious, comic-book hooligans who then managed to veil a conspiracy of such startling proportion for half a century, I doubt there's anything that I or anyone else can say of a rational, reasonable nature that will move you off your position. I apologize for making the conscious choice not to play on your team anymore, but I've tried it and grew tired of never gaining an edge on my opponents.

And for those of you who truly remain undecided, I would like to suggest the two books that enabled me to finally reach a point of closure on the subject. The first is Vincent Bugliosi's *Reclaiming History*. If you are old enough, you may recognize the author's name already—Bugliosi was the prosecutor in the trial of Charles Manson et al for the Tate-LaBianca murders of 1969, and then coauthor of a popular book about it called *Helter Skelter*. In *Reclaiming History*, he draws upon his considerable legal skills to examine, in brain-overloading detail, every conceivable perspective of the event. His second-by-second account of the actual shooting is so thorough you'd think he was there that day, armed with camcorders, microphones, and a small cadre of stenographers. He also takes aim at the many alternate theories that have so entertained the public through the years, blowing each out of the sky like the clay pigeon it is. It took him over twenty years to research and write the book, which boasts an elephantine 1,600-plus page count—not including the endnotes, which are so voluminous they had to be included on a CD—and weighs in at nearly six pounds (also making it a serviceable weapon). First published in 2007, *Reclaiming History* is still widely available and, mercifully, can now be digested in e-book format.

The second title is a bit more elusive, as it has been out of print since 1967. Copics are sometimes available from antiquarian dealers, albeit at prohibitive prices, and I certainly hope a paperback or digital edition (or both) is put forth by the rights holder at some point. The book in question, *Lee: A Portrait of Lee Harvey Oswald by His Brother* was written by the assassin's older brother, Robert. Robert Oswald had a better fly-on-the-wall perspective of the assassin than anyone. He was able to observe Lee, up close and personal, during every stage of his brother's brief and troubled life. This is why I venture the opinion that his book is the singular most important piece of evidence supporting the lone-gunman theory that we have. (If you try and really can't find a copy, then Norman Mailer's 1995 work *Oswald's Tale: An American Mystery* is a very suitable substitute.) To truly understand the horrific act that was carried out in Dealey Plaza that day, you must familiarize yourself with the psyche of the person responsible. Robert Oswald—with tremendous courage and generosity, in my view—provided the raw material to do this and, in turn, gave the definitive testimony on the assassination. While thousands have poured their time and energy into examining grainy photographs, interpreting inconsistent eyewitness accounts, and performing costly reenactments, the key that turned the lock all along has been sitting in the pages of this unjustly forgotten publication, which affords the reader the unparalleled privilege of getting behind the eyes of the man who envisioned the crime, forged the plan, and pulled the trigger.

About the Author

WIL MARA has been writing books for the last twenty-five years. He began in the school-library market, where he has contributed more than seventy-five educational titles for young readers. He entered the fiction world with five ghostwritten titles for the popular Boxcar Children Mysteries series. Wil's first novel for adults was the 2005 disaster thriller *Wave*, which sold through its first printing in less than two months and won the New Jersey Notable Book Award. His next disaster novel, *The Gemini Virus*, was released in October 2012 to rave reviews by critics and consumers alike. Wil also spent twenty years as an editor, working for Scholastic, Harcourt Brace, Prentice Hall, and other publishers. *Frame 232* is the first book in an ongoing suspense series featuring hero Jason Hammond. It is also Wil's first title for Tyndale House.

More information about Wil's work can be found at www.wilmara.com.

BE ON THE LOOKOUT FOR
JASON HAMMOND'S NEXT ADVENTURE

The Nevada Testament

When demolition expert Randy Miller accidentally unearths
cryptic documents from reclusive billionaire Howard Hughes, it
draws the attention of some very powerful people—people who
will stop at nothing to make sure the many truths that lie in
those pages remain lost.

On the run and fearing for his life as well as his family's,
Miller contacts Jason Hammond, a billionaire in his own right
with a reputation for fearlessly digging into history, exposing
the facts, and bringing the unrepentant to justice. This time,
however, Jason will be going up against forces more formidable
than any he's ever encountered and will be drawn into a world
of unimaginable deception, greed, and ruthlessness.

IN BOOKSTORES AND ONLINE SUMMER 2014

TYNDALE
FICTION

www.tyndalefiction.com

CP0653